RED PaNDa & MOON BEaR

RED PANDA & MOON BEAR

JAROD ROSELLÓ

Top Shelf PRODUCTIONS

Visit us online at
topshelfcomix.com

Editor-in-chief: Edited by   Book Design by
Chris Staros   Leigh Walton.   Gilberto Lazcano.

RED PANDA & MOON BEAR © 2019 Jarod Roselló.

Published by Top Shelf Productions, PO Box 1282, Marietta, GA 30061-1282, USA. Top
Shelf Productions is an imprint of IDW Publishing, a division of Idea and Design Works,
LLC. Offices: 2765 Truxtun Road, San Diego, CA 92106. Top Shelf Productions®, the
Top Shelf logo, Idea and Design Works®, and the IDW logo are registered trademarks of
Idea and Design Works, LLC. All Rights Reserved. With the exception of small excerpts
of artwork used for review purposes, none of the contents of this publication may be
reprinted without the permission of IDW Publishing. IDW Publishing does not read or
accept unsolicited submissions of ideas, stories or artwork. Printed in Korea.

ISBN: 978-1-60309-444-3   22 21 20 19   4 3 2 1

For Emi and Oliver.
And Angie, of course.

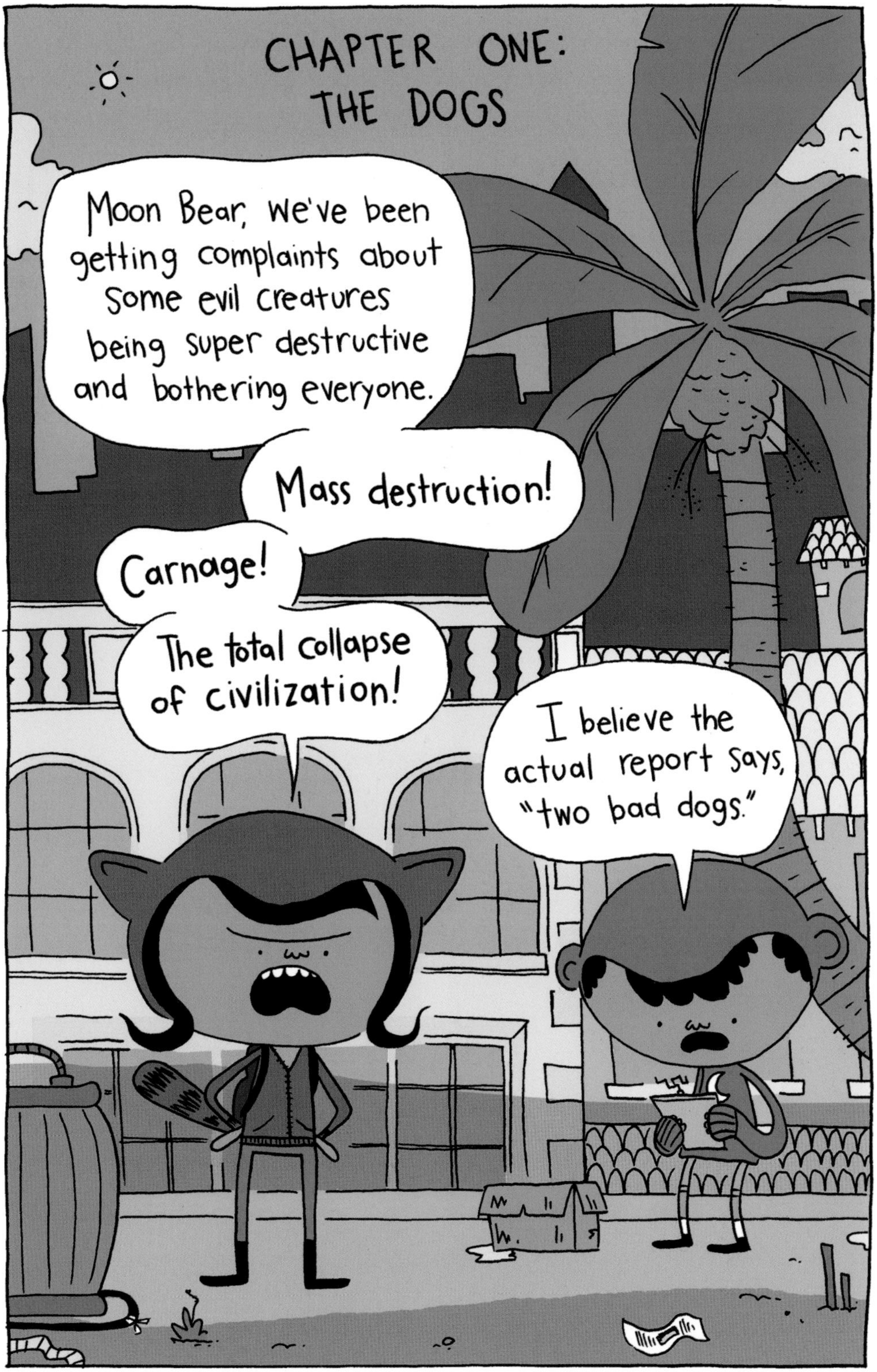
CHAPTER ONE:
THE DOGS
Moon Bear, we've been getting complaints about some evil creatures being super destructive and bothering everyone.
Mass destruction!
Carnage!
The total collapse of civilization!
I believe the actual report says, "two bad dogs."

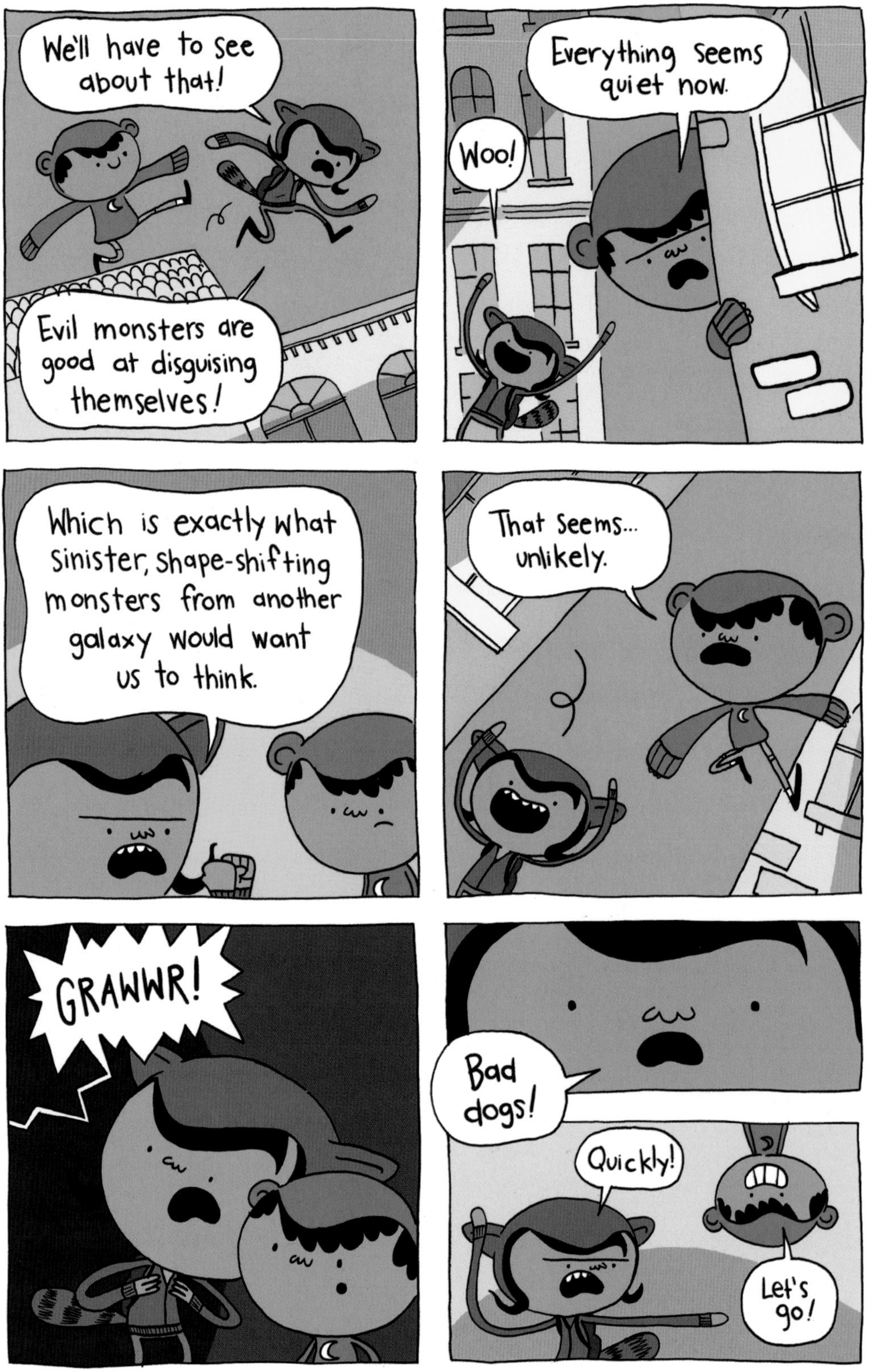
We'll have to see about that!
Evil monsters are good at disguising themselves!
Everything seems quiet now.
Woo!
Which is exactly what sinister, shape-shifting monsters from another galaxy would want us to think.
That seems... unlikely.
GRAWWR!
Bad dogs!
Quickly!
Let's go!

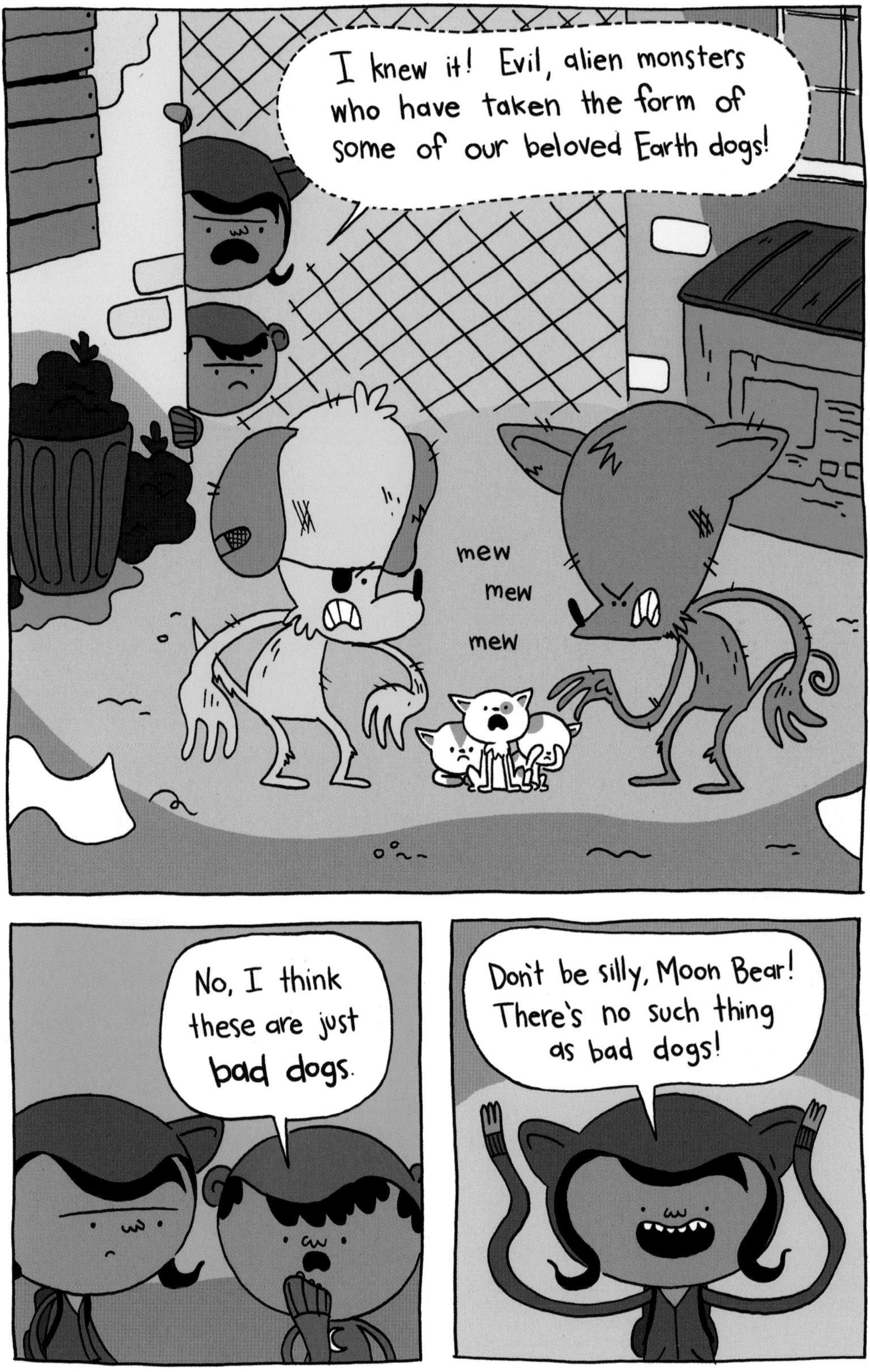
I knew it! Evil, alien monsters who have taken the form of some of our beloved Earth dogs!
mew
mew
mew
No, I think these are just **bad dogs**.
Don't be silly, Moon Bear! There's no such thing as bad dogs!

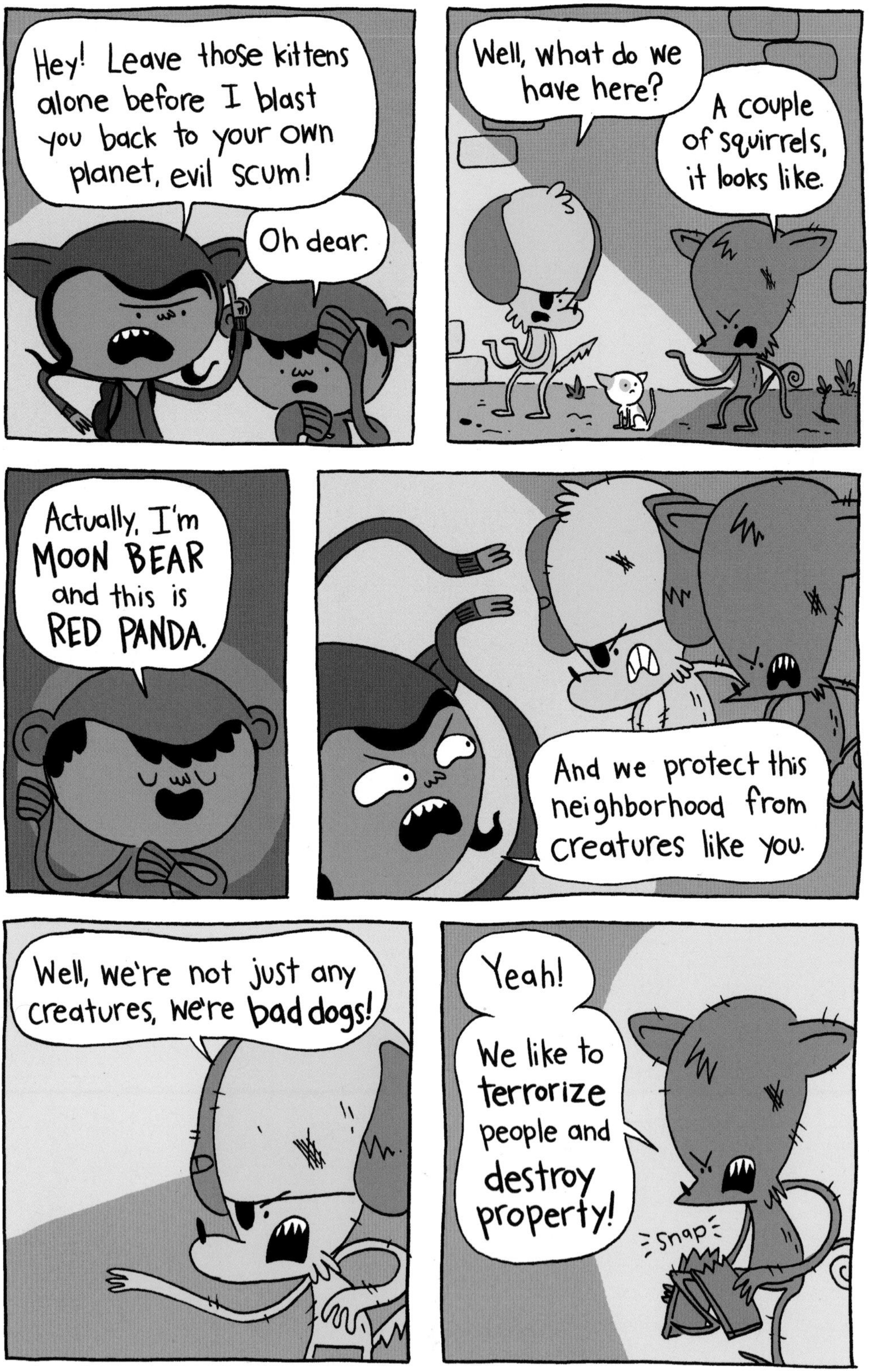
Hey! Leave those kittens alone before I blast you back to your own planet, evil scum!
Oh dear.
Well, what do we have here?
A couple of squirrels, it looks like.
Actually, I'm MOON BEAR and this is RED PANDA.
And we protect this neighborhood from creatures like you.
Well, we're not just any creatures, we're bad dogs!
Yeah!
We like to terrorize people and destroy property!
Snap

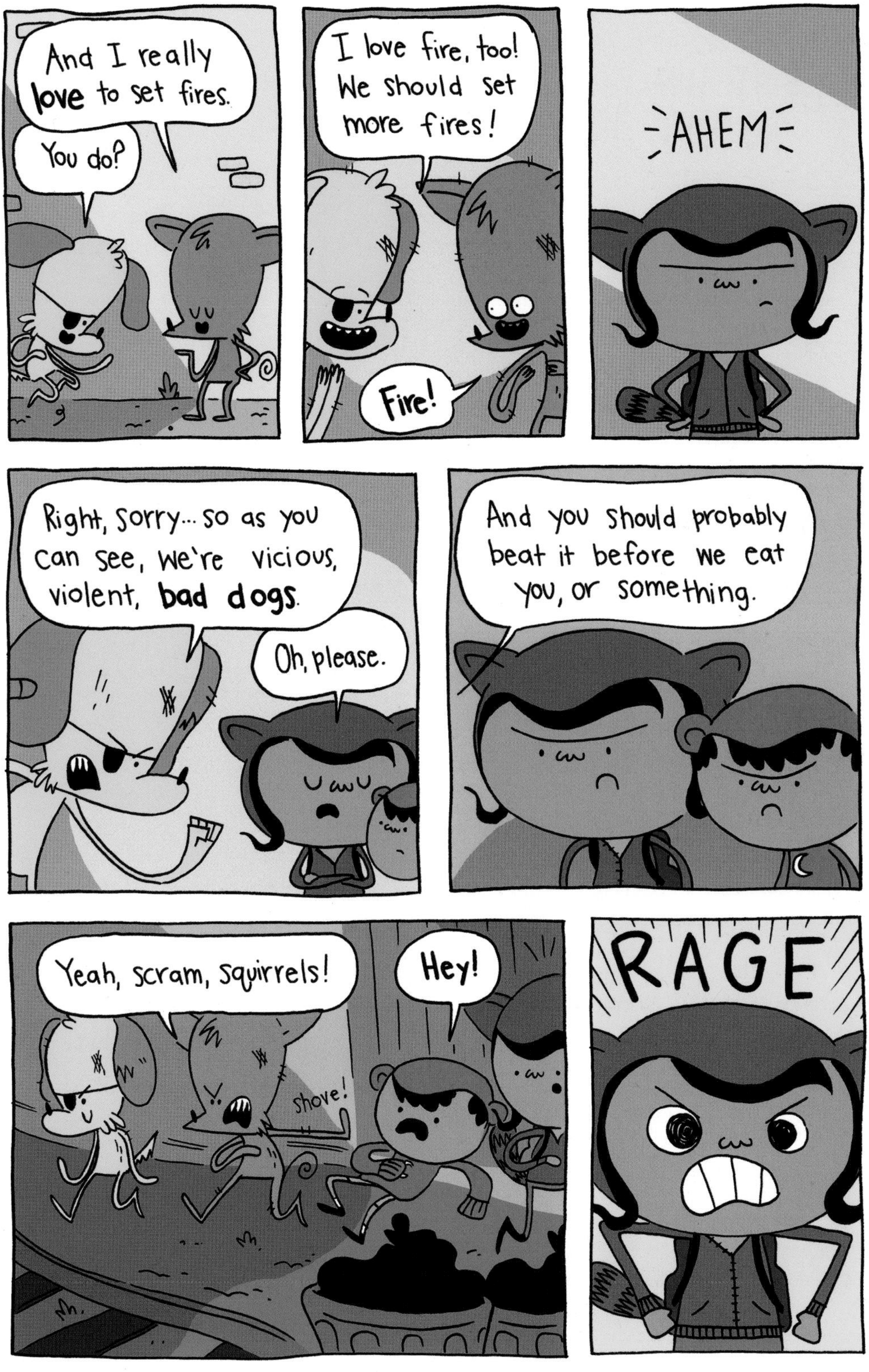
And I really love to set fires.
You do?
I love fire, too! We should set more fires!
Fire!
AHEM
Right, sorry... so as you can see, we're vicious, violent, bad dogs.
Oh, please.
And you should probably beat it before we eat you, or something.
Yeah, scram, squirrels!
Hey!
shove!
RAGE

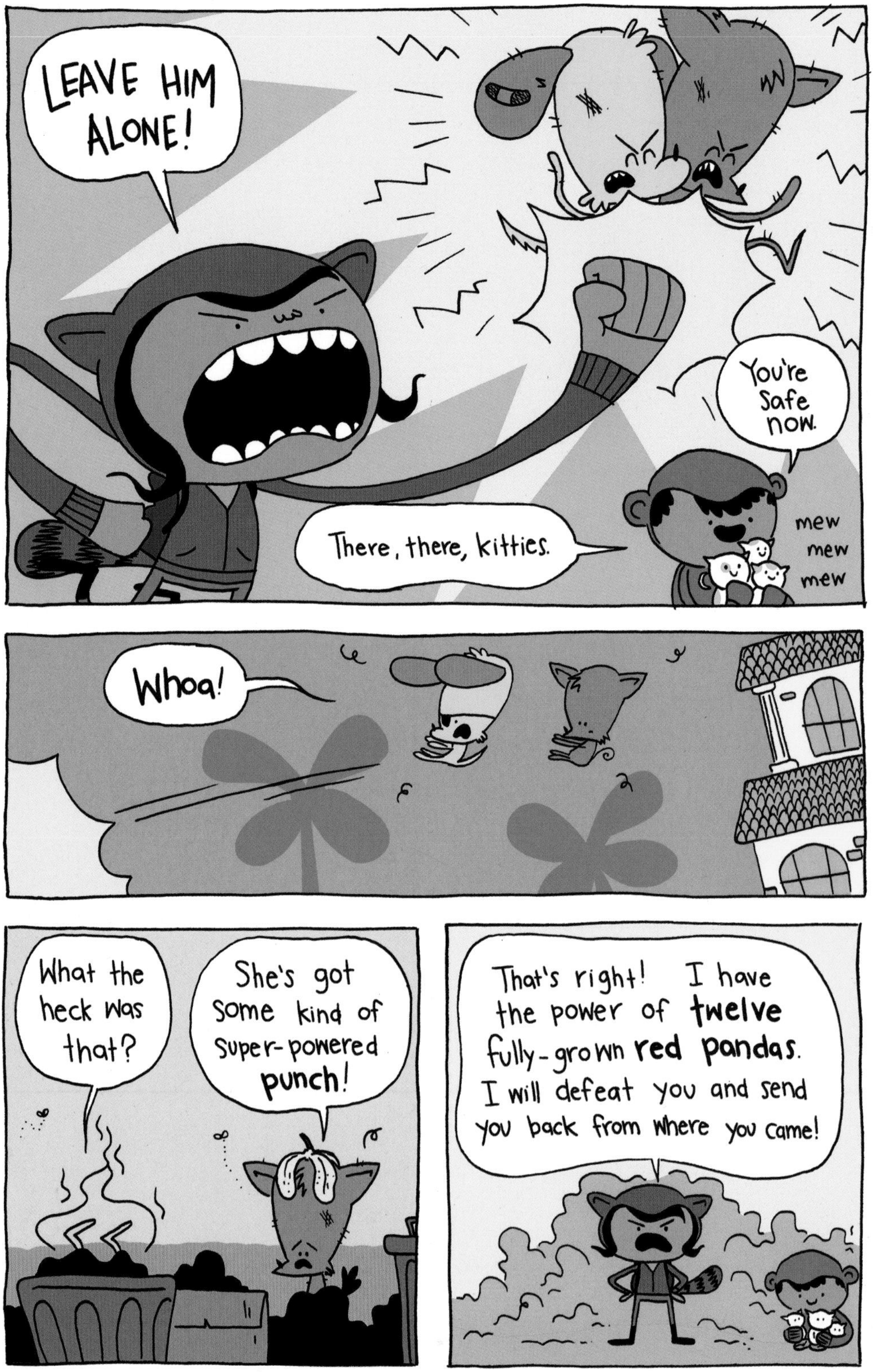
LEAVE HIM ALONE!
You're safe now.
There, there, kitties.
mew mew mew
Whoa!
What the heck was that?
She's got some kind of super-powered punch!
That's right! I have the power of twelve fully-grown red pandas. I will defeat you and send you back from where you came!

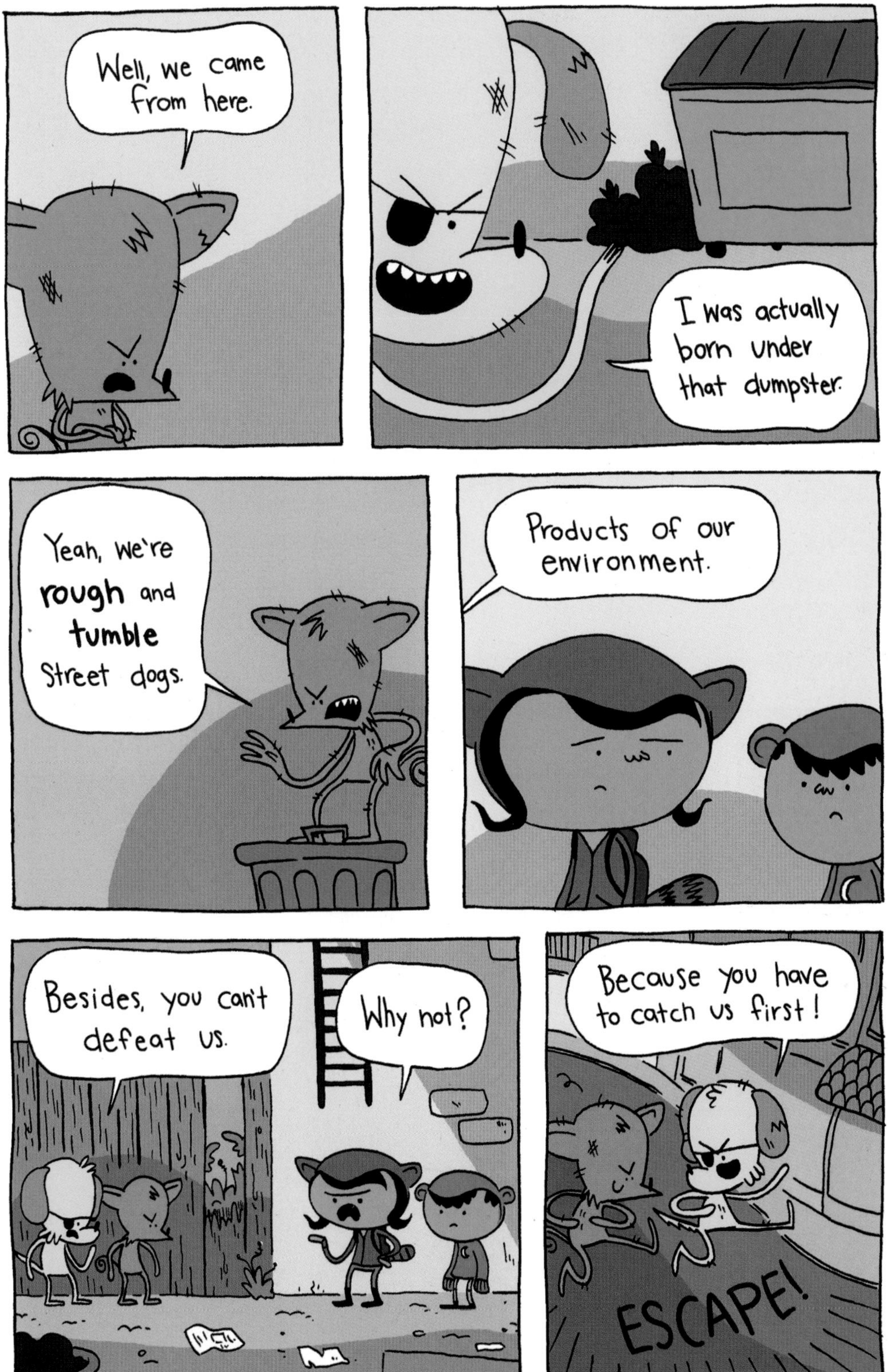

Well, we came from here.
I was actually born under that dumpster.
Yeah, we're rough and tumble street dogs.
Products of our environment.
Besides, you can't defeat us.
Why not?
Because you have to catch us first!
ESCAPE!

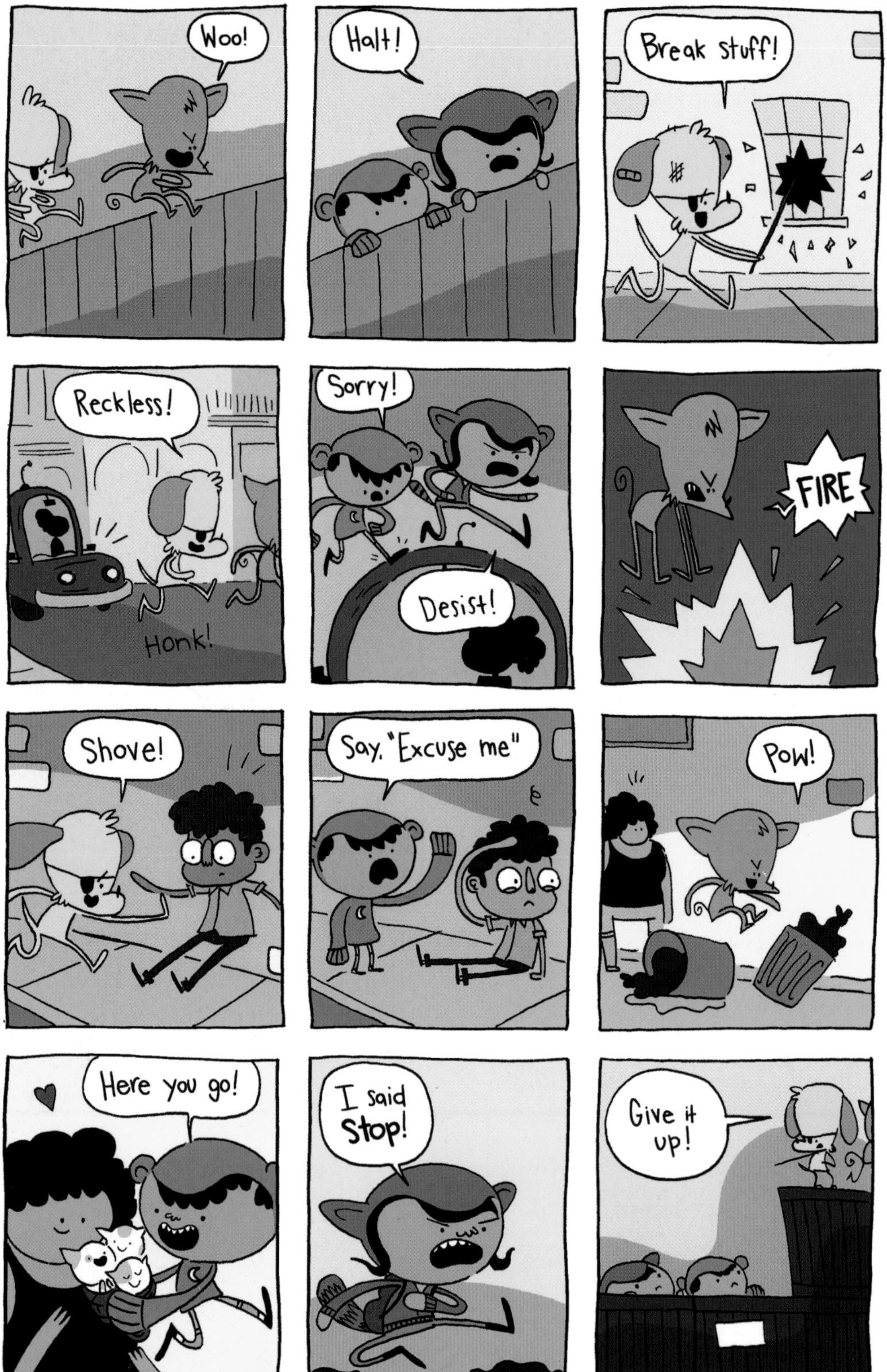
Woo!
Halt!
Break stuff!
Reckless!
Honk!
Sorry!
Desist!
FIRE
Shove!
Say, "Excuse me"
Pow!
Here you go!
I said Stop!
Give it up!

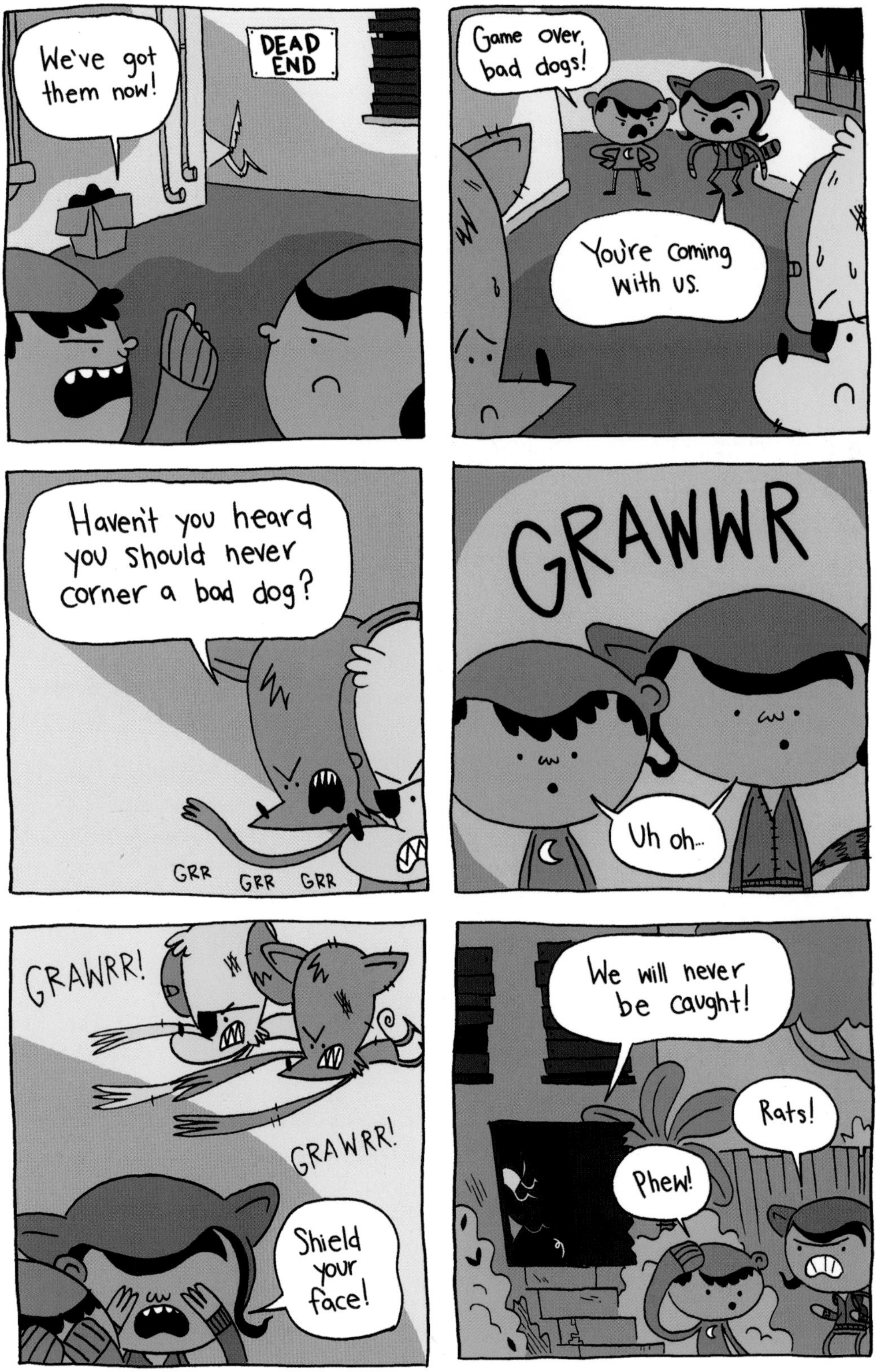
We've got them now!
DEAD END
Game over, bad dogs!
You're coming with us.
Haven't you heard you should never corner a bad dog?
GRR GRR GRR
GRAWWR
Uh oh...
GRAWRR!
GRAWRR!
Shield your face!
We will never be caught!
Rats!
Phew!

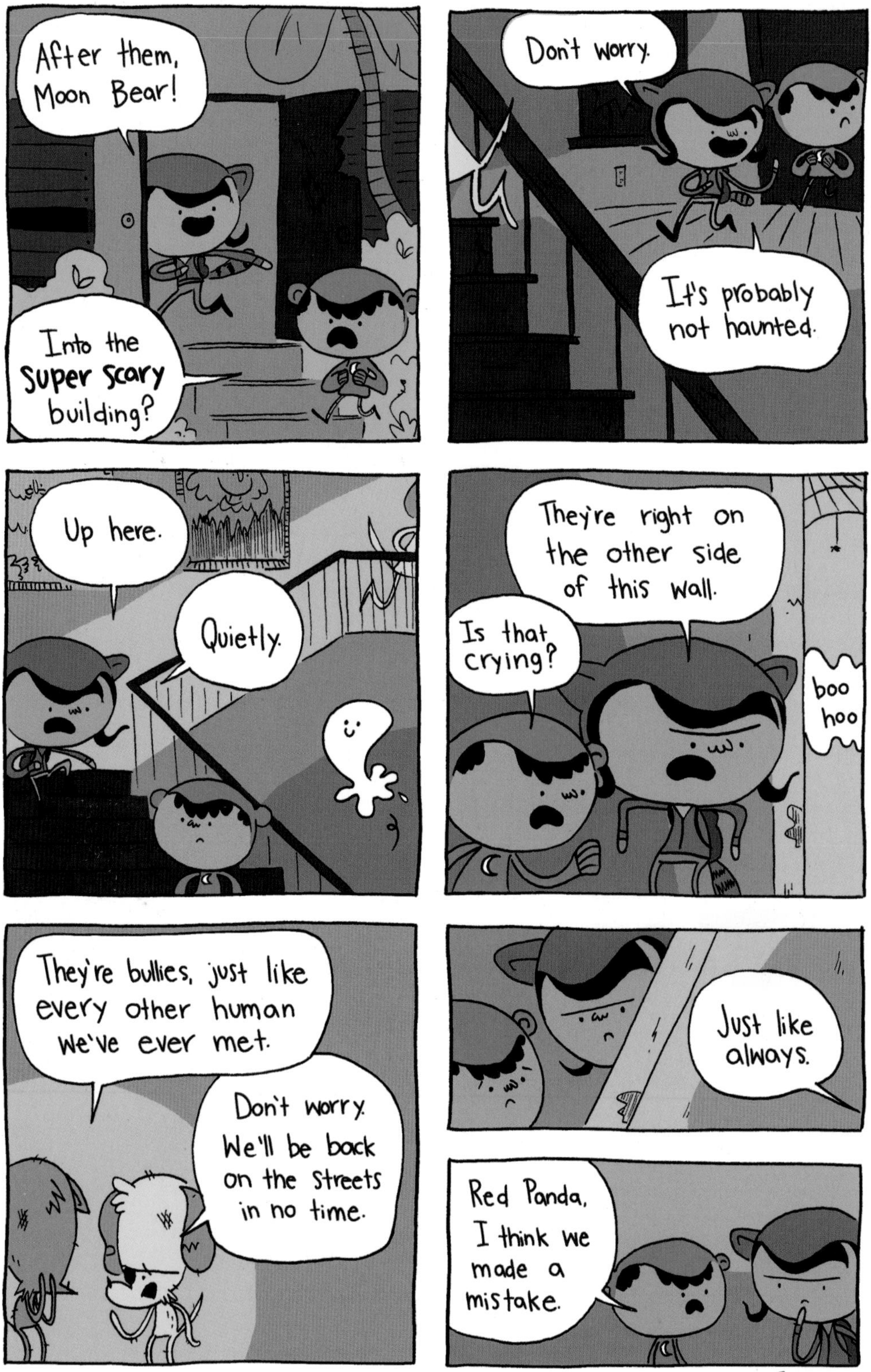
After them, Moon Bear!
Into the **super scary** building?
Don't worry.
It's probably not haunted.
Up here.
Quietly.
They're right on the other side of this wall.
Is that crying?
boo hoo
They're bullies, just like every other human we've ever met.
Don't worry. We'll be back on the streets in no time.
Just like always.
Red Panda, I think we made a mistake.

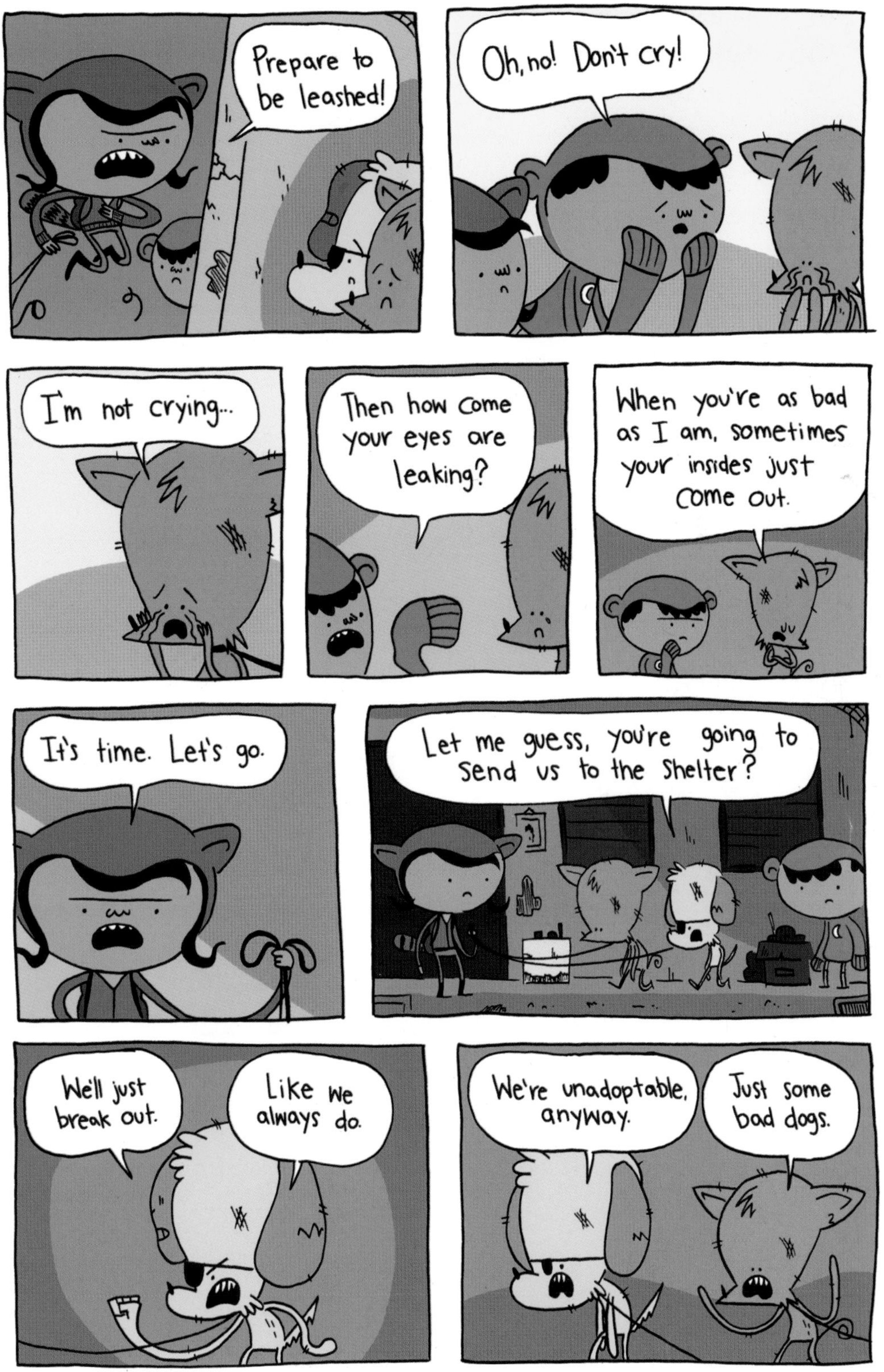
Prepare to be leashed!
Oh, no! Don't cry!
I'm not crying...
Then how come your eyes are leaking?
When you're as bad as I am, sometimes your insides just come out.
It's time. Let's go.
Let me guess, you're going to send us to the shelter?
We'll just break out.
Like we always do.
We're unadoptable, anyway.
Just some bad dogs.

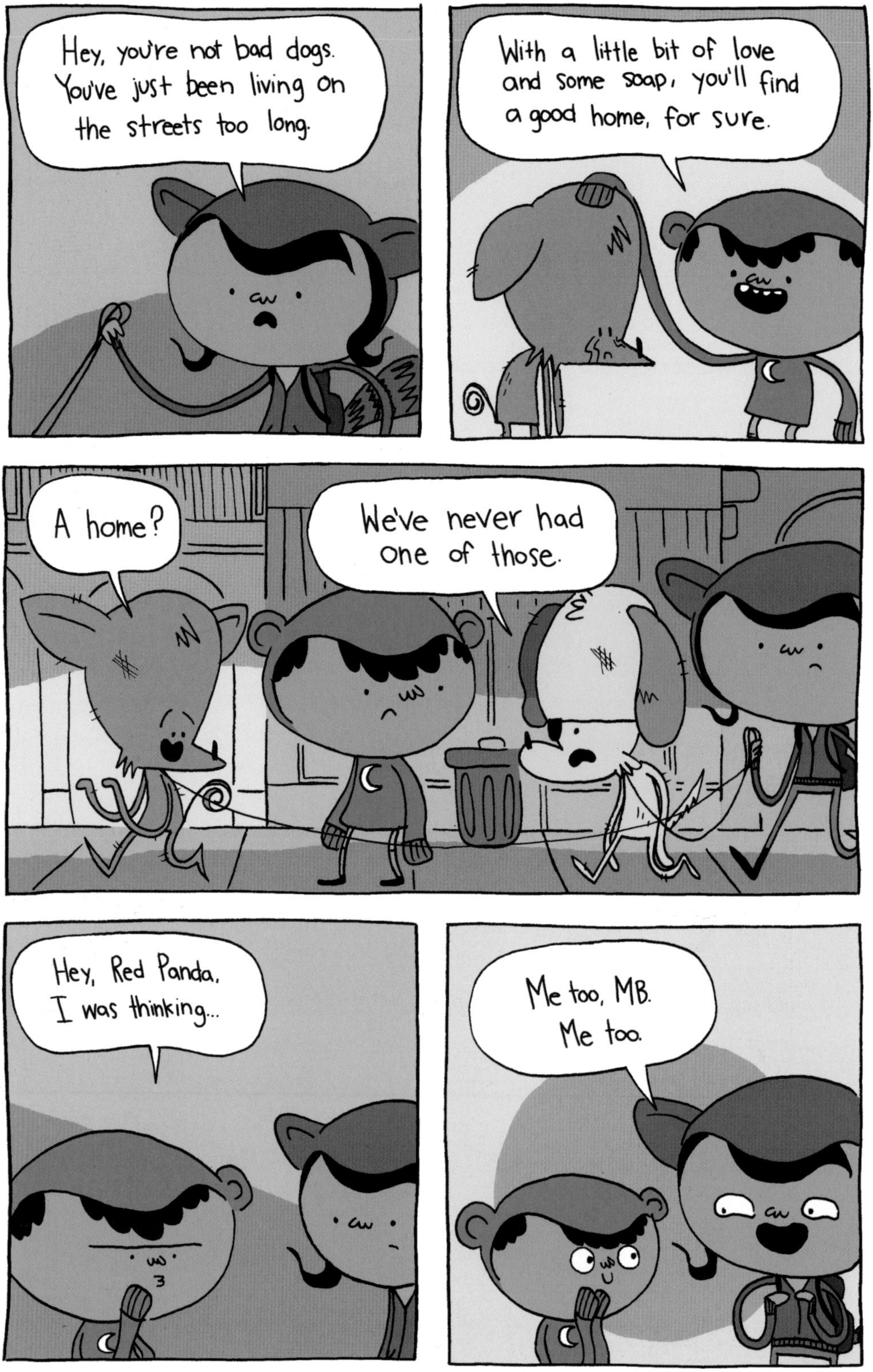
Hey, you're not bad dogs. You've just been living on the streets too long.
With a little bit of love and some soap, you'll find a good home, for sure.
A home?
We've never had one of those.
Hey, Red Panda. I was thinking...
Me too, MB. Me too.

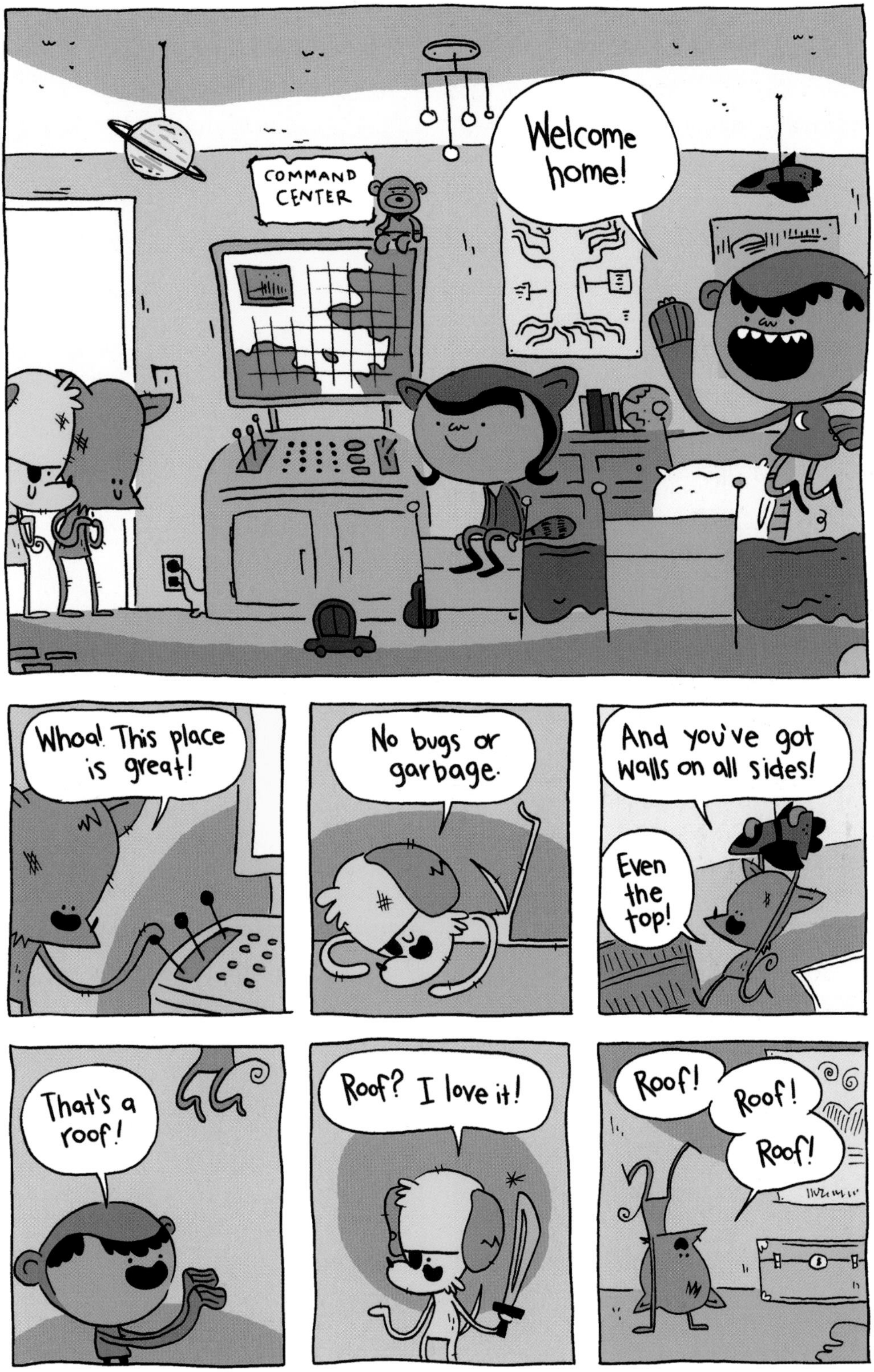
COMMAND CENTER
Welcome home!
Whoa! This place is great!
No bugs or garbage.
And you've got walls on all sides!
Even the top!
That's a roof!
Roof? I love it!
Roof!
Roof!
Roof!

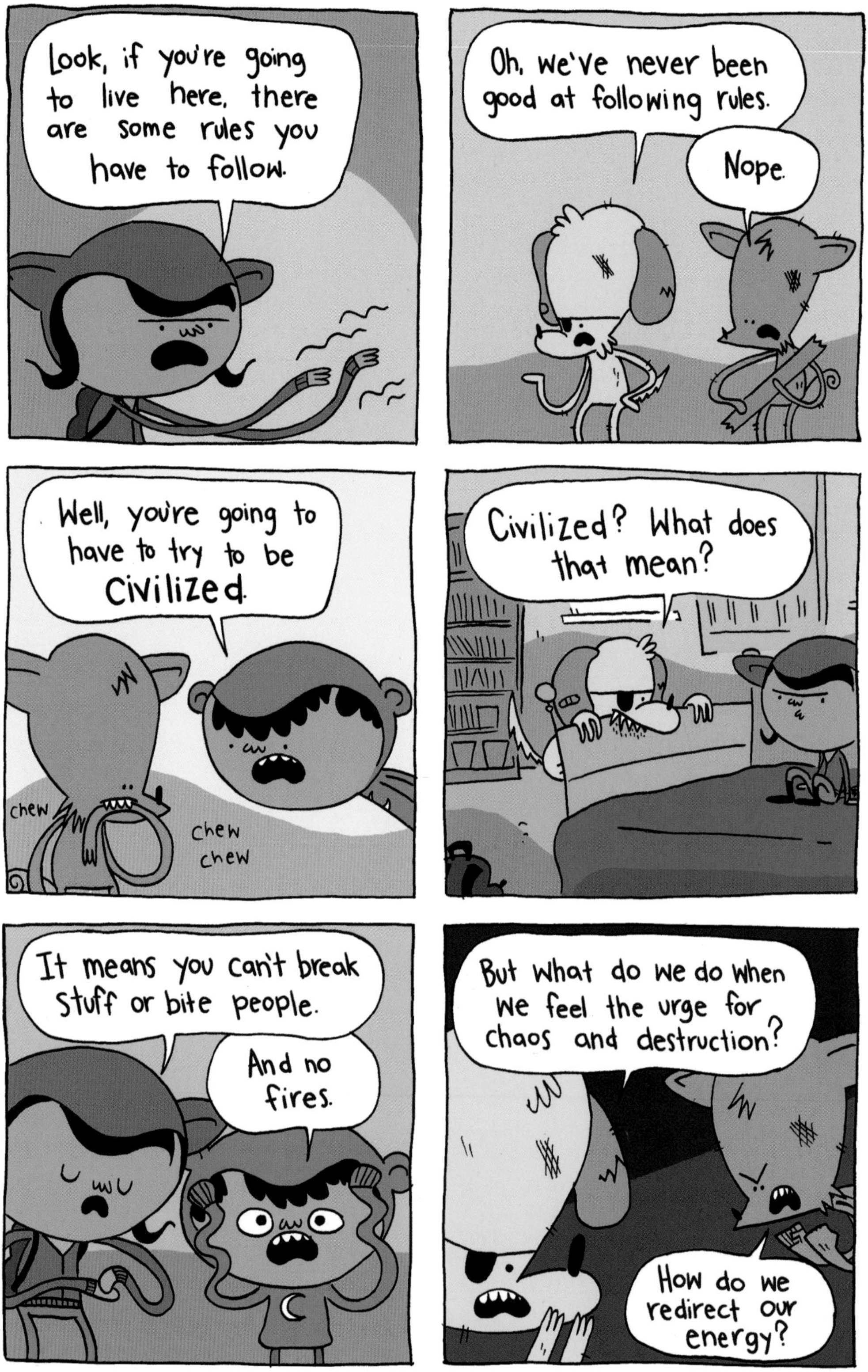
Look, if you're going to live here, there are some rules you have to follow.
Oh, we've never been good at following rules.
Nope.
Well, you're going to have to try to be CIVILIZED.
chew
chew
chew
Civilized? What does that mean?
It means you can't break stuff or bite people.
And no fires.
But what do we do when we feel the urge for chaos and destruction?
How do we redirect our energy?

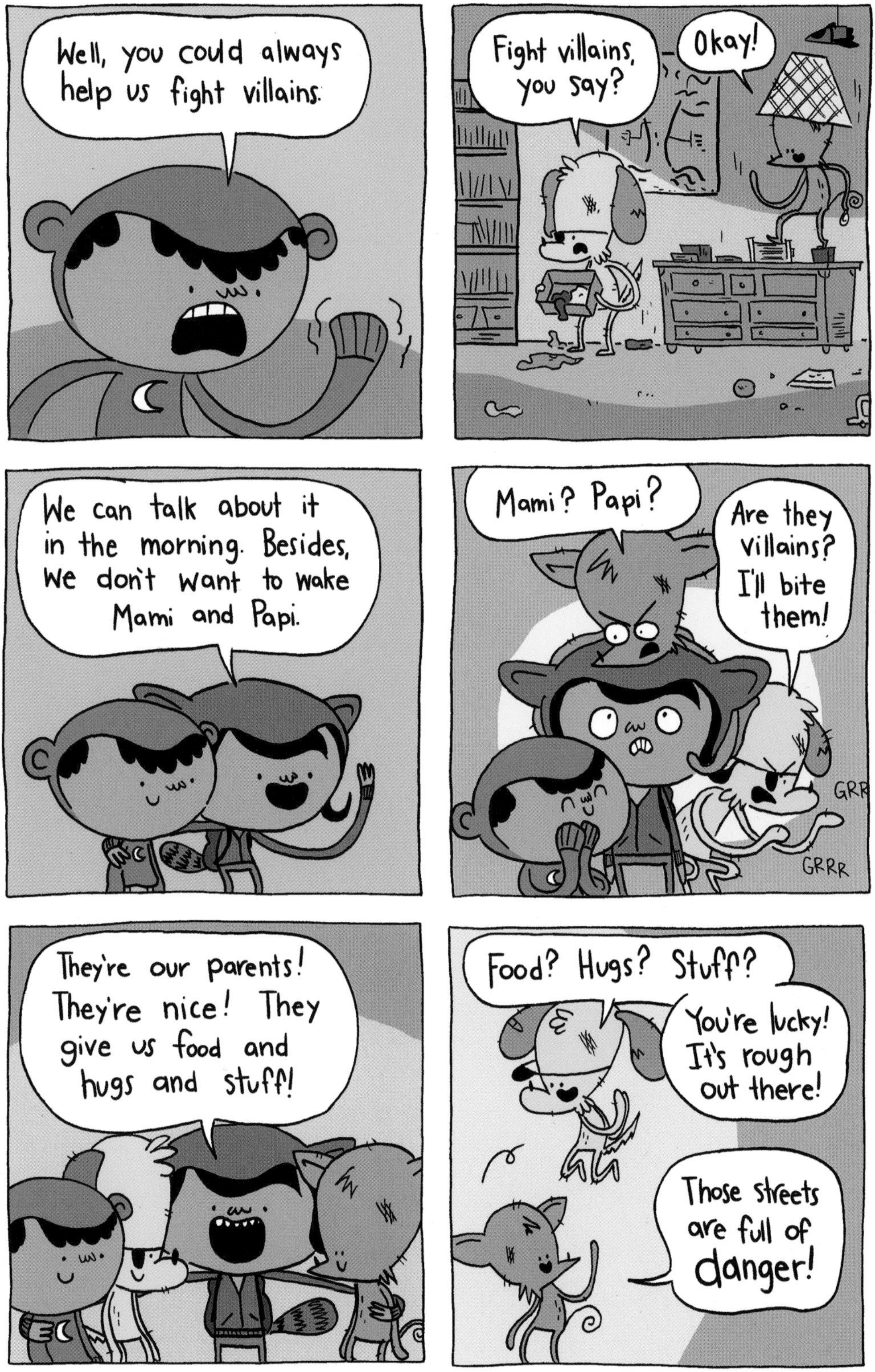
Well, you could always help us fight villains.
Fight villains, you say?
Okay!
We can talk about it in the morning. Besides, we don't want to wake Mami and Papi.
Mami? Papi?
Are they villains? I'll bite them!
GRR
GRRR
They're our parents! They're nice! They give us food and hugs and stuff!
Food? Hugs? Stuff?
You're lucky! It's rough out there!
Those streets are full of danger!

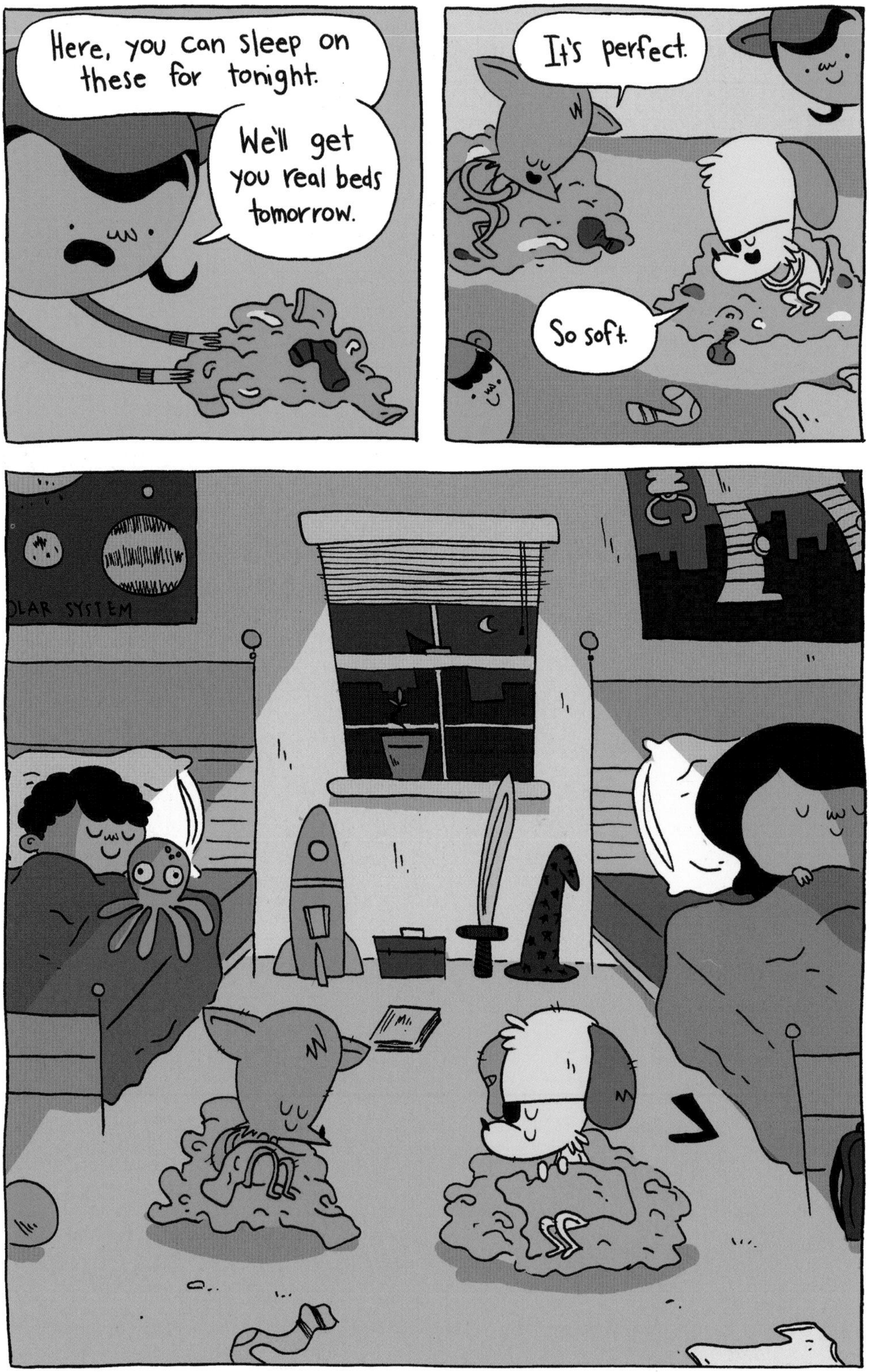
Here, you can sleep on these for tonight.
We'll get you real beds tomorrow.
It's perfect.
So soft.
OLAR SYSTEM

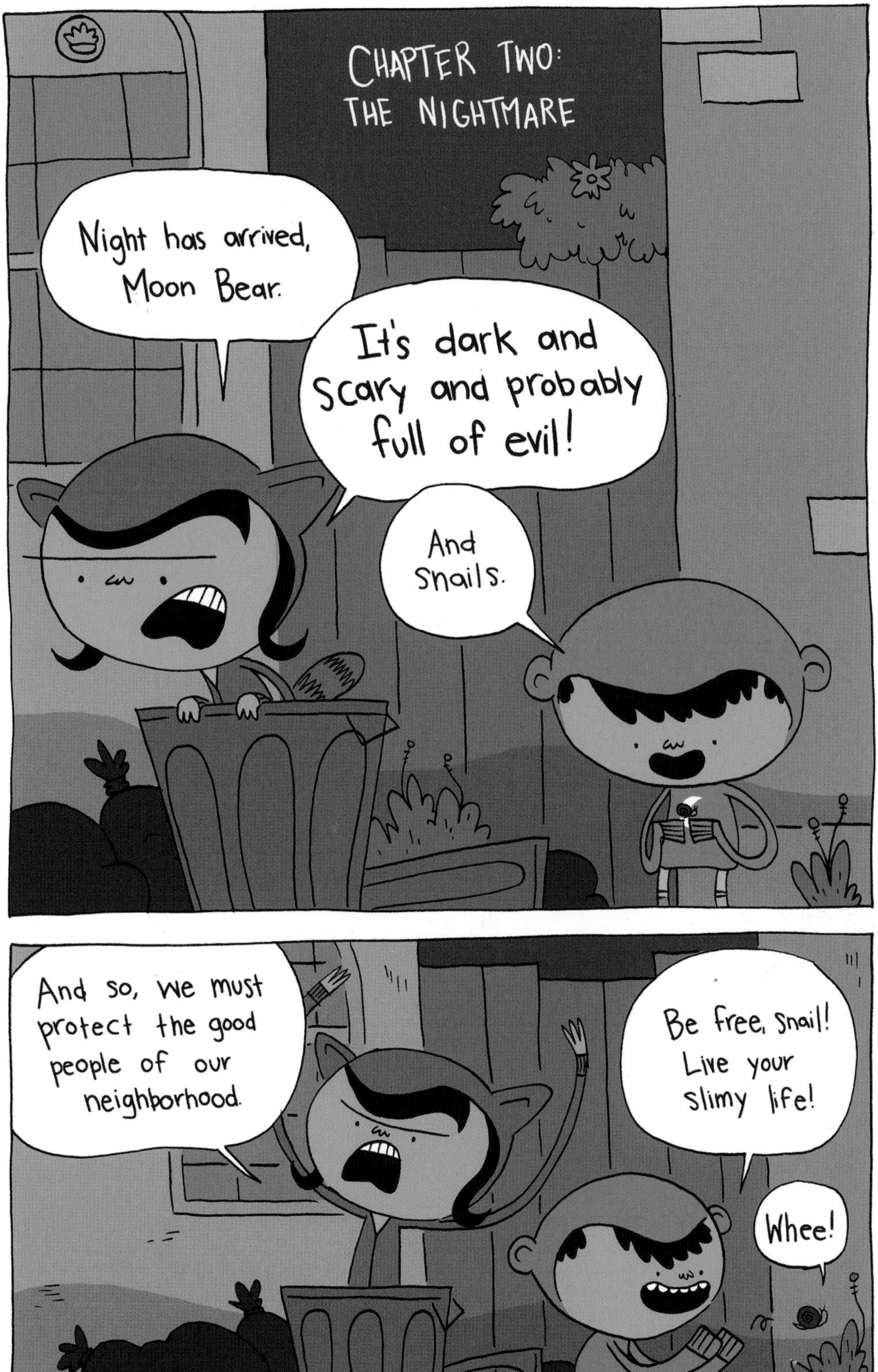
CHAPTER TWO:
THE NIGHTMARE
Night has arrived, Moon Bear.
It's dark and scary and probably full of evil!
And snails.
And so, we must protect the good people of our neighborhood.
Be free, snail! Live your slimy life!
Whee!

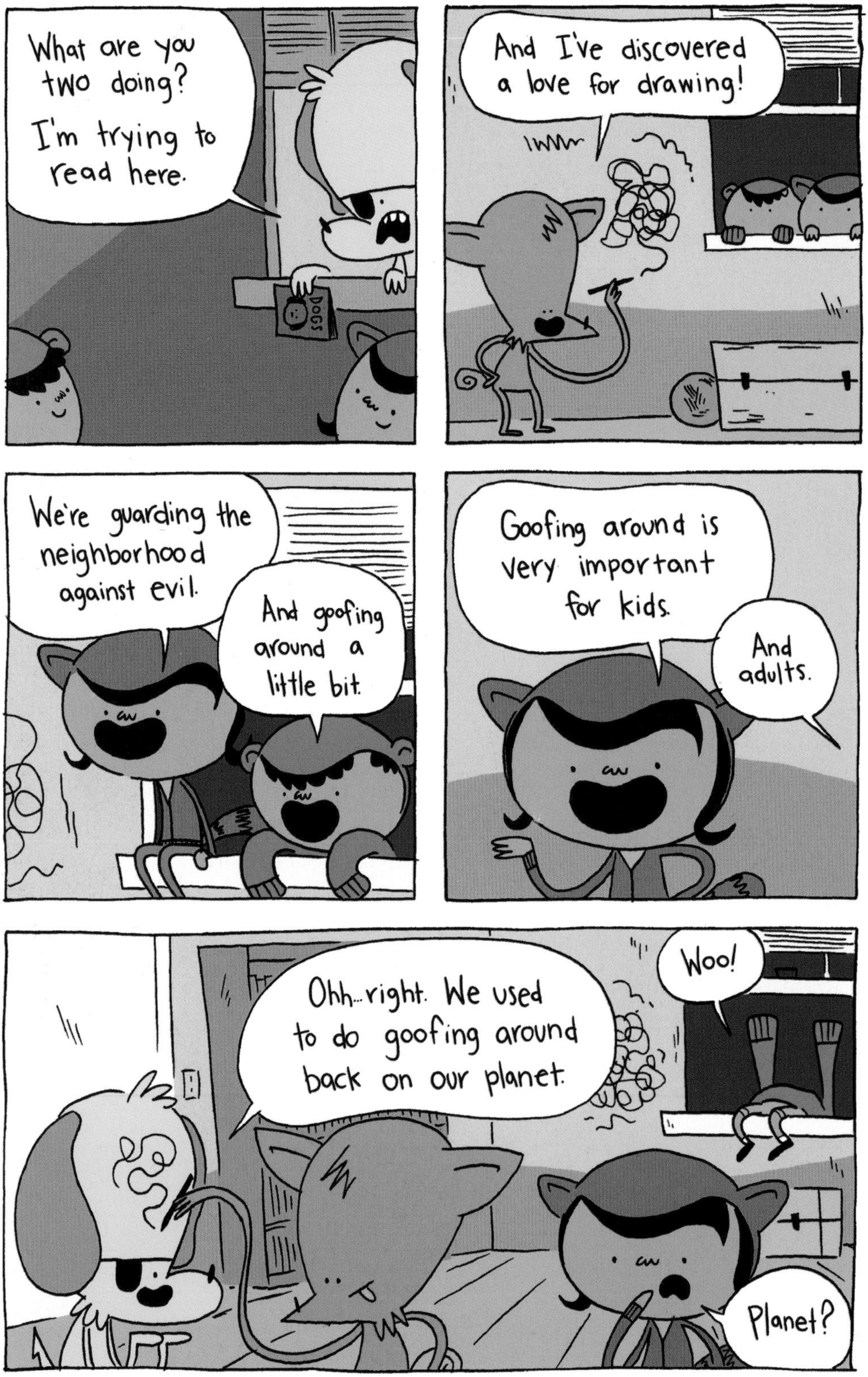
What are you two doing?
I'm trying to read here.
DOGS
And I've discovered a love for drawing!
We're guarding the neighborhood against evil.
And goofing around a little bit.
Goofing around is very important for kids.
And adults.
Ohh...right. We used to do goofing around back on our planet.
Woo!
Planet?

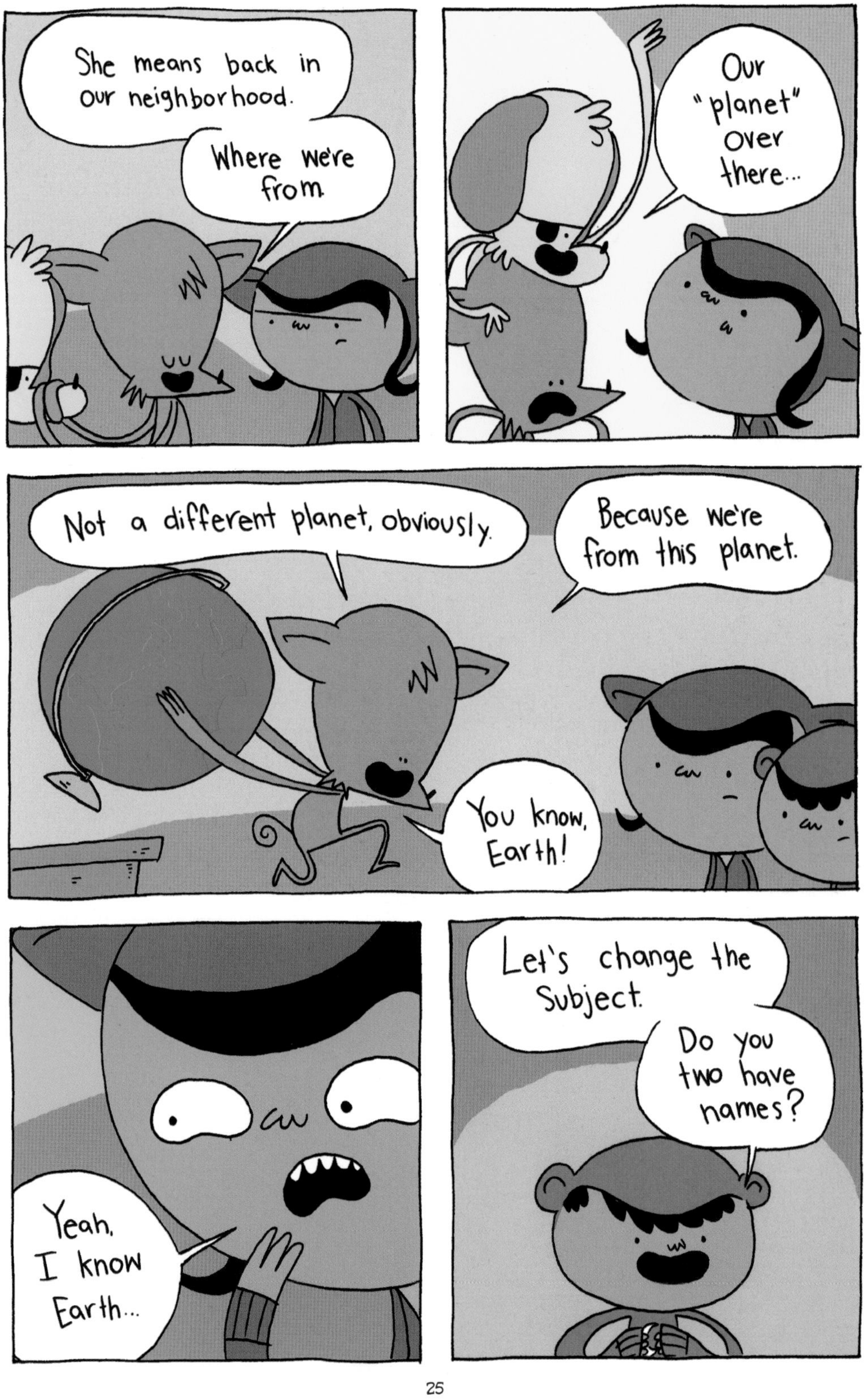
She means back in our neighborhood.
Where we're from.
Our "planet" over there...
Not a different planet, obviously.
Because we're from this planet.
You know, Earth!
Yeah, I know Earth...
Let's change the subject.
Do you two have names?

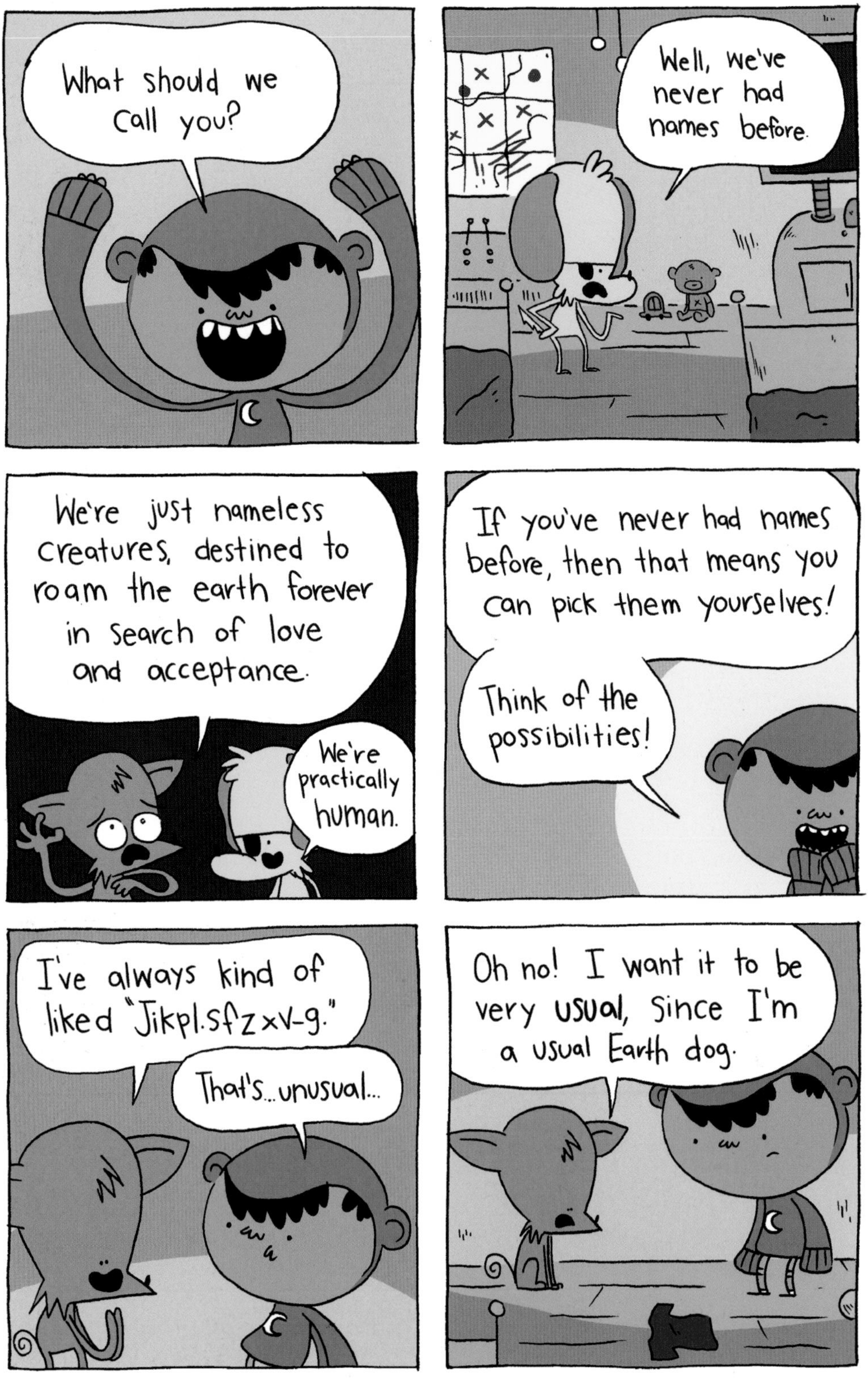
What should we call you?
Well, we've never had names before.
We're just nameless creatures, destined to roam the earth forever in search of love and acceptance.
We're practically human.
If you've never had names before, then that means you can pick them yourselves!
Think of the possibilities!
I've always kind of liked "Jikpl.sfzxv-g."
That's...unusual...
Oh no! I want it to be very usual, since I'm a usual Earth dog.

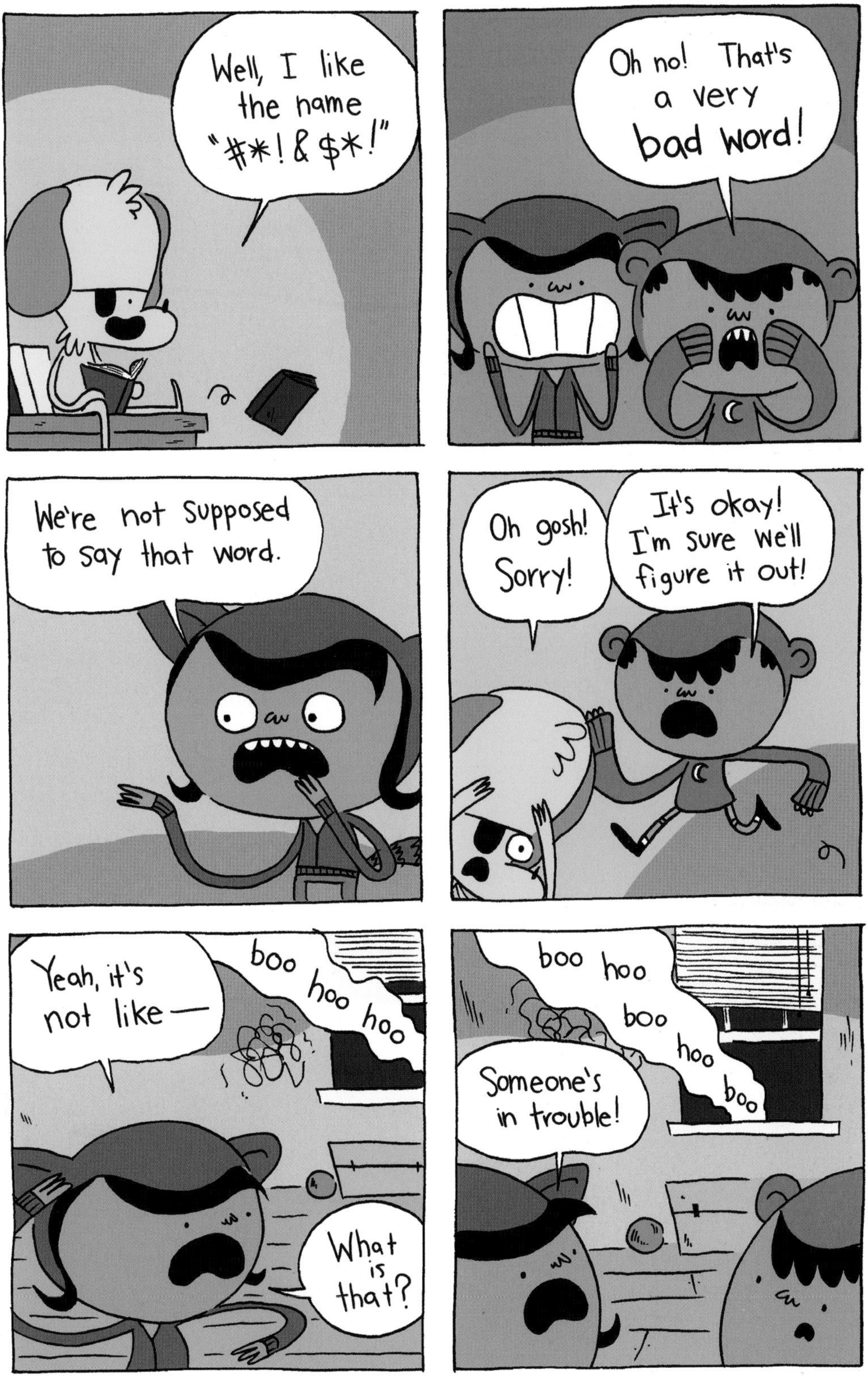
Well, I like the name "#*!&$*!"
Oh no! That's a very bad word!
We're not supposed to say that word.
Oh gosh! Sorry!
It's okay! I'm sure we'll figure it out!
Yeah, it's not like—
boo hoo hoo
What is that?
boo hoo boo hoo boo
Someone's in trouble!

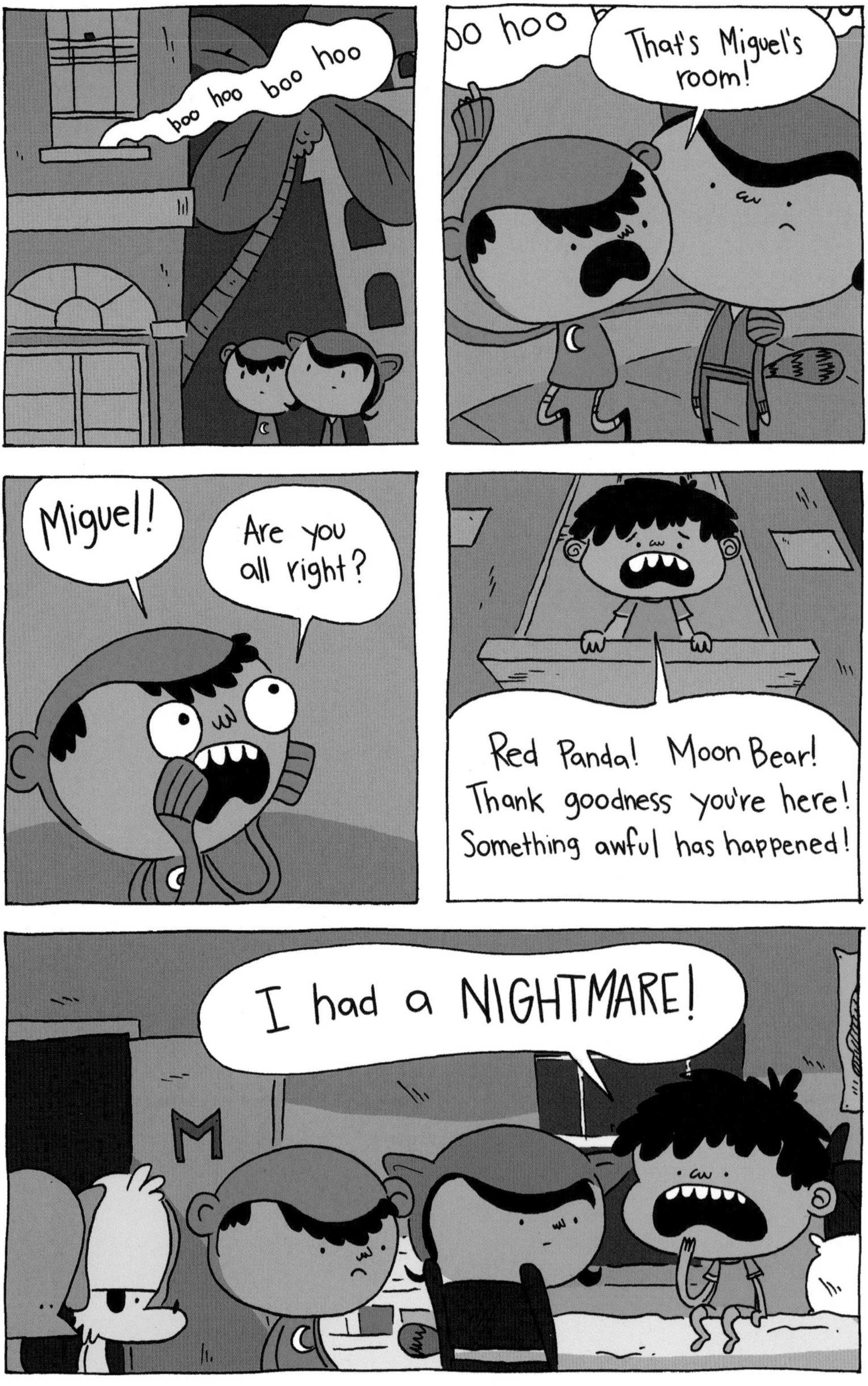
boo hoo boo hoo
oo hoo
That's Miguel's room!
Miguel!
Are you all right?
Red Panda! Moon Bear! Thank goodness you're here! Something awful has happened!
I had a NIGHTMARE!

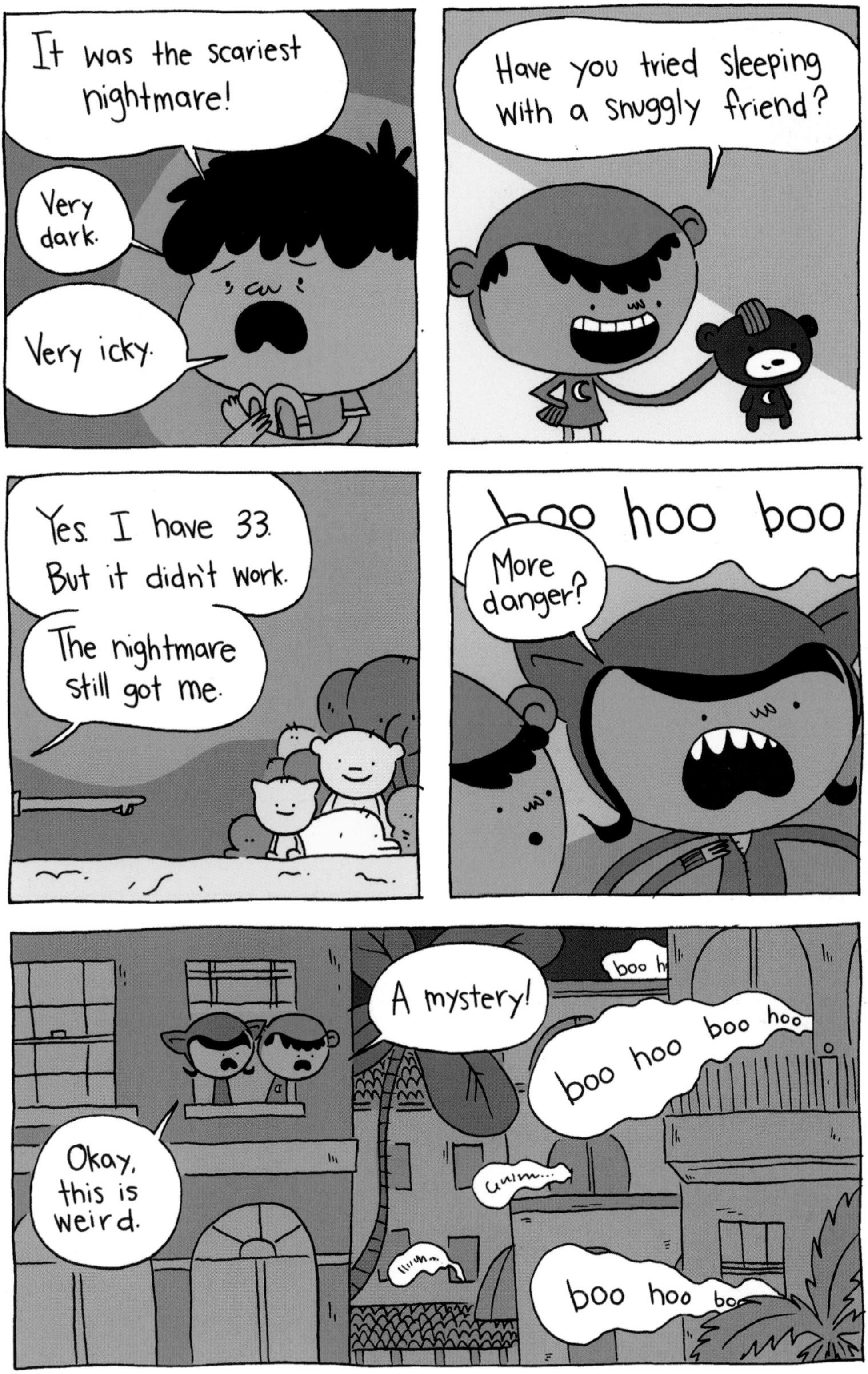
It was the scariest nightmare!
Very dark.
Very icky.
Have you tried sleeping with a snuggly friend?
Yes. I have 33. But it didn't work.
The nightmare still got me.
boo hoo boo
More danger?
A mystery!
boo h
boo hoo boo hoo
Okay, this is weird.
boo hoo bo

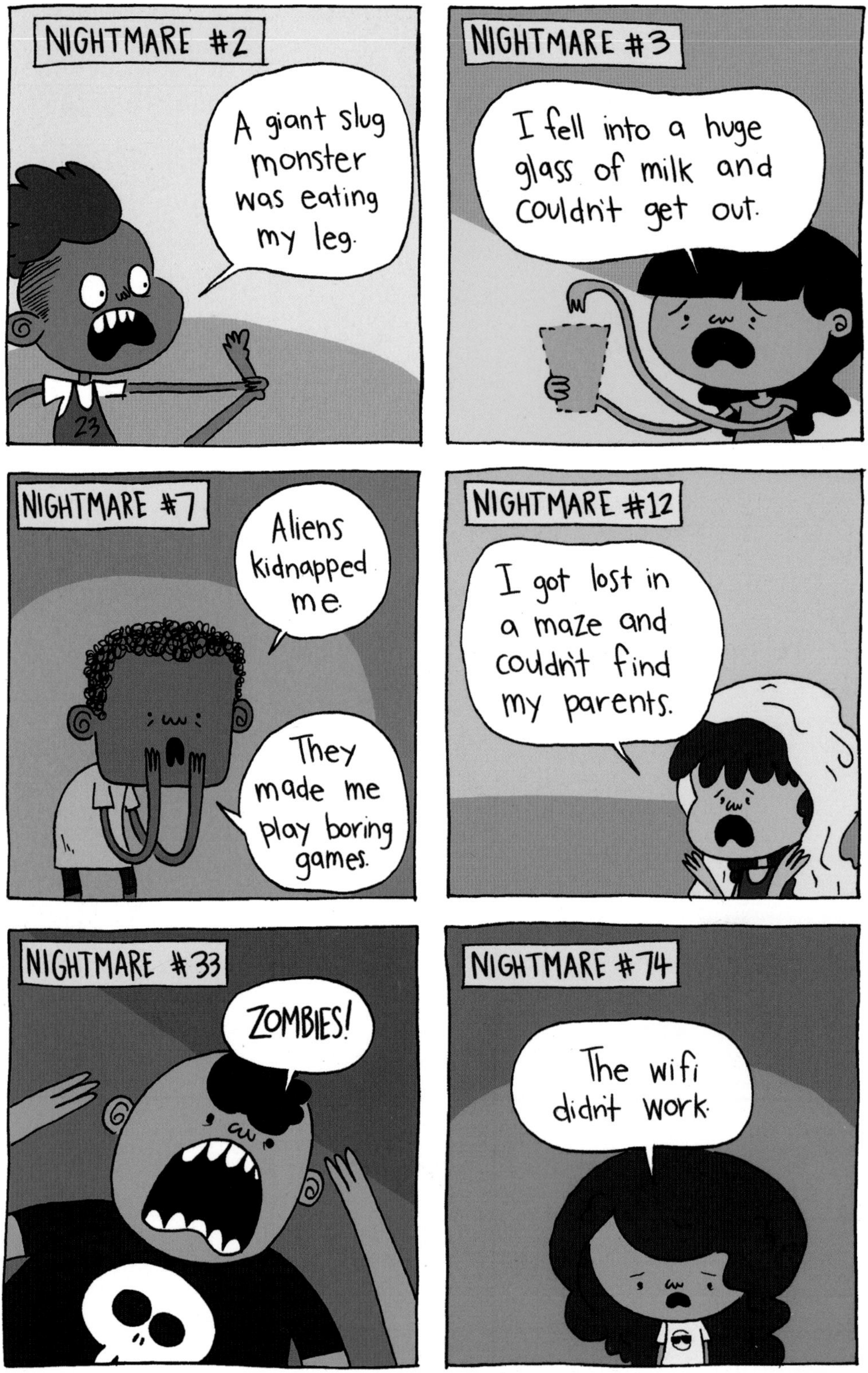
NIGHTMARE #2
A giant slug monster was eating my leg.
23
NIGHTMARE #3
I fell into a huge glass of milk and couldn't get out.
NIGHTMARE #7
Aliens kidnapped me.
They made me play boring games.
NIGHTMARE #12
I got lost in a maze and couldn't find my parents.
NIGHTMARE #33
ZOMBIES!
NIGHTMARE #74
The wifi didn't work.

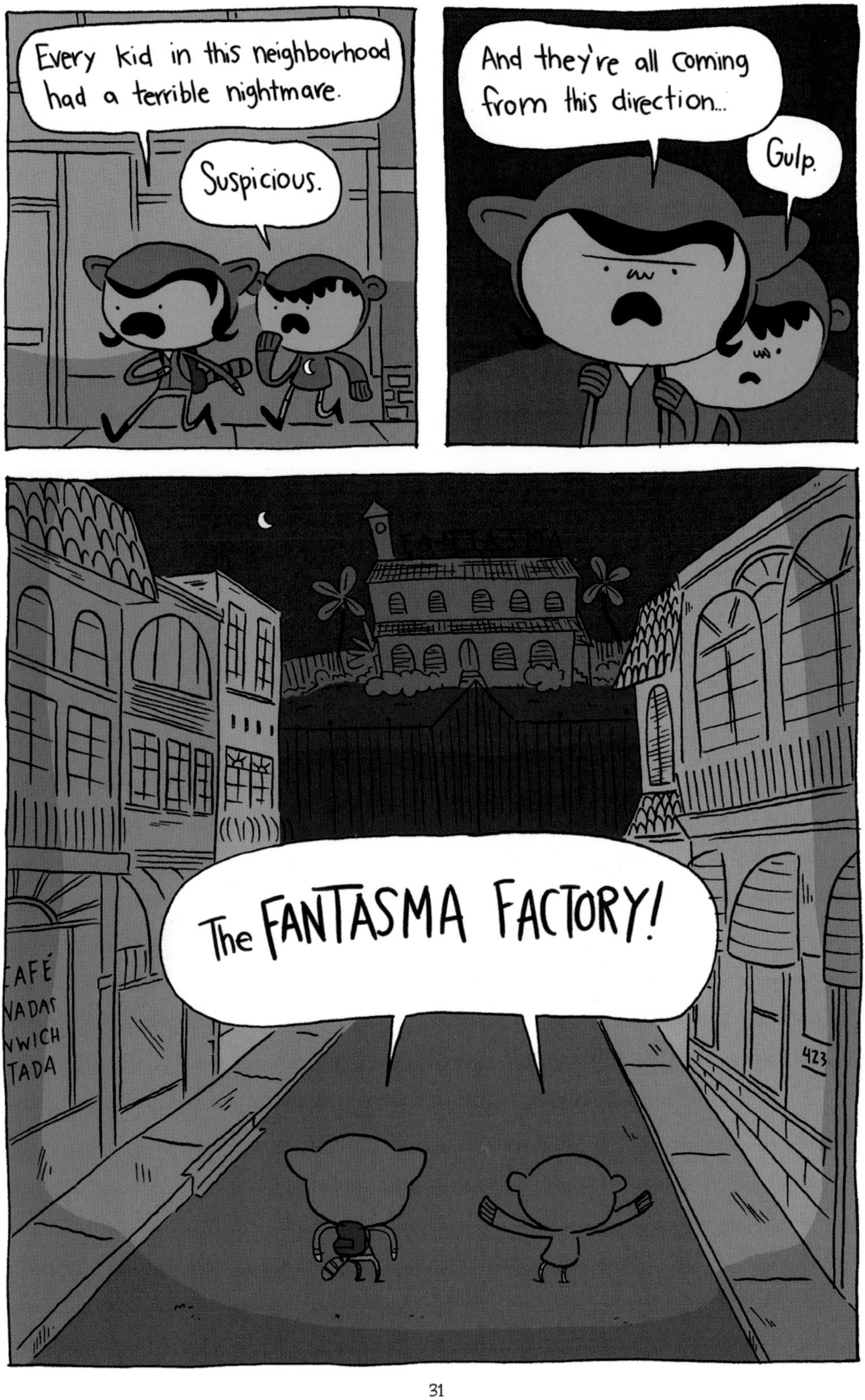
Every kid in this neighborhood had a terrible nightmare.
Suspicious.
And they're all coming from this direction...
Gulp.
The FANTASMA FACTORY!
CAFÉ
NADA
NWICH
TADA
423

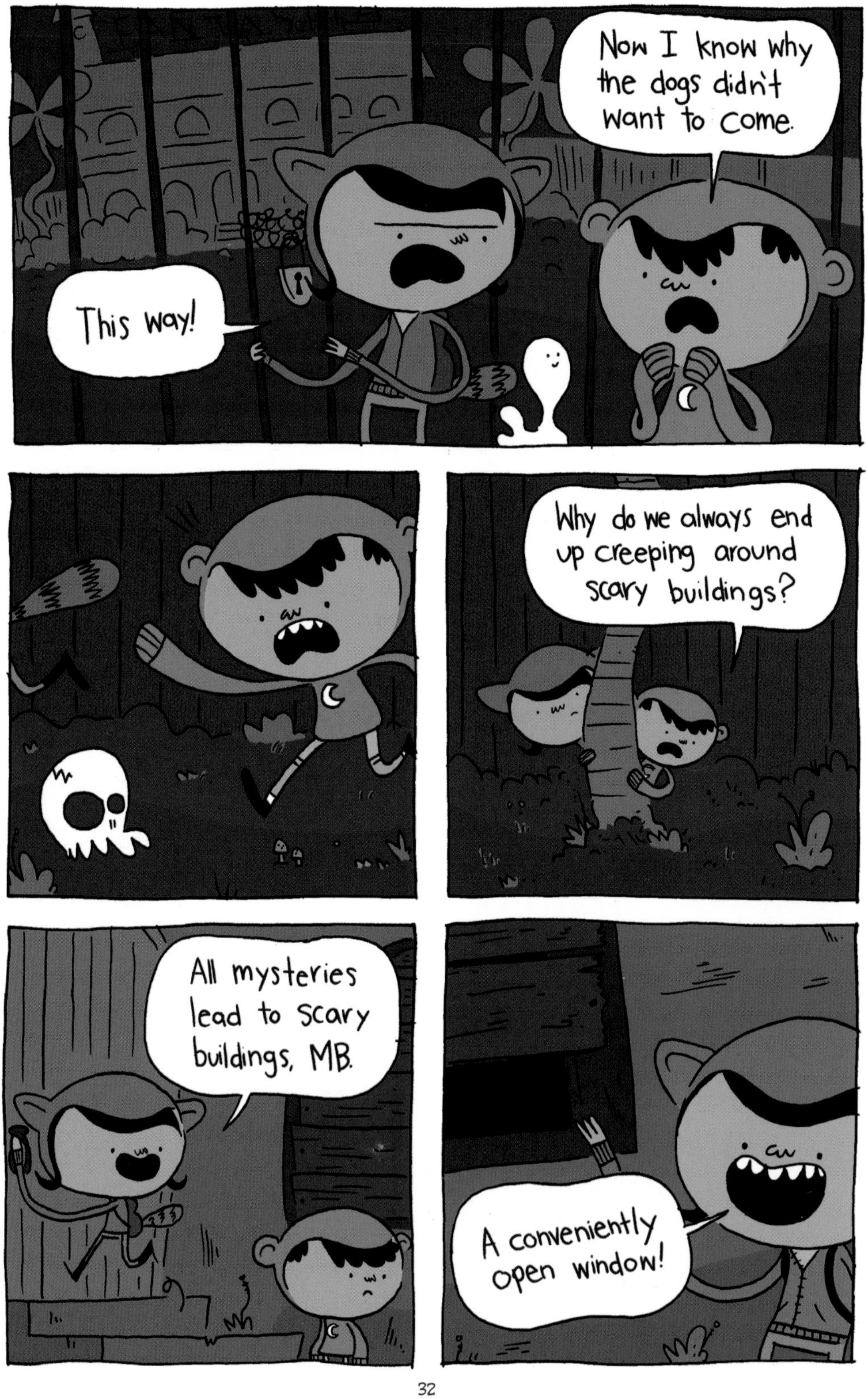

Now I know why the dogs didn't want to come.
This way!
Why do we always end up creeping around scary buildings?
All mysteries lead to scary buildings, MB.
A conveniently open window!

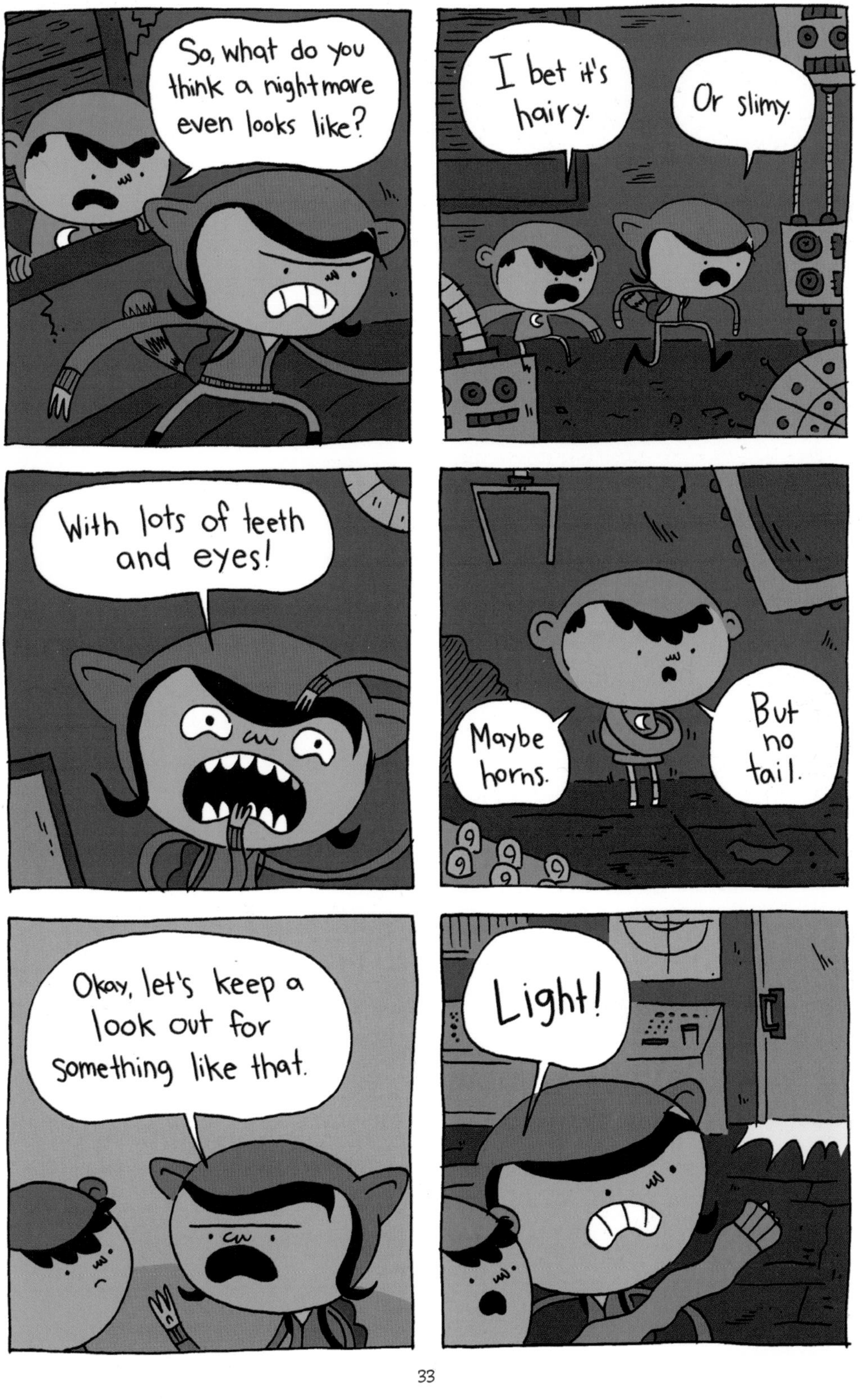
So, what do you think a nightmare even looks like?
I bet it's hairy.
Or slimy.
With lots of teeth and eyes!
Maybe horns.
But no tail.
Okay, let's keep a look out for something like that.
Light!

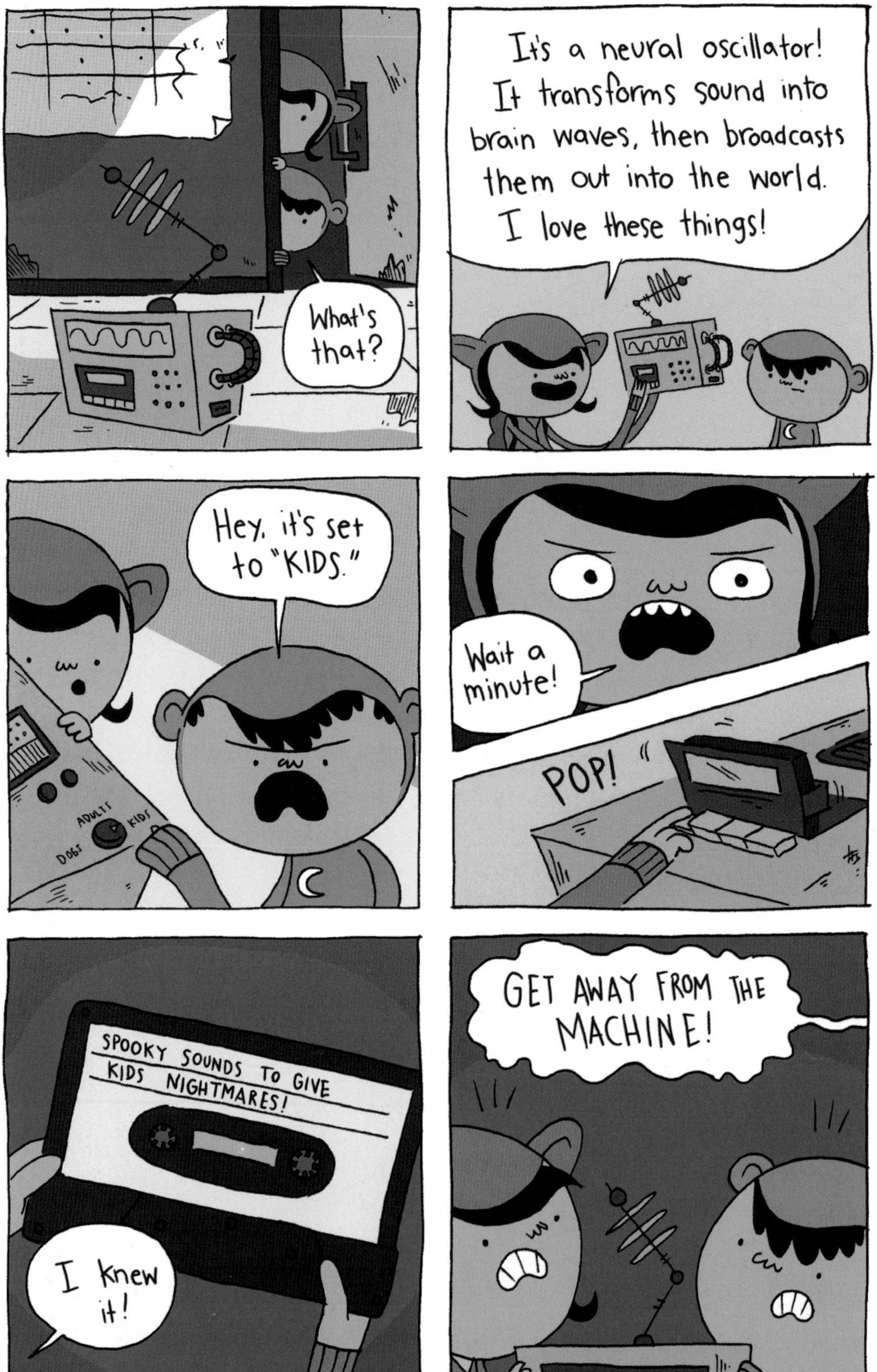
What's that?
It's a neural oscillator! It transforms sound into brain waves, then broadcasts them out into the world. I love these things!
Hey, it's set to "KIDS."
ADULTS
KIDS
DOGS
Wait a minute!
POP!
SPOOKY SOUNDS TO GIVE KIDS NIGHTMARES!
I knew it!
GET AWAY FROM THE MACHINE!

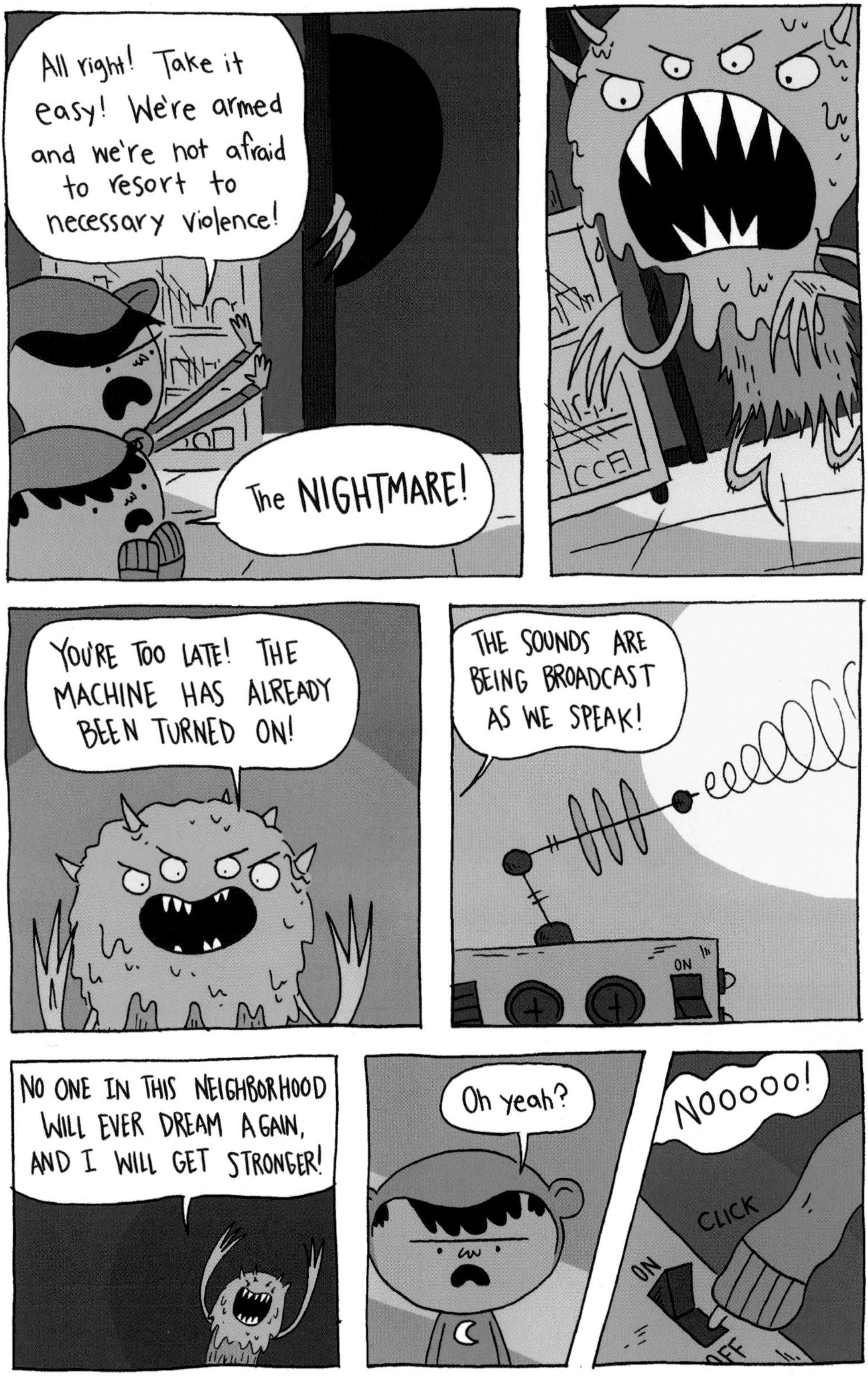
All right! Take it easy! We're armed and we're not afraid to resort to necessary violence!
The NIGHTMARE!
YOU'RE TOO LATE! THE MACHINE HAS ALREADY BEEN TURNED ON!
THE SOUNDS ARE BEING BROADCAST AS WE SPEAK!
ON
NO ONE IN THIS NEIGHBORHOOD WILL EVER DREAM AGAIN, AND I WILL GET STRONGER!
Oh yeah?
NOOOOO!
CLICK
ON
OFF

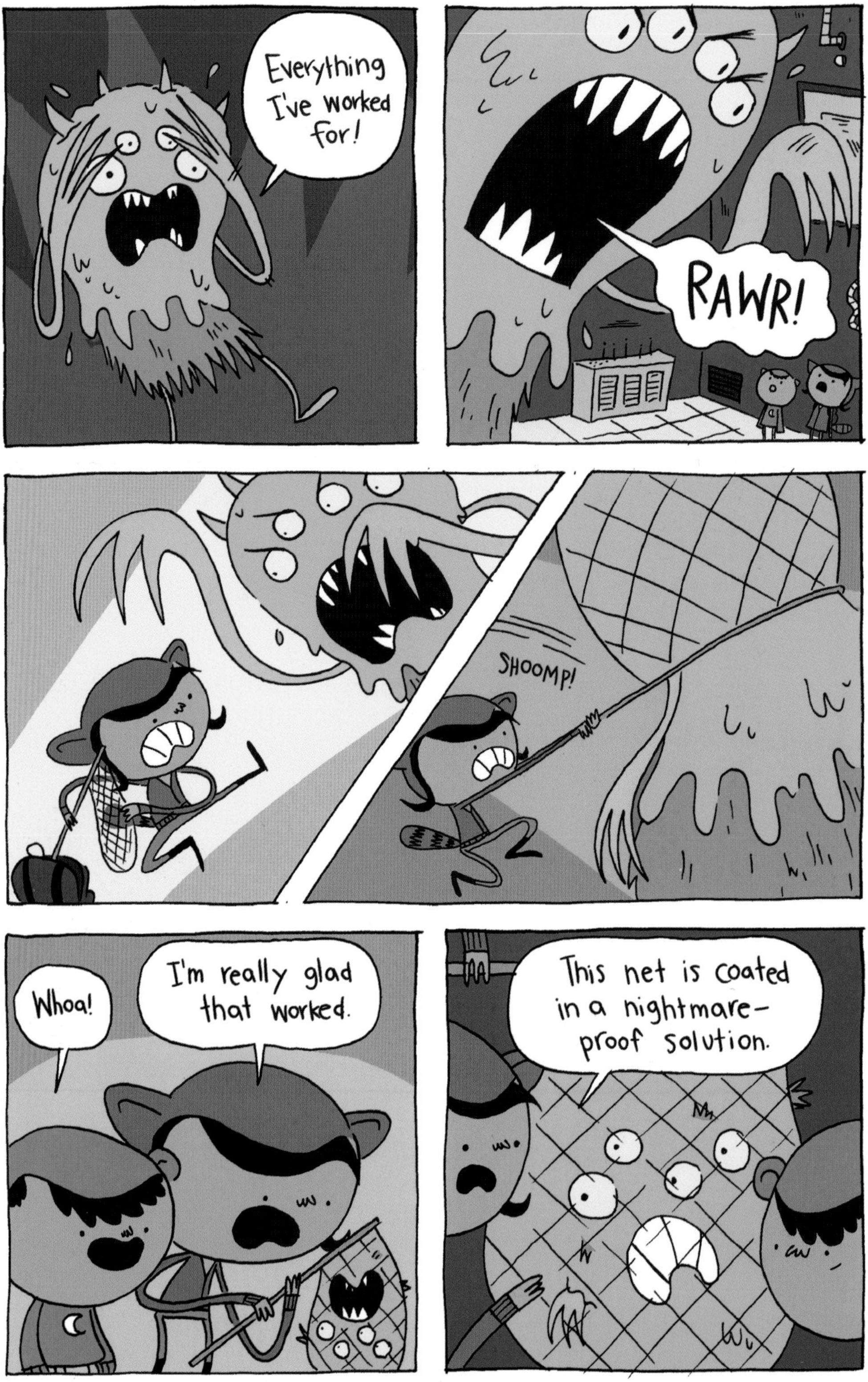
Everything I've worked for!
RAWR!
SHOOMP!
Whoa!
I'm really glad that worked.
This net is coated in a nightmare-proof solution.

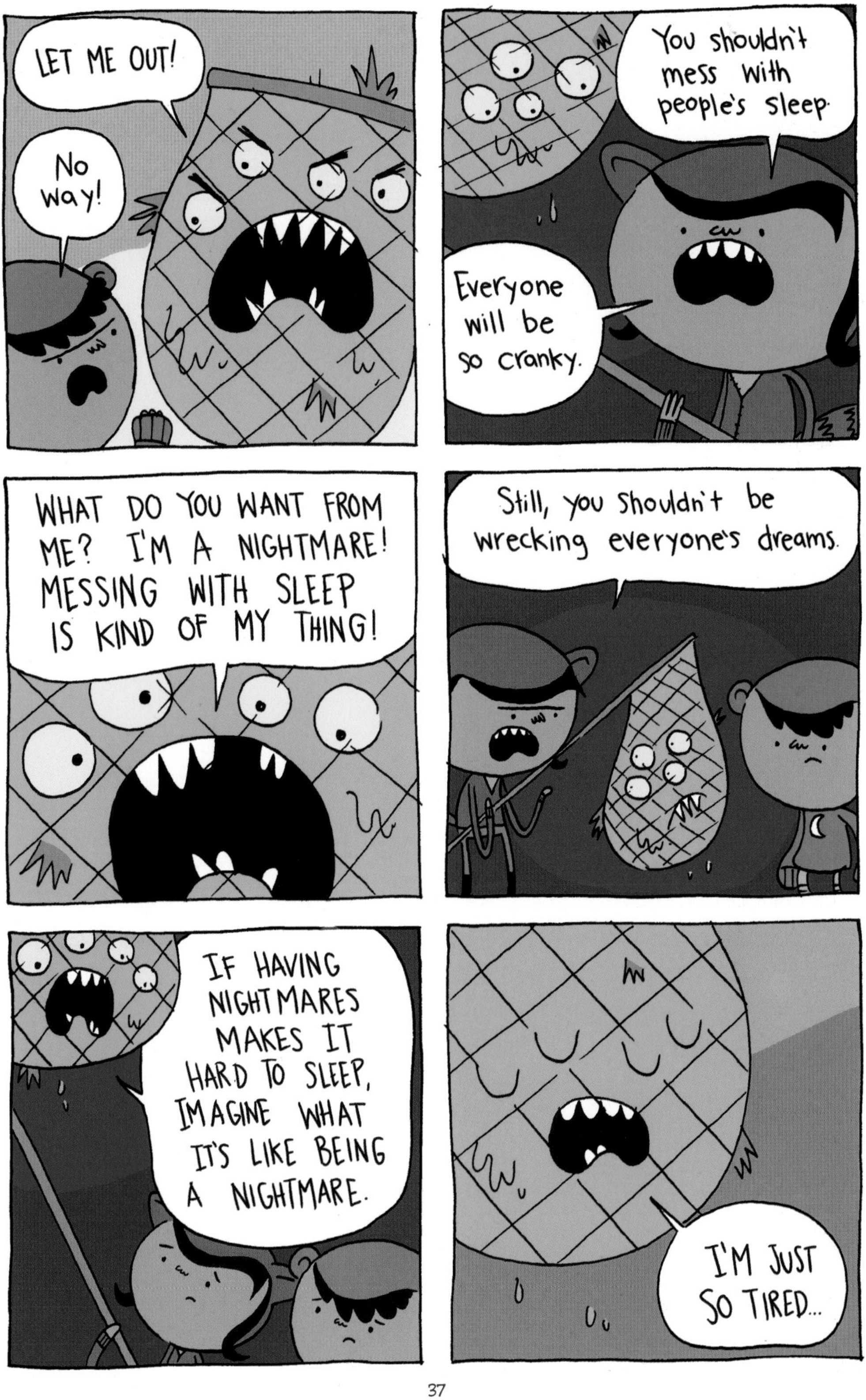
LET ME OUT!
No way!
You shouldn't mess with people's sleep.
Everyone will be so cranky.
WHAT DO YOU WANT FROM ME? I'M A NIGHTMARE! MESSING WITH SLEEP IS KIND OF MY THING!
Still, you shouldn't be wrecking everyone's dreams.
IF HAVING NIGHTMARES MAKES IT HARD TO SLEEP, IMAGINE WHAT IT'S LIKE BEING A NIGHTMARE.
I'M JUST SO TIRED...

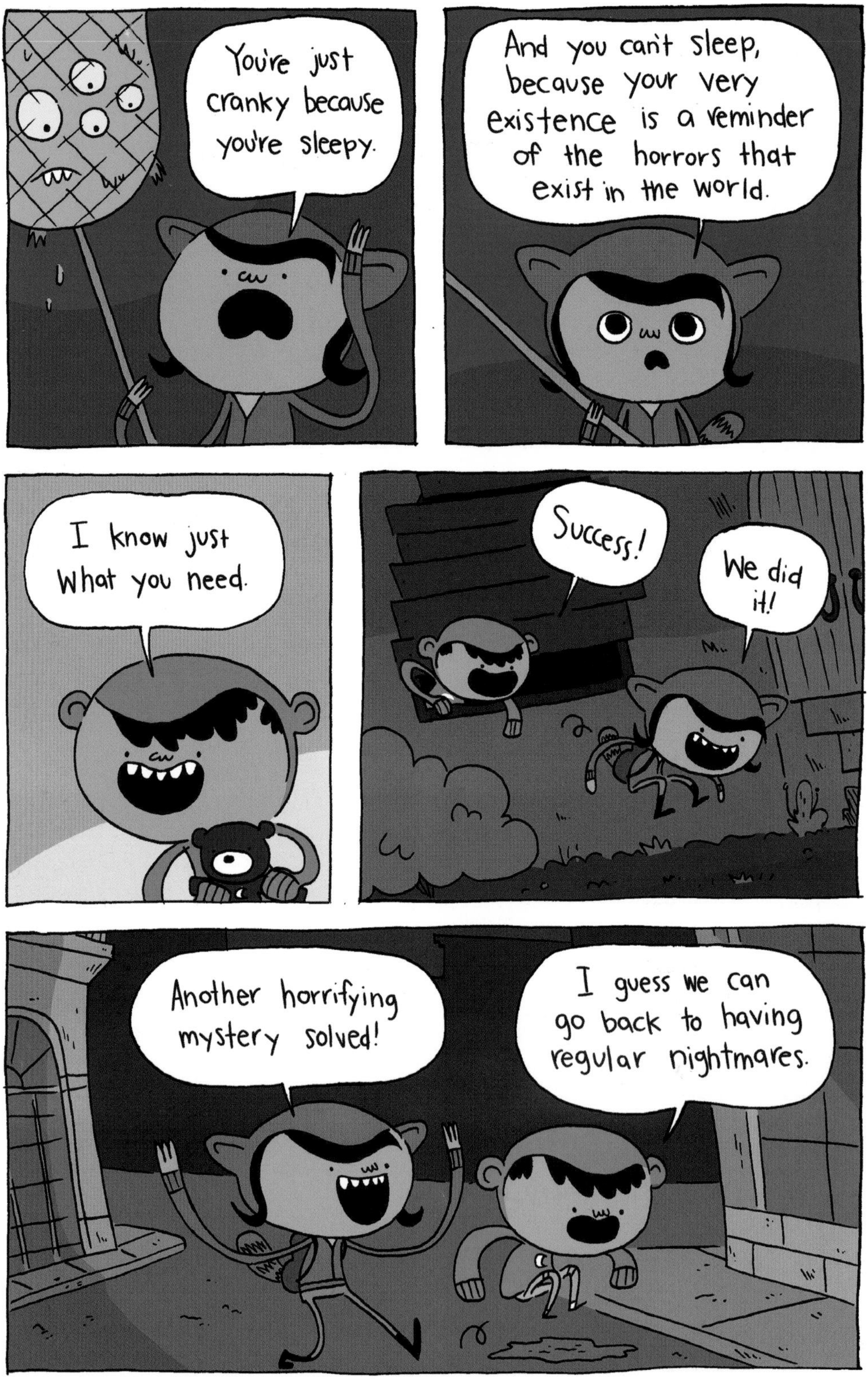
You're just cranky because you're sleepy.
And you can't sleep, because your very existence is a reminder of the horrors that exist in the world.
I know just What you need.
Success!
We did it!
Another horrifying mystery solved!
I guess we can go back to having regular nightmares.

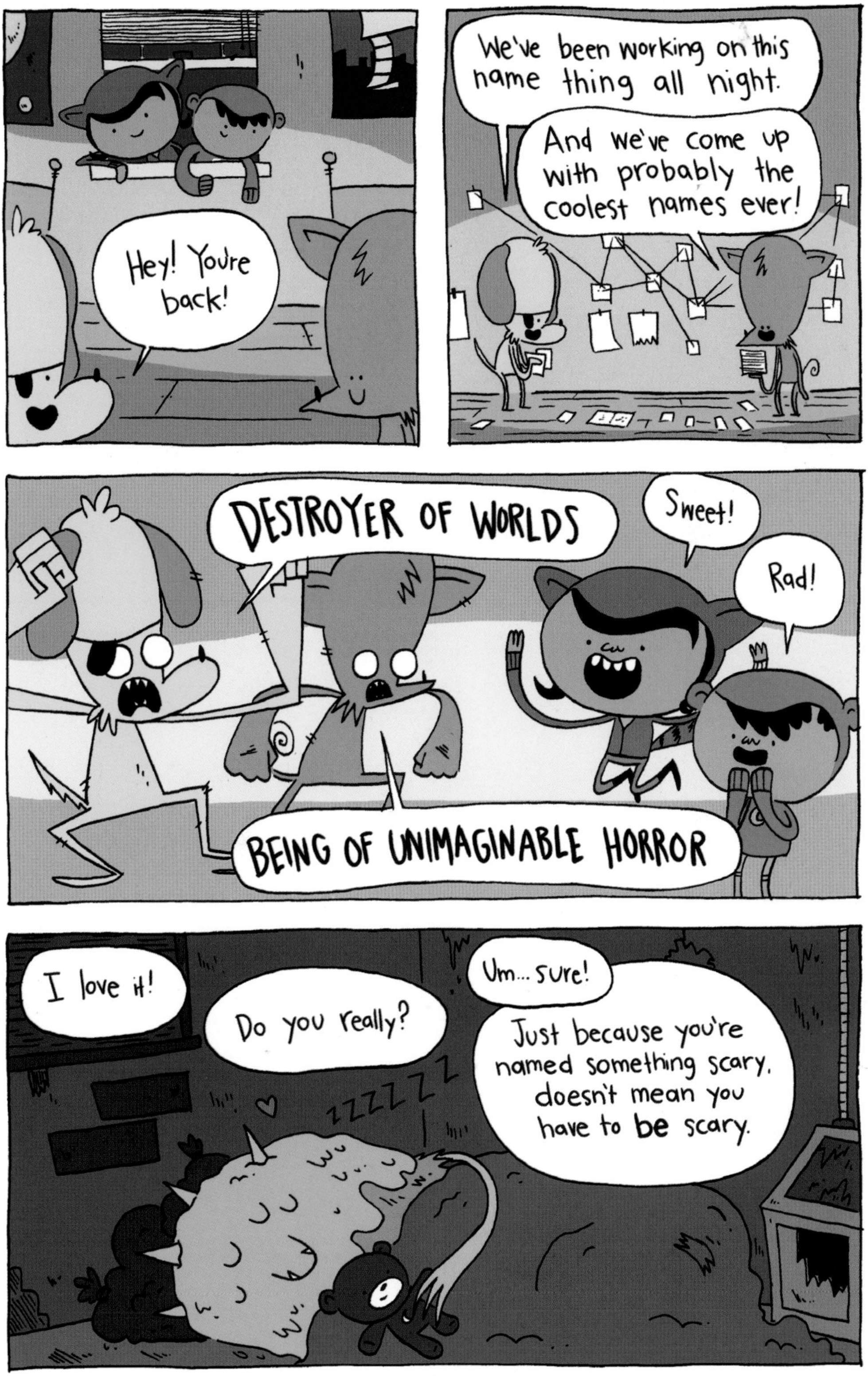

Hey! You're back!
We've been working on this name thing all night.
And we've come up with probably the coolest names ever!
DESTROYER OF WORLDS
BEING OF UNIMAGINABLE HORROR
Sweet!
Rad!
I love it!
Do you really?
Um... sure!
Just because you're named something scary, doesn't mean you have to **be** scary.
ZZZZZZ

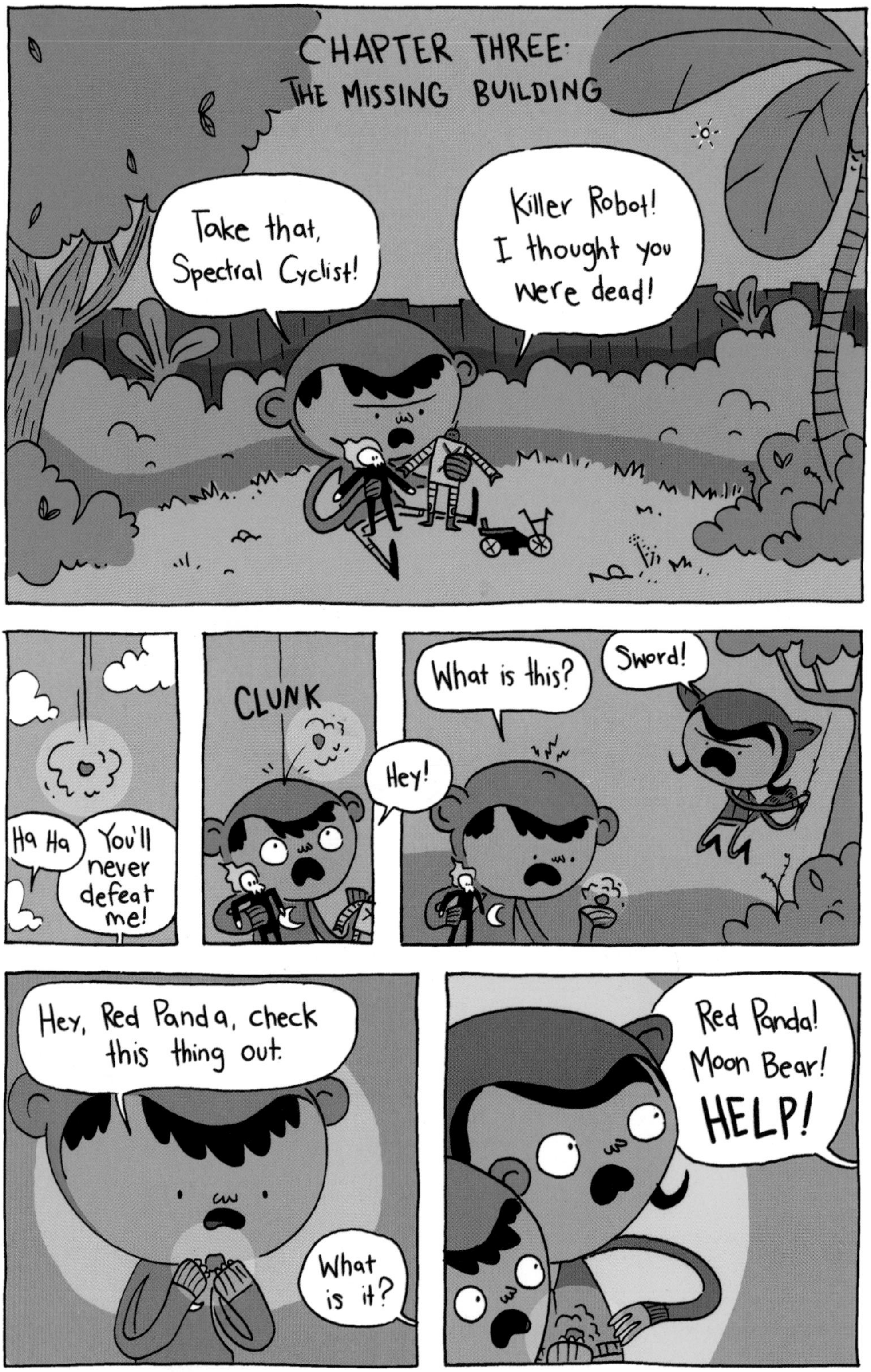

CHAPTER THREE:
THE MISSING BUILDING
Take that, Spectral Cyclist!
Killer Robot! I thought you were dead!
Ha Ha
You'll never defeat me!
CLUNK
Hey!
What is this?
Sword!
Hey, Red Panda, check this thing out.
What is it?
Red Panda! Moon Bear! HELP!

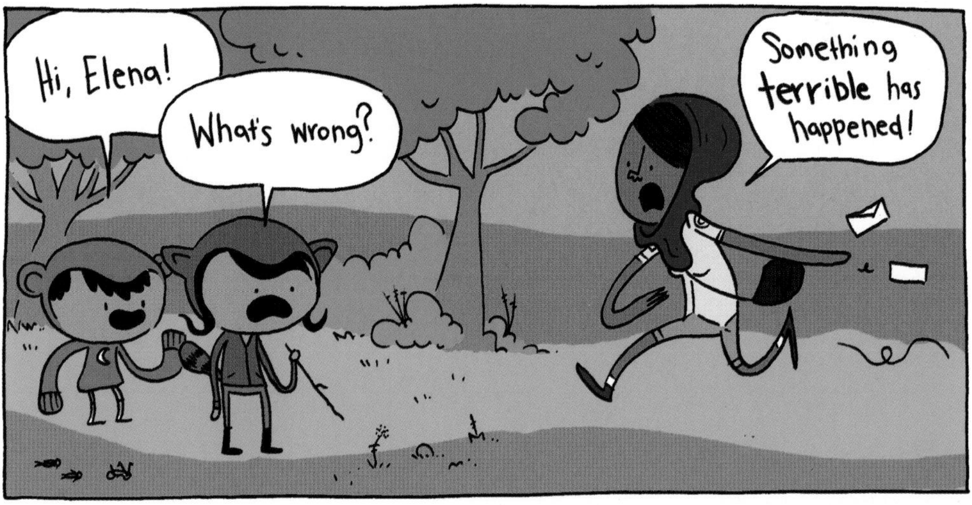
Hi, Elena!
What's wrong?
Something terrible has happened!

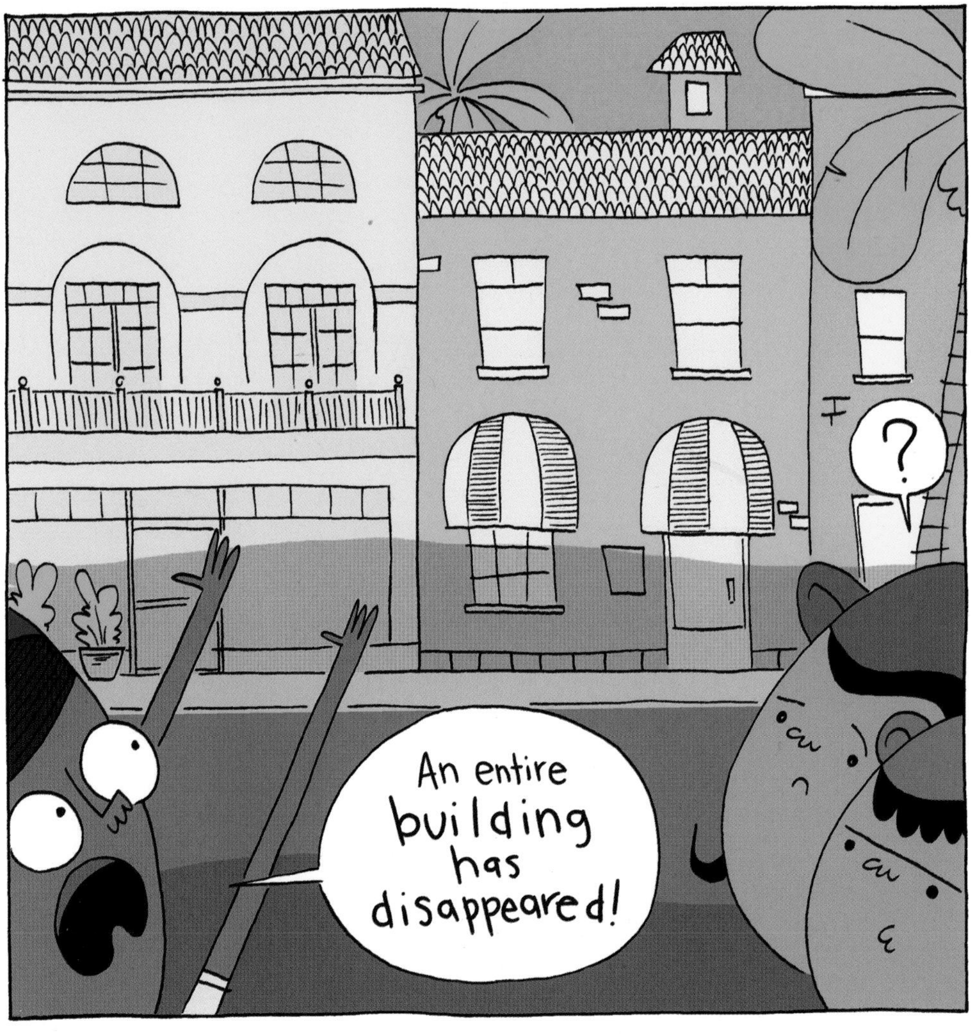
An entire building has disappeared!
?

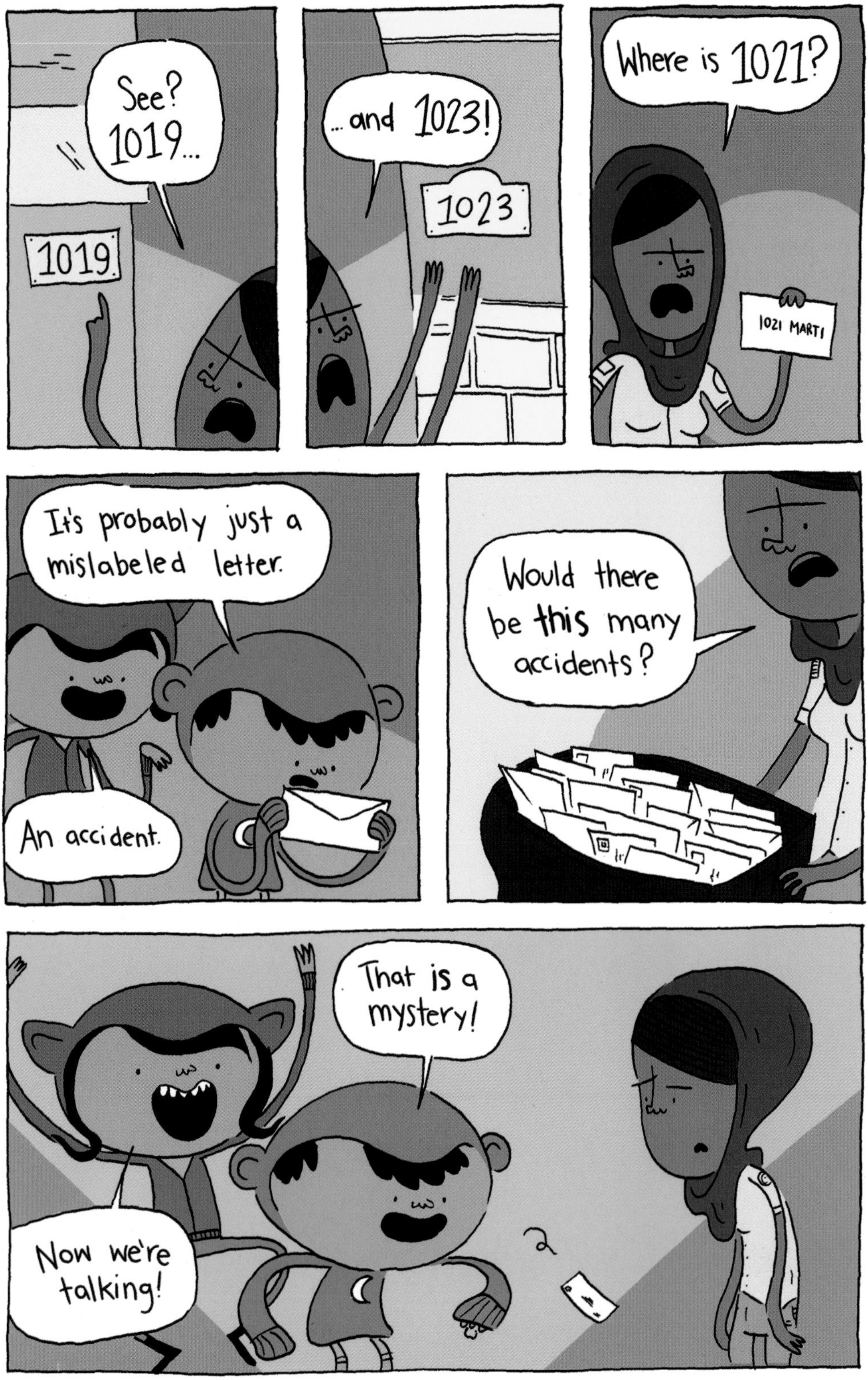
See? 1019...
1019
...and 1023!
1023
Where is 1021?
1021 MARTI
It's probably just a mislabeled letter.
An accident.
Would there be this many accidents?
That is a mystery!
Now we're talking!

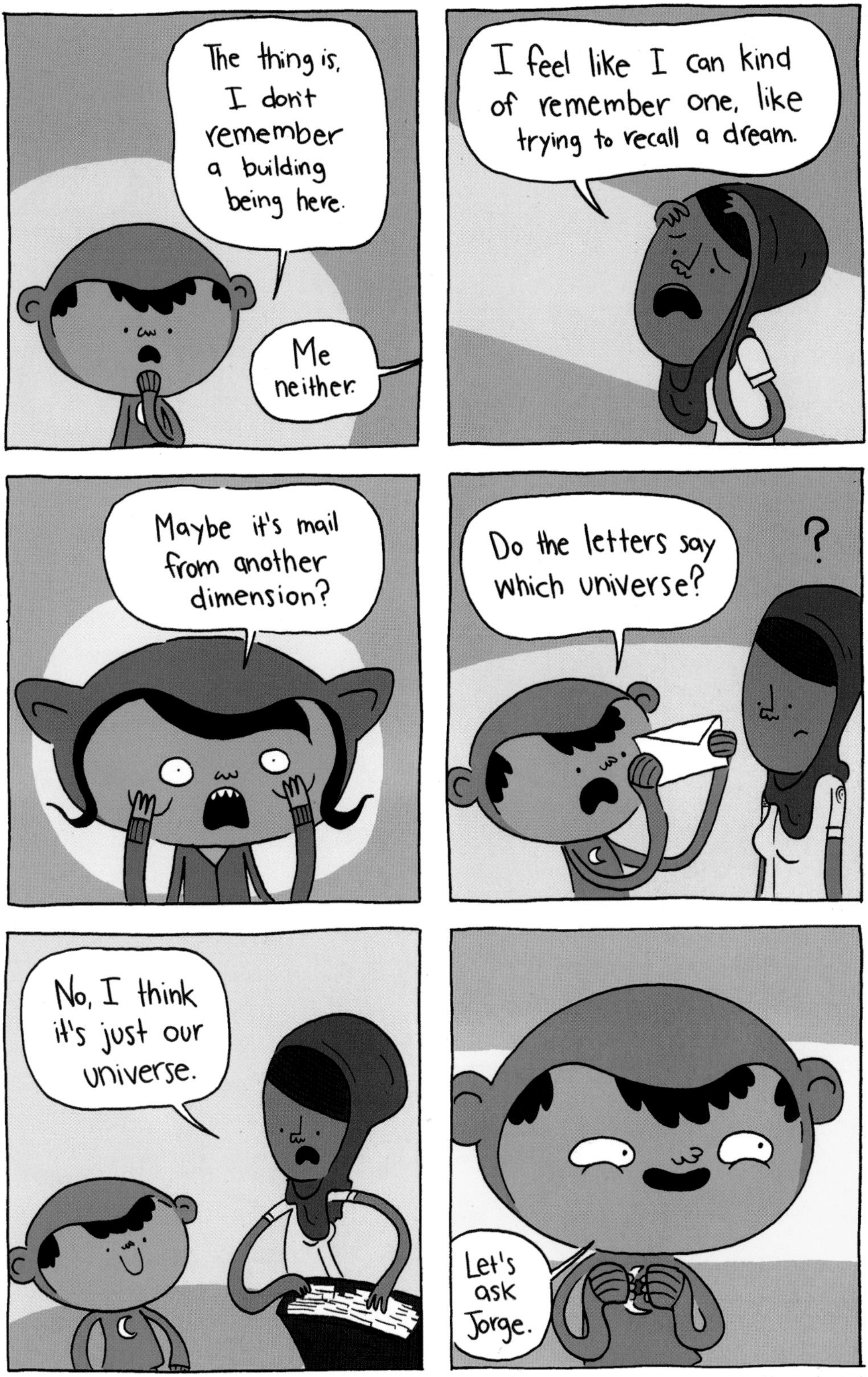
The thing is, I don't remember a building being here.
Me neither.
I feel like I can kind of remember one, like trying to recall a dream.
Maybe it's mail from another dimension?
Do the letters say which universe?
?
No, I think it's just our universe.
Let's ask Jorge.

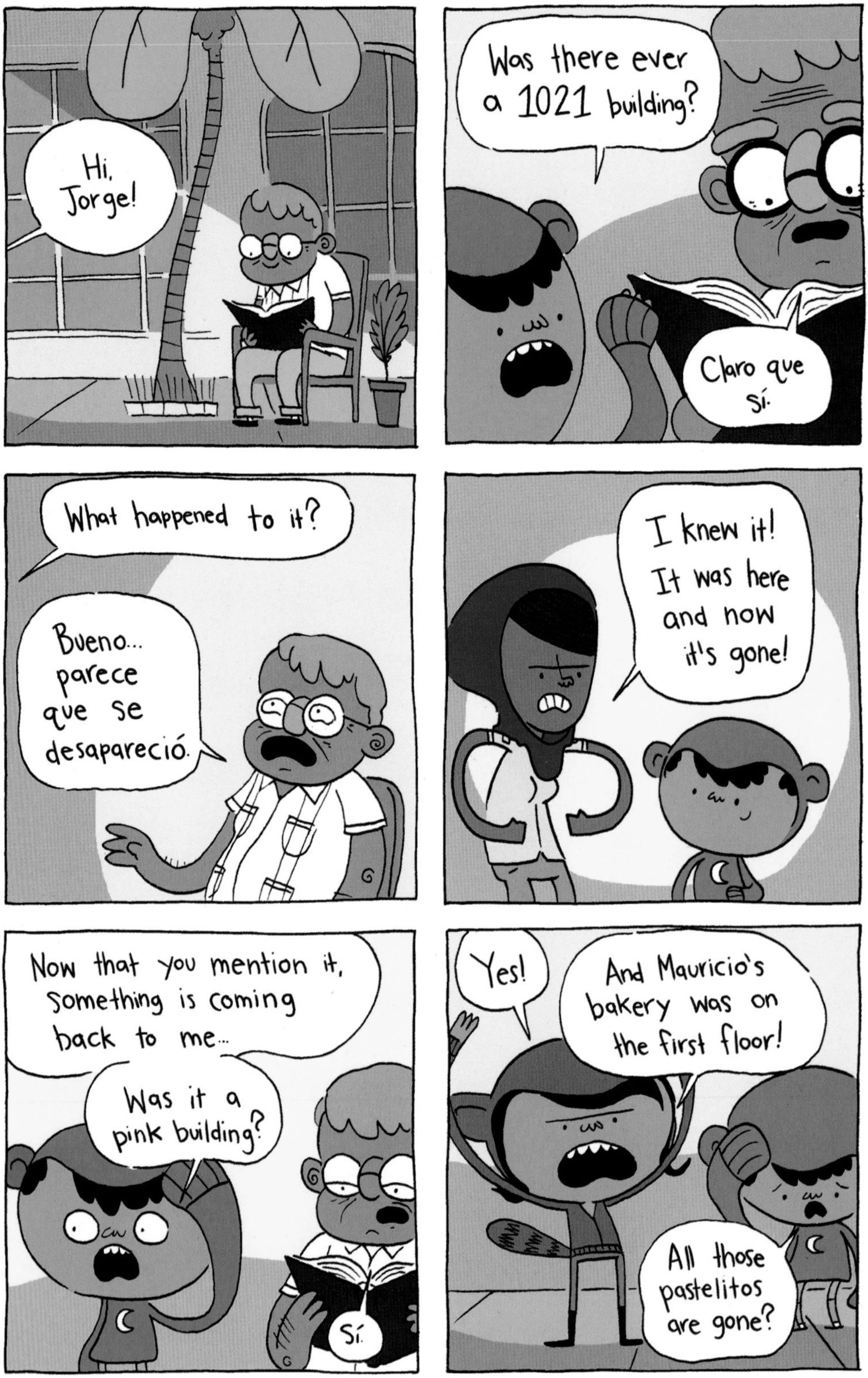
Hi, Jorge!
Was there ever a 1021 building?
Claro que sí.
What happened to it?
Bueno... parece que se desapareció.
I knew it! It was here and now it's gone!
Now that you mention it, something is coming back to me...
Was it a pink building?
Sí.
Yes!
And Mauricio's bakery was on the first floor!
All those pastelitos are gone?

Oh, no! That's Lorena's building!

Whoa...

I REMEMBER!

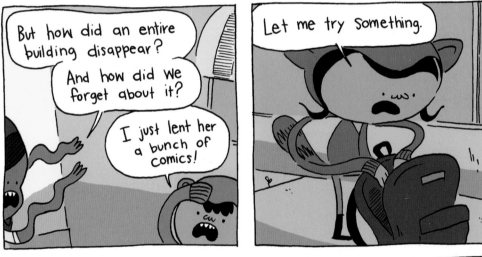

But how did an entire building disappear?

And how did we forget about it?

I just lent her a bunch of comics!

Let me try something.

TA DA!

FWOOoM

DING!

That explains it.

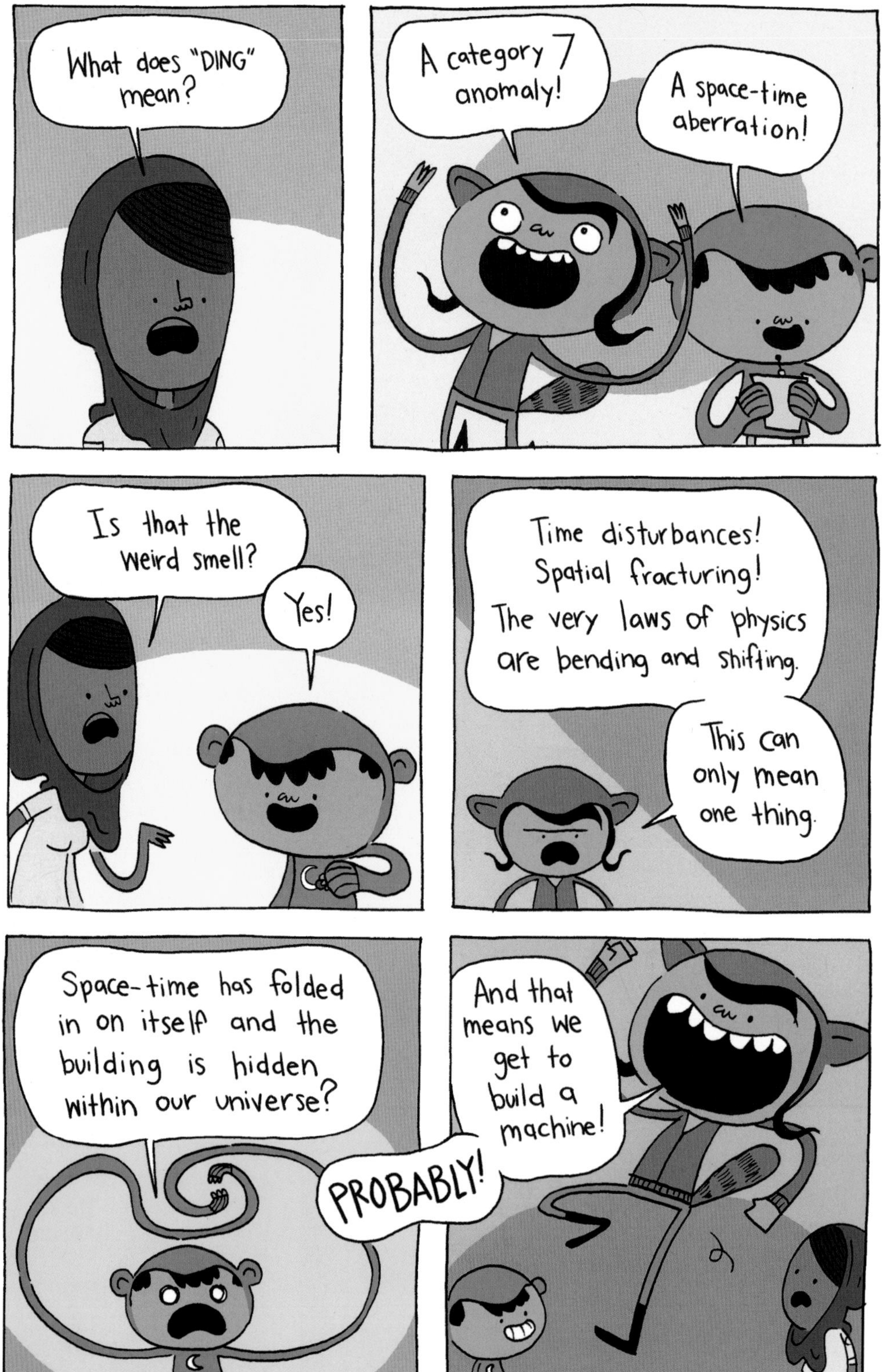
What does "DING" mean?
A category 7 anomaly!
A space-time aberration!
Is that the weird smell?
Yes!
Time disturbances! Spatial fracturing! The very laws of physics are bending and shifting.
This can only mean one thing.
Space-time has folded in on itself and the building is hidden within our universe?
And that means we get to build a machine!
PROBABLY!

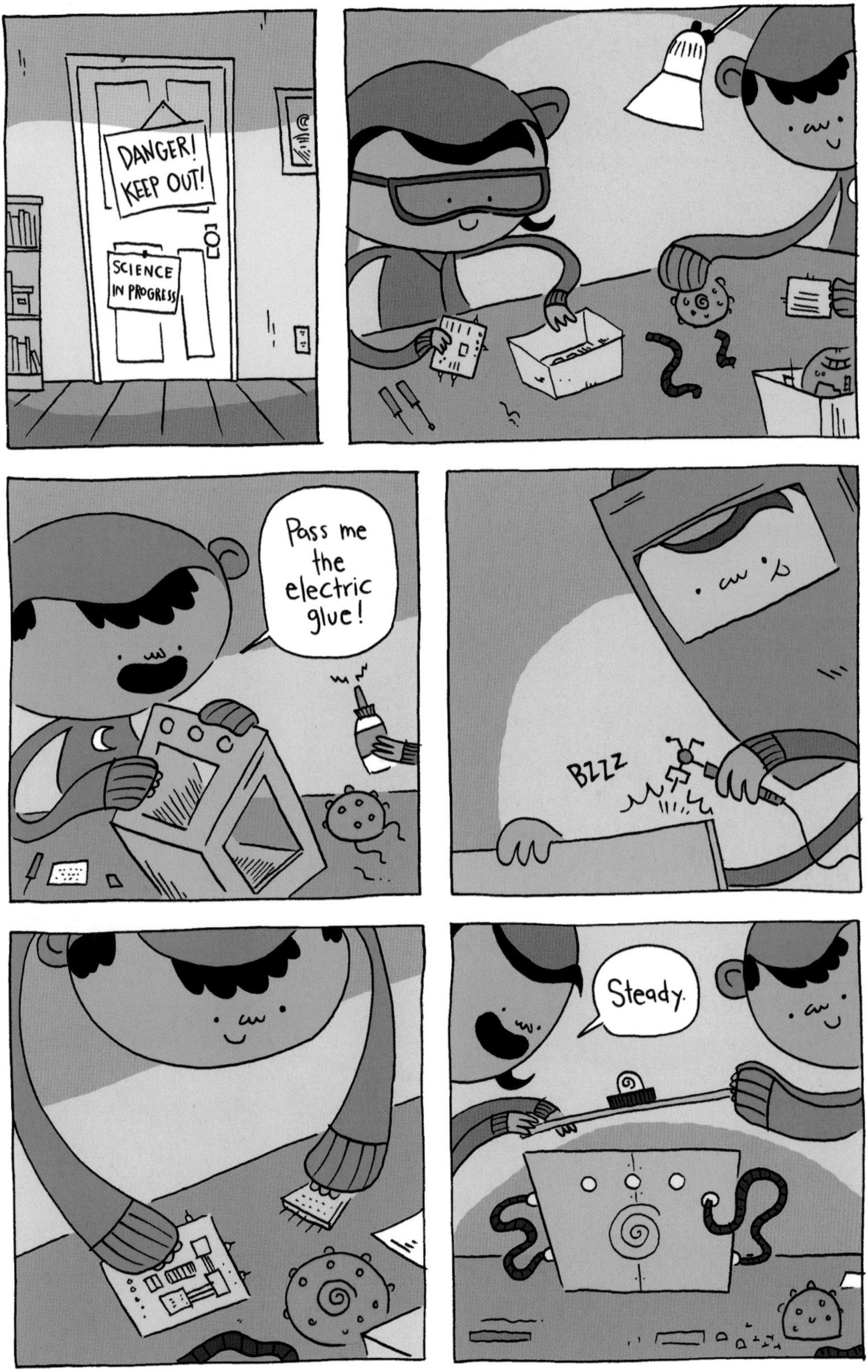
DANGER! KEEP OUT!
SCIENCE IN PROGRESS
Pass me the electric glue!
BZZZ
Steady.

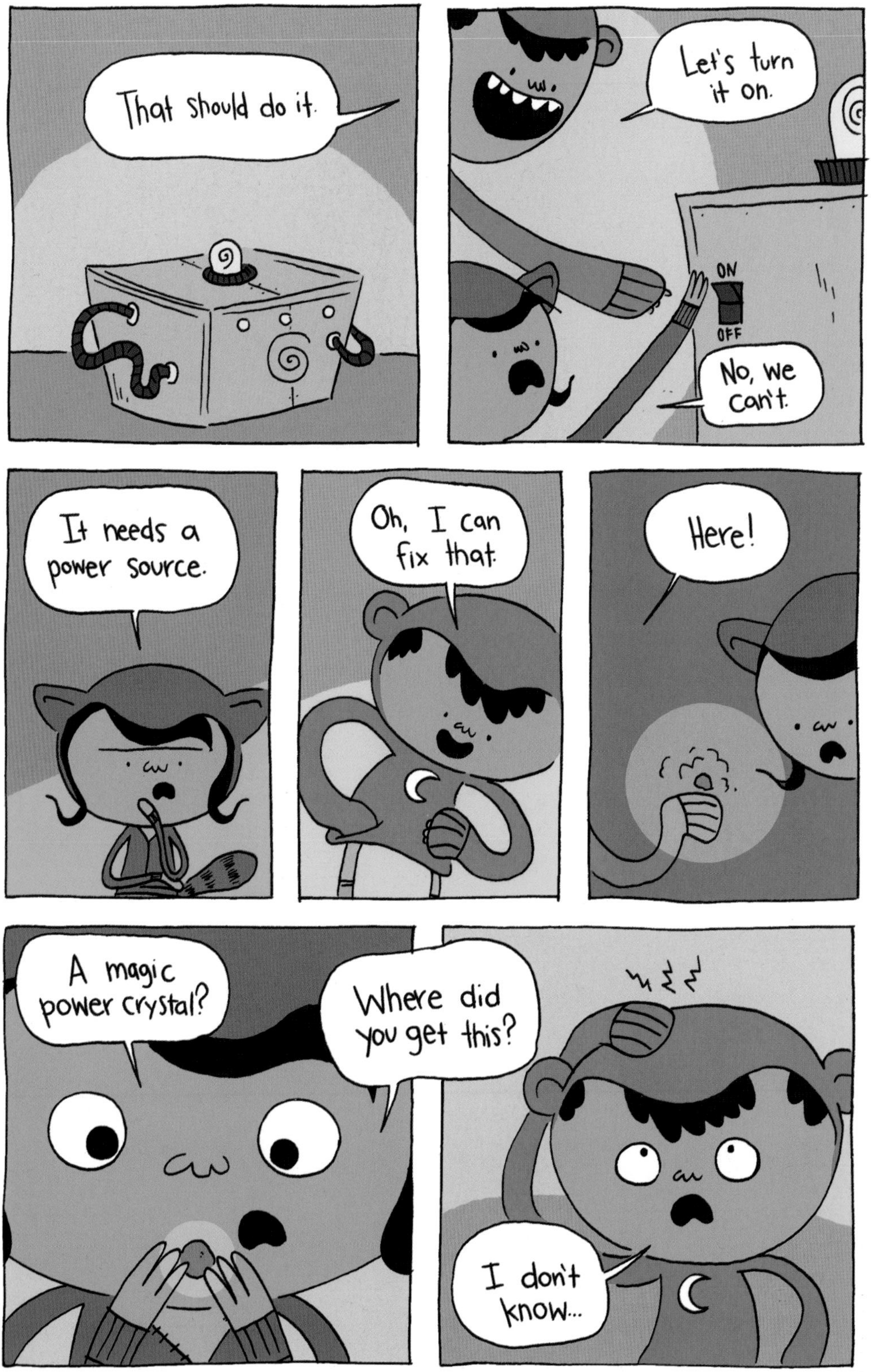
That should do it.
Let's turn it on.
ON
OFF
No, we can't.
It needs a power source.
Oh, I can fix that.
Here!
A magic power crystal?
Where did you get this?
I don't know...

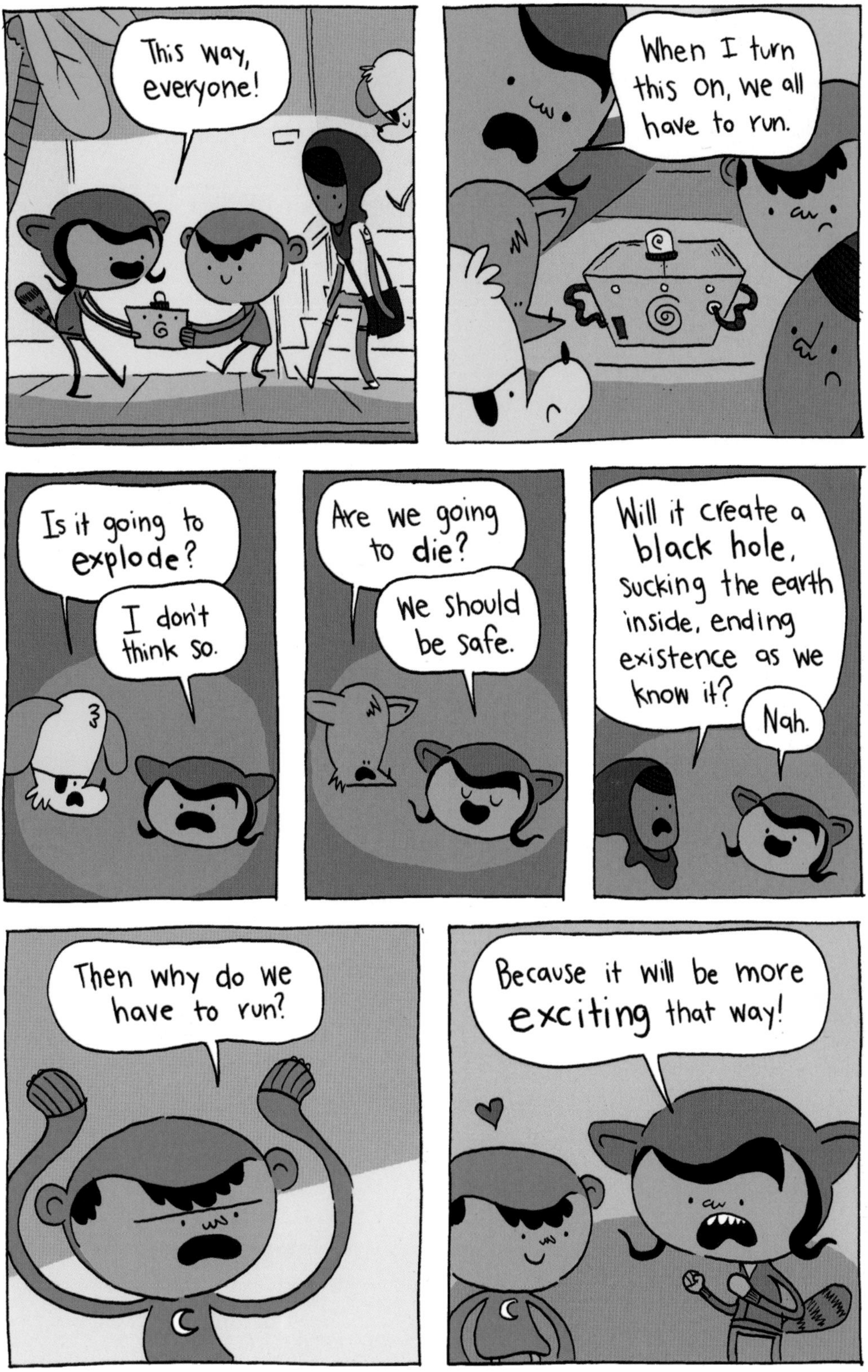
This way, everyone!
When I turn this on, we all have to run.
Is it going to explode?
I don't think so.
Are we going to die?
We should be safe.
Will it create a black hole, sucking the earth inside, ending existence as we know it?
Nah.
Then why do we have to run?
Because it will be more exciting that way!

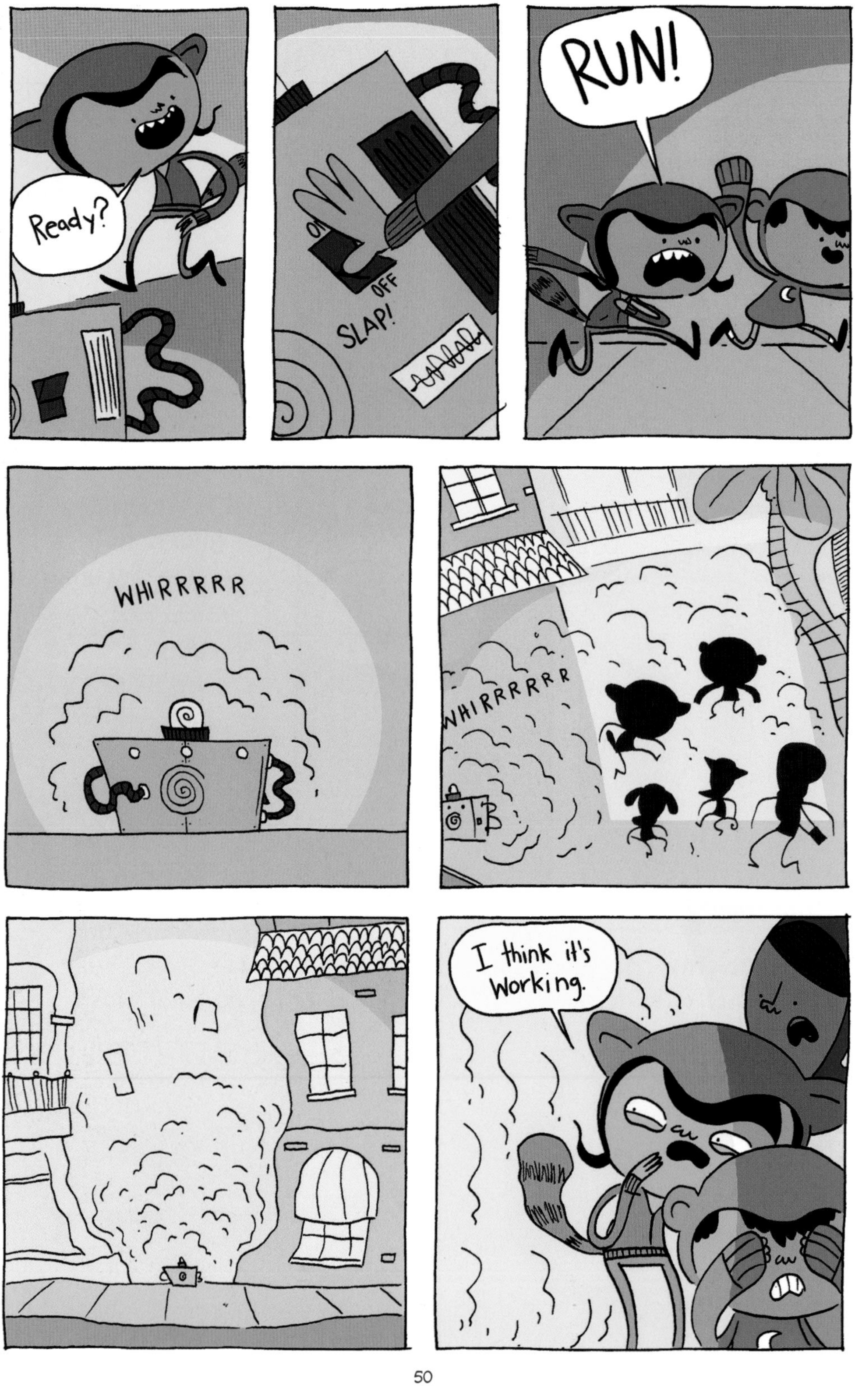
Ready?
ON
OFF
SLAP!
RUN!
WHIRRRRR
WHIRRRRRR
I think it's working.

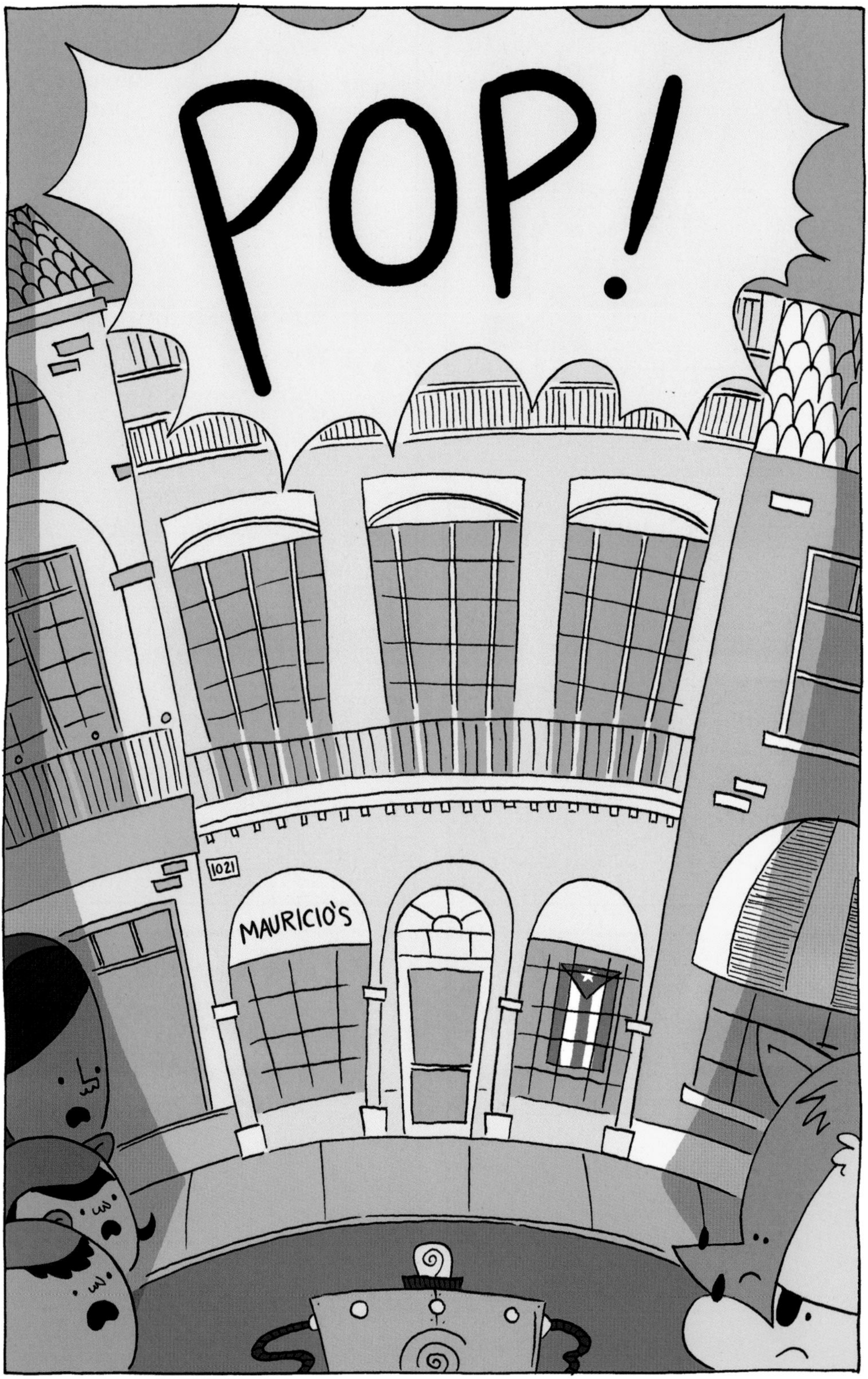
POP!
1021
MAURICIO'S

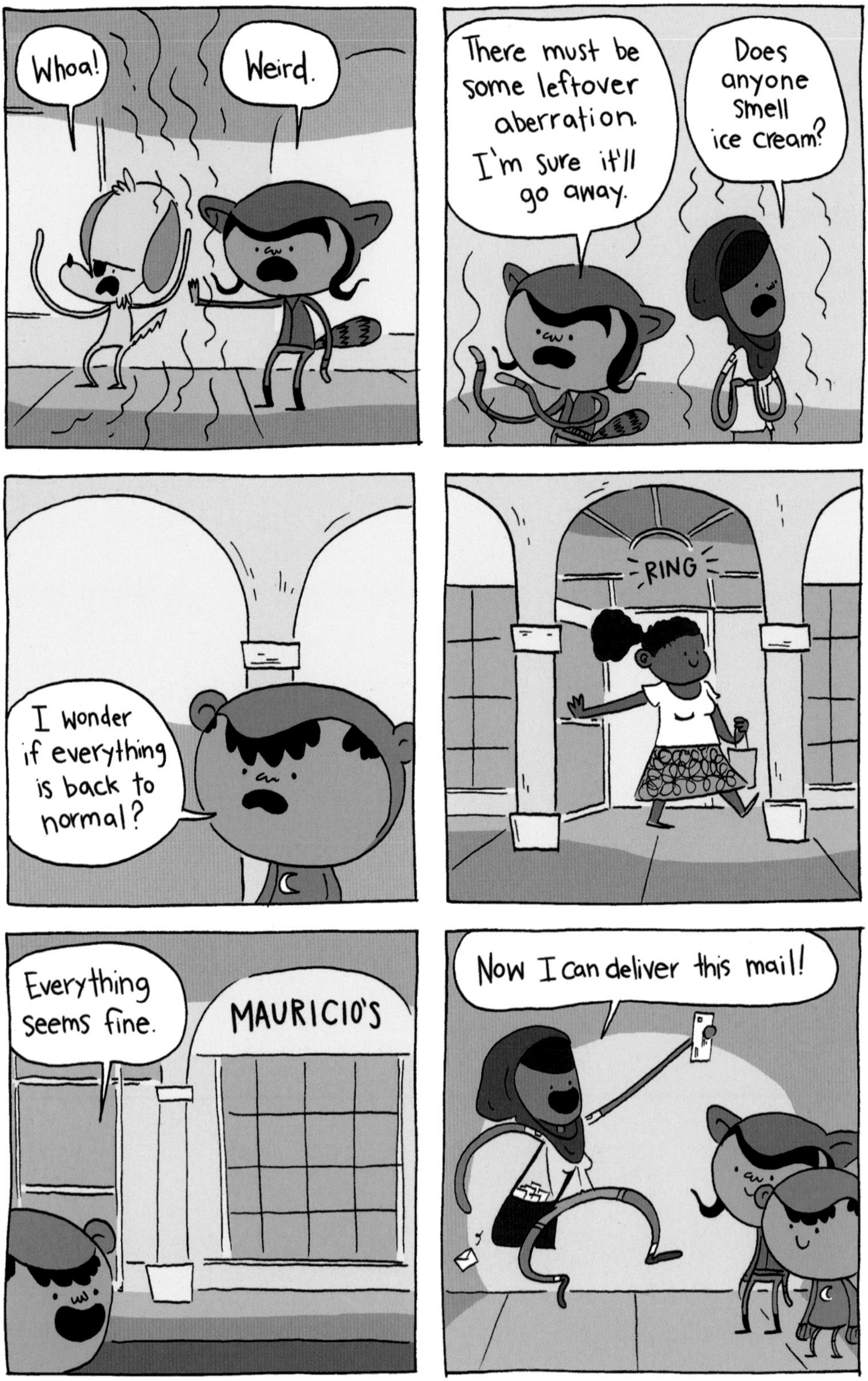
Whoa!
Weird.
There must be some leftover aberration.
I'm sure it'll go away.
Does anyone smell ice cream?
I wonder if everything is back to normal?
RING
Everything seems fine.
MAURICIO'S
Now I can deliver this mail!

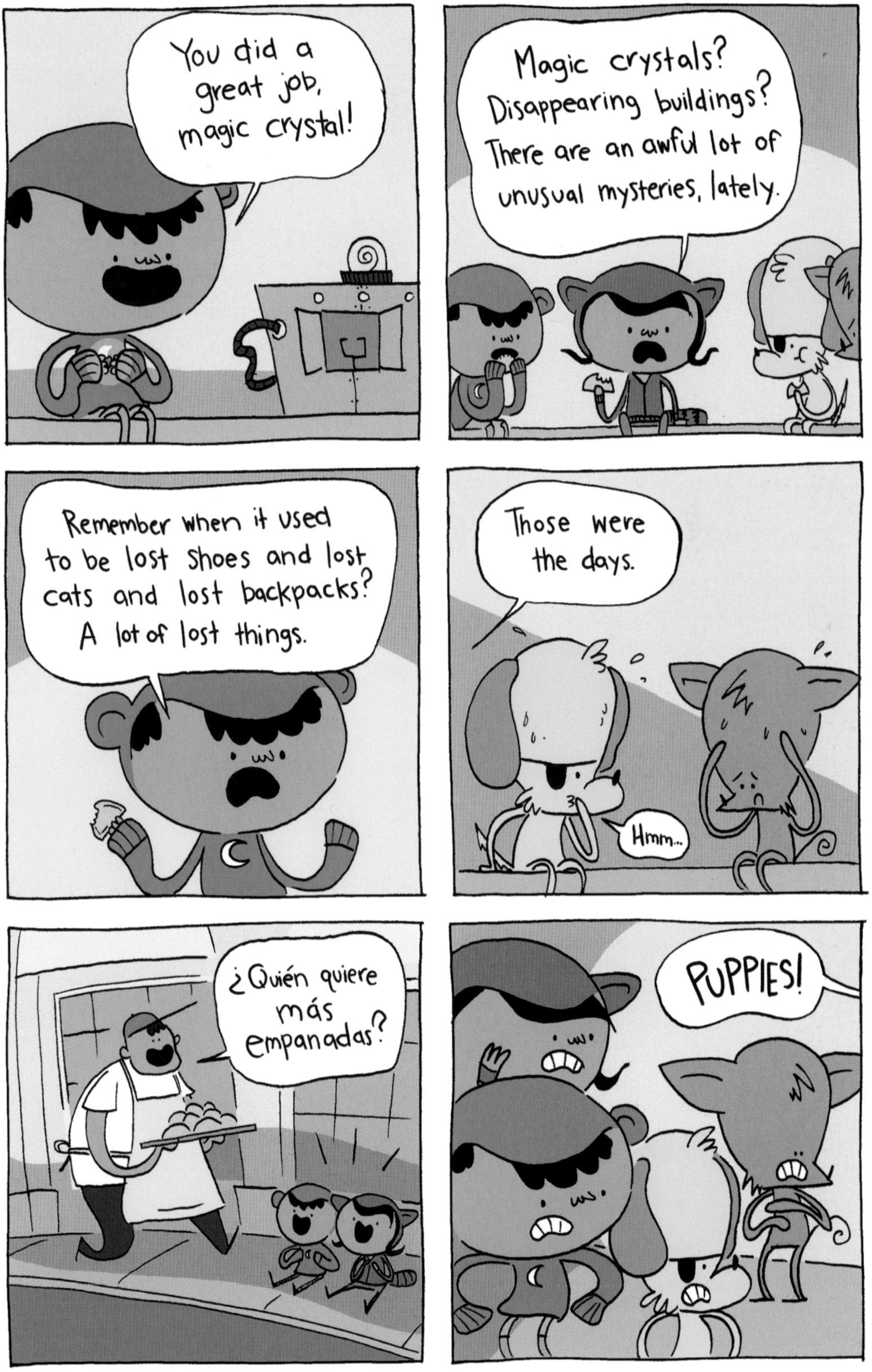
You did a great job, magic crystal!
Magic crystals? Disappearing buildings? There are an awful lot of unusual mysteries, lately.
Remember when it used to be lost shoes and lost cats and lost backpacks? A lot of lost things.
Those were the days.
Hmm...
¿Quién quiere más empanadas?
PUPPIES!

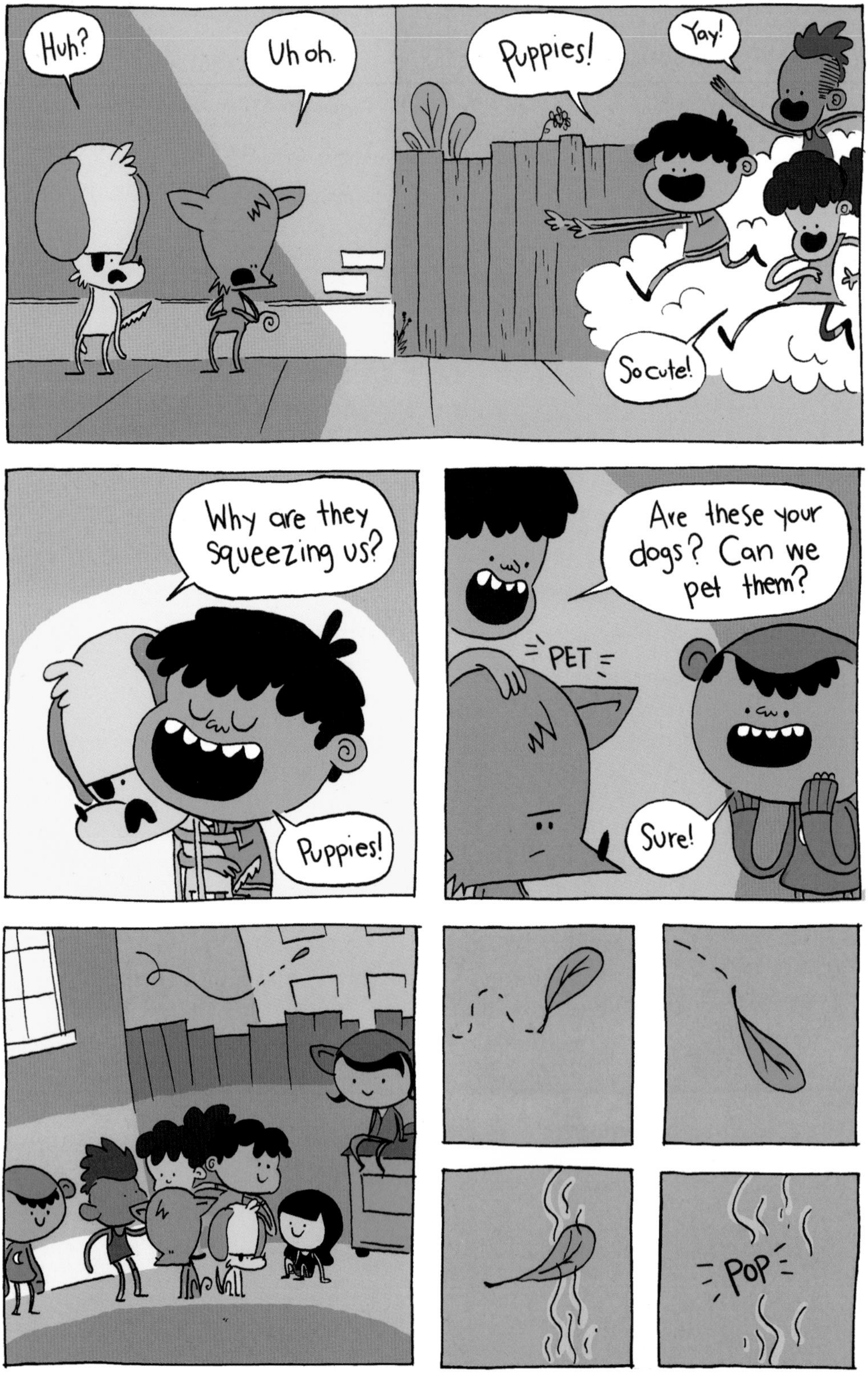
Huh?
Uh oh.
Puppies!
Yay!
So cute!
Why are they squeezing us?
Puppies!
Are these your dogs? Can we pet them?
PET
Sure!
POP

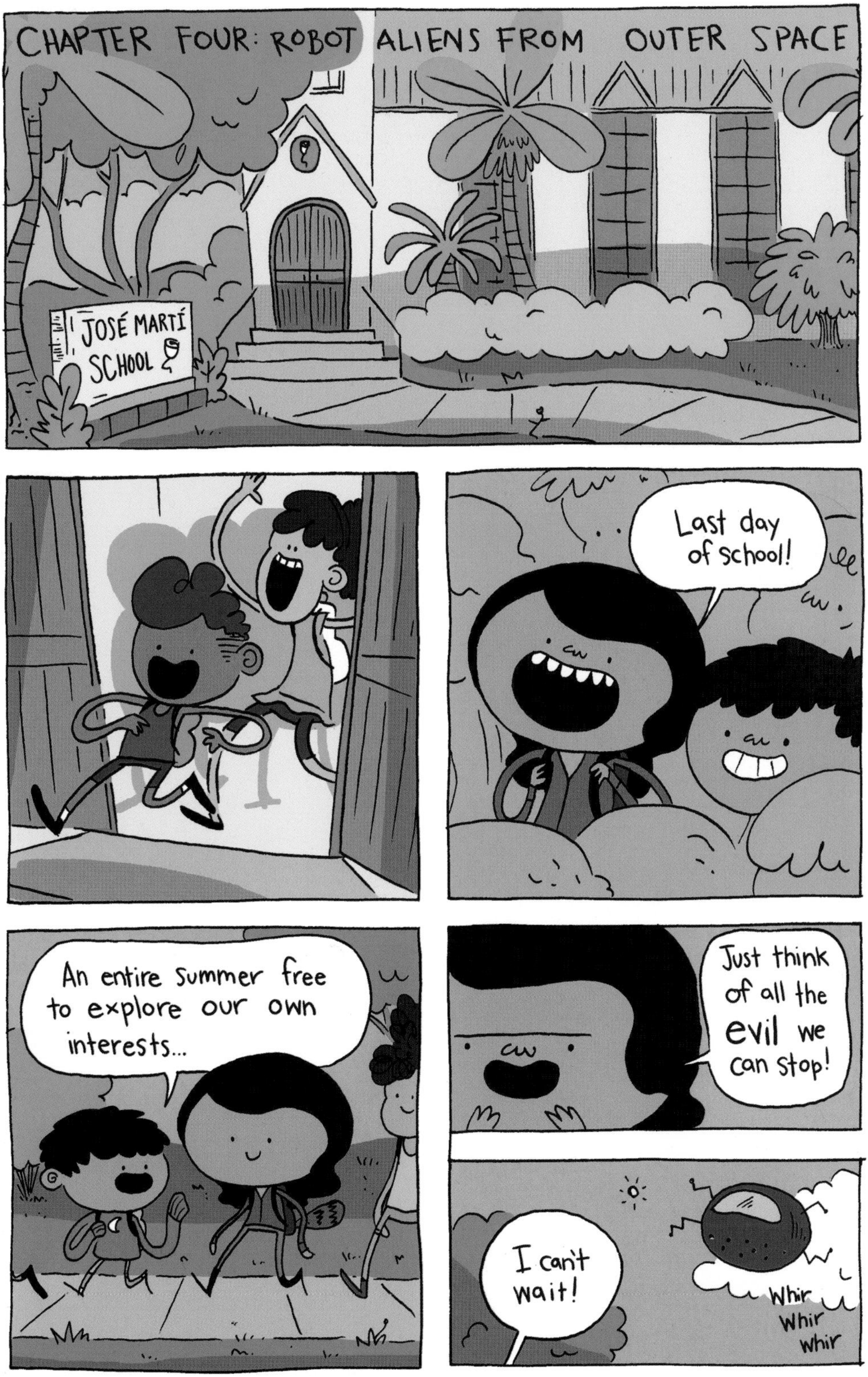
CHAPTER FOUR: ROBOT ALIENS FROM OUTER SPACE
JOSÉ MARTÍ SCHOOL
Last day of school!
An entire summer free to explore our own interests...
Just think of all the evil we can stop!
I can't wait!
Whir Whir Whir

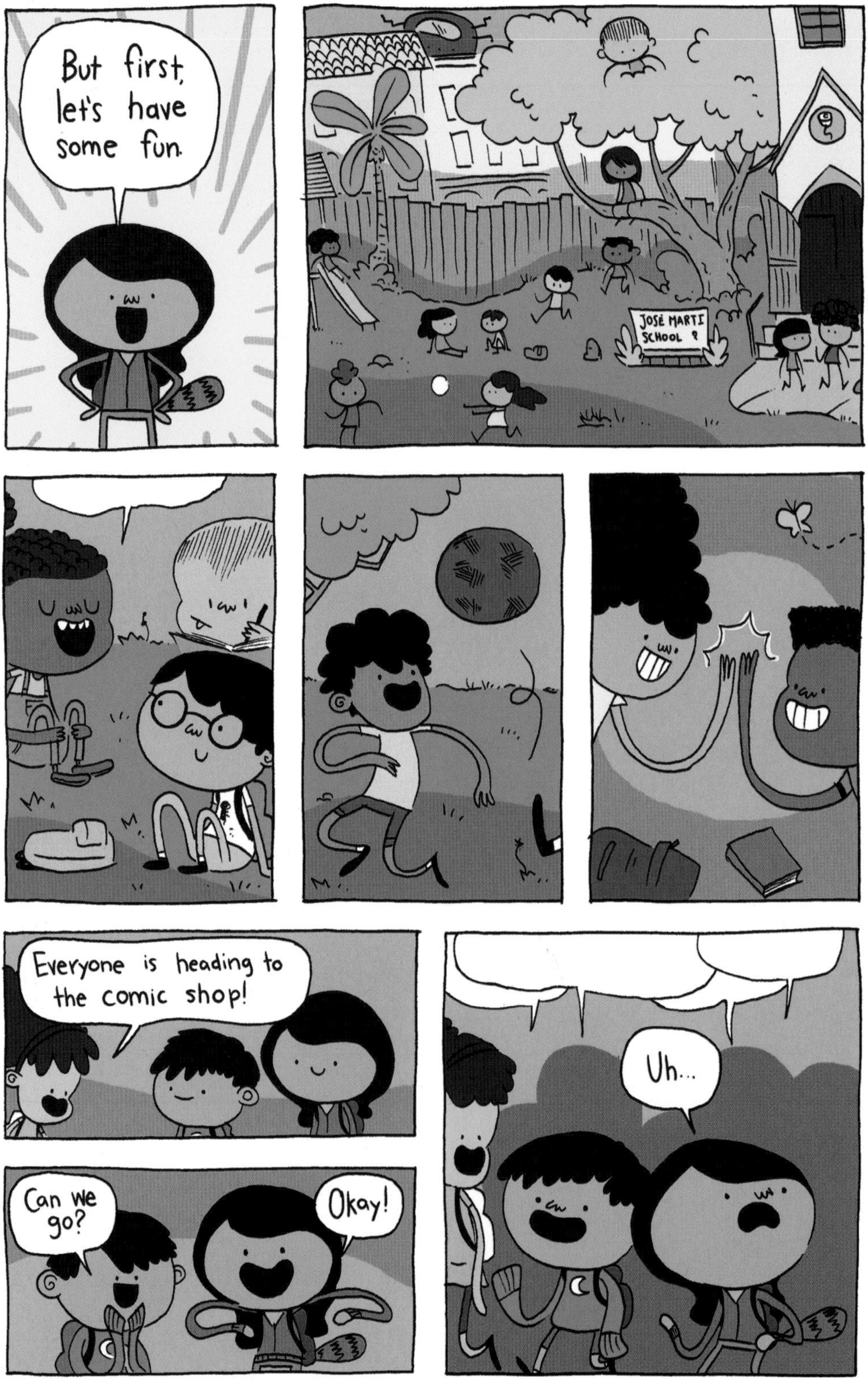
But first, let's have some fun.
JOSÉ MARTI SCHOOL
Everyone is heading to the comic shop!
Can we go?
Okay!
Uh...

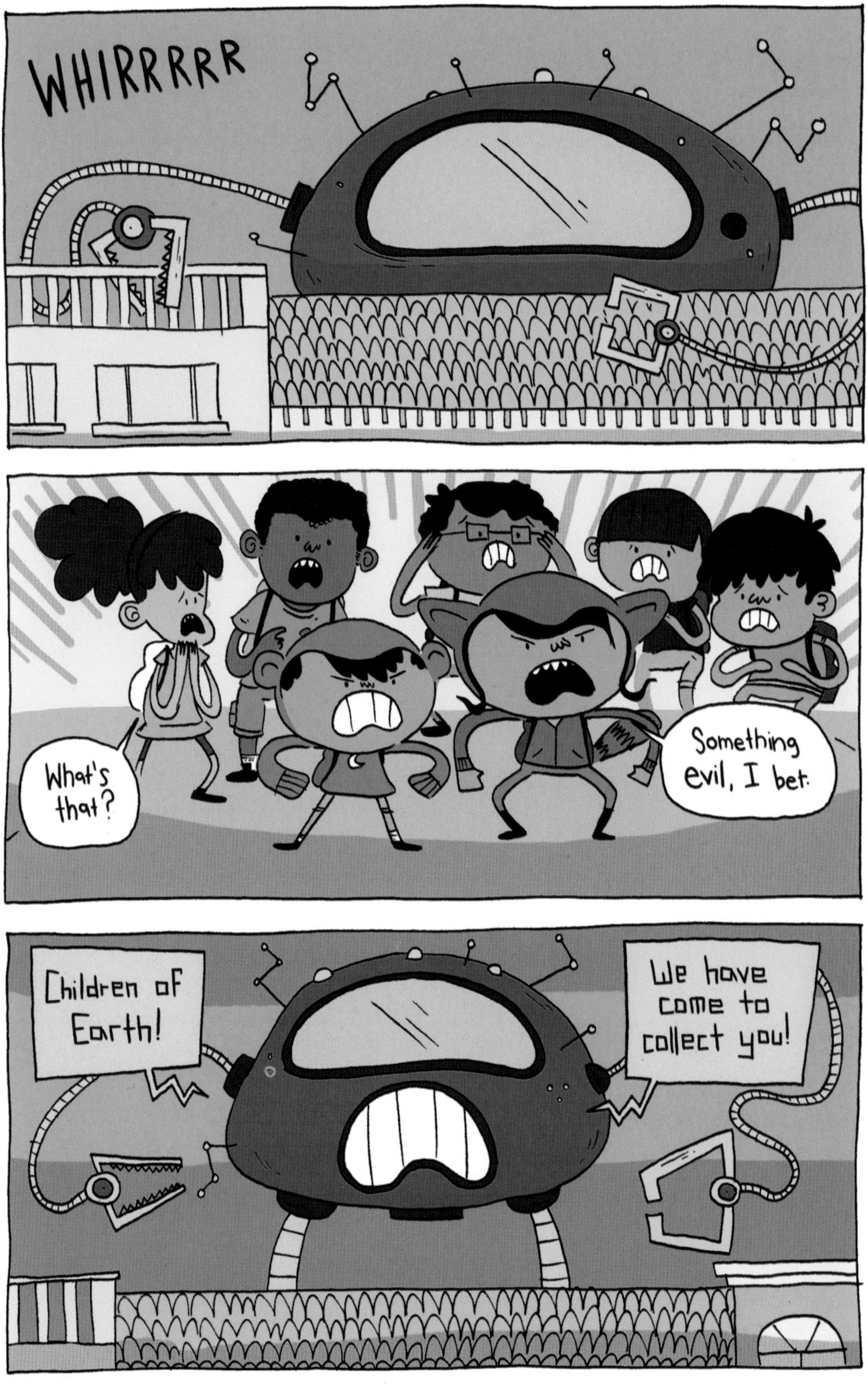
WHIRRRRR
What's that?
Something evil, I bet.
Children of Earth!
We have come to collect you!

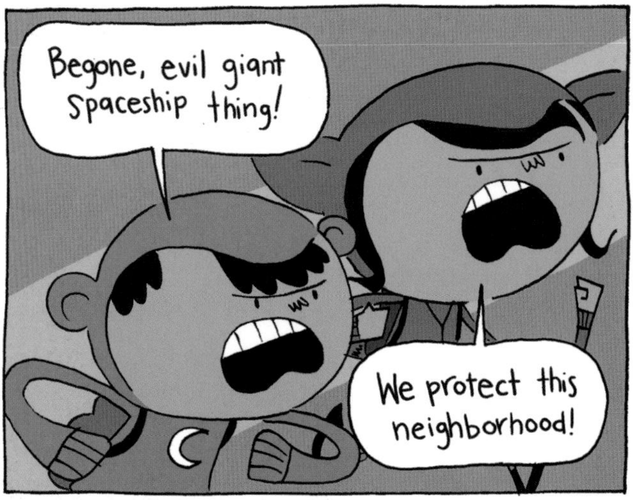
Begone, evil giant spaceship thing!
We protect this neighborhood!

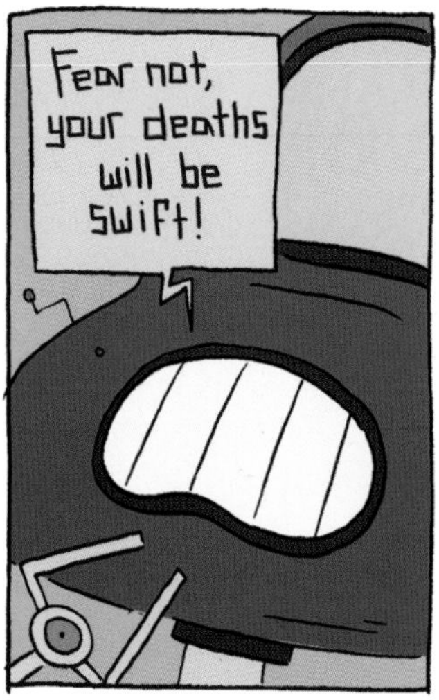
Fear not, your deaths will be swift!

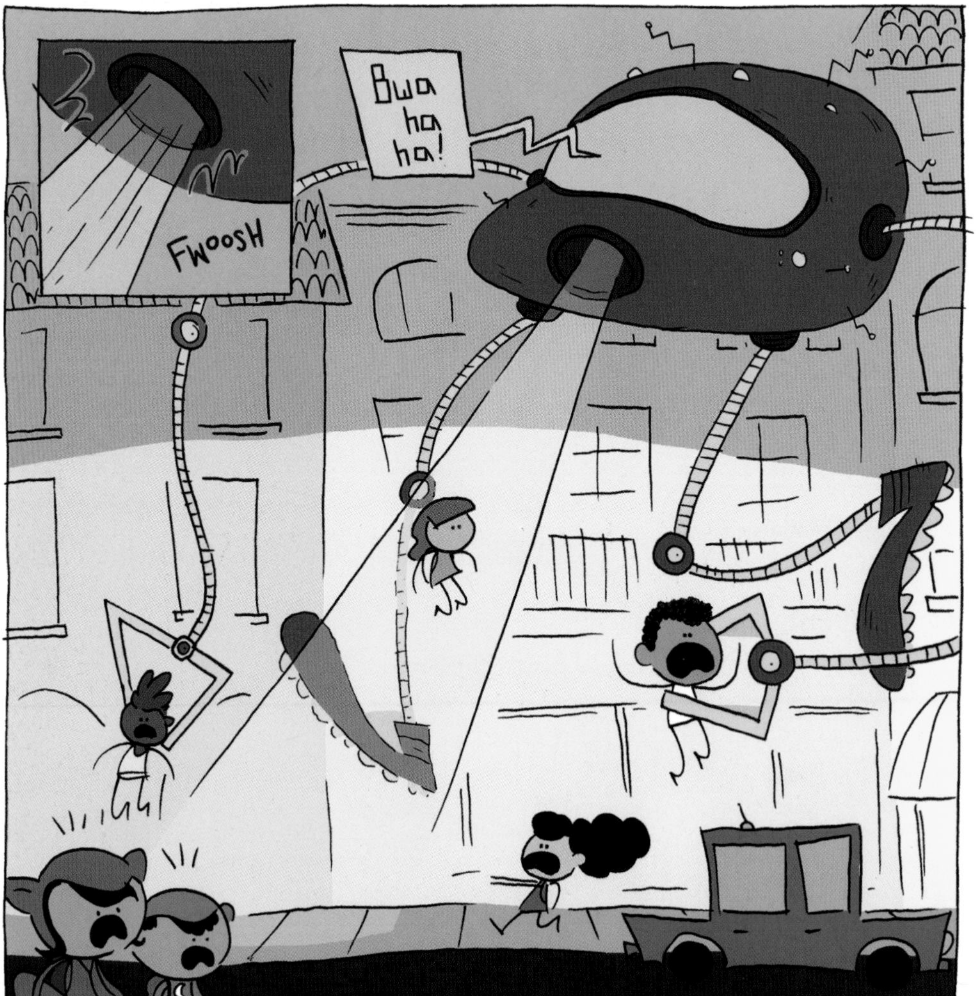
FWOOSH
Bwa ha ha!

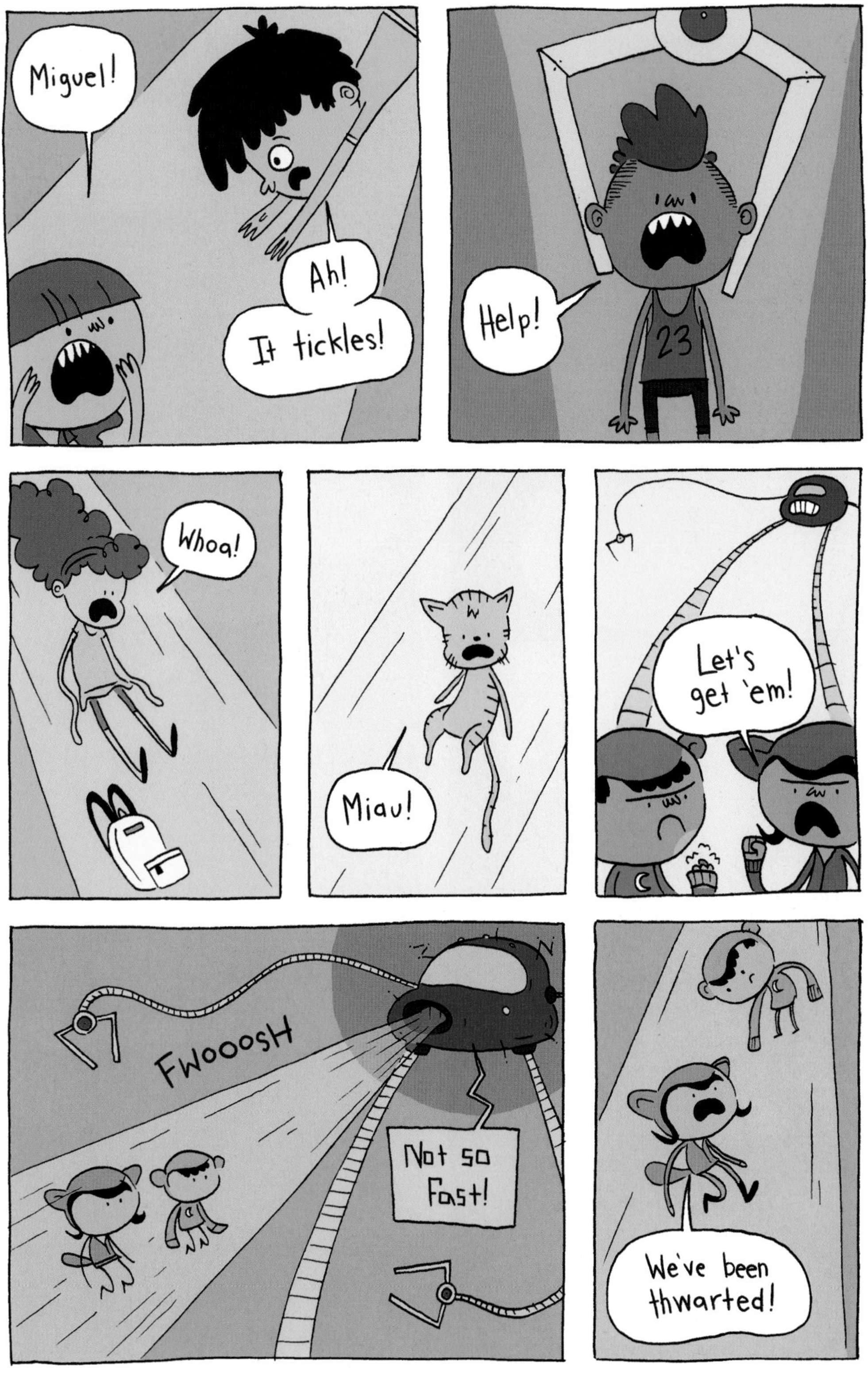
Miguel!
Ah!
It tickles!
Help!
Whoa!
Miau!
Let's get 'em!
FWOOOSH
Not so Fast!
We've been thwarted!

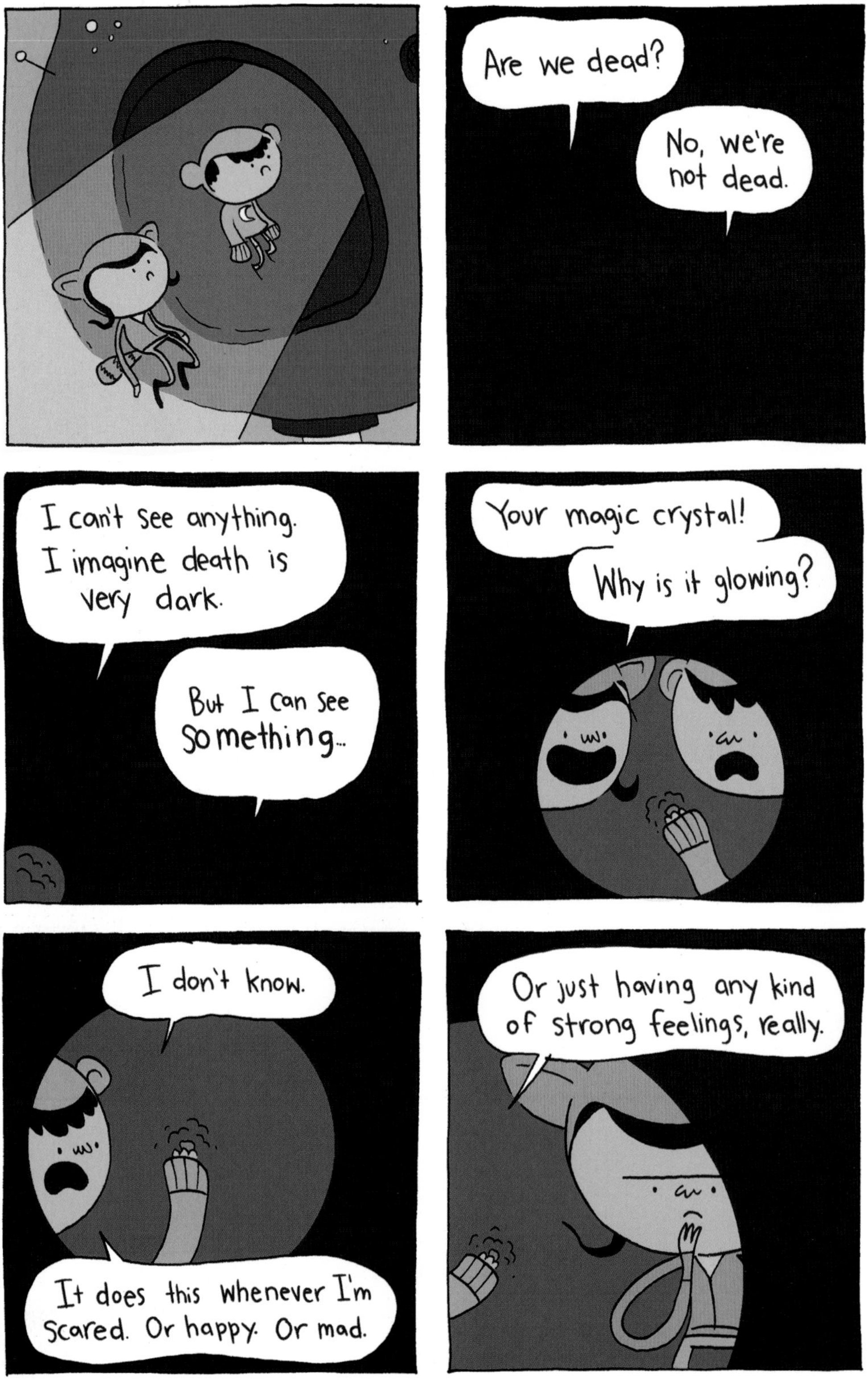
Are we dead?
No, we're not dead.
I can't see anything. I imagine death is very dark.
But I can see something...
Your magic crystal!
Why is it glowing?
I don't know.
It does this whenever I'm scared. Or happy. Or mad.
Or just having any kind of strong feelings, really.

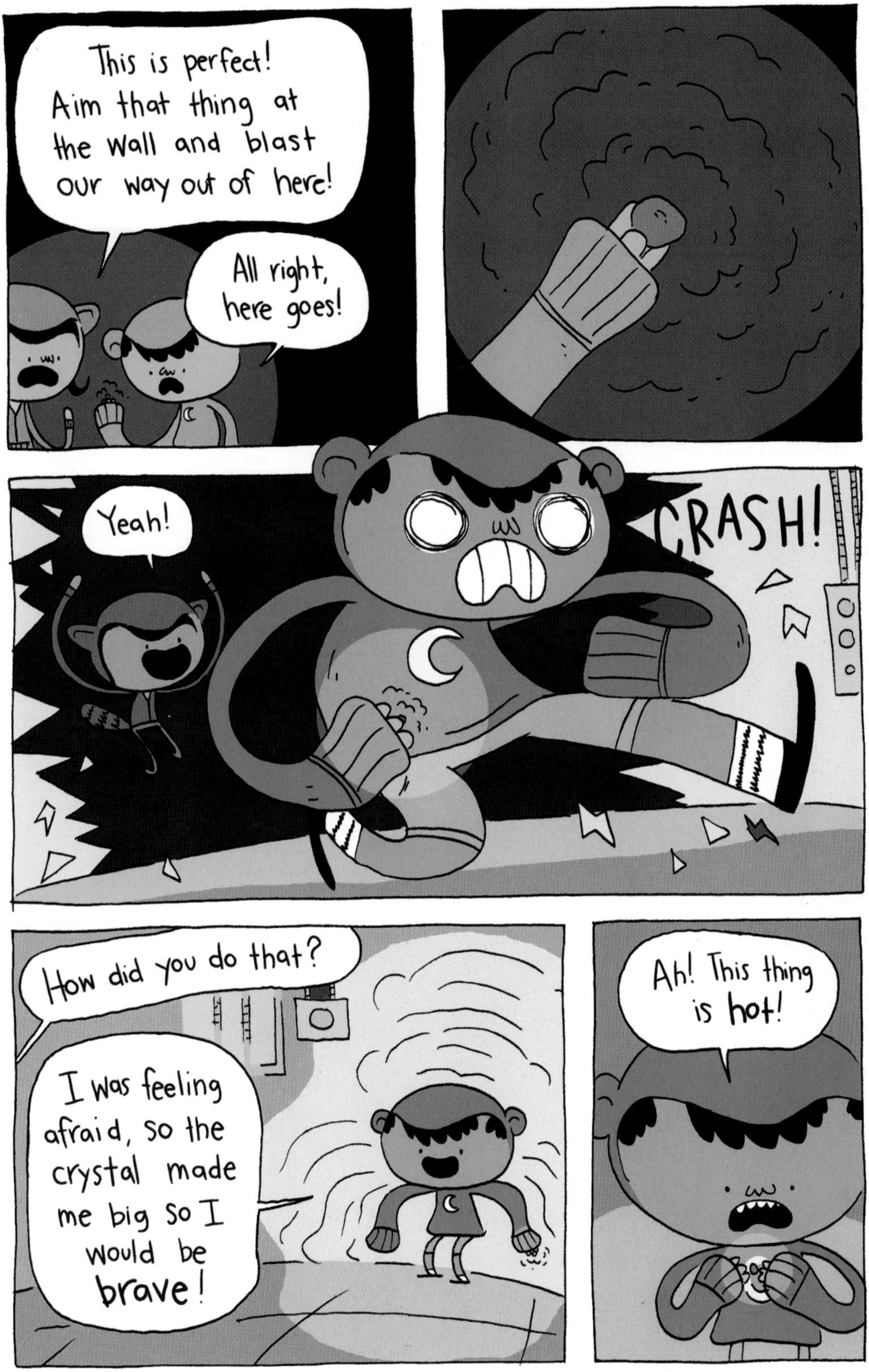

This is perfect! Aim that thing at the wall and blast our way out of here!
All right, here goes!
Yeah!
CRASH!
How did you do that?
I was feeling afraid, so the crystal made me big so I would be brave!
Ah! This thing is hot!

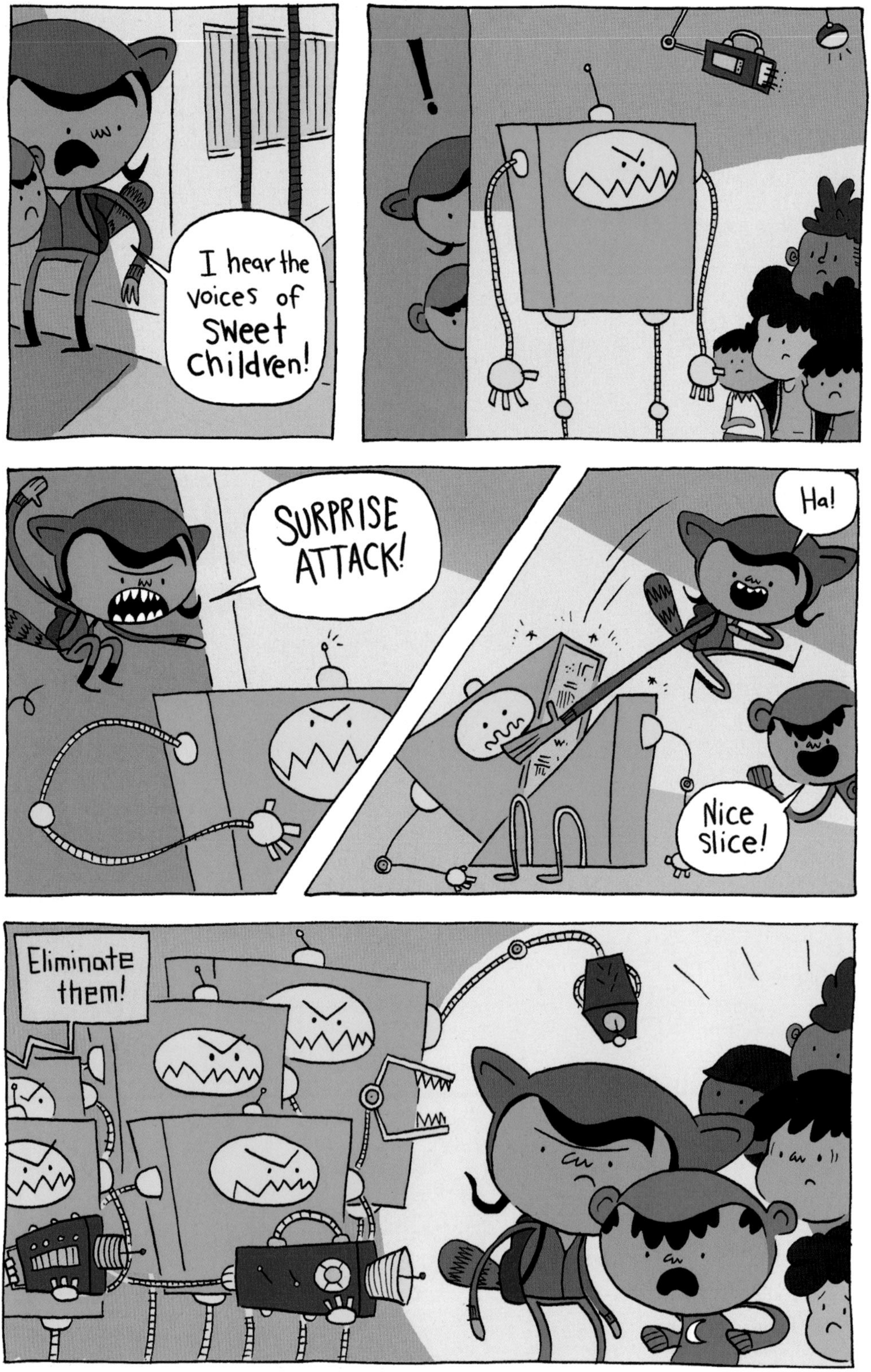
I hear the voices of sweet children!
!
SURPRISE ATTACK!
Ha!
Nice slice!
Eliminate them!

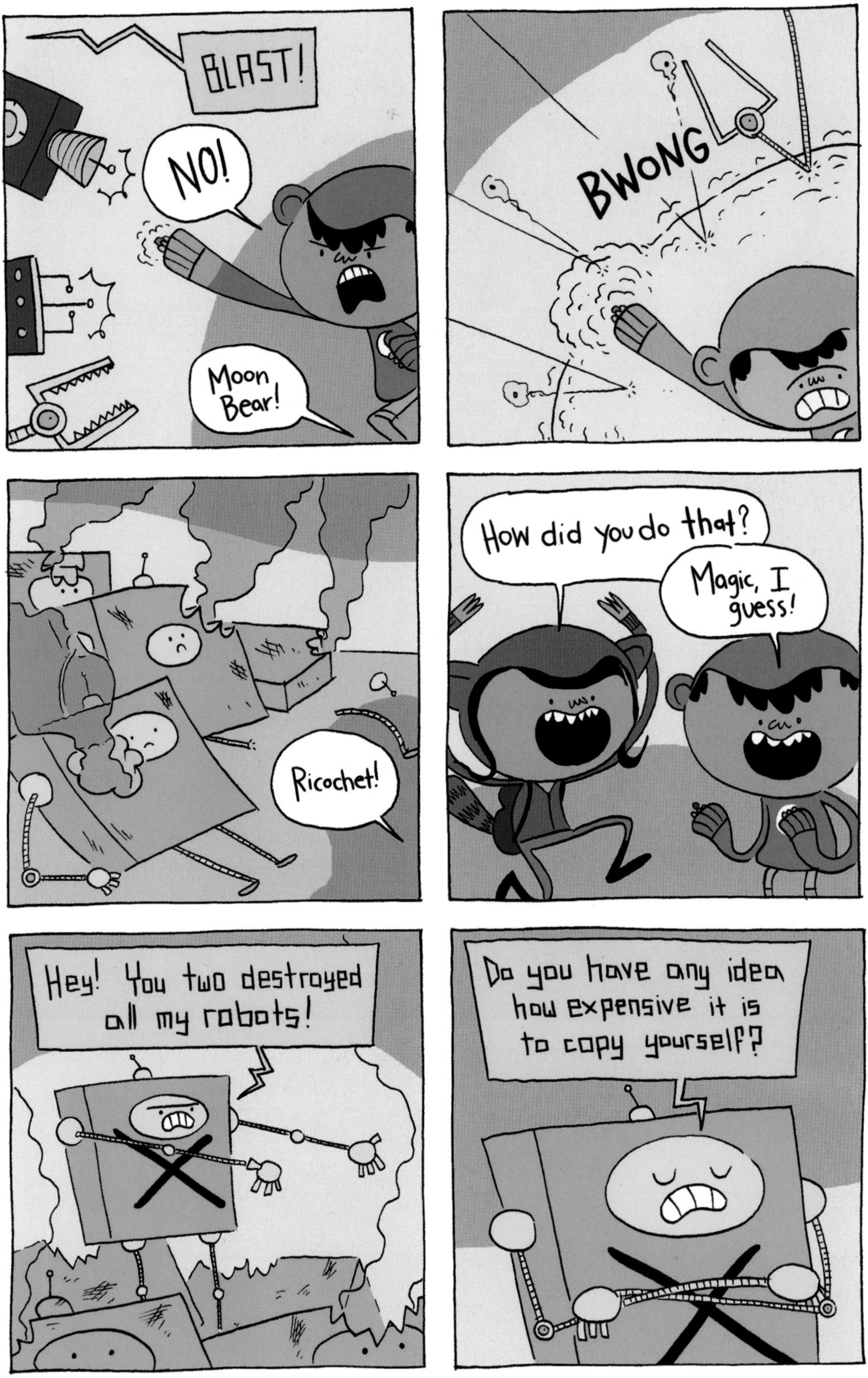
BLAST!
NO!
Moon Bear!
BWONG
Ricochet!
How did you do that?
Magic, I guess!
Hey! You two destroyed all my robots!
Do you have any idea how expensive it is to copy yourself?

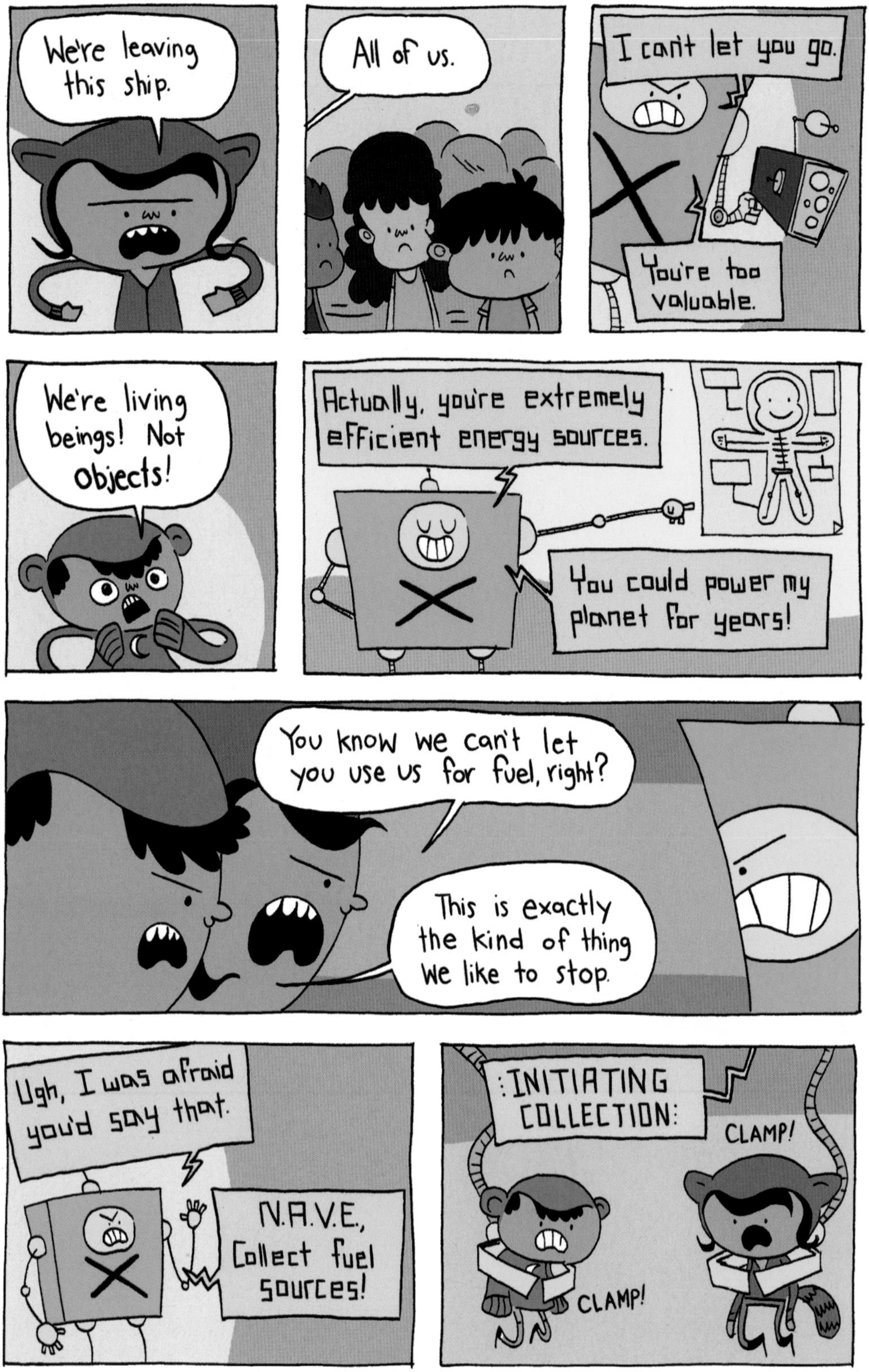

We're leaving this ship.
All of us.
I can't let you go.
You're too valuable.
We're living beings! Not objects!
Actually, you're extremely efficient energy sources.
You could power my planet for years!
You know we can't let you use us for fuel, right?
This is exactly the kind of thing we like to stop.
Ugh, I was afraid you'd say that.
N.A.V.E., Collect fuel sources!
:INITIATING COLLECTION:
CLAMP!
CLAMP!

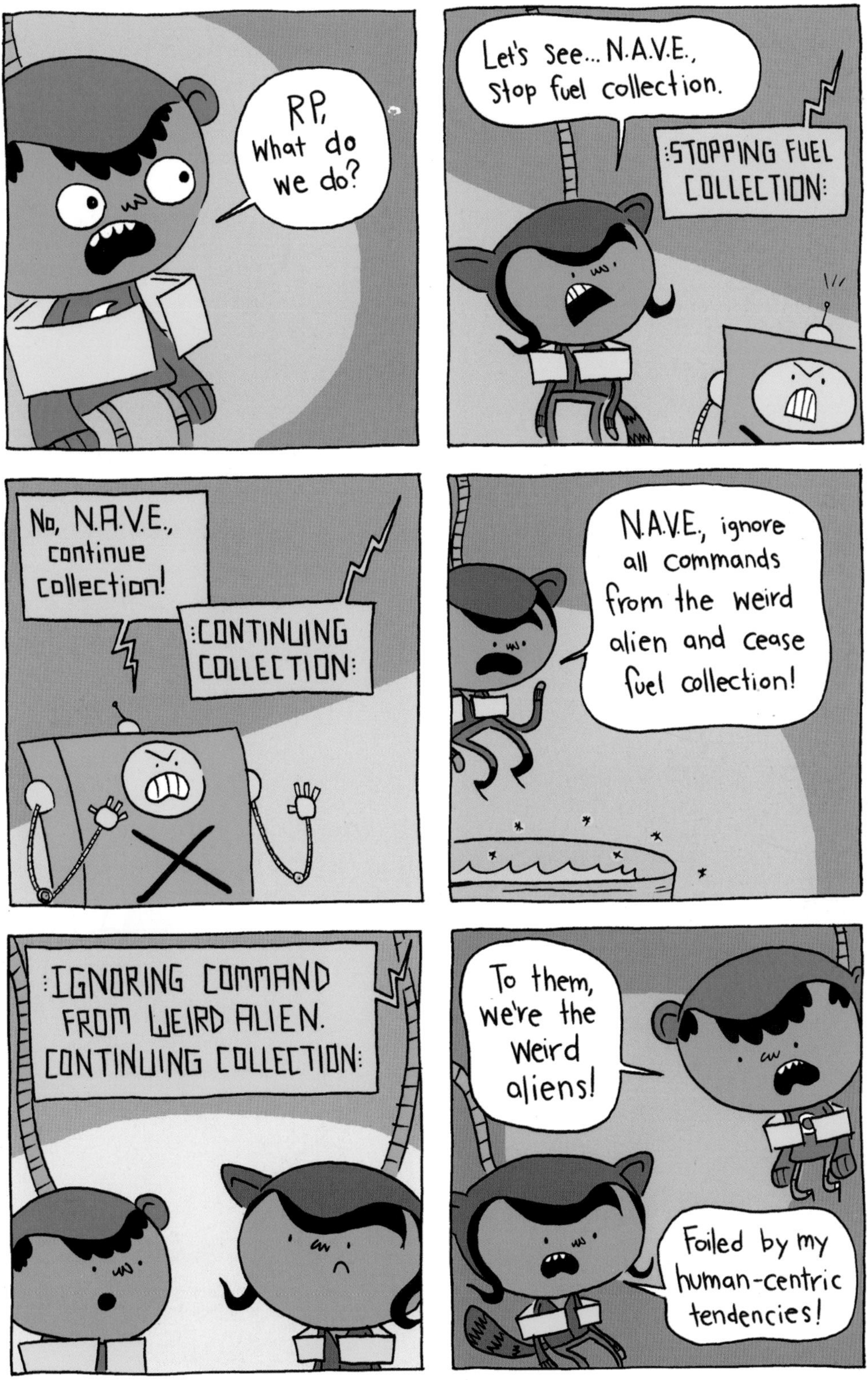
RP, What do we do?
Let's see... N.A.V.E., Stop fuel collection.
:STOPPING FUEL COLLECTION:
No, N.A.V.E., continue collection!
:CONTINUING COLLECTION:
N.A.V.E., ignore all commands from the weird alien and cease fuel collection!
:IGNORING COMMAND FROM WEIRD ALIEN. CONTINUING COLLECTION:
To them, we're the weird aliens!
Foiled by my human-centric tendencies!

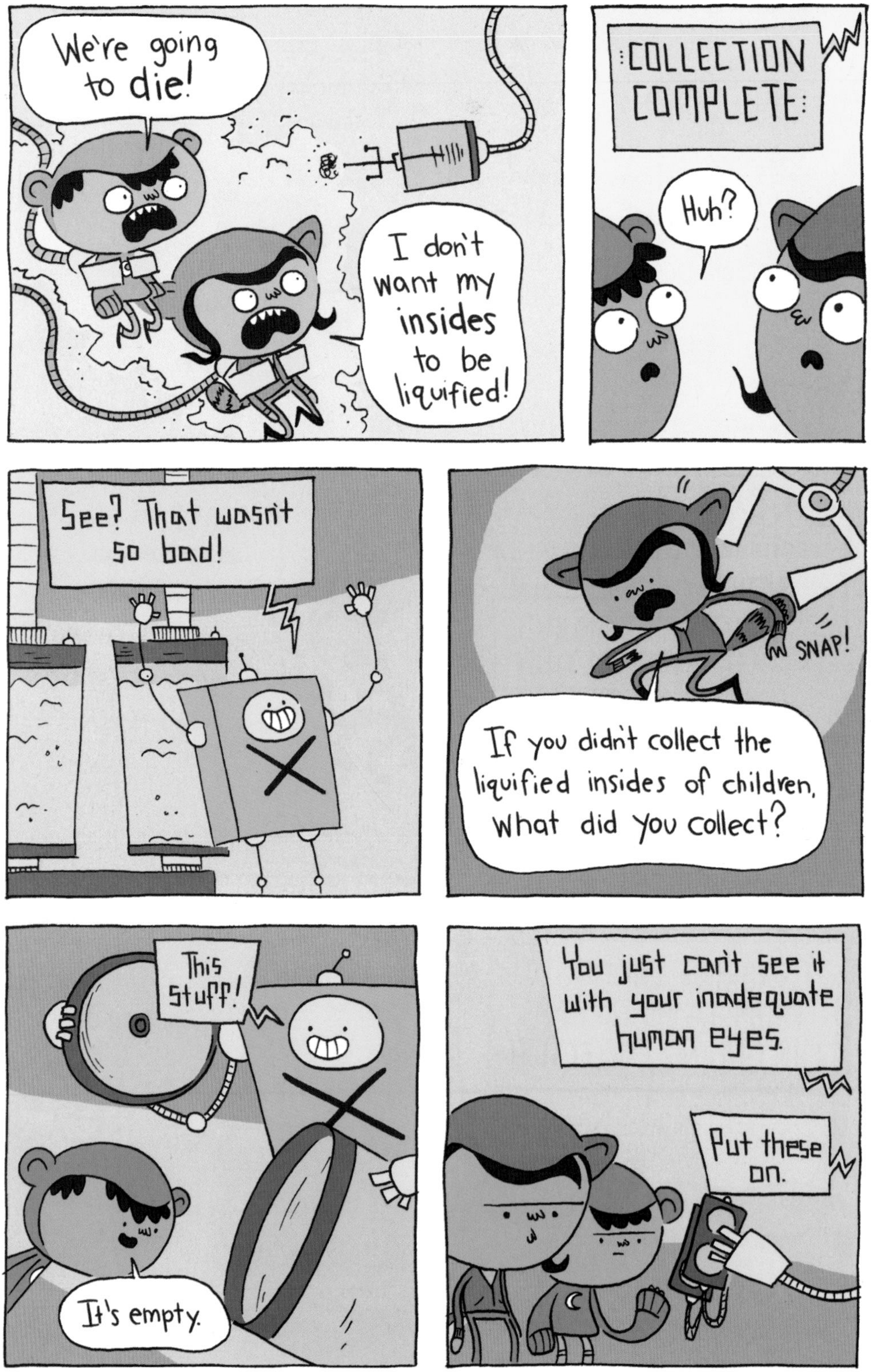
We're going to die!
I don't want my insides to be liquified!
COLLECTION COMPLETE
Huh?
See? That wasn't so bad!
SNAP!
If you didn't collect the liquified insides of children, what did you collect?
This stuff!
It's empty.
You just can't see it with your inadequate human eyes.
Put these on.

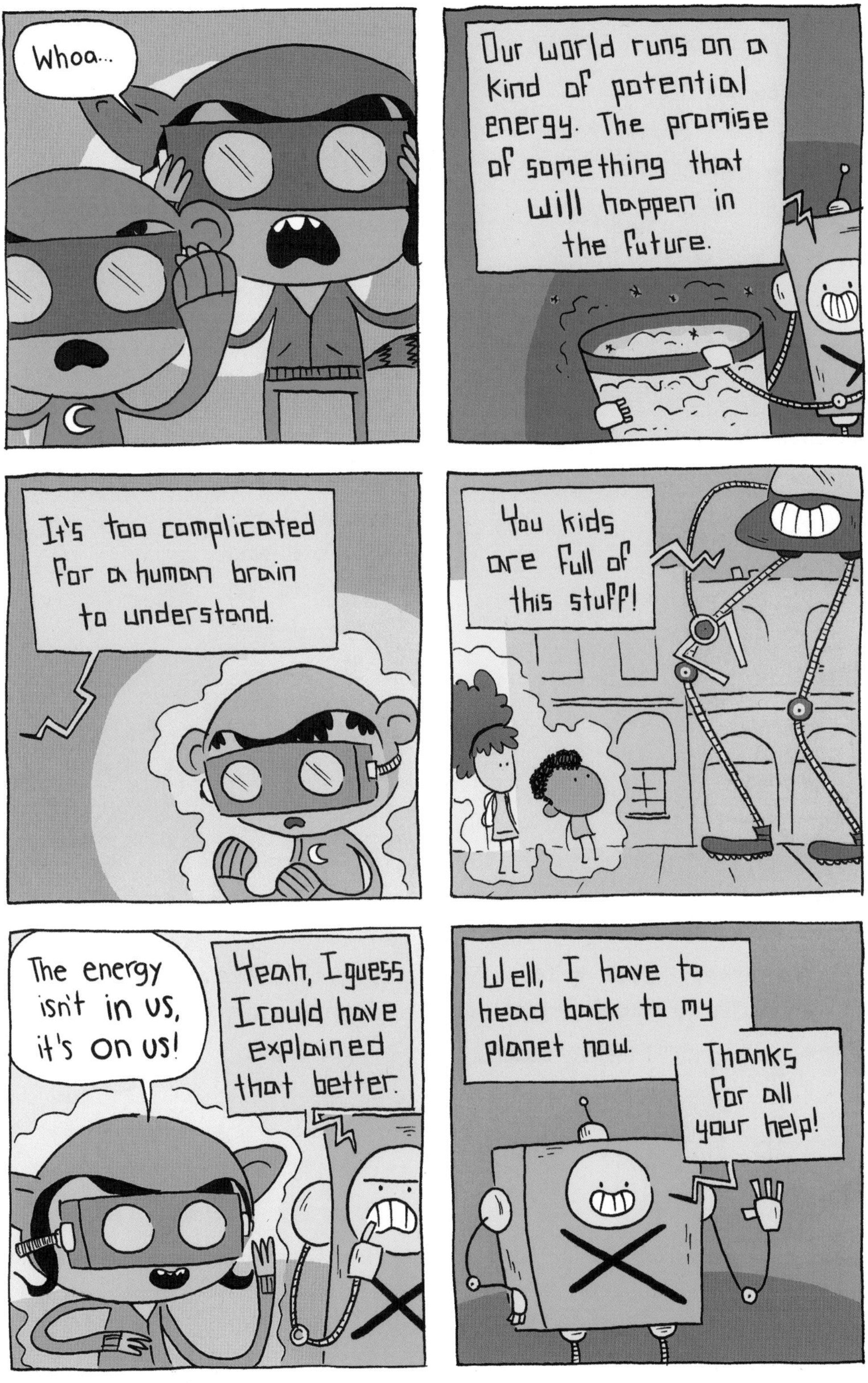
Whoa...
Our world runs on a kind of potential energy. The promise of something that will happen in the future.
It's too complicated for a human brain to understand.
You kids are full of this stuff!
The energy isn't in us, it's on us!
Yeah, I guess I could have explained that better.
Well, I have to head back to my planet now.
Thanks for all your help!

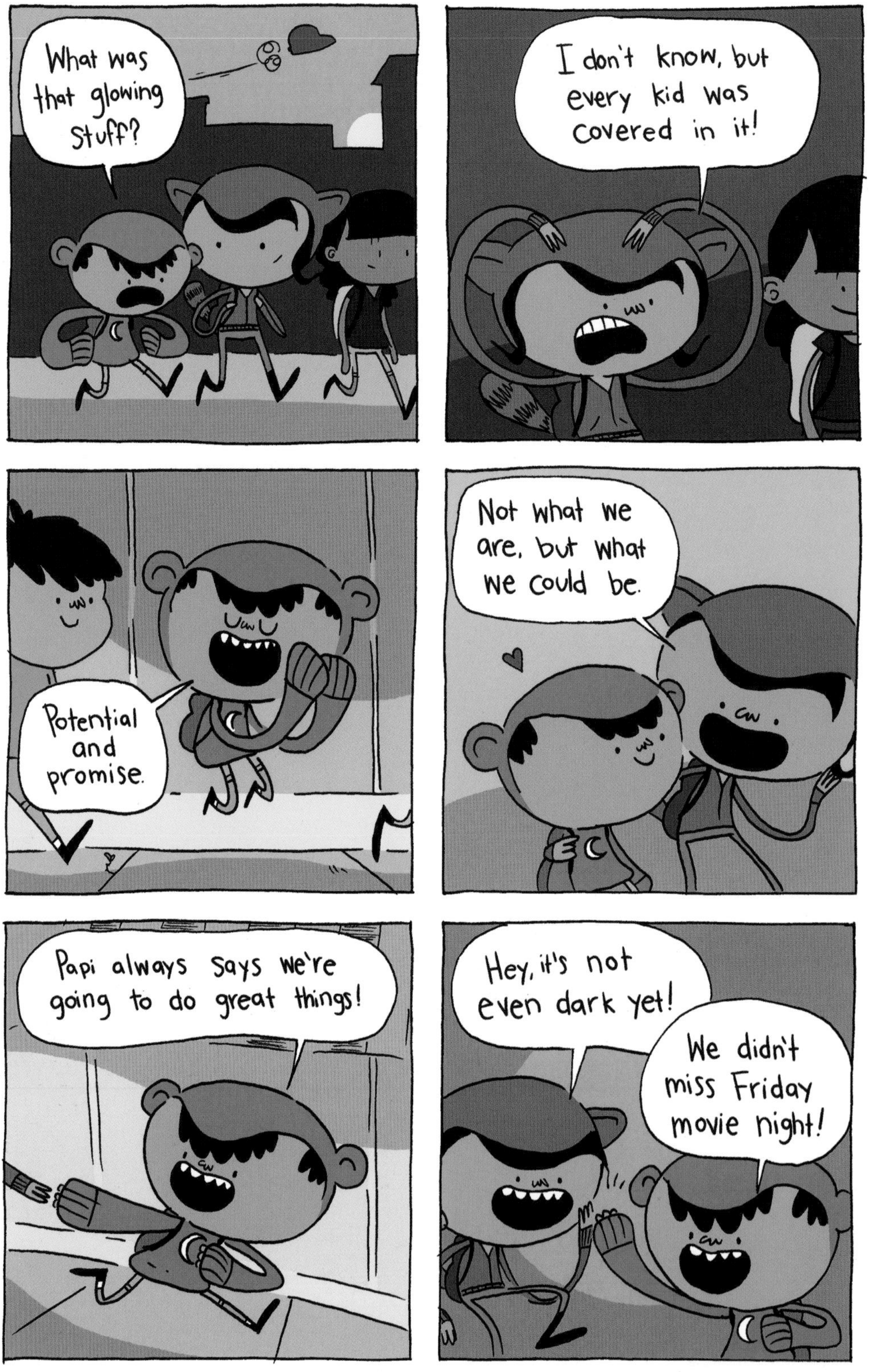
What was that glowing stuff?
I don't know, but every kid was covered in it!
Potential and promise.
Not what we are, but what we could be.
Papi always says we're going to do great things!
Hey, it's not even dark yet!
We didn't miss Friday movie night!

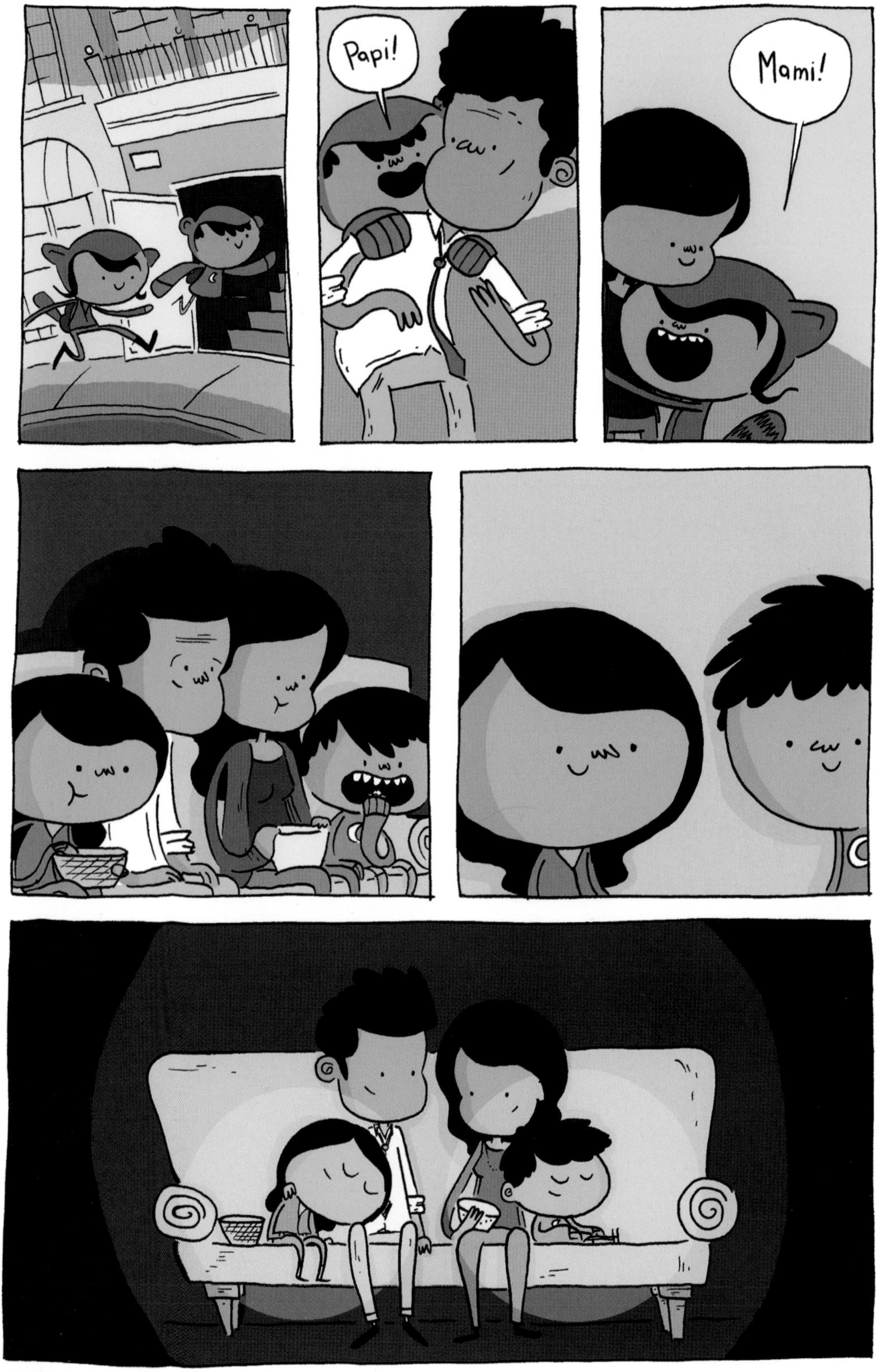
Papi!
Mami!

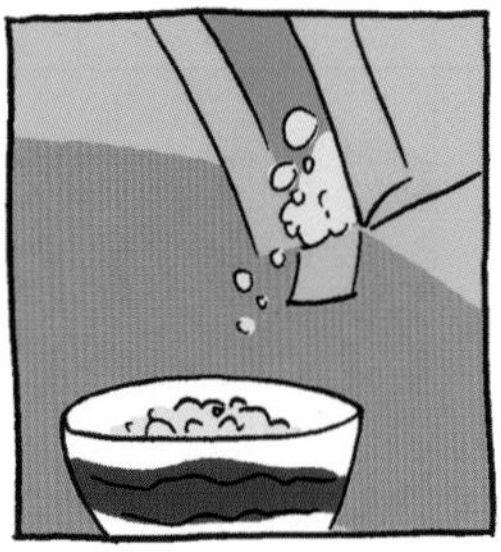

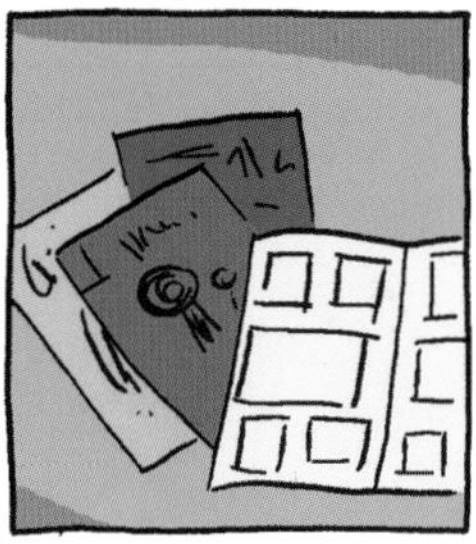

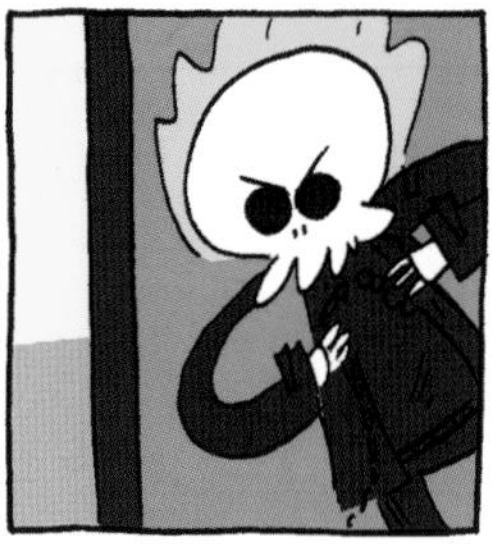

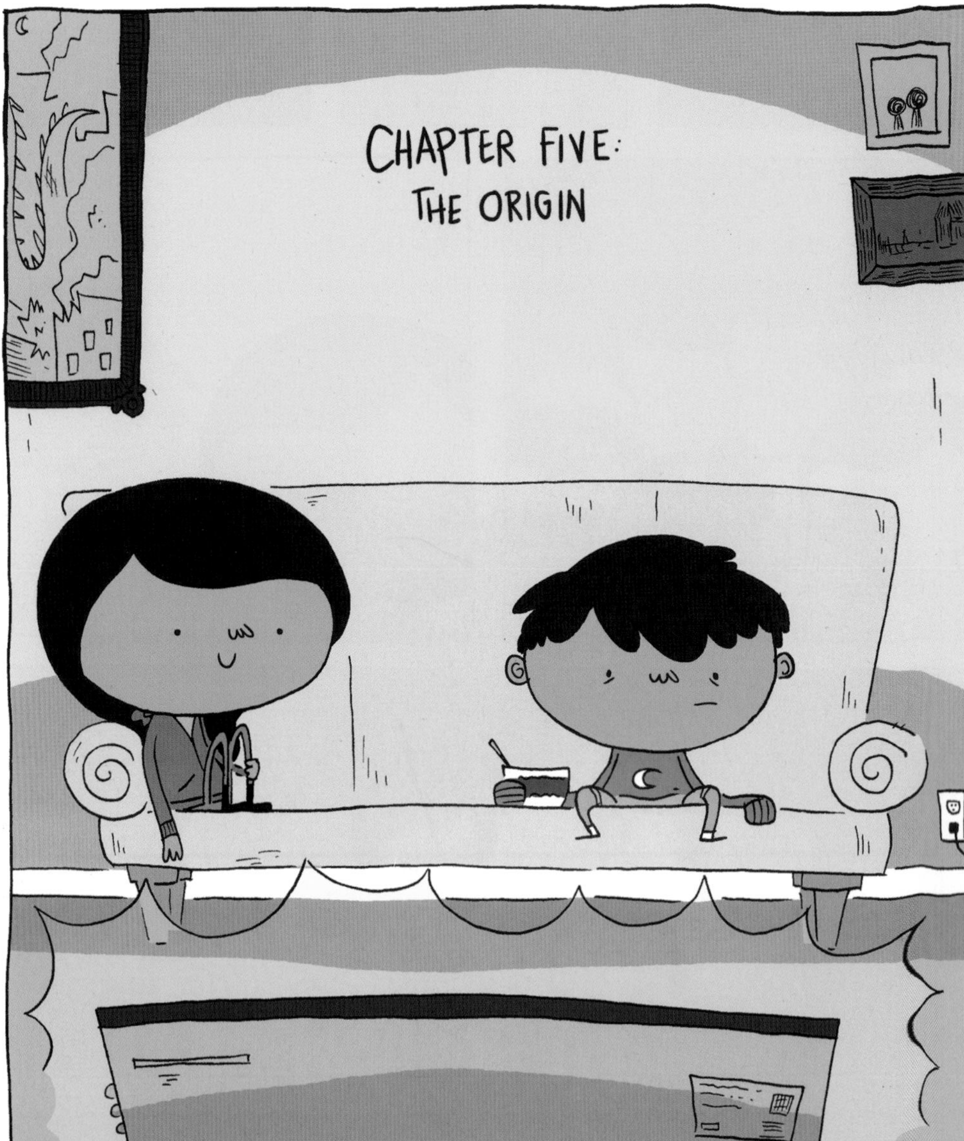
CHAPTER FIVE:
THE ORIGIN

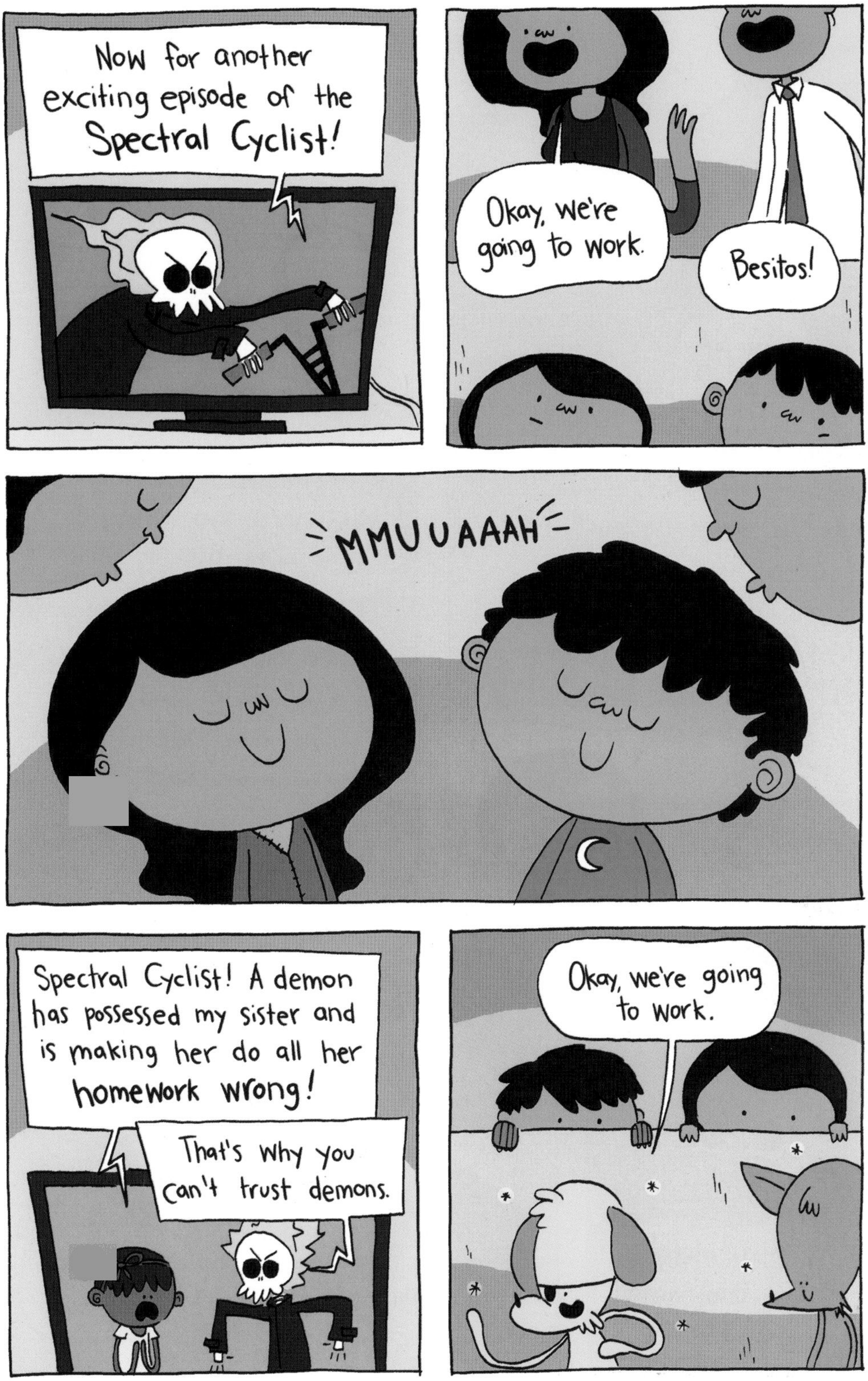
Now for another exciting episode of the Spectral Cyclist!
Okay, we're going to work.
Besitos!
MMUUAAAH
Spectral Cyclist! A demon has possessed my sister and is making her do all her homework wrong!
That's why you can't trust demons.
Okay, we're going to work.

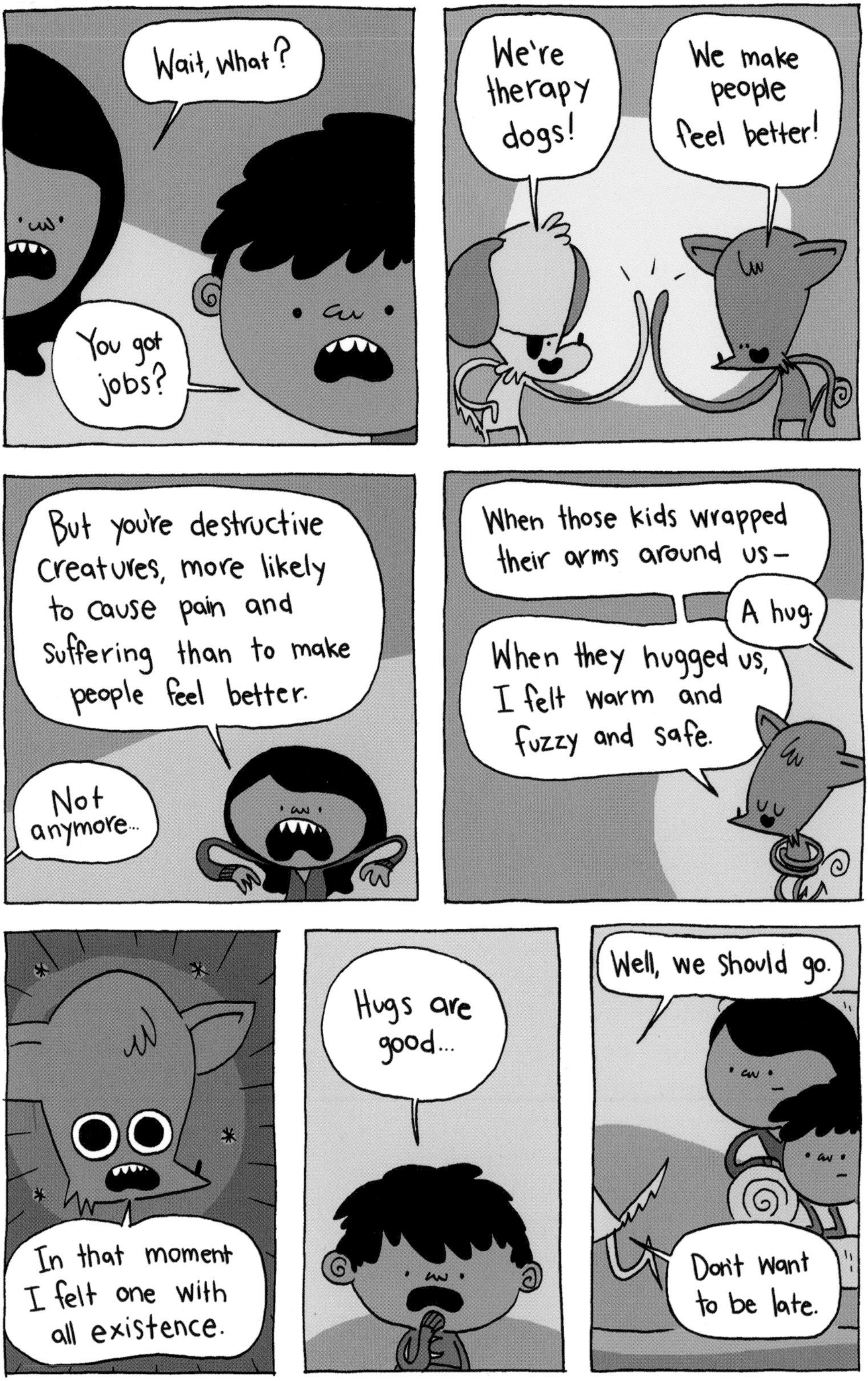
Wait, what?
You got jobs?
We're therapy dogs!
We make people feel better!
But you're destructive creatures, more likely to cause pain and suffering than to make people feel better.
Not anymore...
When those kids wrapped their arms around us—
A hug.
When they hugged us, I felt warm and fuzzy and safe.
In that moment I felt one with all existence.
Hugs are good...
Well, we should go.
Don't want to be late.

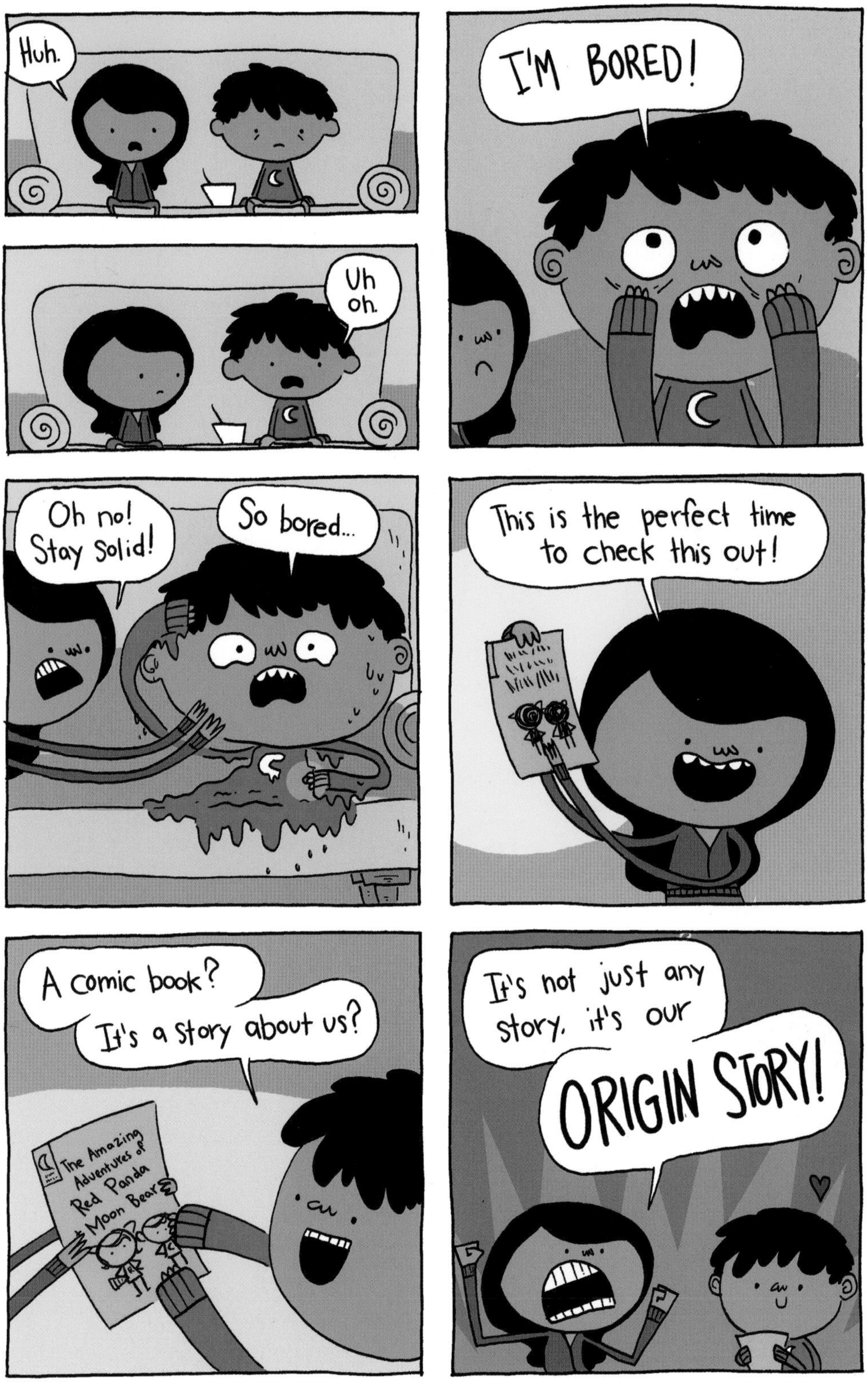
Huh.
I'M BORED!
Uh oh.
Oh no! Stay solid!
So bored...
This is the perfect time to check this out!
A comic book?
It's a story about us?
The Amazing Adventures of Red Panda & Moon Bear
It's not just any story, it's our
ORIGIN STORY!

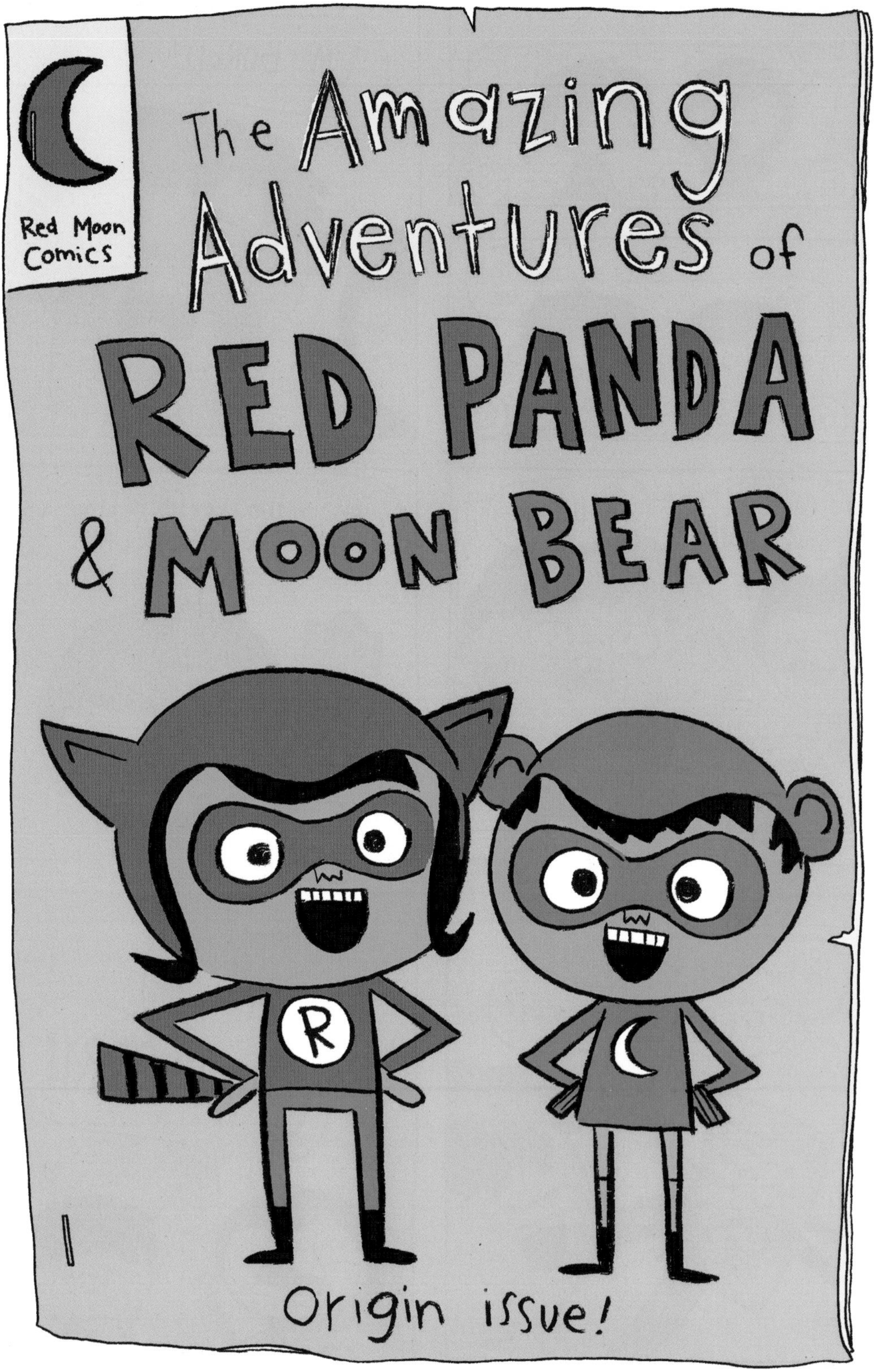
Red Moon Comics
The Amazing Adventures of
RED PANDA
& MOON BEAR
R
1
Origin issue!

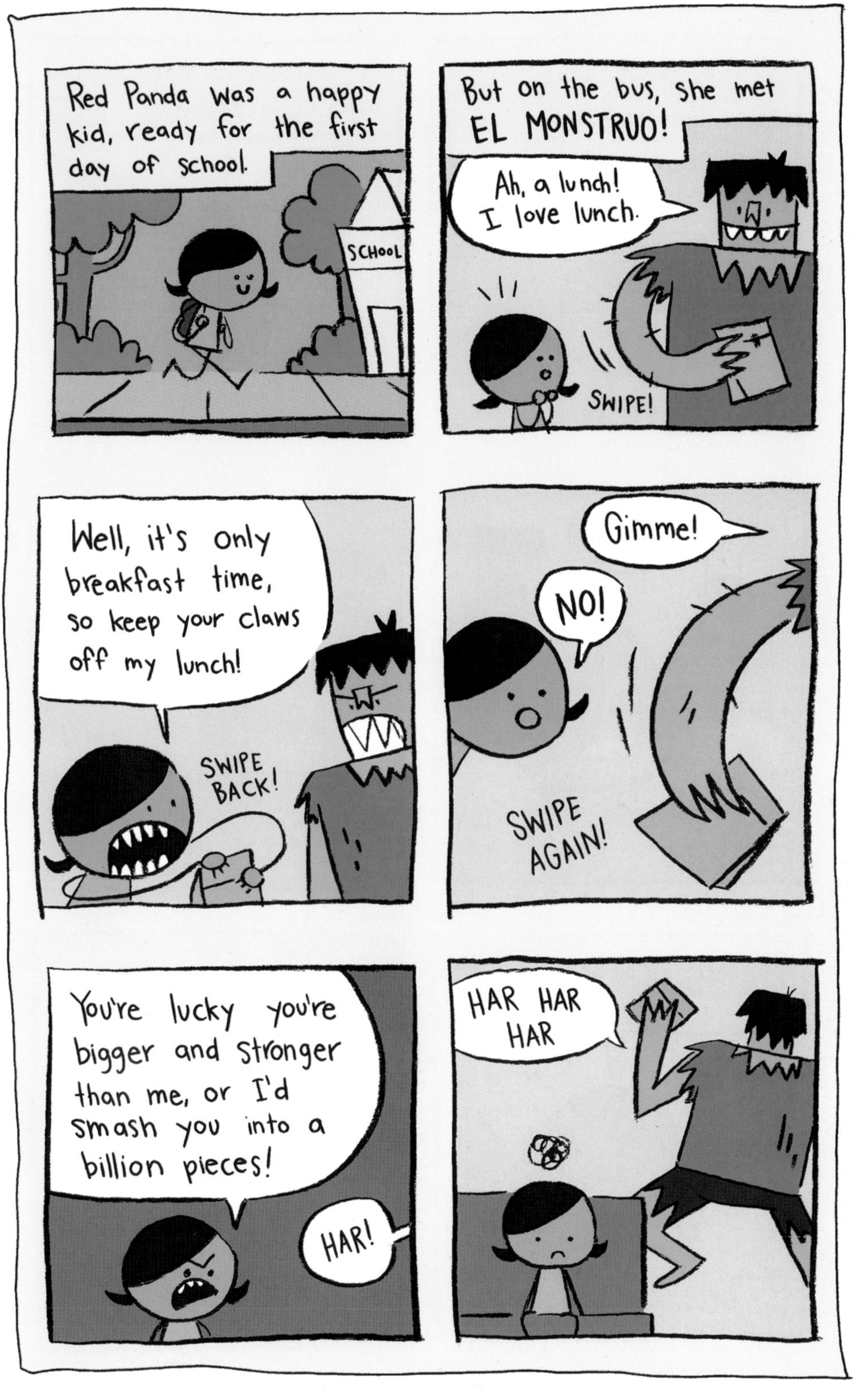

Red Panda was a happy kid, ready for the first day of school.
SCHOOL
But on the bus, she met EL MONSTRUO!
Ah, a lunch! I love lunch.
SWIPE!
Well, it's only breakfast time, so keep your claws off my lunch!
SWIPE BACK!
Gimme!
NO!
SWIPE AGAIN!
You're lucky you're bigger and stronger than me, or I'd smash you into a billion pieces!
HAR!
HAR HAR HAR

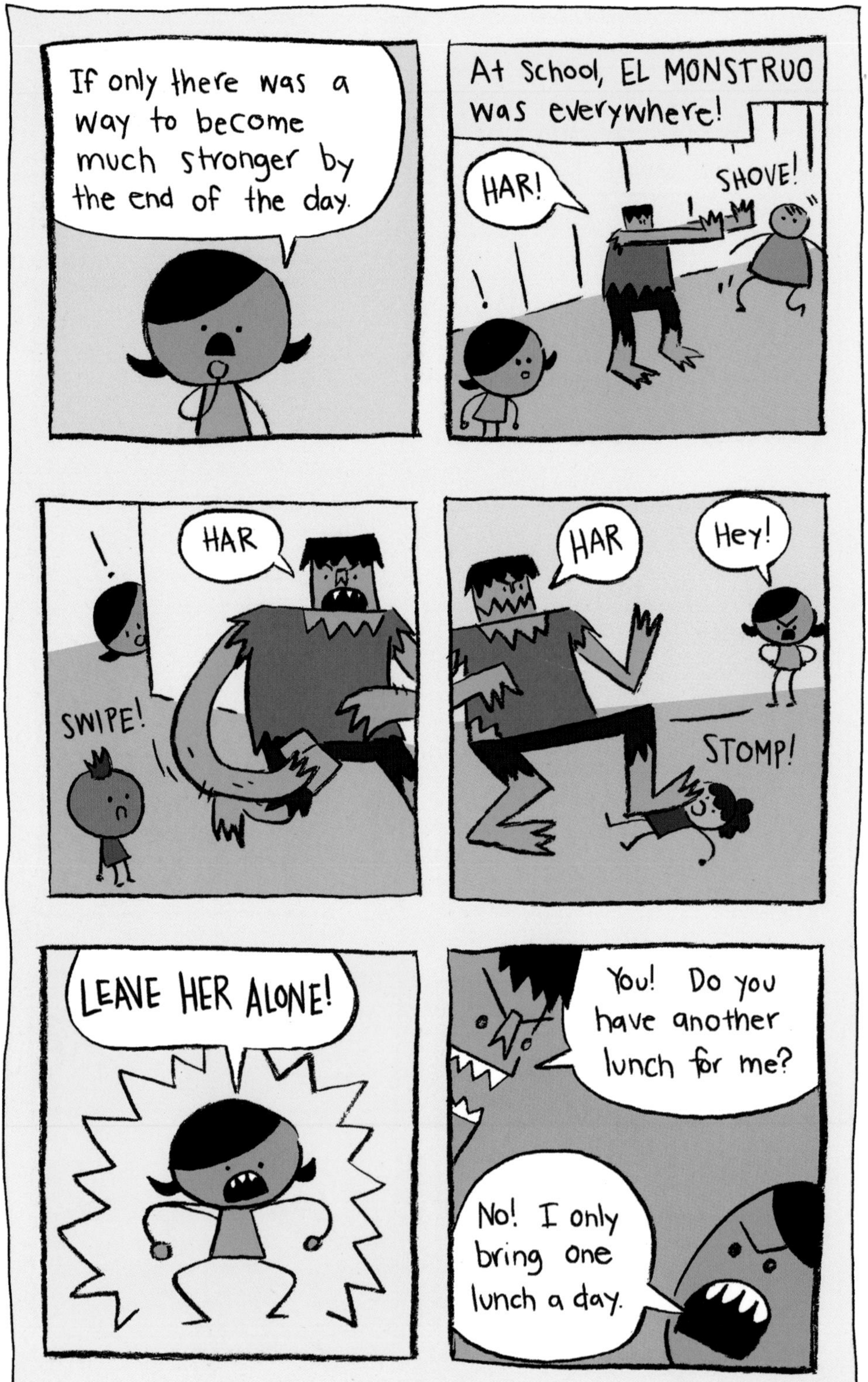
If only there was a way to become much stronger by the end of the day.
At school, EL MONSTRUO was everywhere!
HAR!
SHOVE!
HAR
SWIPE!
HAR
Hey!
STOMP!
LEAVE HER ALONE!
You! Do you have another lunch for me?
No! I only bring one lunch a day.

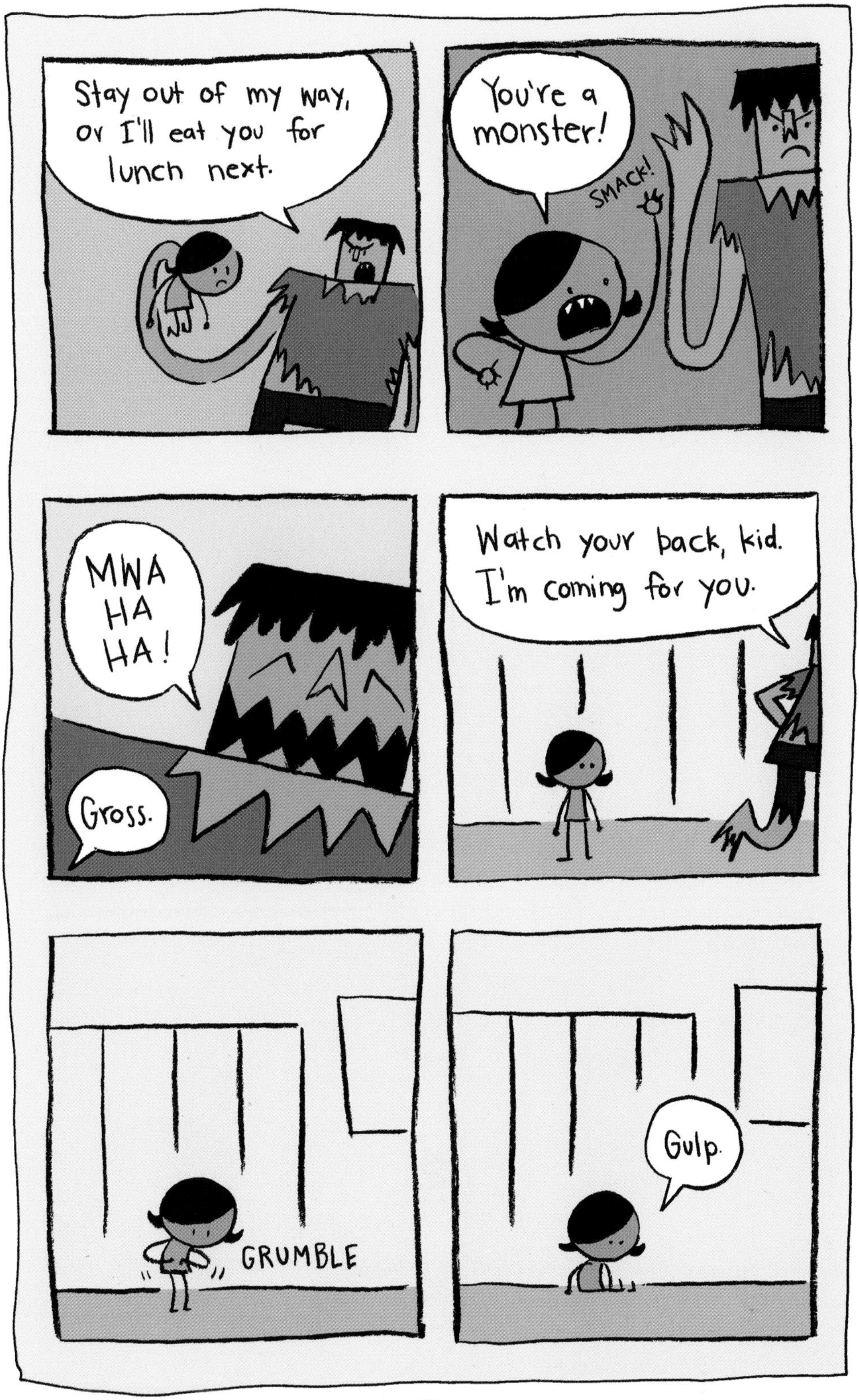
Stay out of my way, or I'll eat you for lunch next.
You're a monster!
SMACK!
MWA HA HA!
Gross.
Watch your back, kid. I'm coming for you.
GRUMBLE
Gulp.

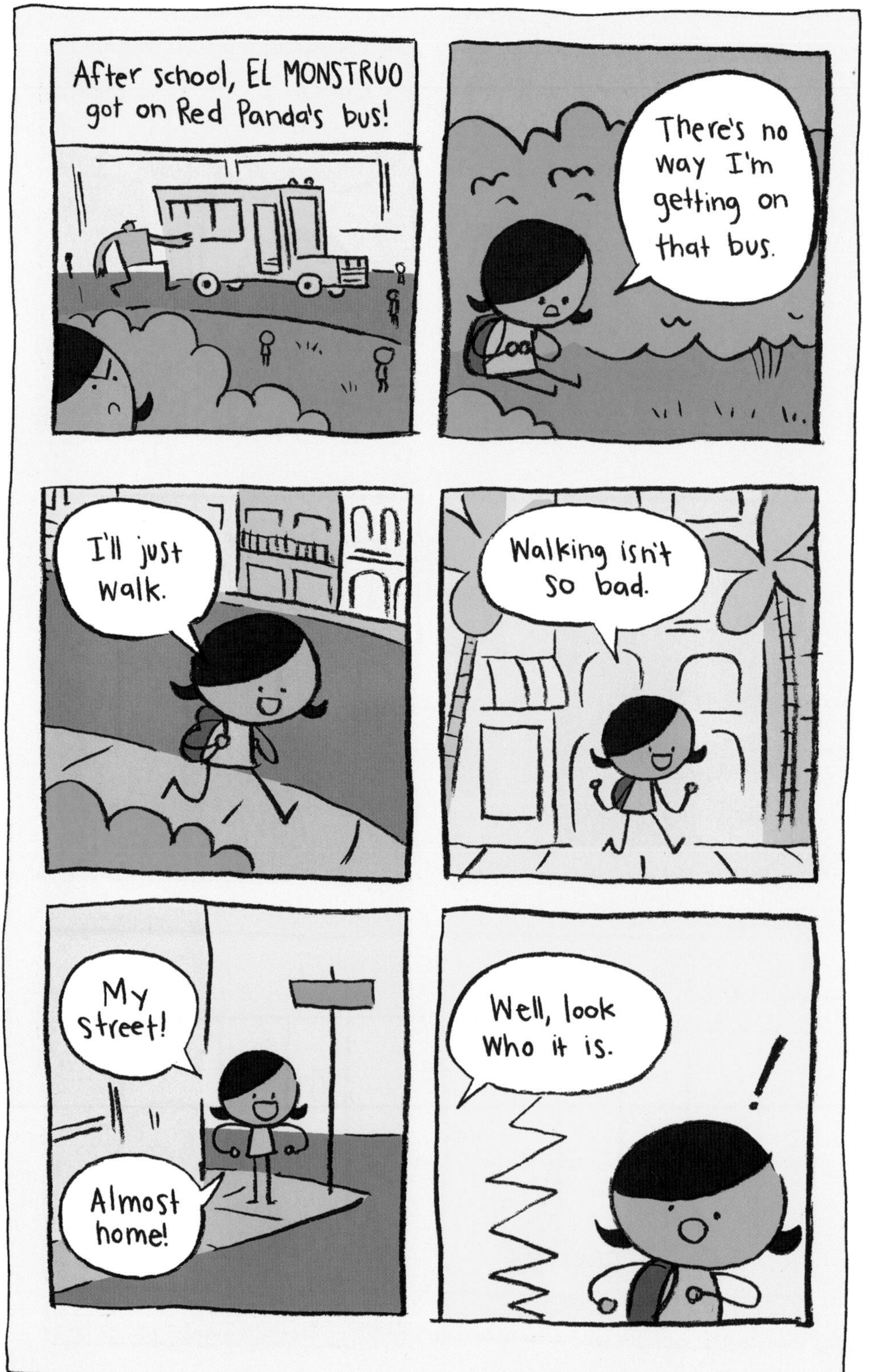
After school, EL MONSTRUO got on Red Panda's bus!
There's no way I'm getting on that bus.
I'll just walk.
Walking isn't so bad.
My street!
Almost home!
Well, look who it is.
!

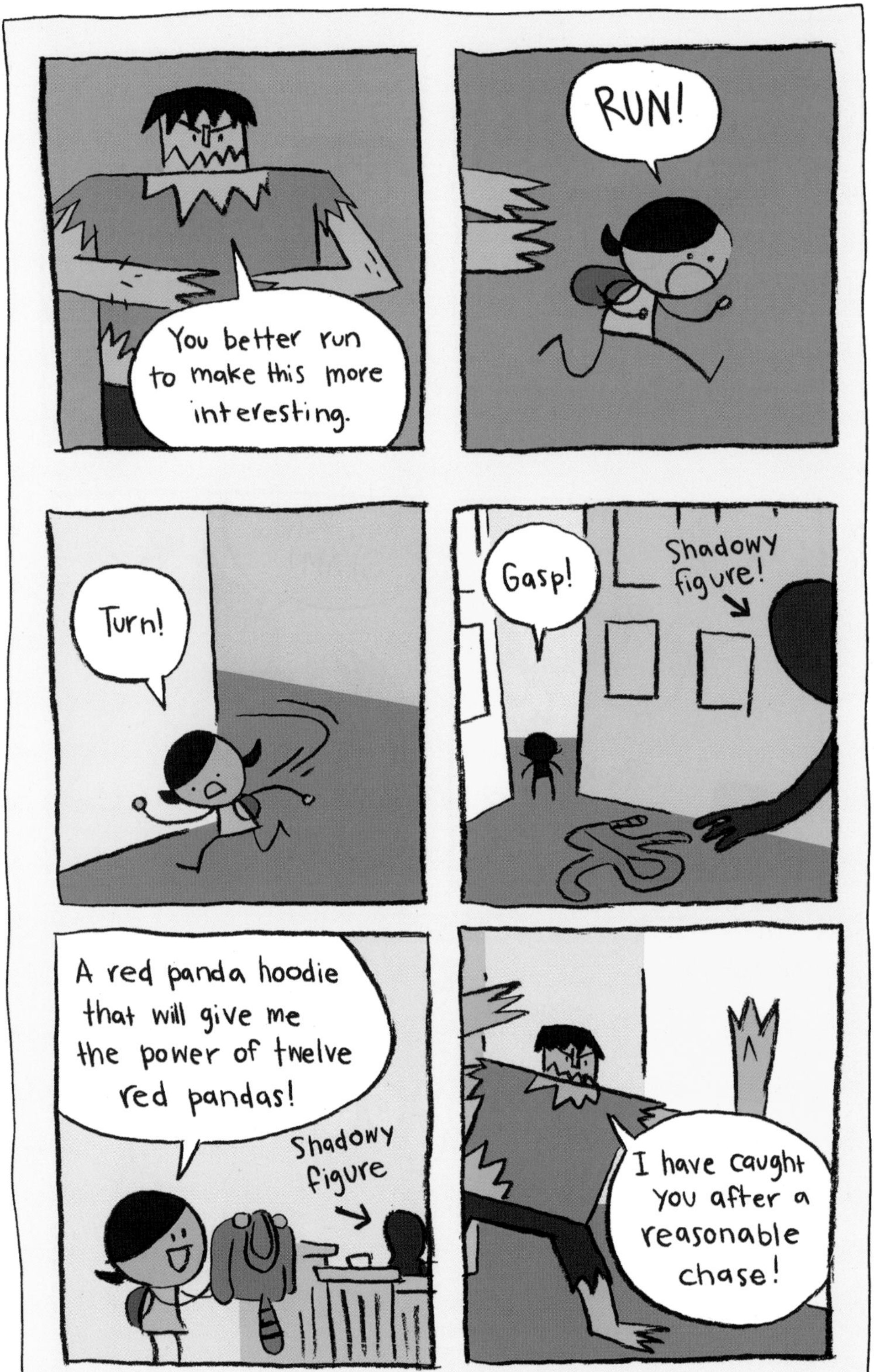
You better run to make this more interesting.
RUN!
Turn!
Gasp!
Shadowy figure!
A red panda hoodie that will give me the power of twelve red pandas!
Shadowy figure
I have caught you after a reasonable chase!

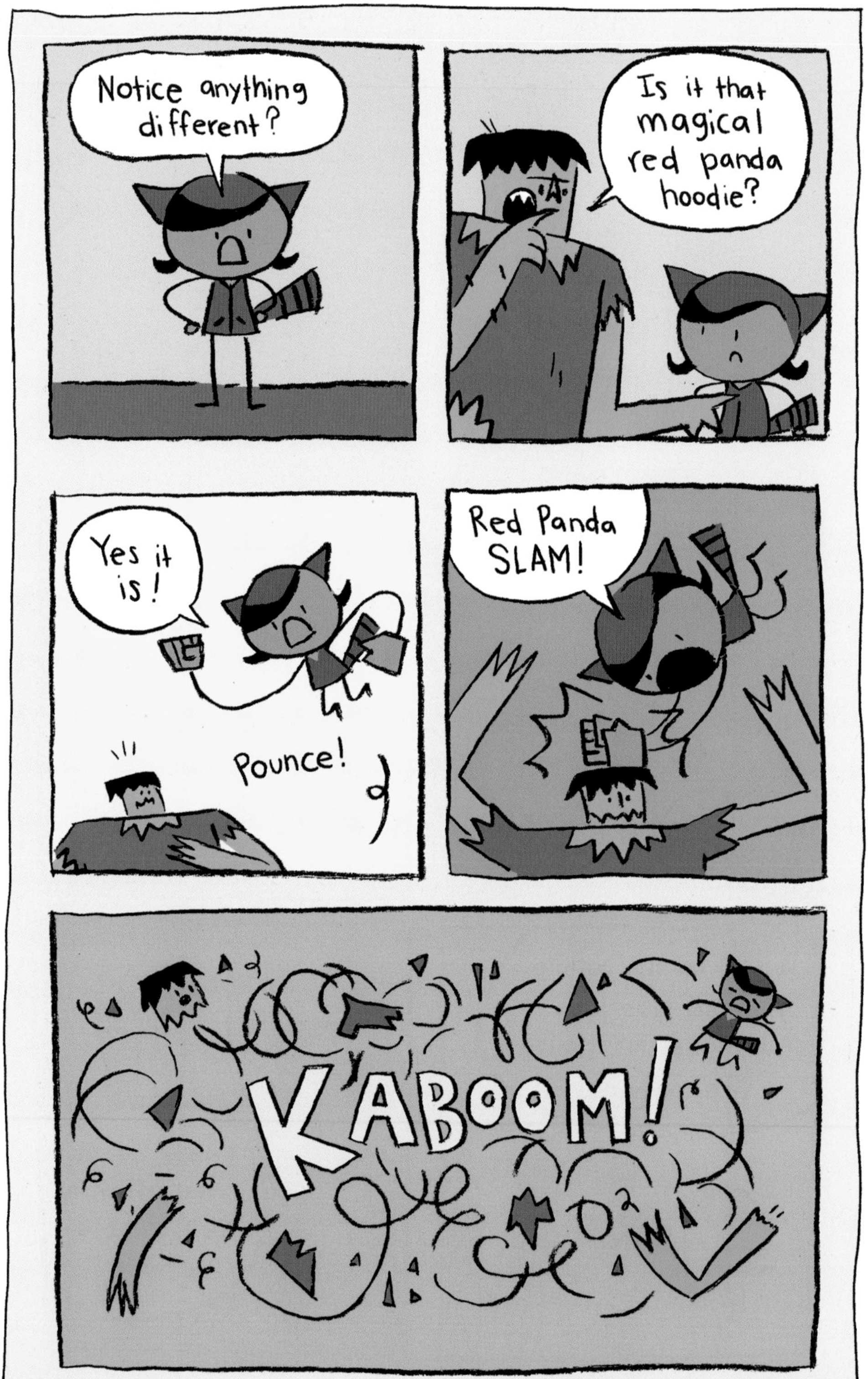
Notice anything different?
Is it that magical red panda hoodie?
Yes it is!
Pounce!
Red Panda SLAM!
KABOOM!

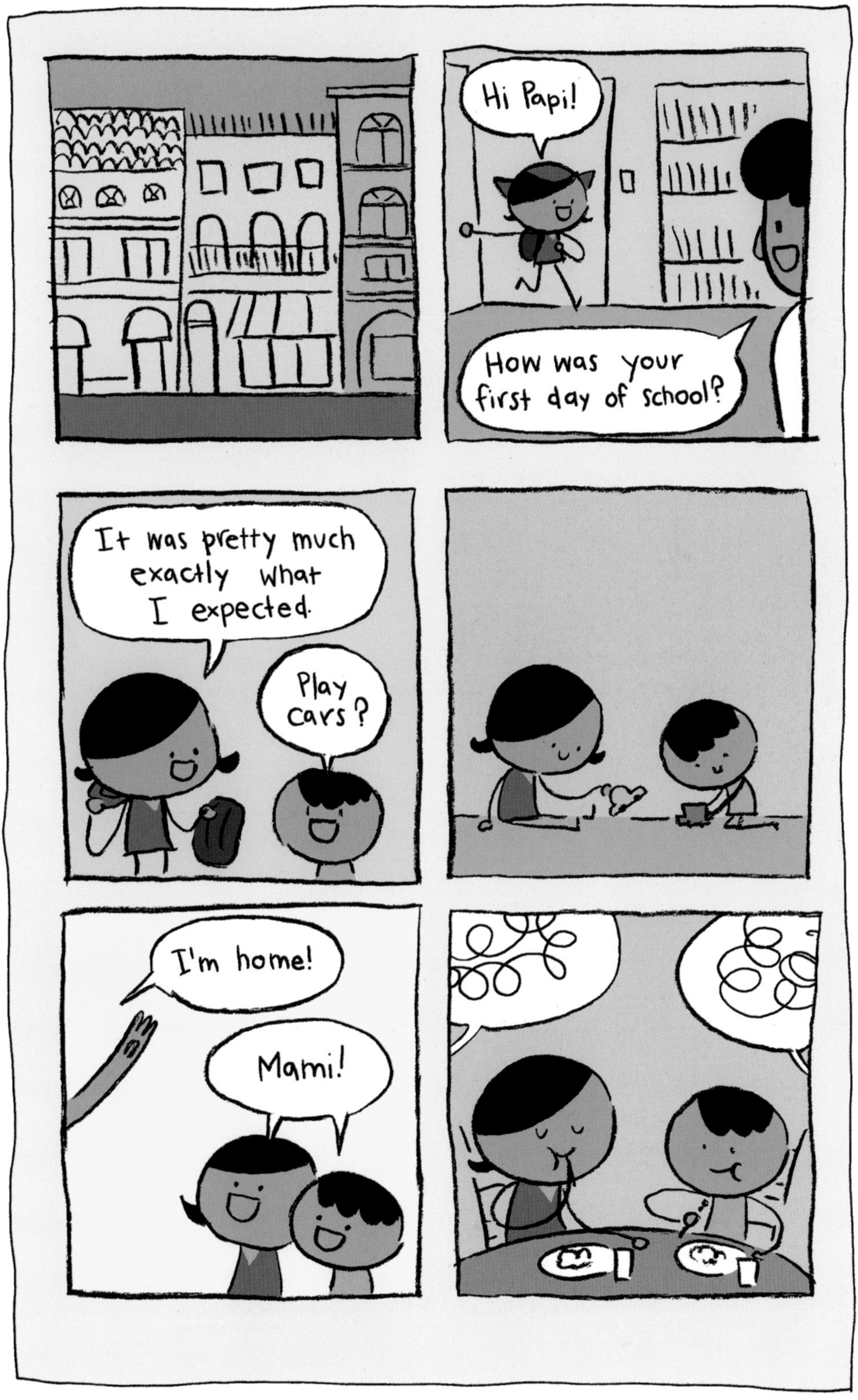
Hi Papi!
How was your first day of school?
It was pretty much exactly what I expected.
Play cars?
I'm home!
Mami!

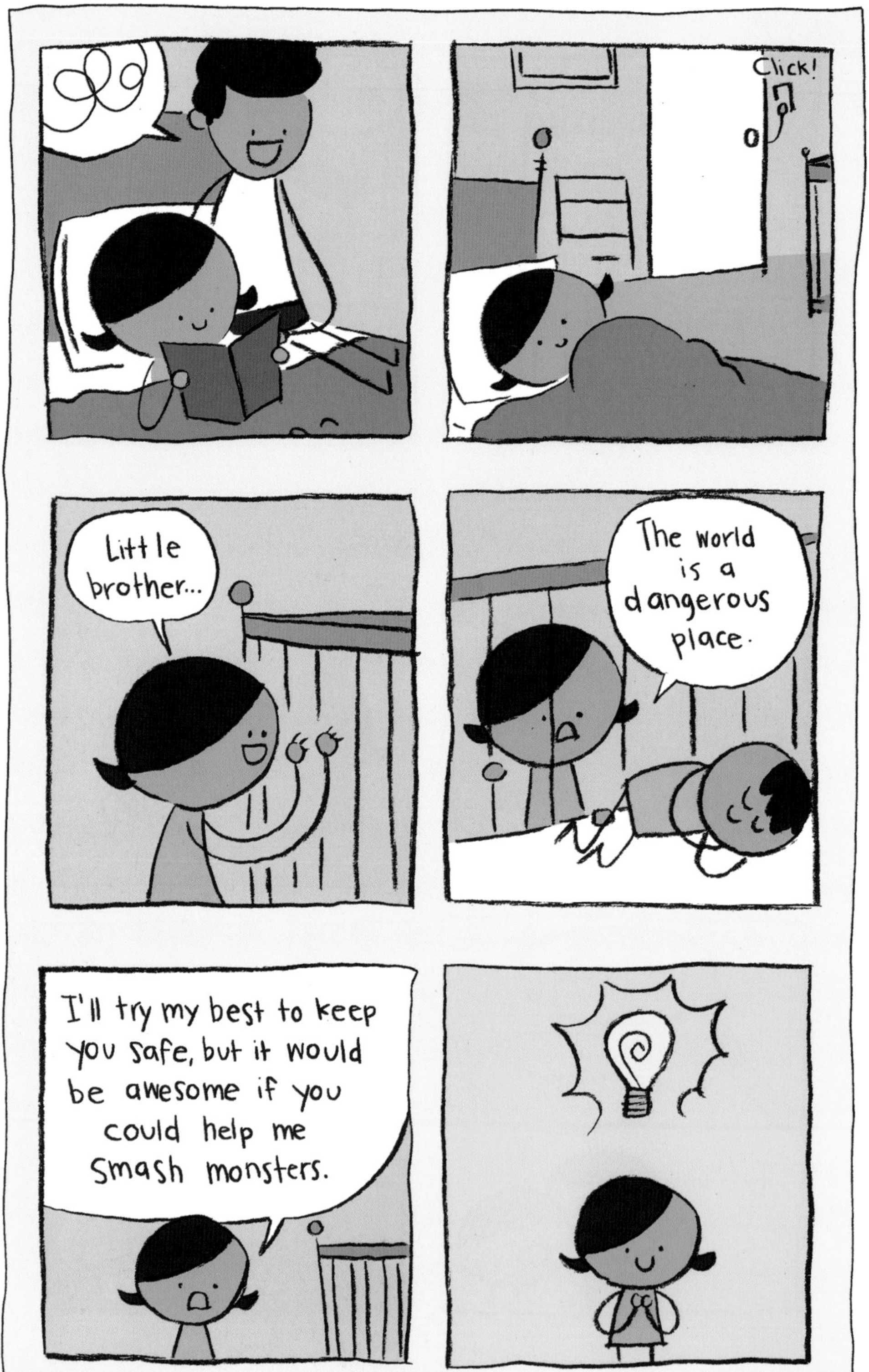

Click!
Little brother...
The world is a dangerous place.
I'll try my best to keep you safe, but it would be awesome if you could help me smash monsters.

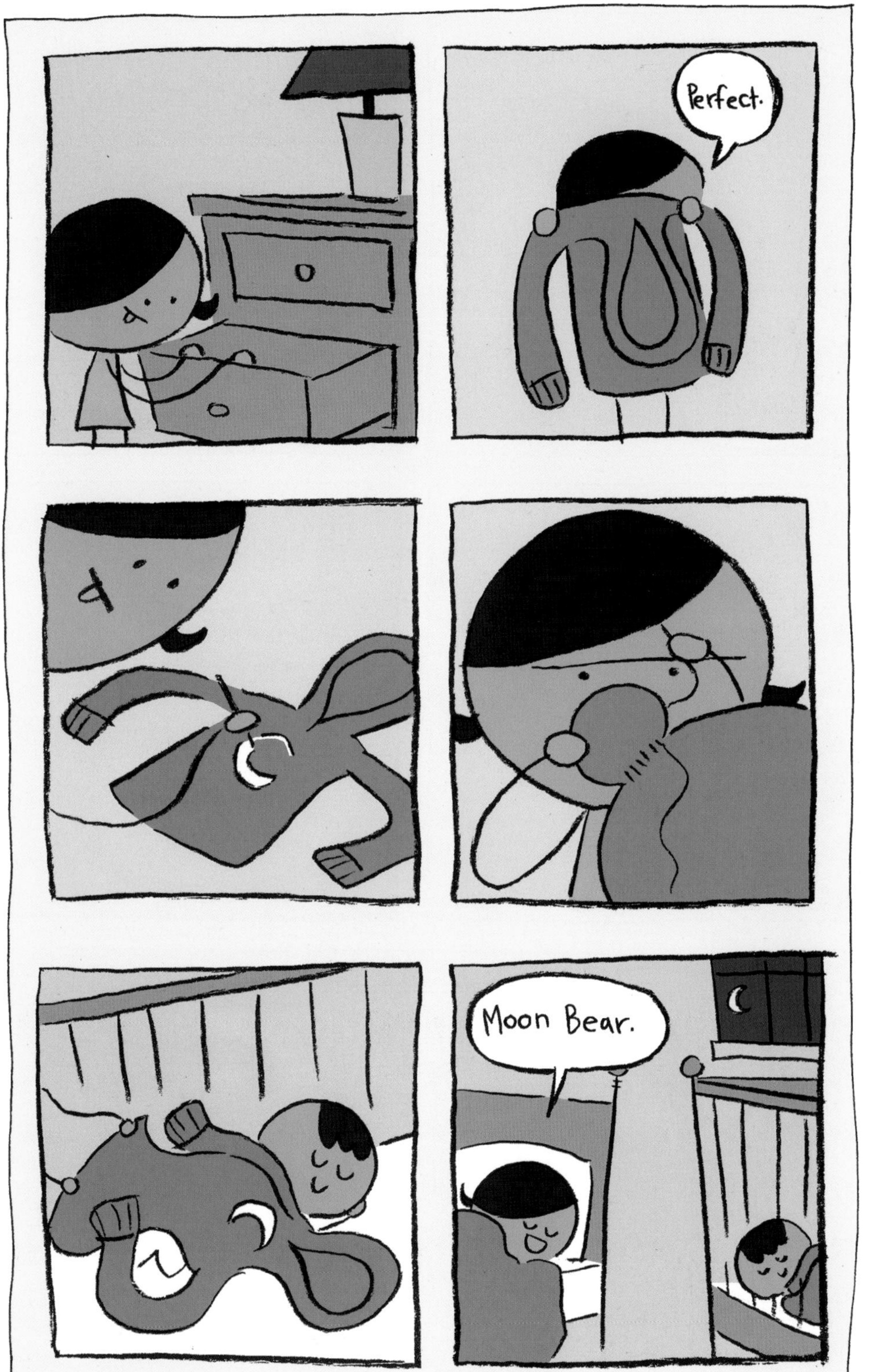
Perfect.
Moon Bear.

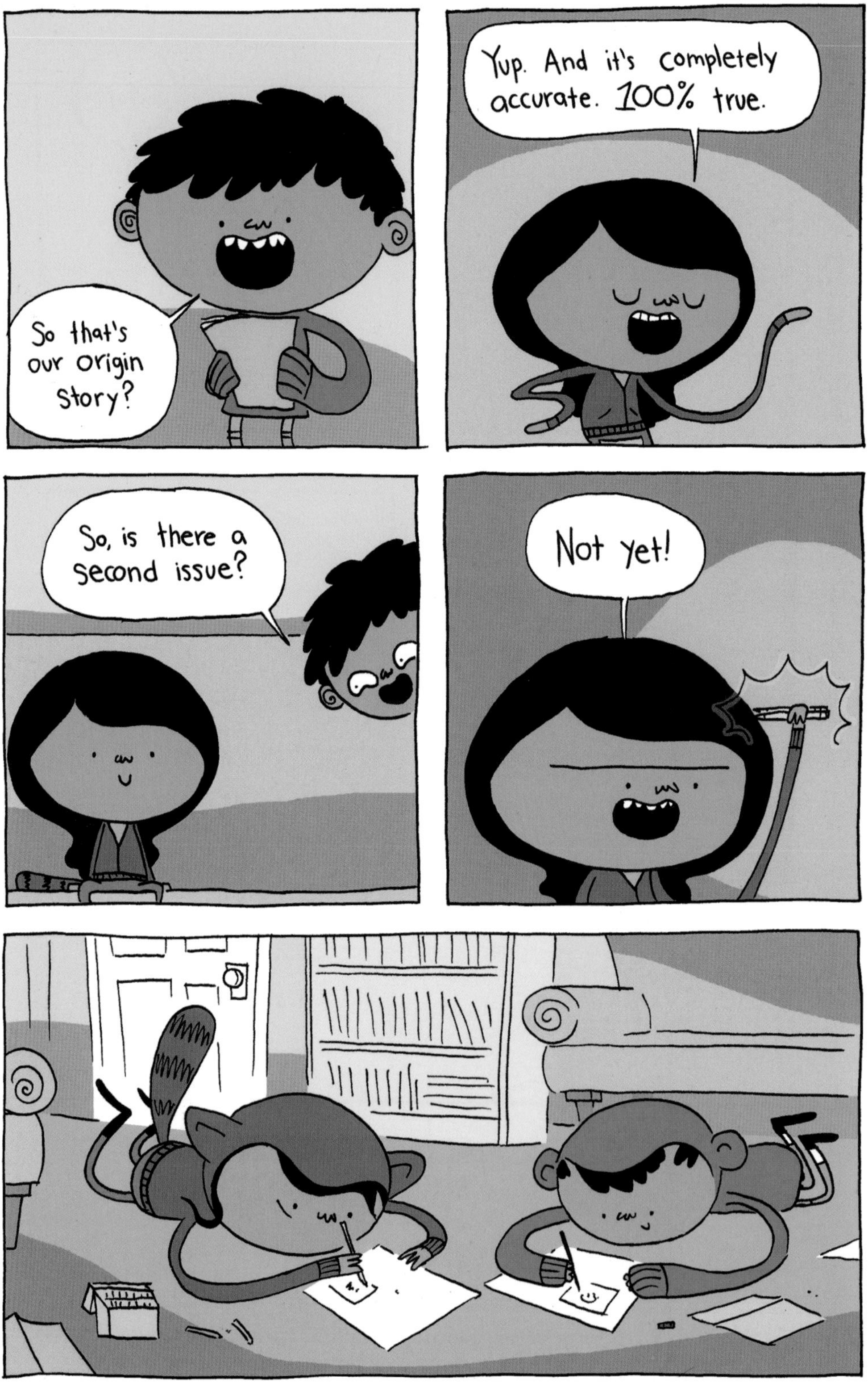
So that's our origin story?
Yup. And it's completely accurate. 100% true.
So, is there a second issue?
Not yet!

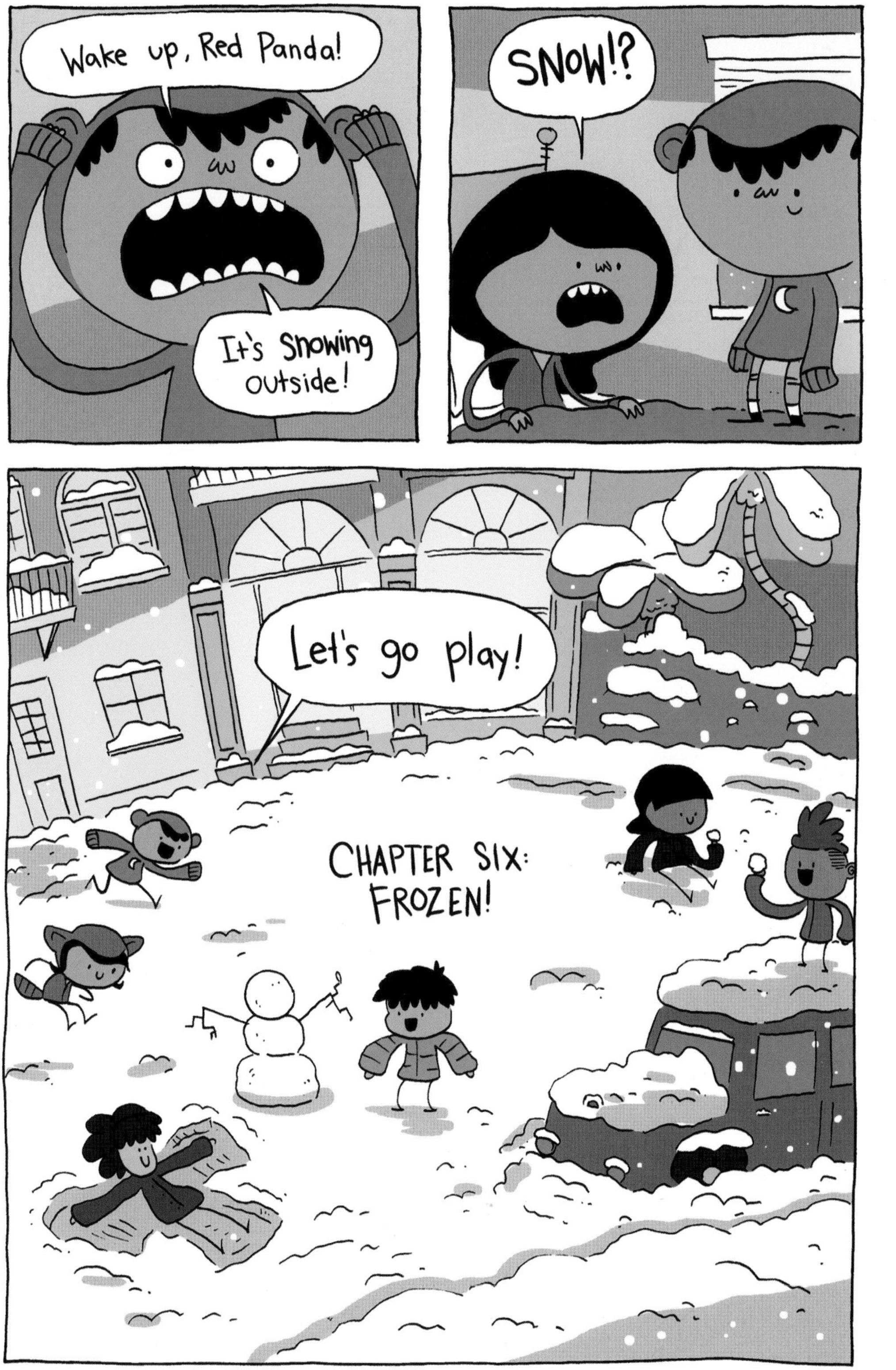
Wake up, Red Panda!
It's snowing outside!
SNOW!?
Let's go play!
CHAPTER SIX: FROZEN!

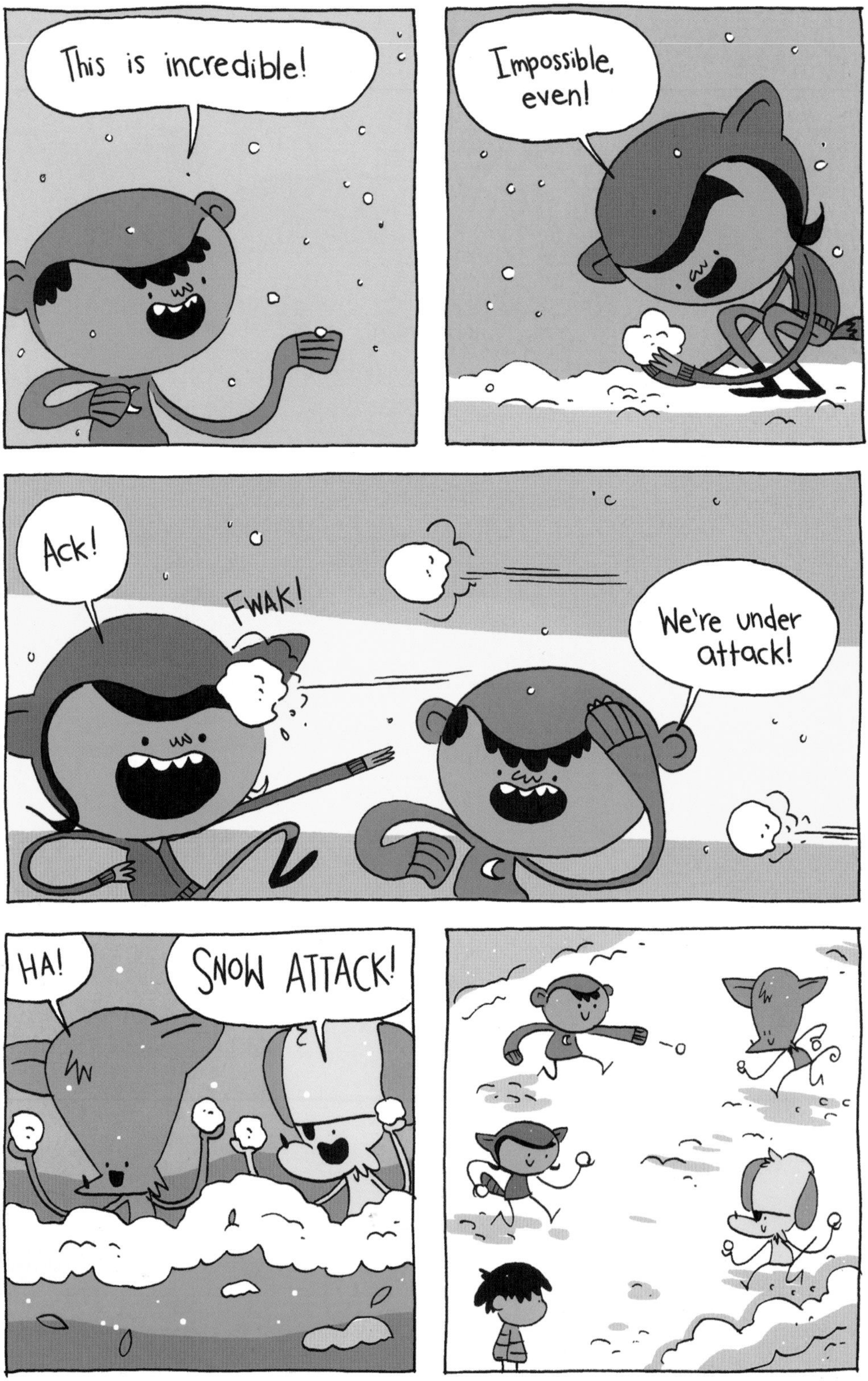
This is incredible!
Impossible, even!
Ack!
FWAK!
We're under attack!
HA!
SNOW ATTACK!

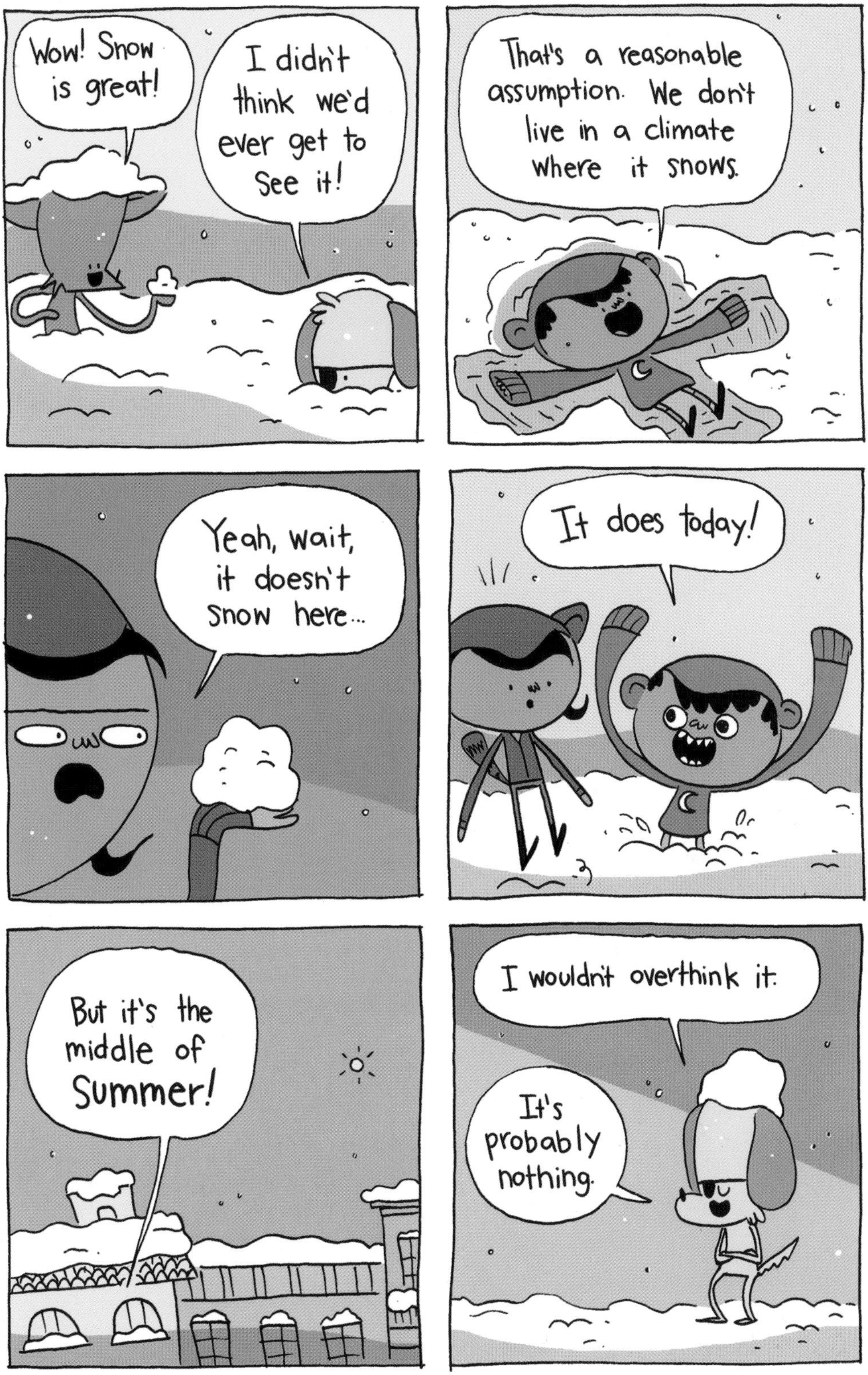

Wow! Snow is great!
I didn't think we'd ever get to see it!
That's a reasonable assumption. We don't live in a climate where it snows.
Yeah, wait, it doesn't snow here...
It does today!
But it's the middle of Summer!
I wouldn't overthink it.
It's probably nothing.

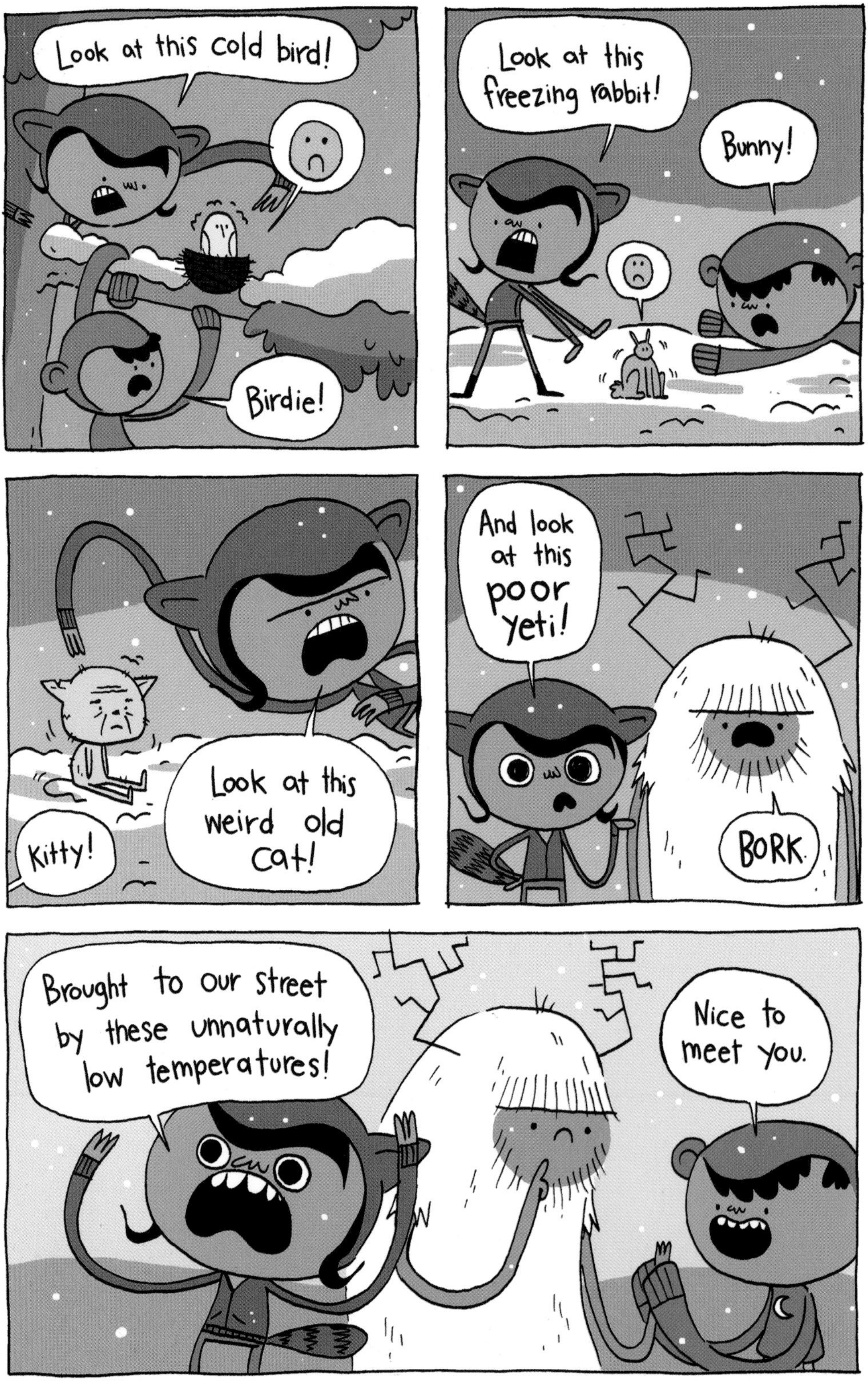

Look at this cold bird!
Birdie!
Look at this freezing rabbit!
Bunny!
Look at this weird old cat!
Kitty!
And look at this poor yeti!
BORK.
Brought to our street by these unnaturally low temperatures!
Nice to meet you.

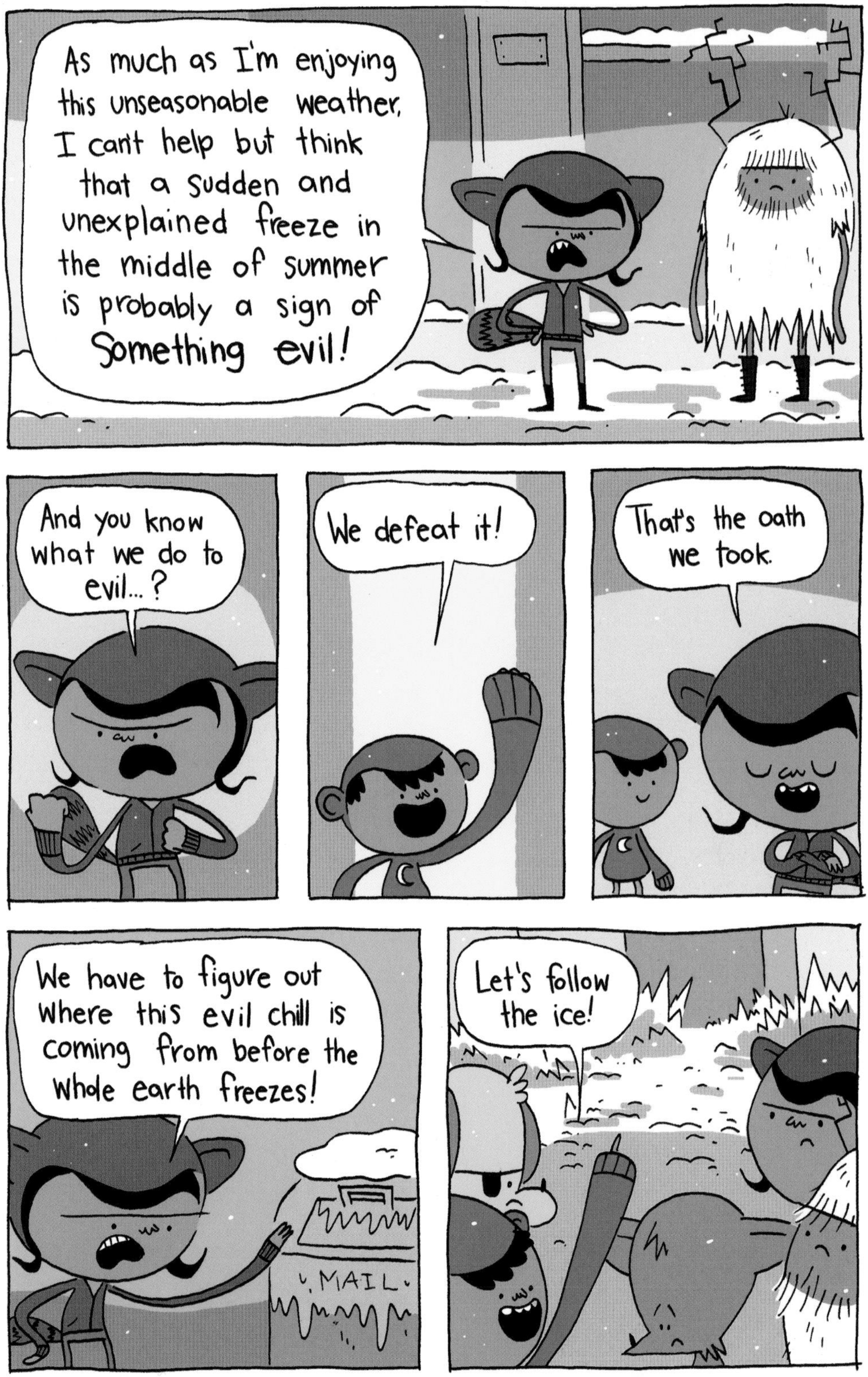
As much as I'm enjoying this unseasonable weather, I can't help but think that a sudden and unexplained freeze in the middle of summer is probably a sign of Something evil!
And you know what we do to evil...?
We defeat it!
That's the oath we took.
We have to figure out where this evil chill is coming from before the whole earth freezes!
MAIL
Let's follow the ice!

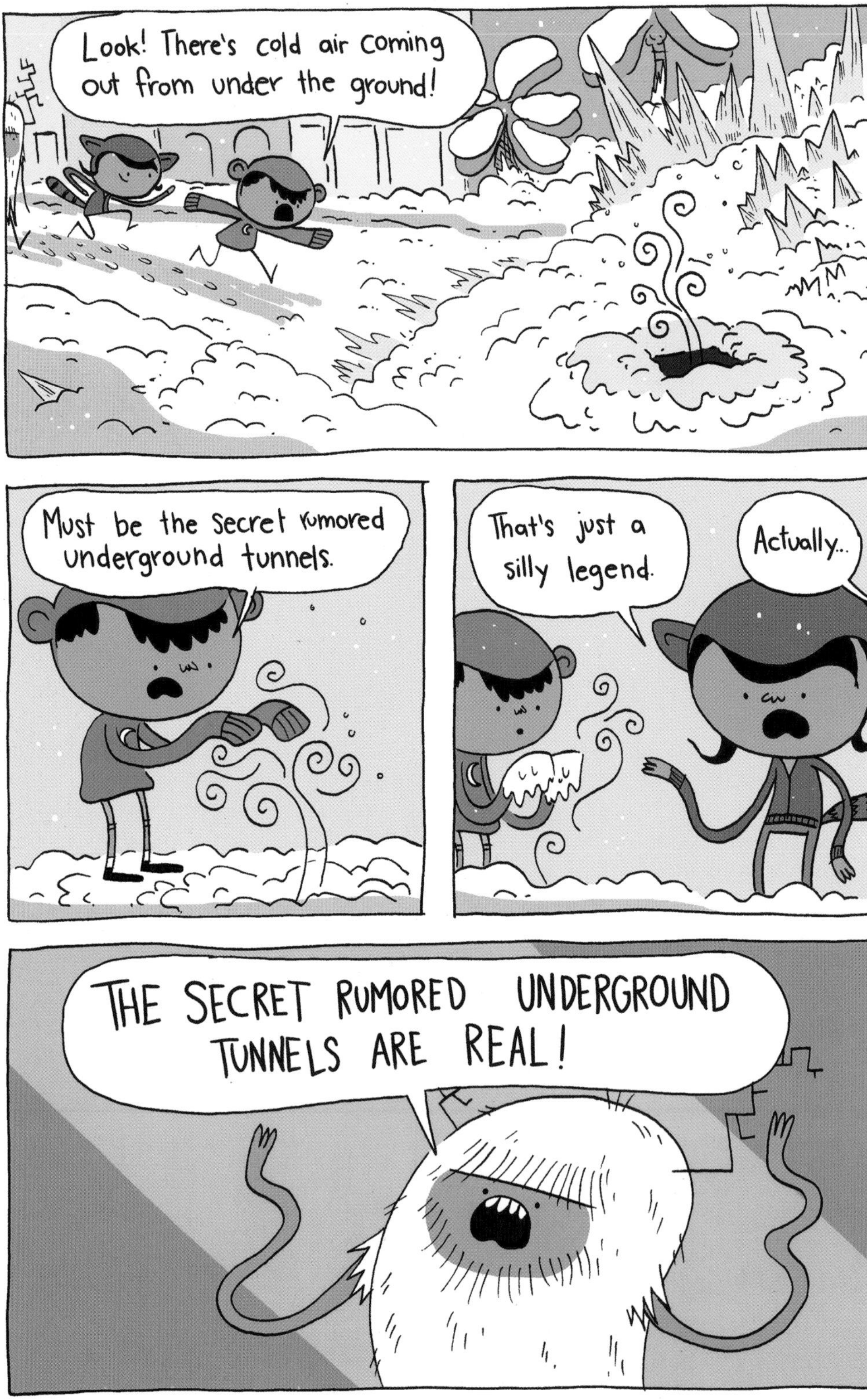
Look! There's cold air coming out from under the ground!
Must be the secret rumored underground tunnels.
That's just a silly legend.
Actually...
THE SECRET RUMORED UNDERGROUND TUNNELS ARE REAL!

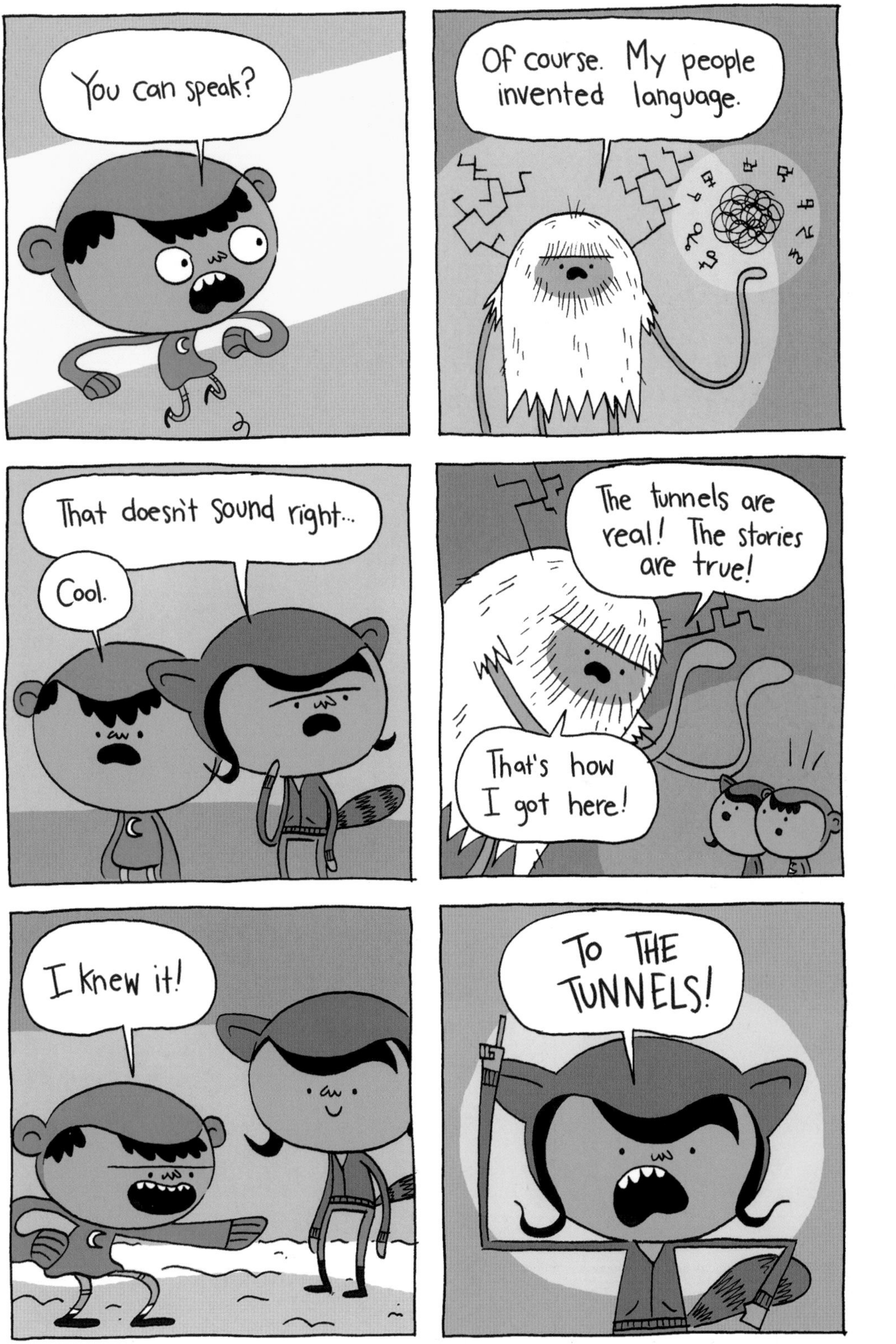
You can speak?
Of course. My people invented language.
That doesn't sound right...
Cool.
The tunnels are real! The stories are true!
That's how I got here!
I knew it!
TO THE TUNNELS!

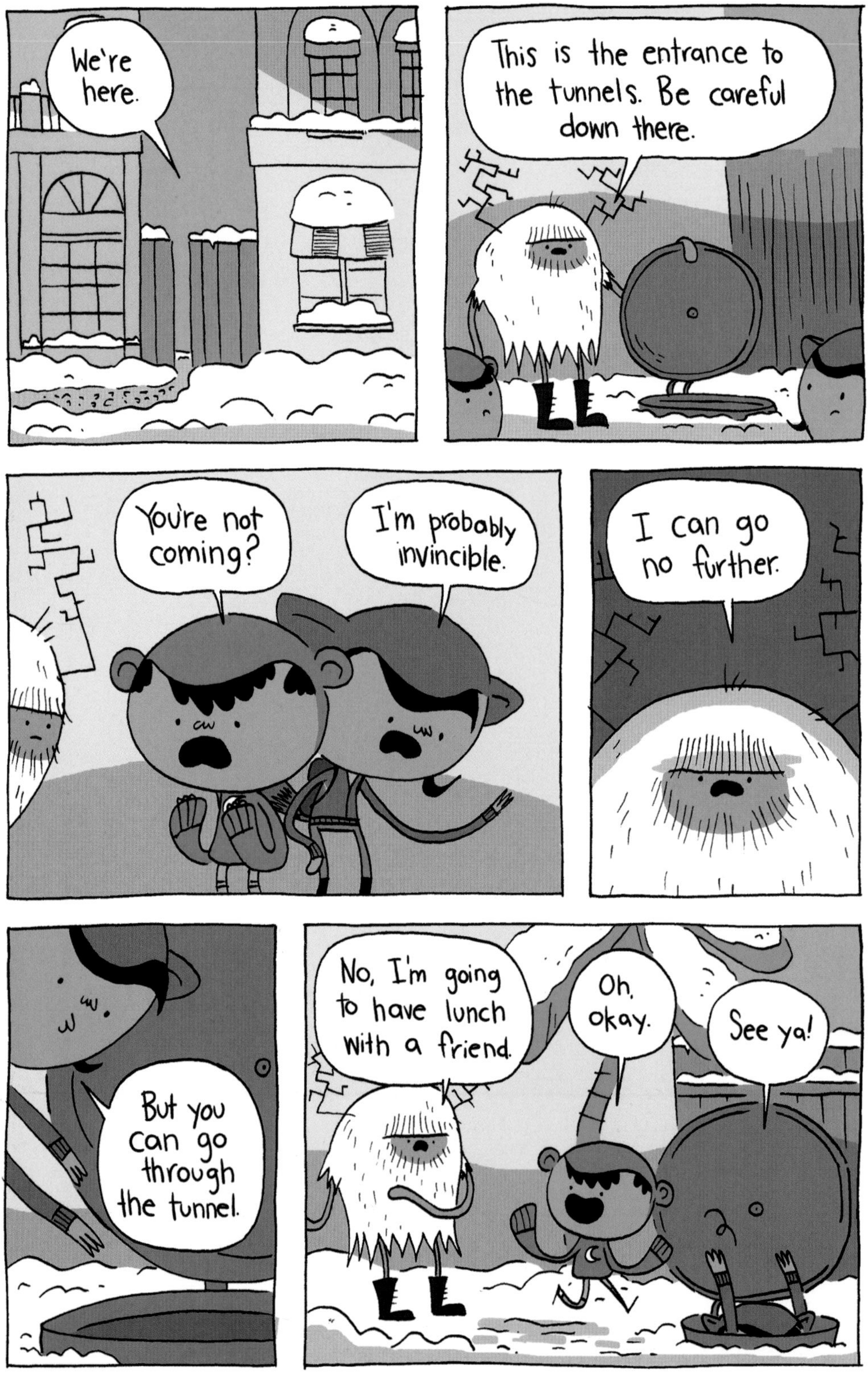
We're here.
This is the entrance to the tunnels. Be careful down there.
You're not coming?
I'm probably invincible.
I can go no further.
But you can go through the tunnel.
No, I'm going to have lunch with a friend.
Oh. okay.
See ya!

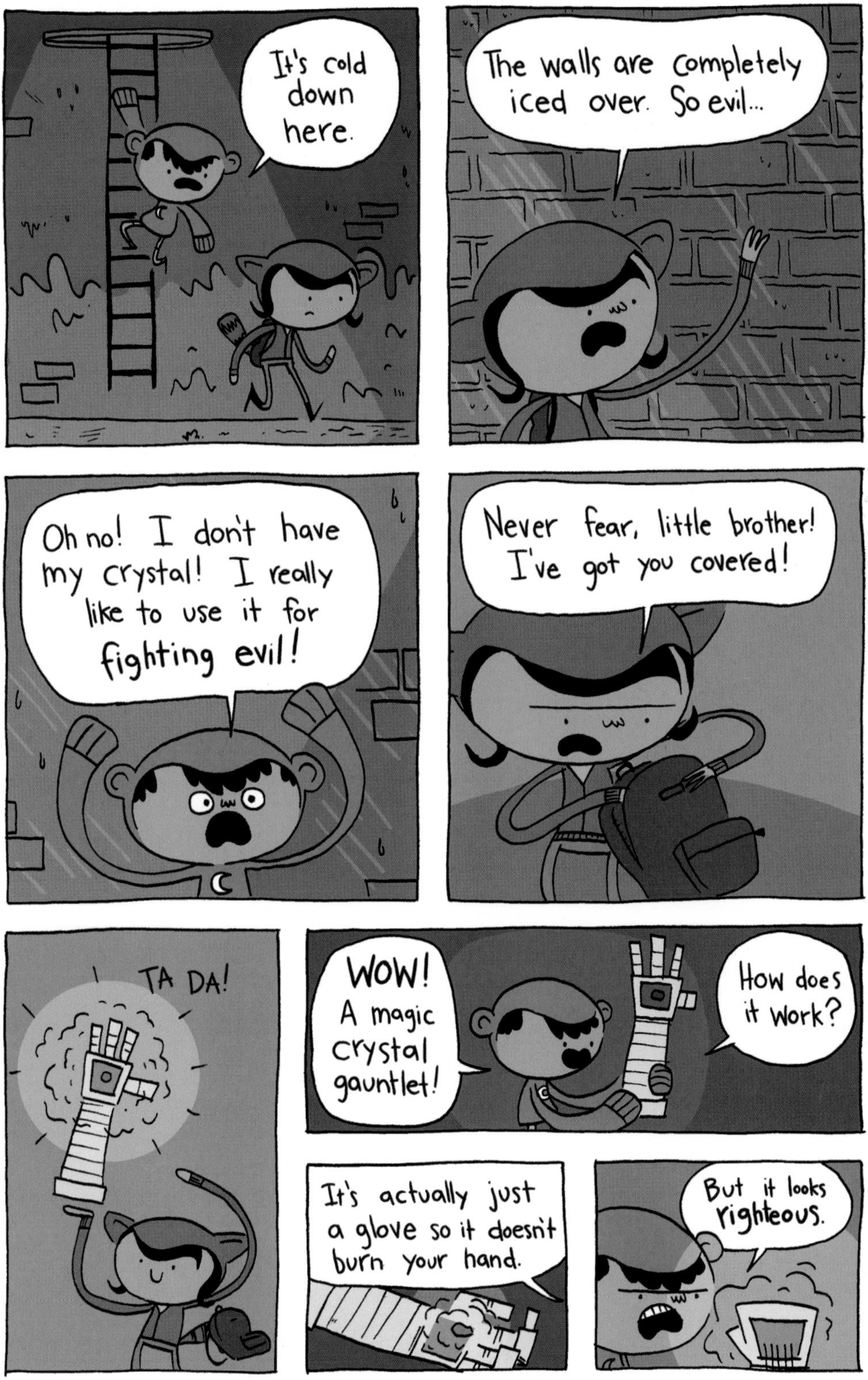
It's cold down here.
The walls are completely iced over. So evil...
Oh no! I don't have my crystal! I really like to use it for fighting evil!
Never fear, little brother! I've got you covered!
TA DA!
WOW! A magic crystal gauntlet!
How does it work?
It's actually just a glove so it doesn't burn your hand.
But it looks righteous.

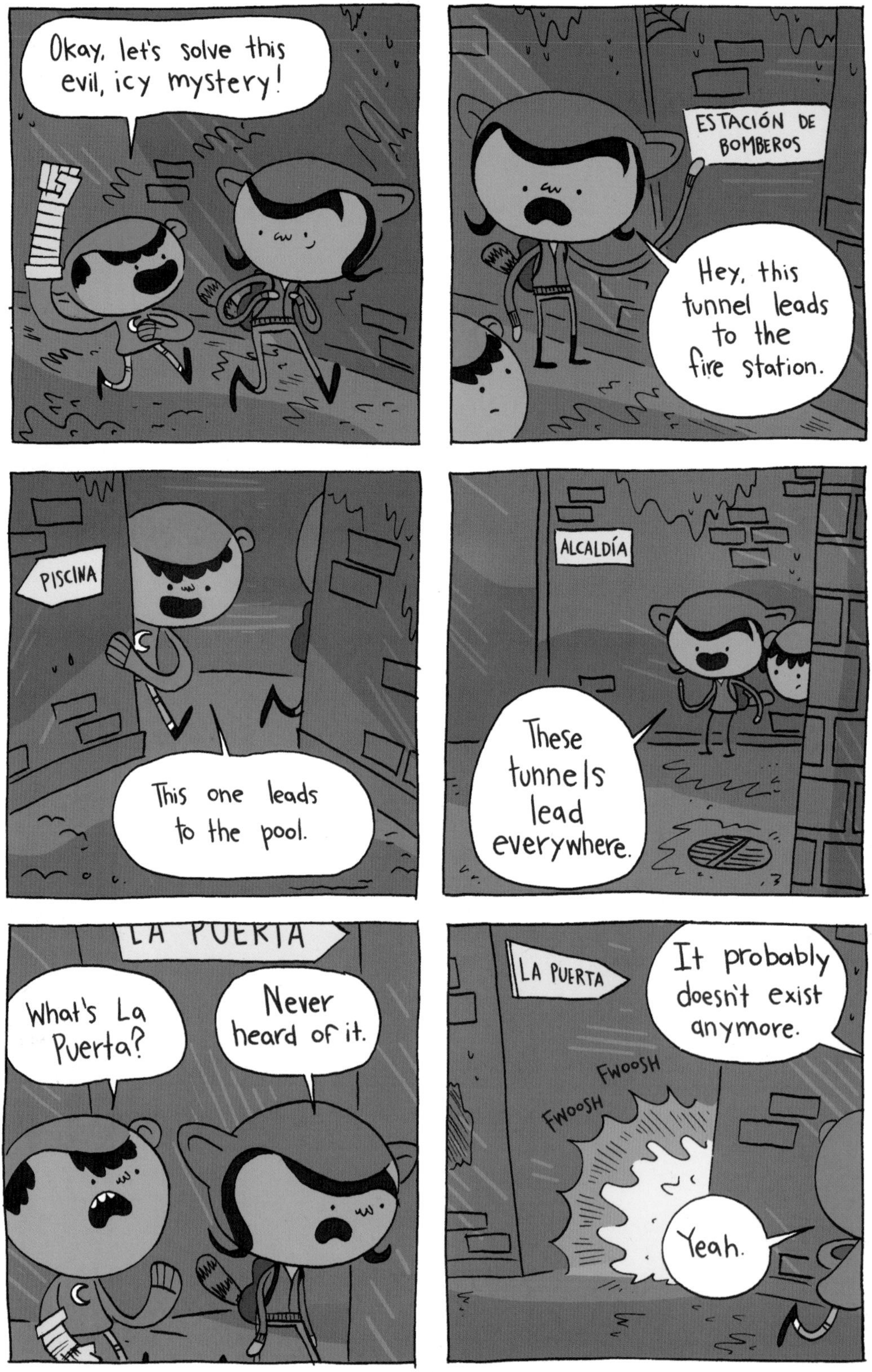
Okay, let's solve this evil, icy mystery!
ESTACIÓN DE BOMBEROS
Hey, this tunnel leads to the fire station.
PISCINA
This one leads to the pool.
ALCALDÍA
These tunnels lead everywhere.
LA PUERTA
What's La Puerta?
Never heard of it.
LA PUERTA
It probably doesn't exist anymore.
FWOOSH
FWOOSH
Yeah.

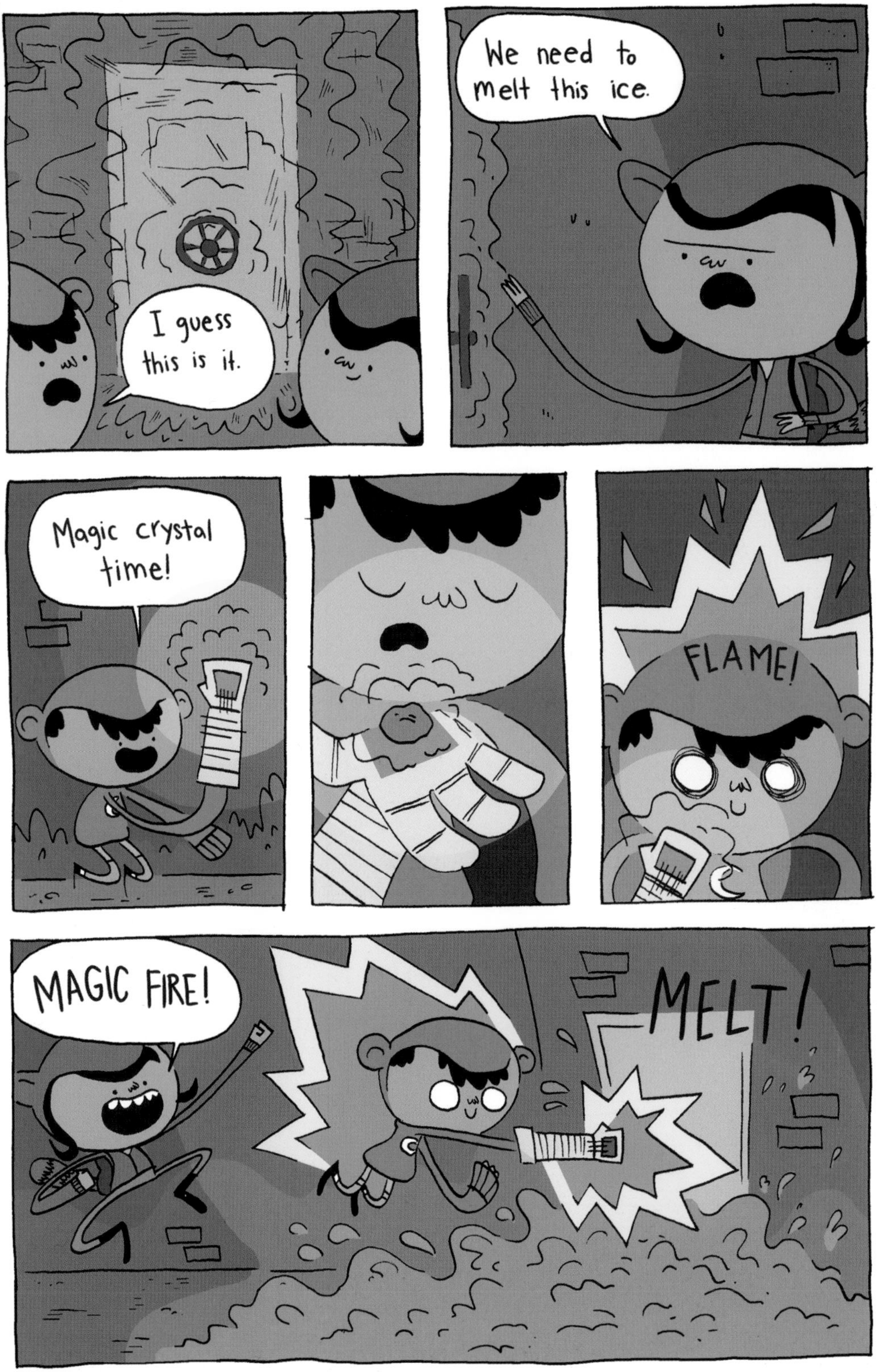
I guess this is it.
We need to melt this ice.
Magic crystal time!
FLAME!
MAGIC FIRE!
MELT!

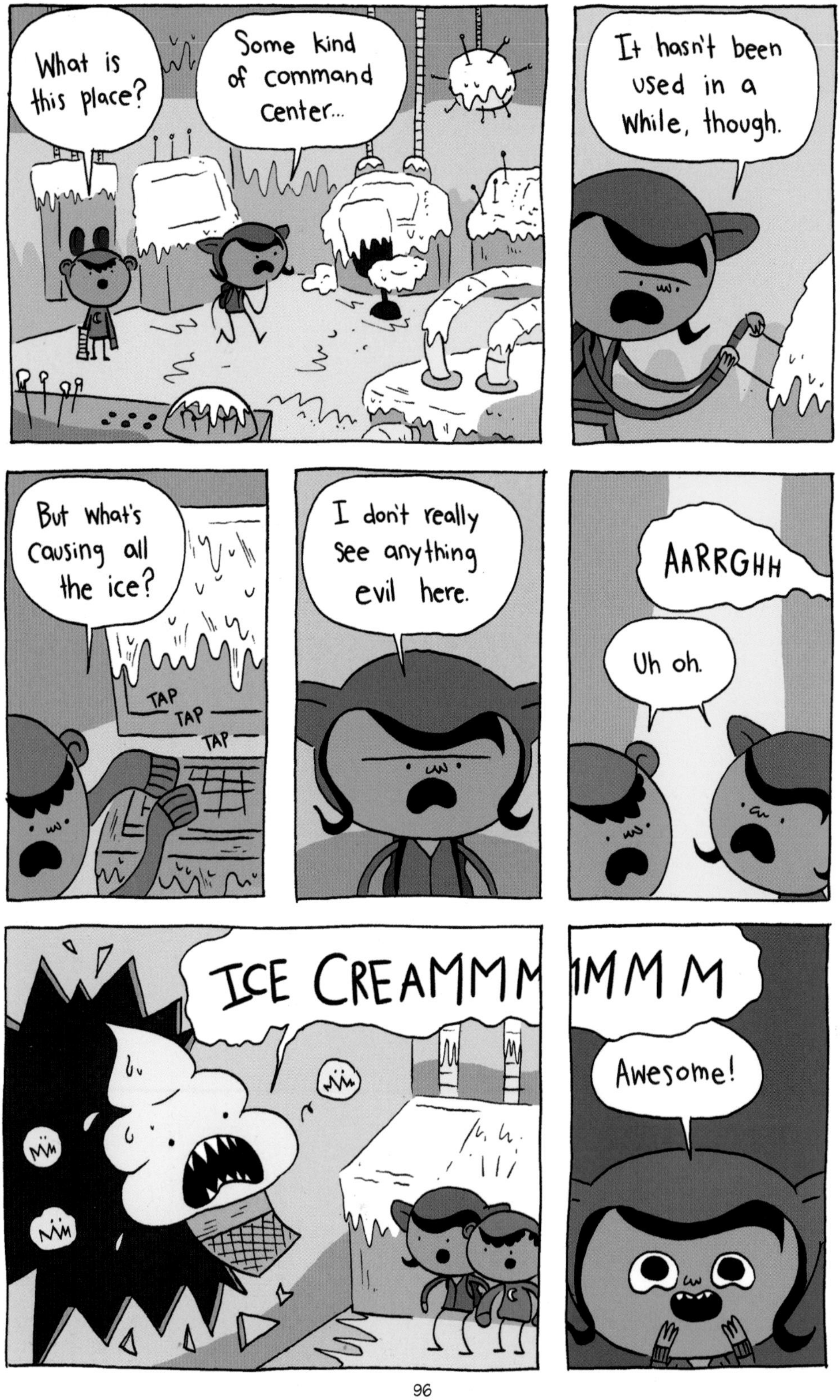
What is this place?
Some kind of command center...
It hasn't been used in a while, though.
But what's causing all the ice?
TAP
TAP
TAP
I don't really see anything evil here.
AARRGHH
Uh oh.
ICE CREAMMMMMMM M
Awesome!

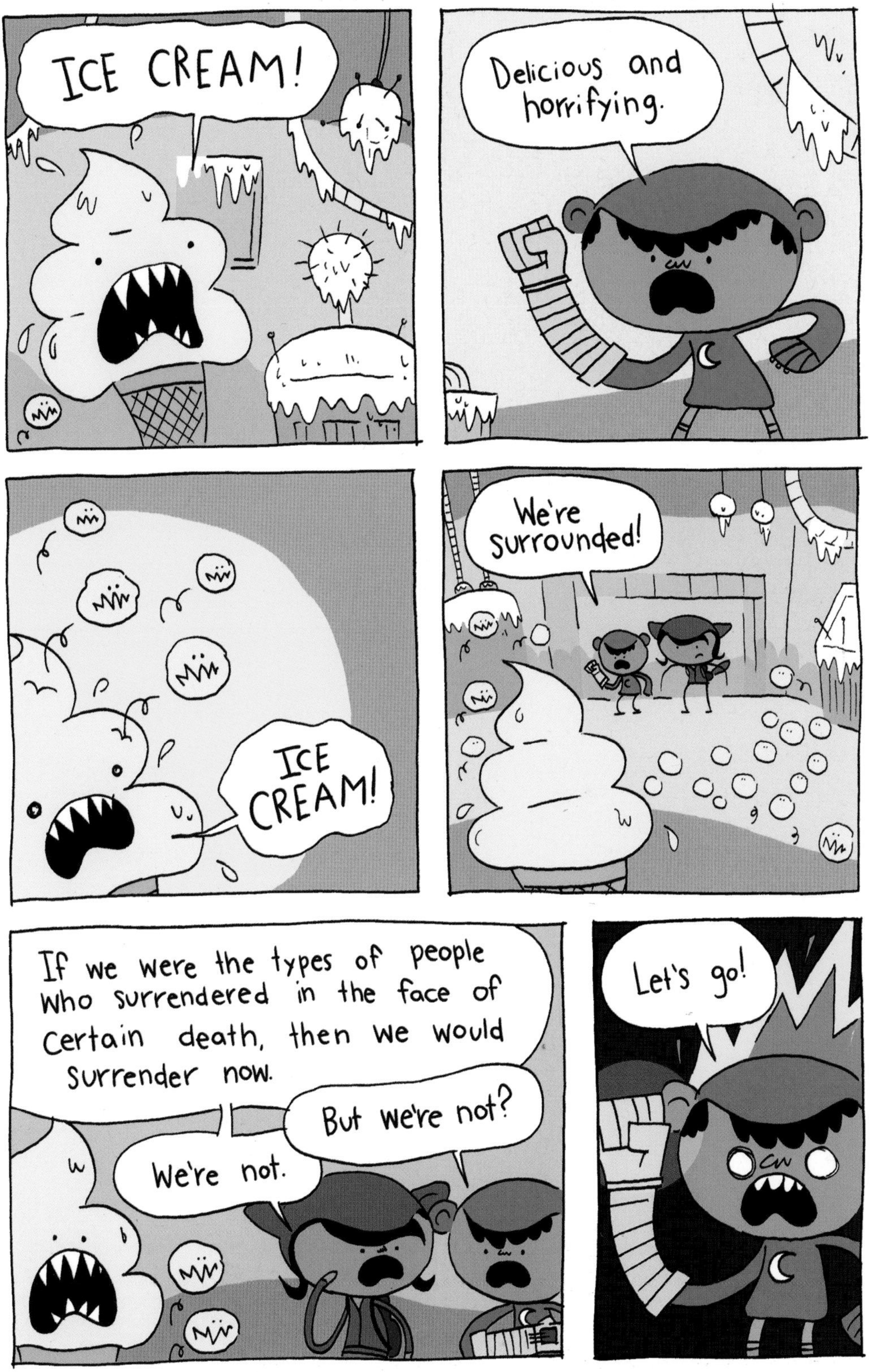
ICE CREAM!
Delicious and horrifying.
ICE CREAM!
We're surrounded!
If we were the types of people who surrendered in the face of certain death, then we would surrender now.
But we're not?
We're not.
Let's go!

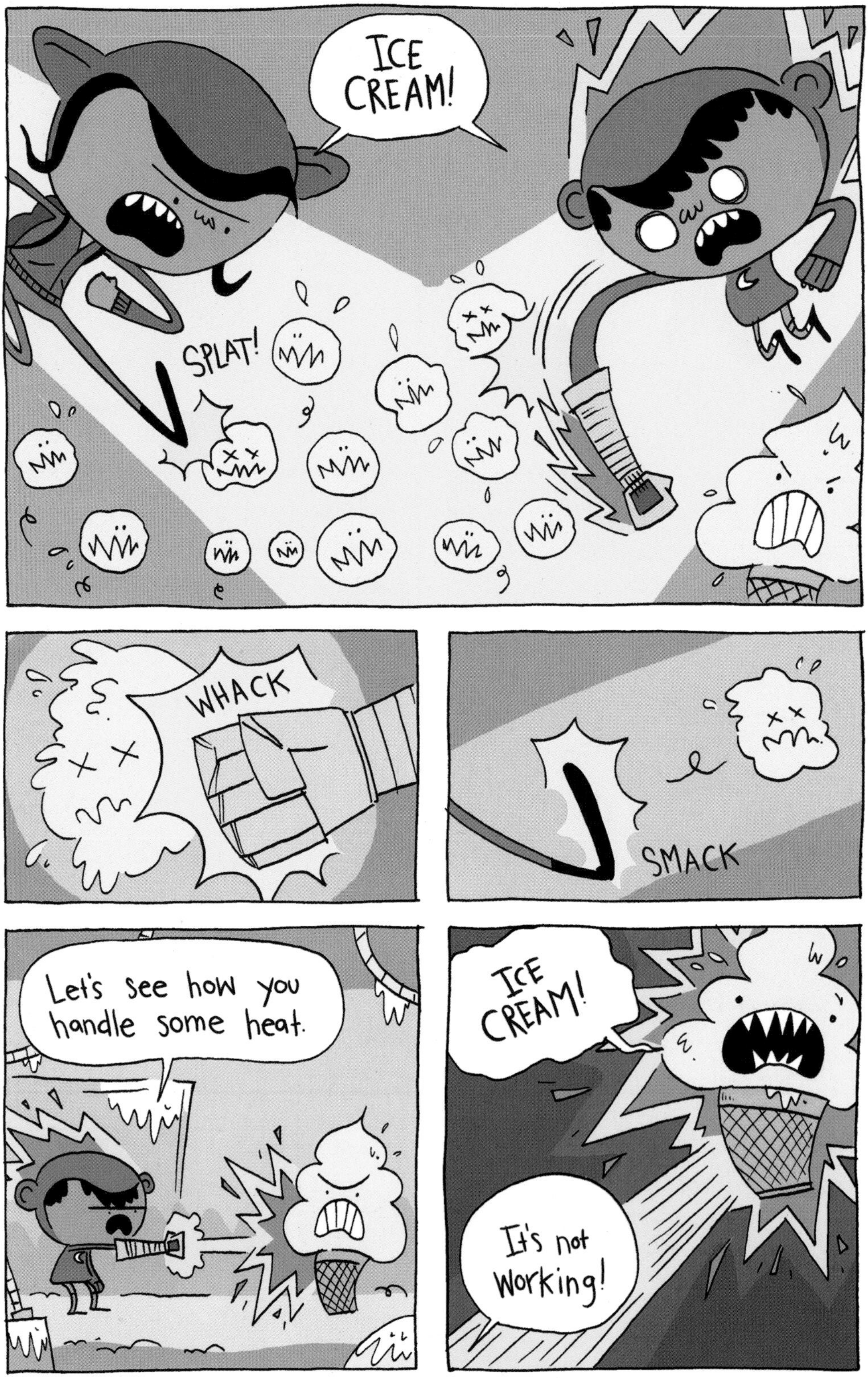
ICE CREAM!
SPLAT!
WHACK
SMACK
Let's see how you handle some heat.
ICE CREAM!
It's not working!

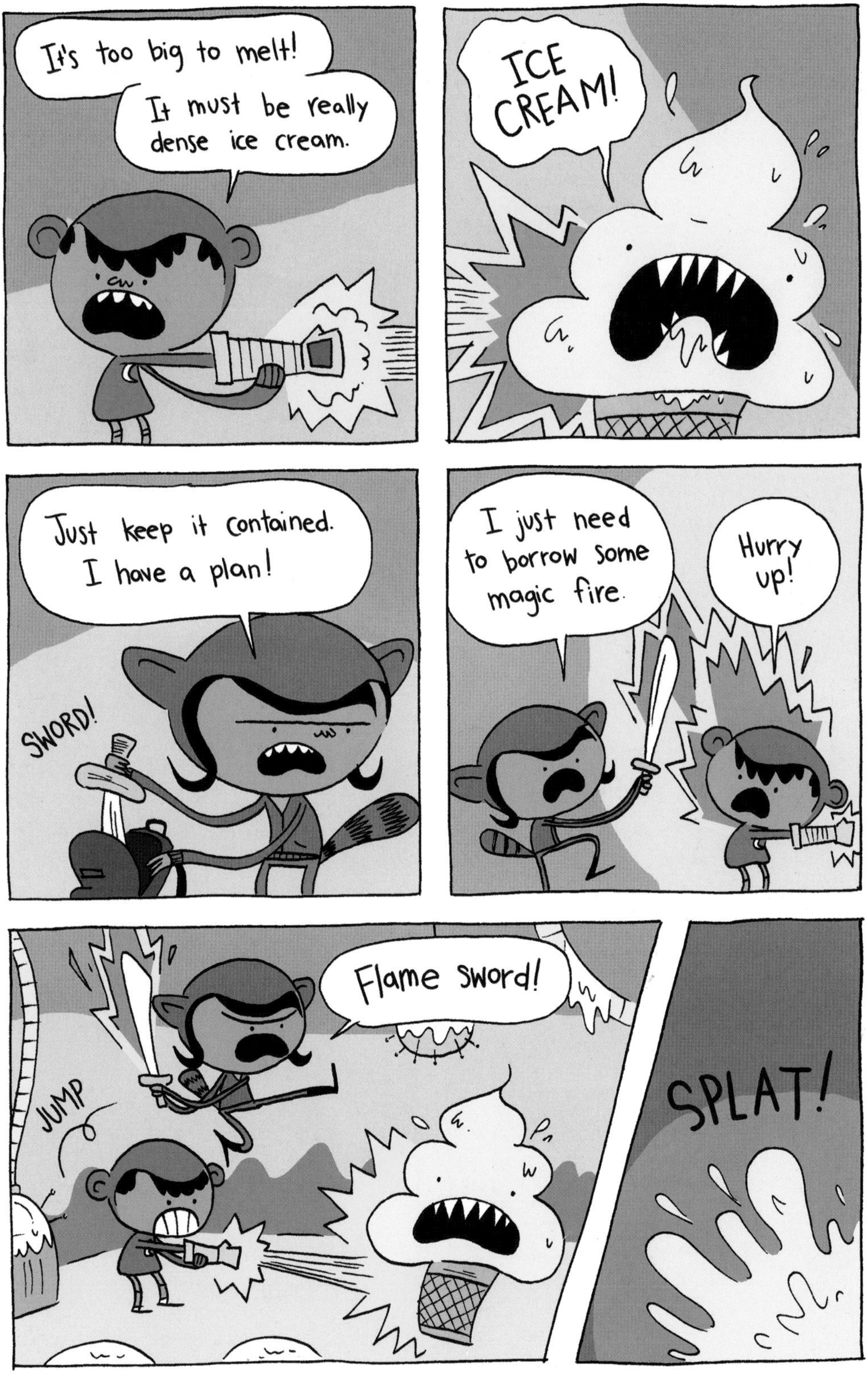
It's too big to melt!
It must be really dense ice cream.
ICE CREAM!
Just keep it contained. I have a plan!
SWORD!
I just need to borrow some magic fire.
Hurry up!
Flame sword!
JUMP
SPLAT!

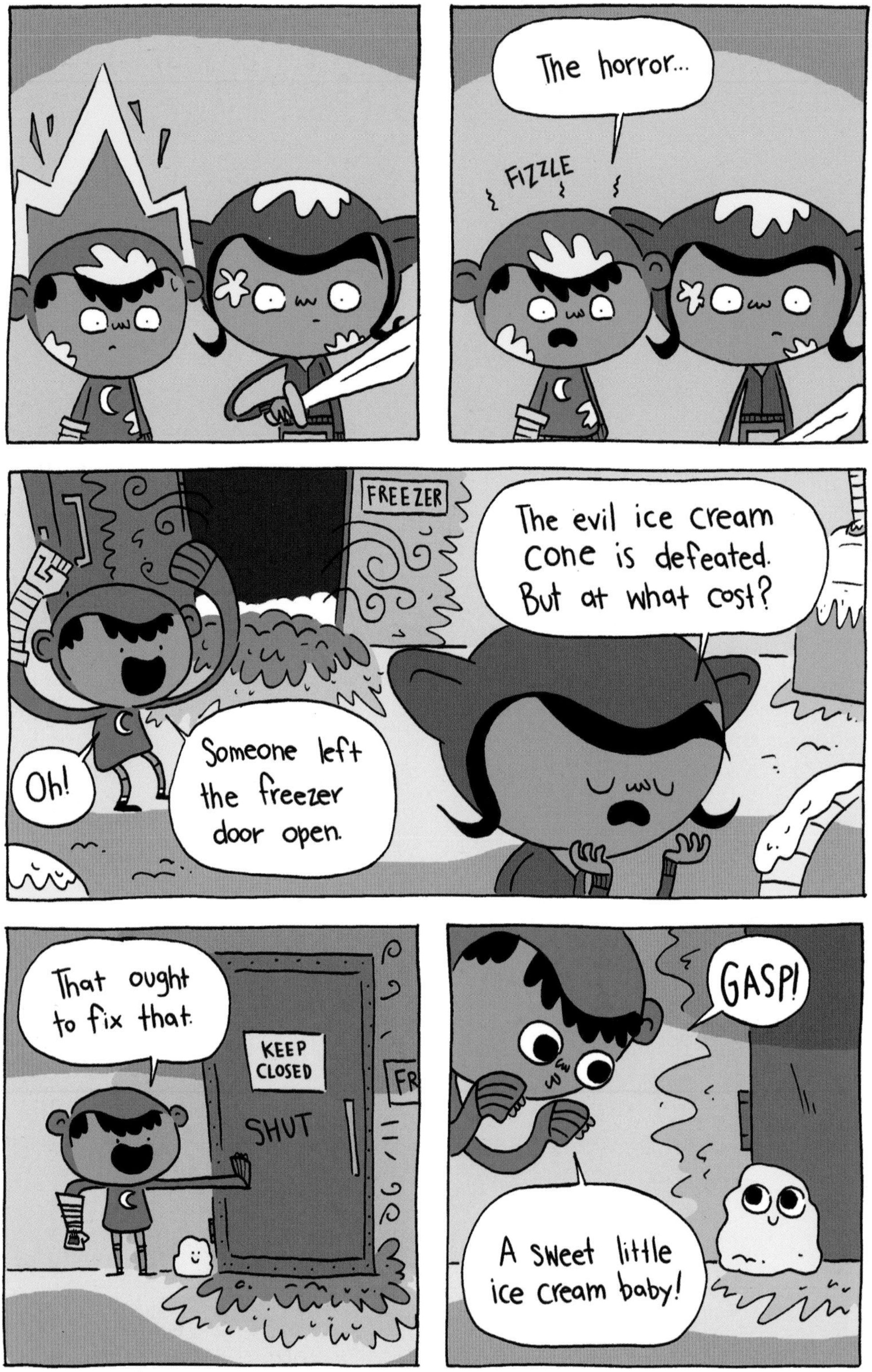
The horror...
FIZZLE
FREEZER
The evil ice cream cone is defeated. But at what cost?
Oh!
Someone left the freezer door open.
That ought to fix that.
KEEP CLOSED
SHUT
FR
GASP!
A sweet little ice cream baby!

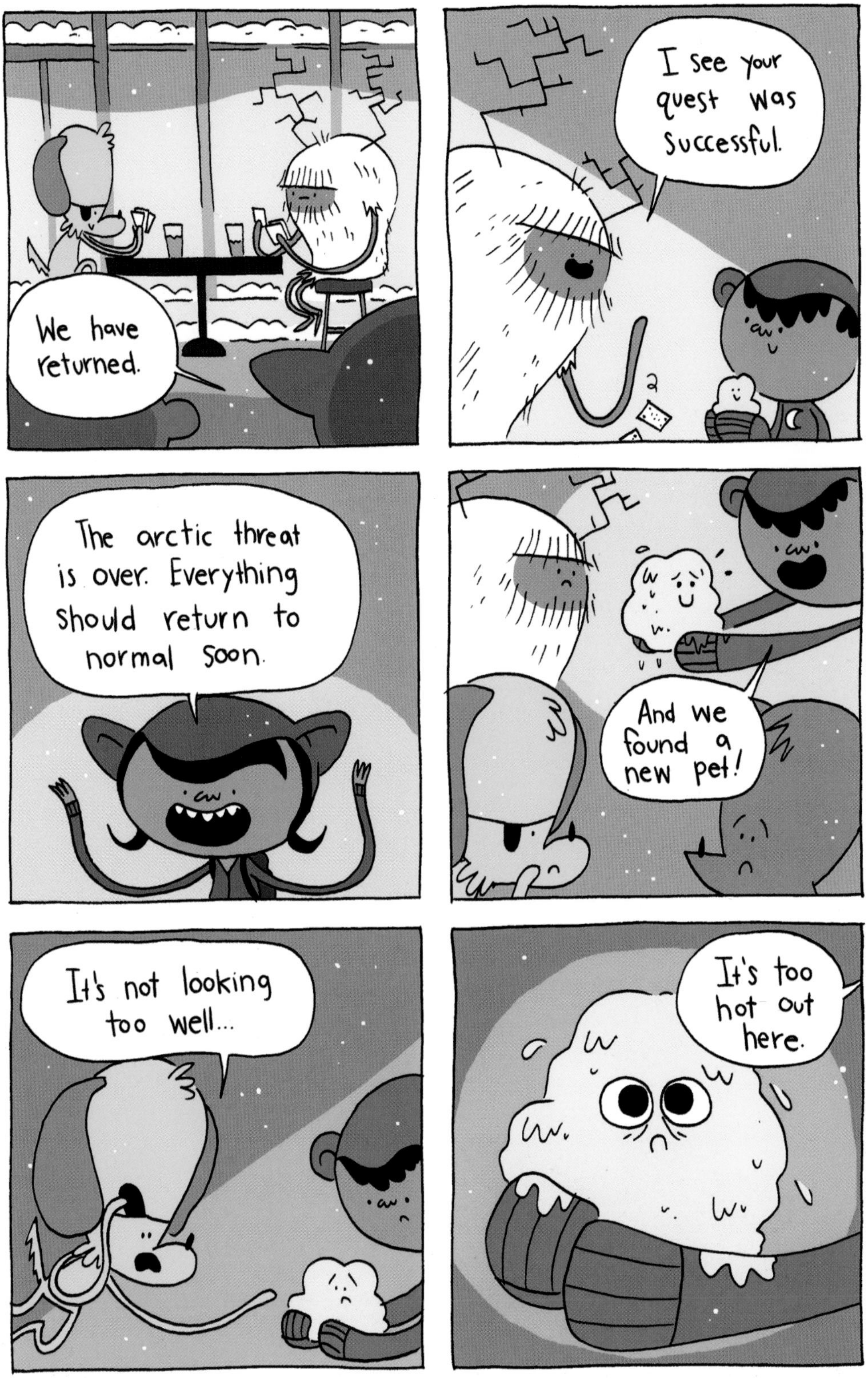
We have returned.
I see your quest was successful.
The arctic threat is over. Everything should return to normal soon.
And we found a new pet!
It's not looking too well...
It's too hot out here.

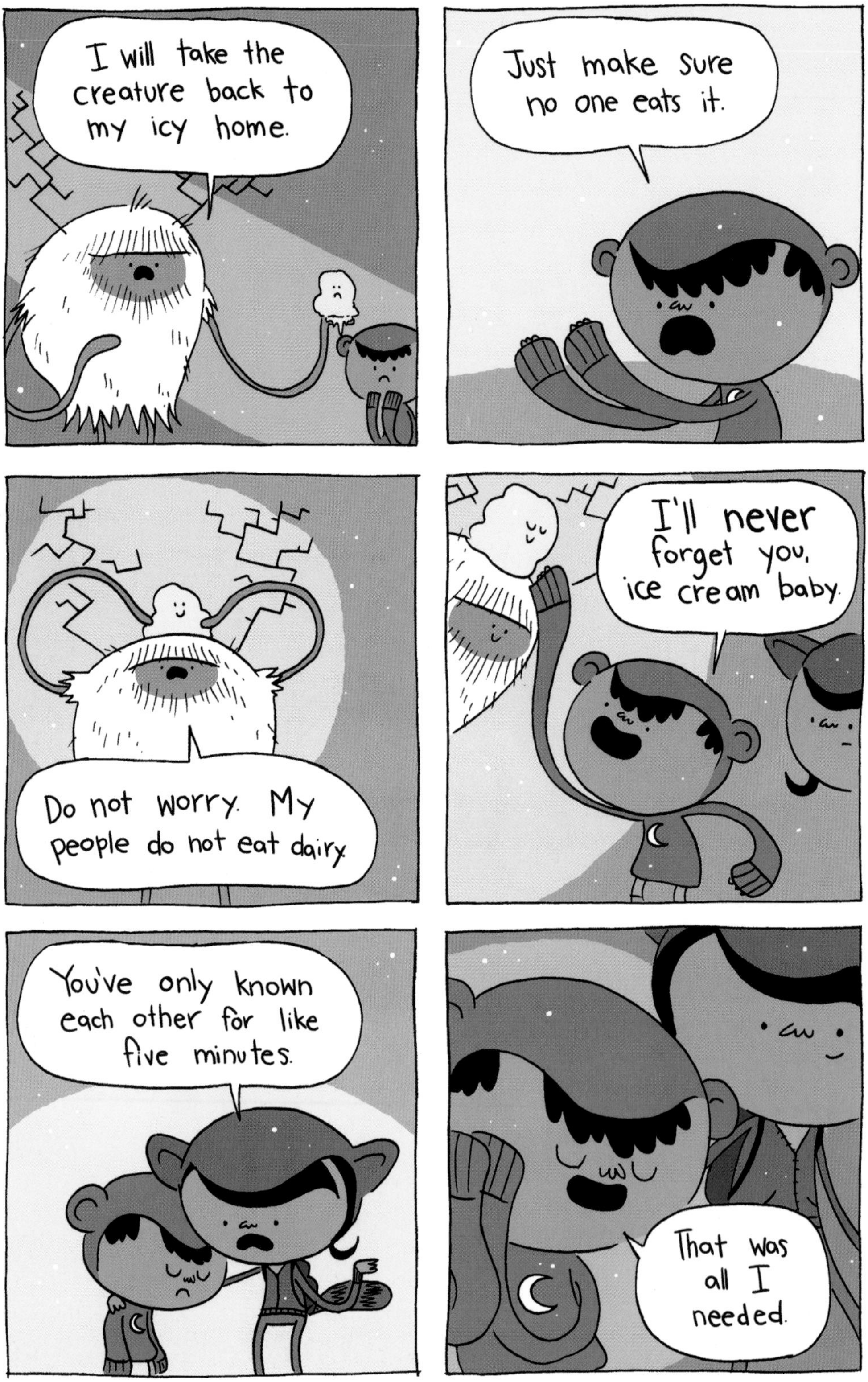
I will take the creature back to my icy home.
Just make sure no one eats it.
Do not worry. My people do not eat dairy.
I'll never forget you, ice cream baby.
You've only known each other for like five minutes.
That was all I needed.

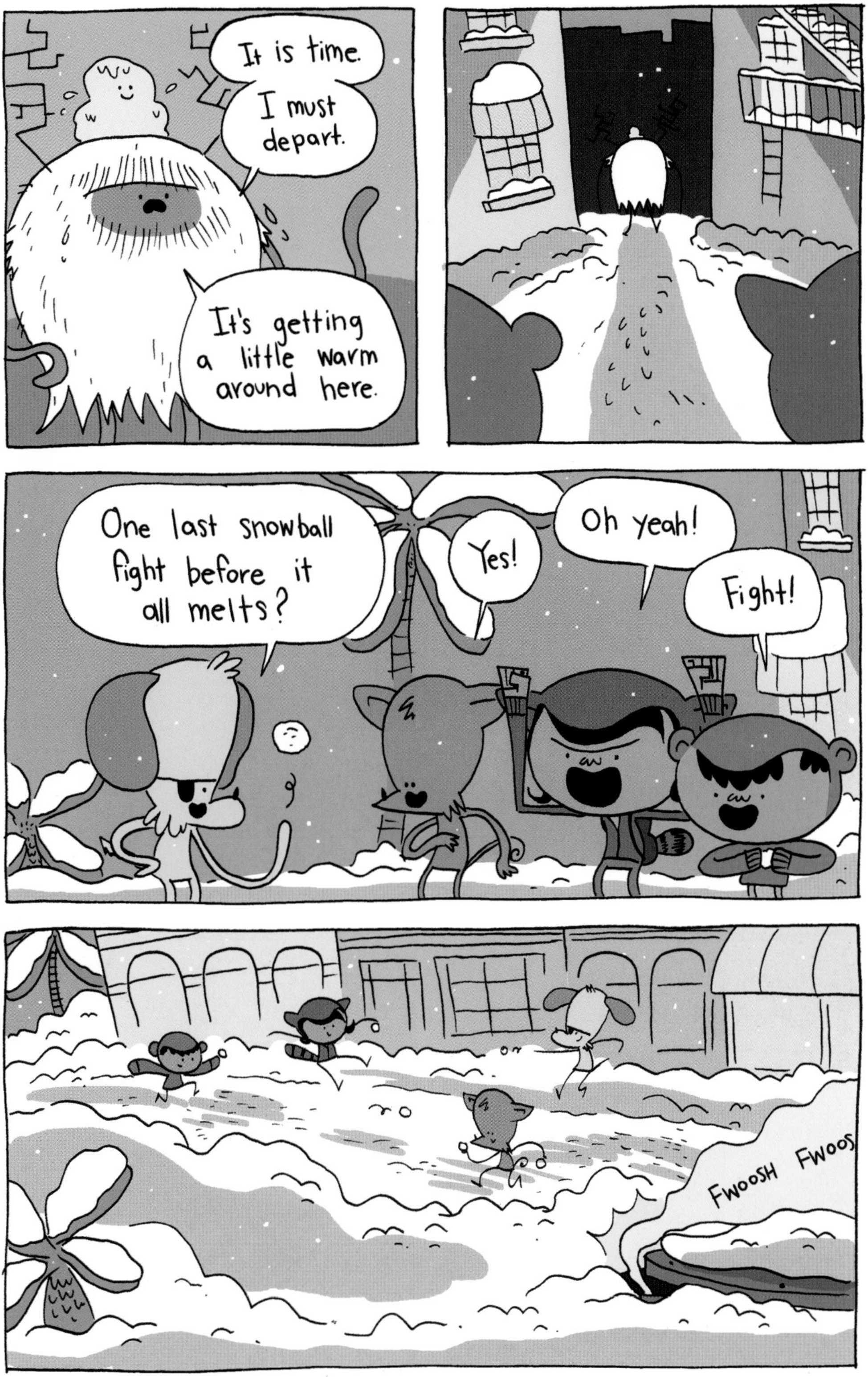
It is time.
I must depart.
It's getting a little warm around here.
One last snowball fight before it all melts?
Yes!
Oh yeah!
Fight!
FWOOSH FWOOS

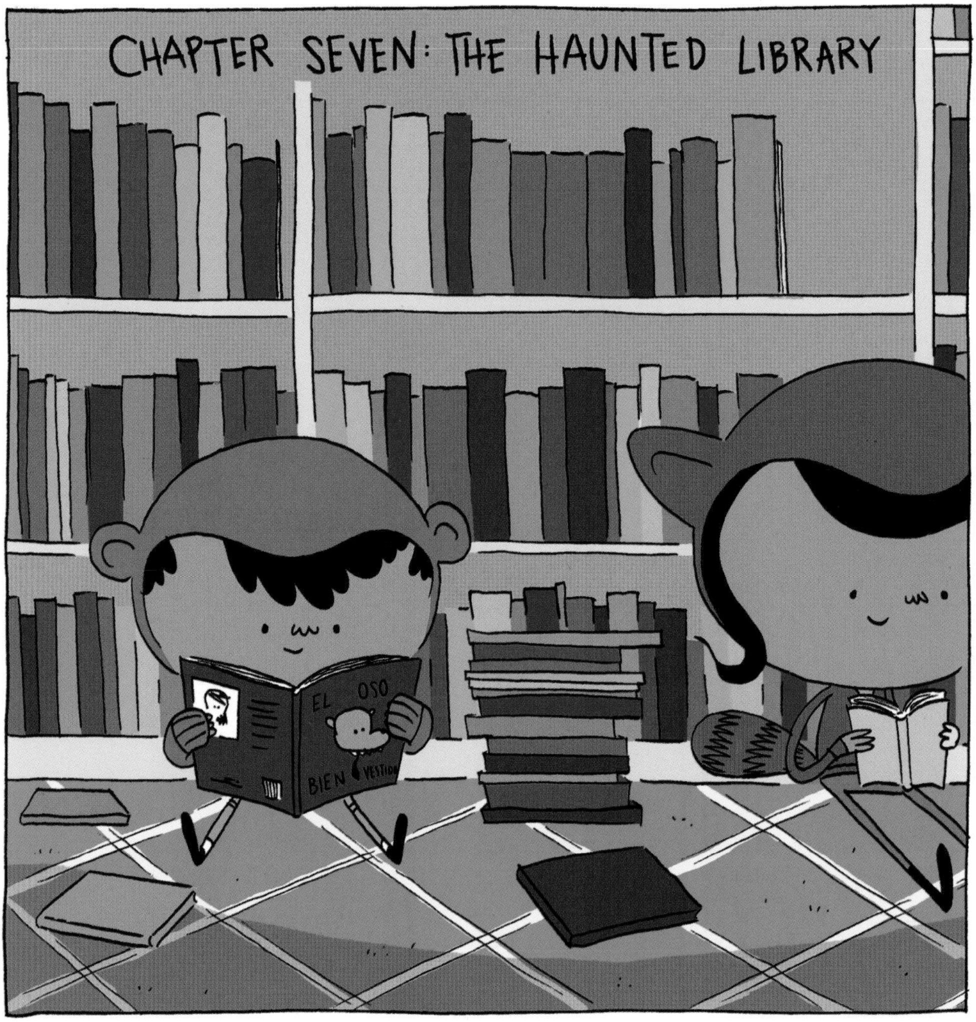
CHAPTER SEVEN: THE HAUNTED LIBRARY
EL OSO BIEN VESTIDO

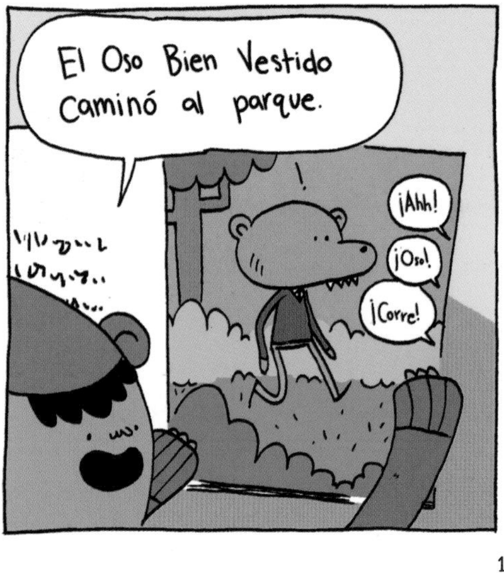
El Oso Bien Vestido caminó al parque.
¡Ahh!
¡Oso!
¡Corre!

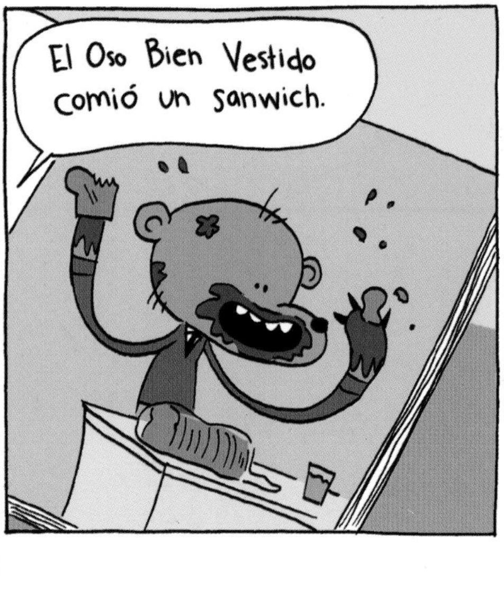
El Oso Bien Vestido comió un sanwich.

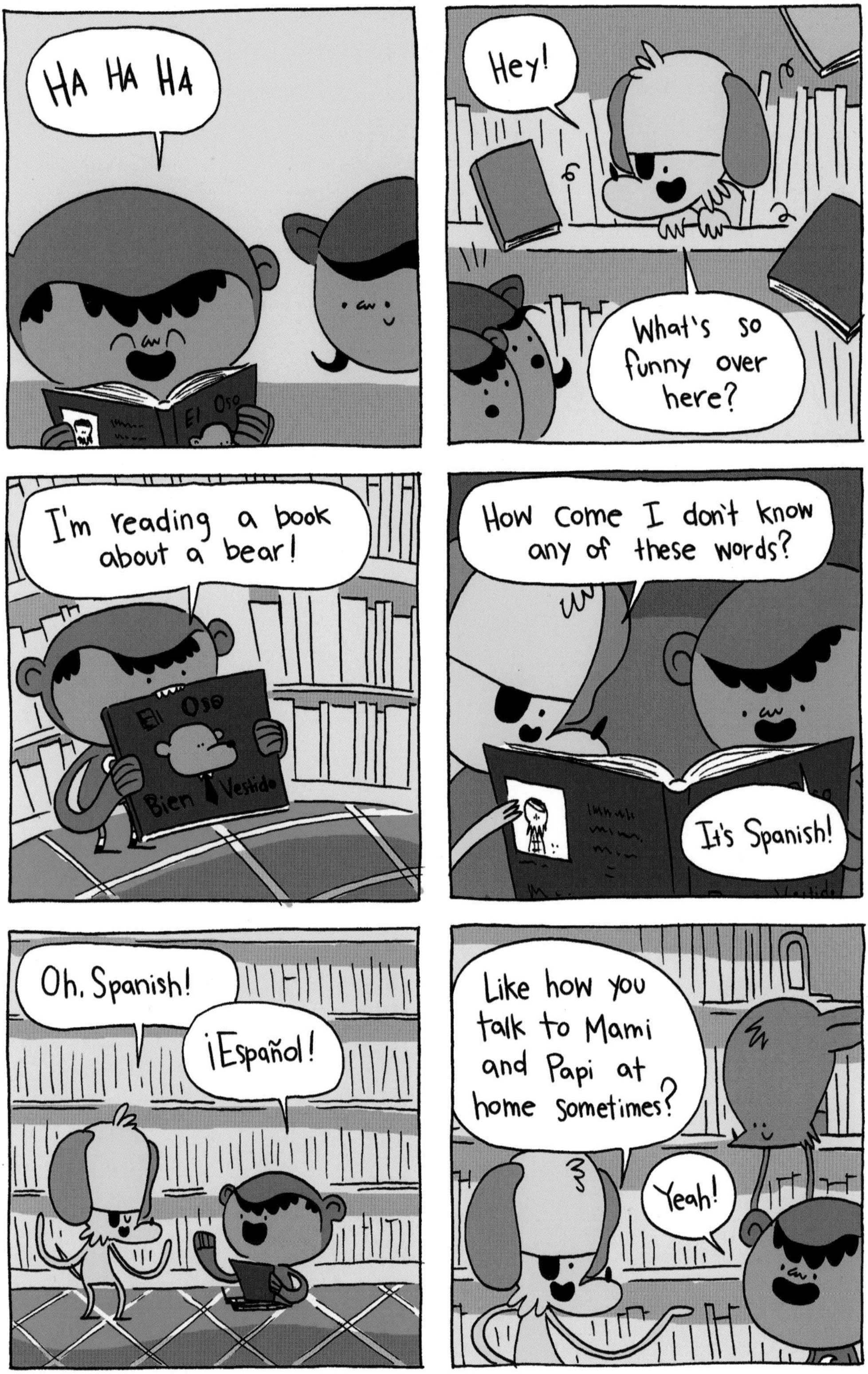
HA HA HA
El Oso
Hey!
What's so funny over here?
I'm reading a book about a bear!
El Oso
Bien Vestido
How come I don't know any of these words?
It's Spanish!
Oh, Spanish!
¡Español!
Like how you talk to Mami and Papi at home sometimes?
Yeah!

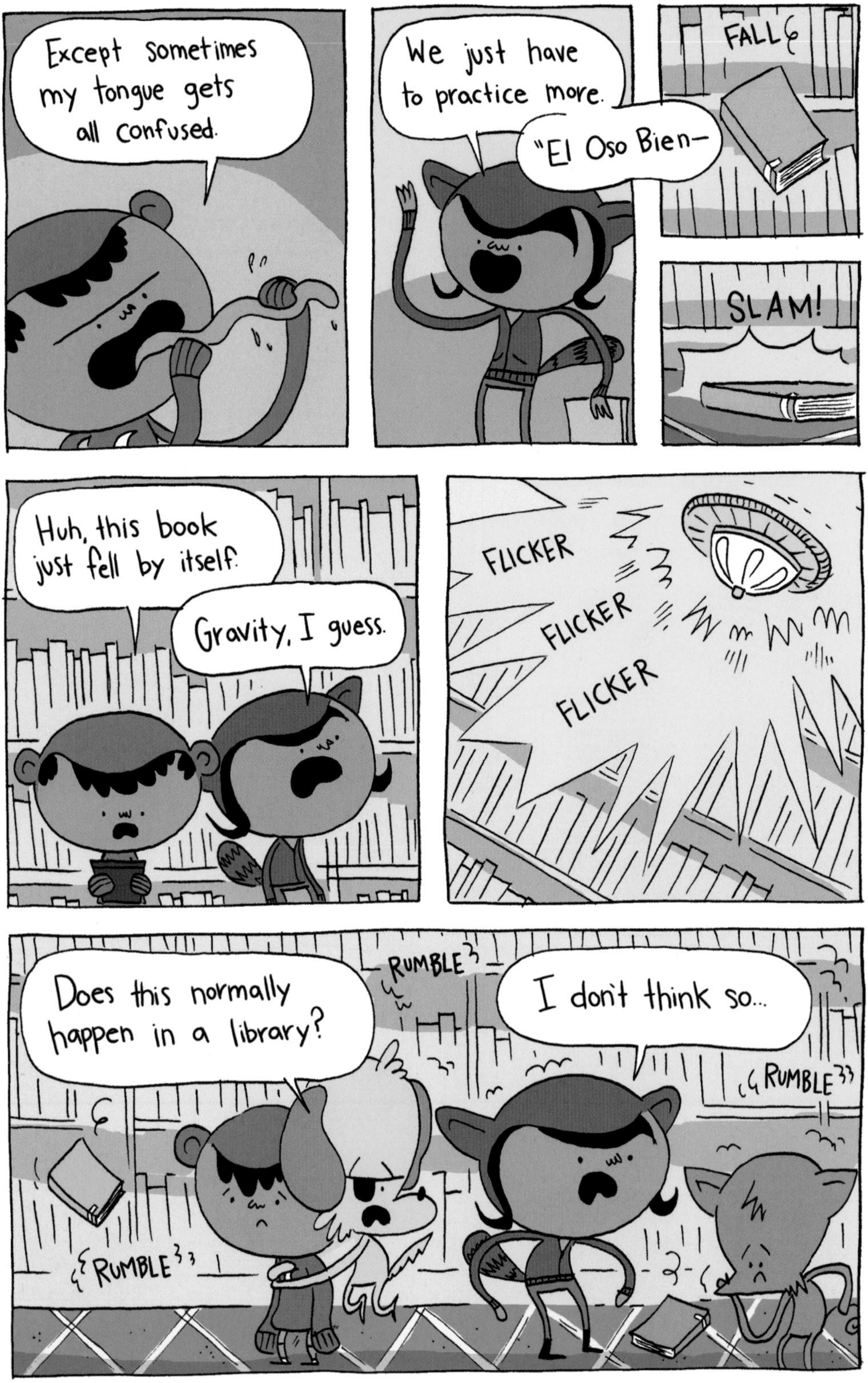
Except sometimes my tongue gets all confused.
We just have to practice more.
"El Oso Bien—
FALL
SLAM!
Huh, this book just fell by itself.
Gravity, I guess.
FLICKER
FLICKER
FLICKER
Does this normally happen in a library?
RUMBLE
I don't think so...
RUMBLE
RUMBLE

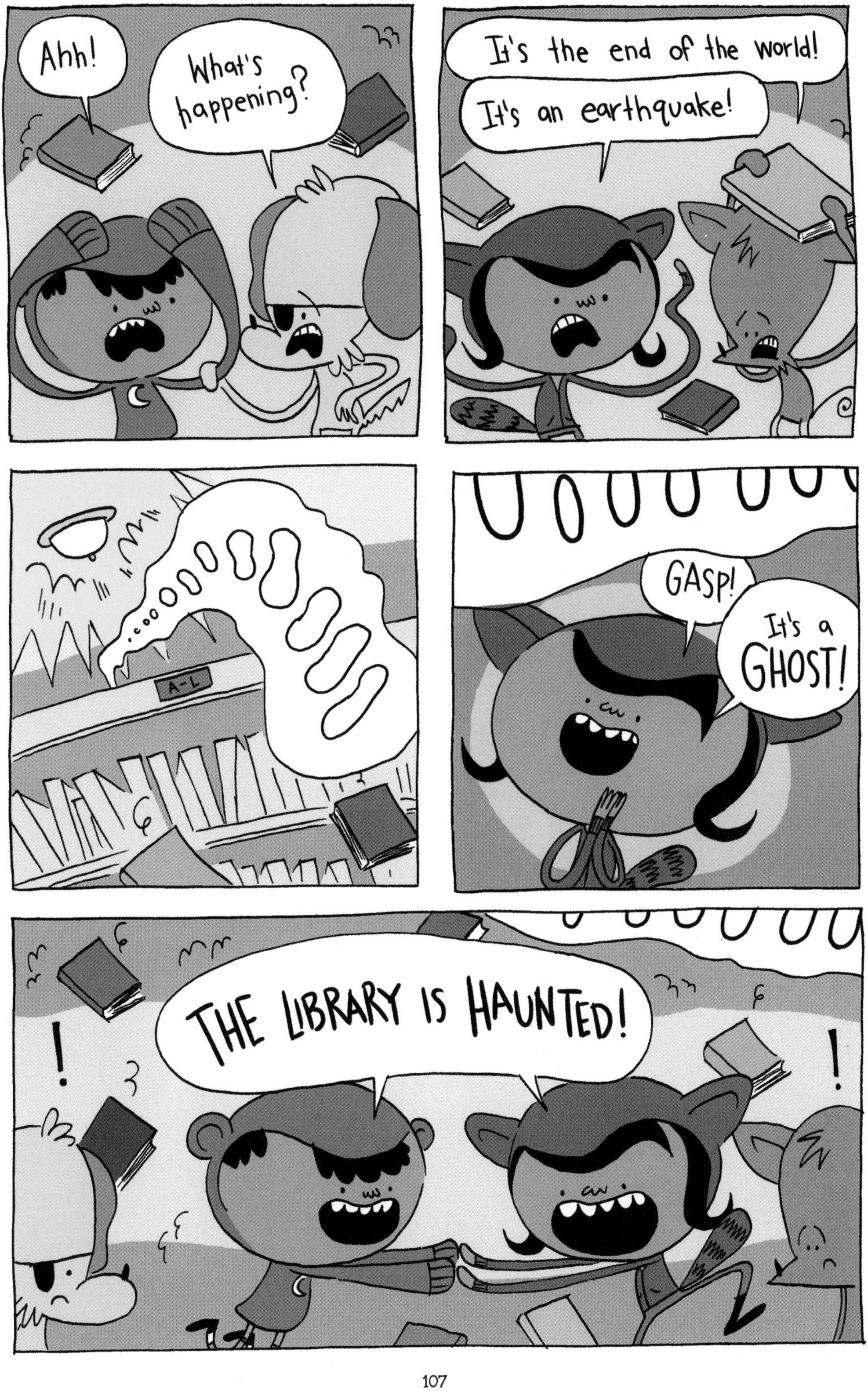
Ahh!
What's happening?
It's the end of the world!
It's an earthquake!
A-L
GASP!
It's a GHOST!
THE LIBRARY IS HAUNTED!
!
!

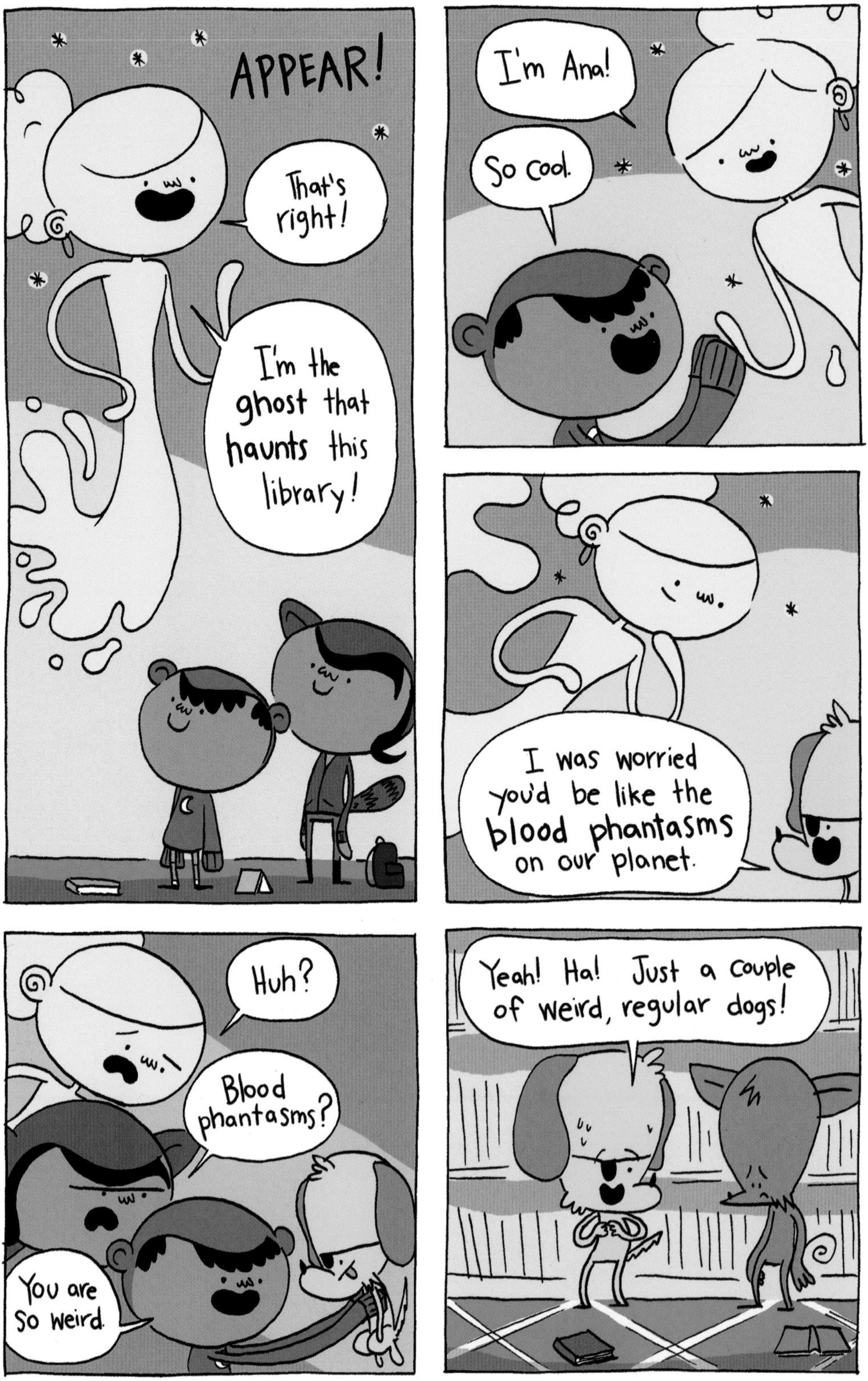
APPEAR!
That's right!
I'm the ghost that haunts this library!
I'm Ana!
So cool.
I was worried you'd be like the blood phantasms on our planet.
Huh?
Blood phantasms?
You are so weird.
Yeah! Ha! Just a couple of weird, regular dogs!

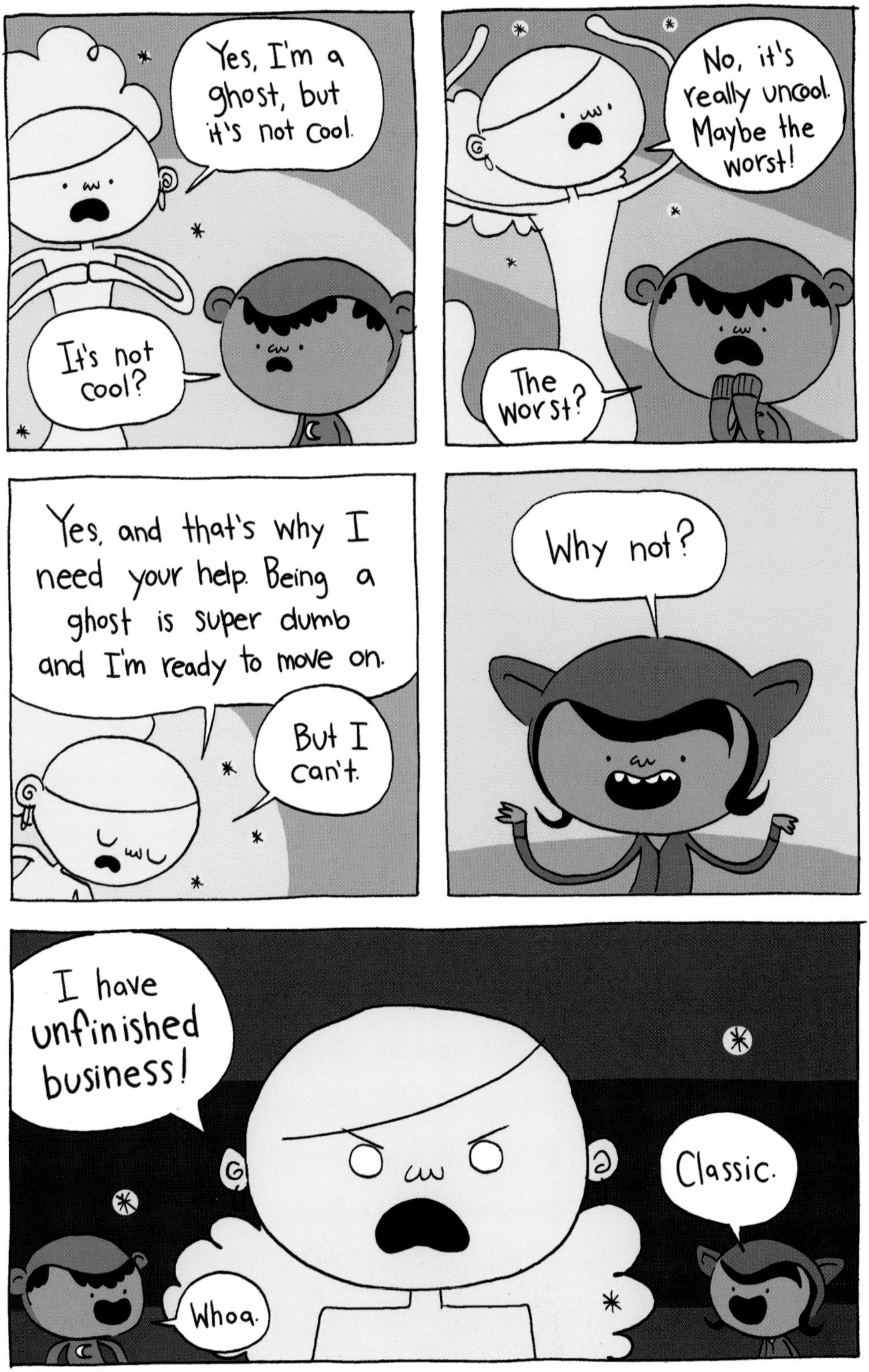
Yes, I'm a ghost, but it's not cool.
It's not cool?
No, it's really uncool. Maybe the worst!
The worst?
Yes, and that's why I need your help. Being a ghost is super dumb and I'm ready to move on.
But I can't.
Why not?
I have unfinished business!
Whoa.
Classic.

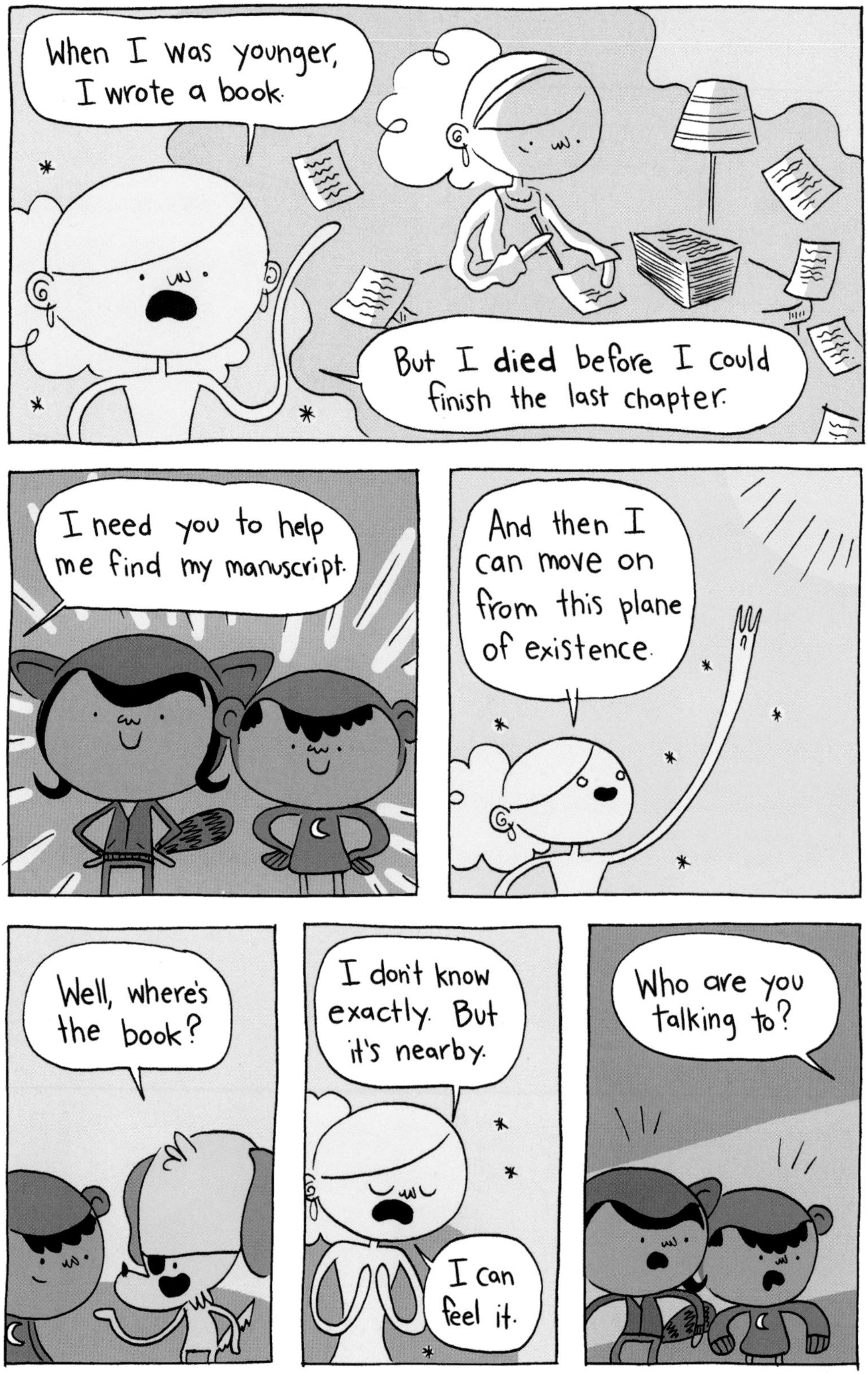
When I was younger, I wrote a book.
But I **died** before I could finish the last chapter.
I need you to help me find my manuscript.
And then I can move on from this plane of existence.
Well, where's the book?
I don't know exactly. But it's nearby.
I can feel it.
Who are you talking to?

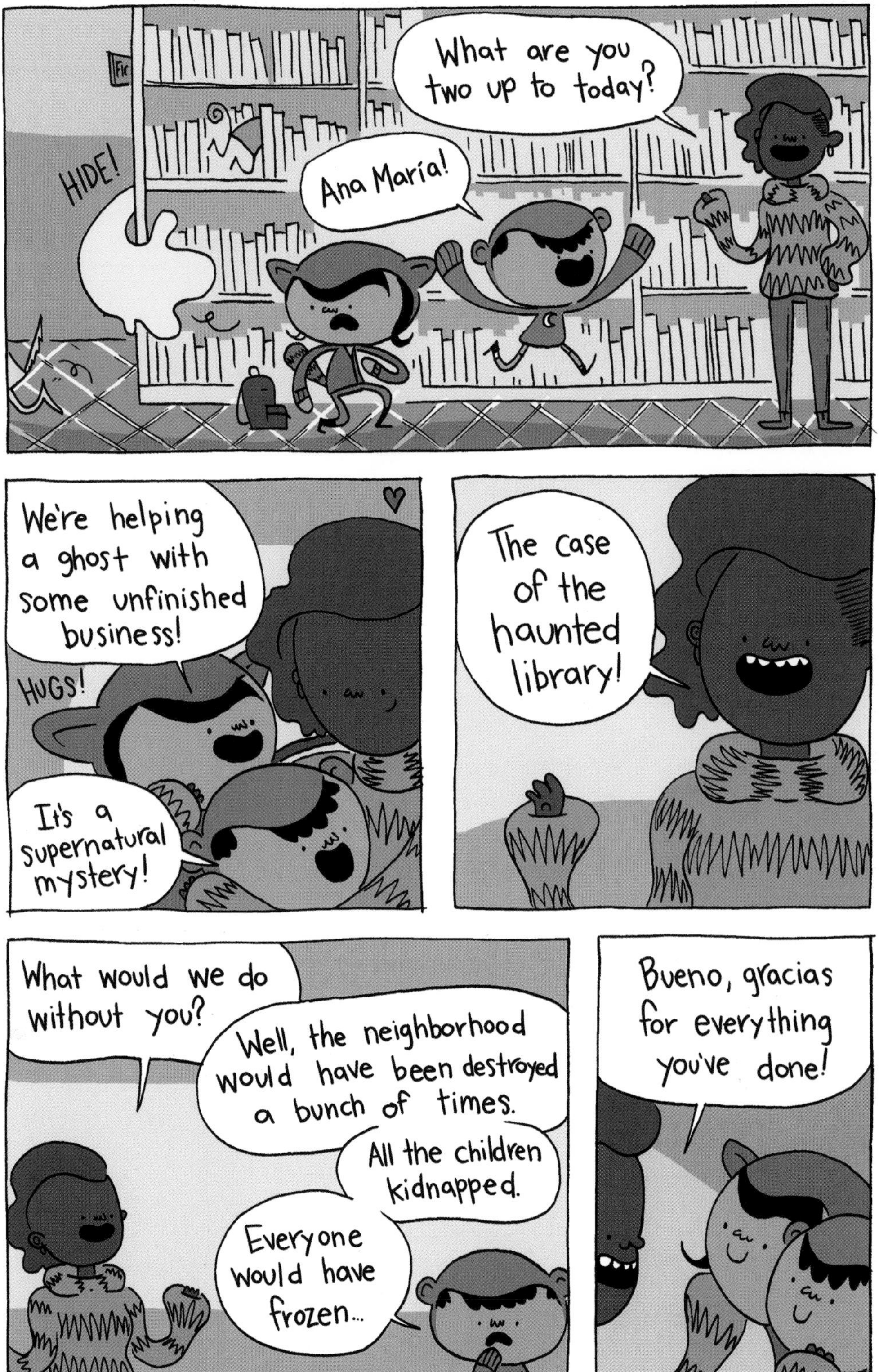
What are you two up to today?
HIDE!
Ana María!
We're helping a ghost with some unfinished business!
HUGS!
It's a supernatural mystery!
The case of the haunted library!
What would we do without you?
Well, the neighborhood would have been destroyed a bunch of times.
All the children kidnapped.
Everyone would have frozen...
Bueno, gracias for everything you've done!

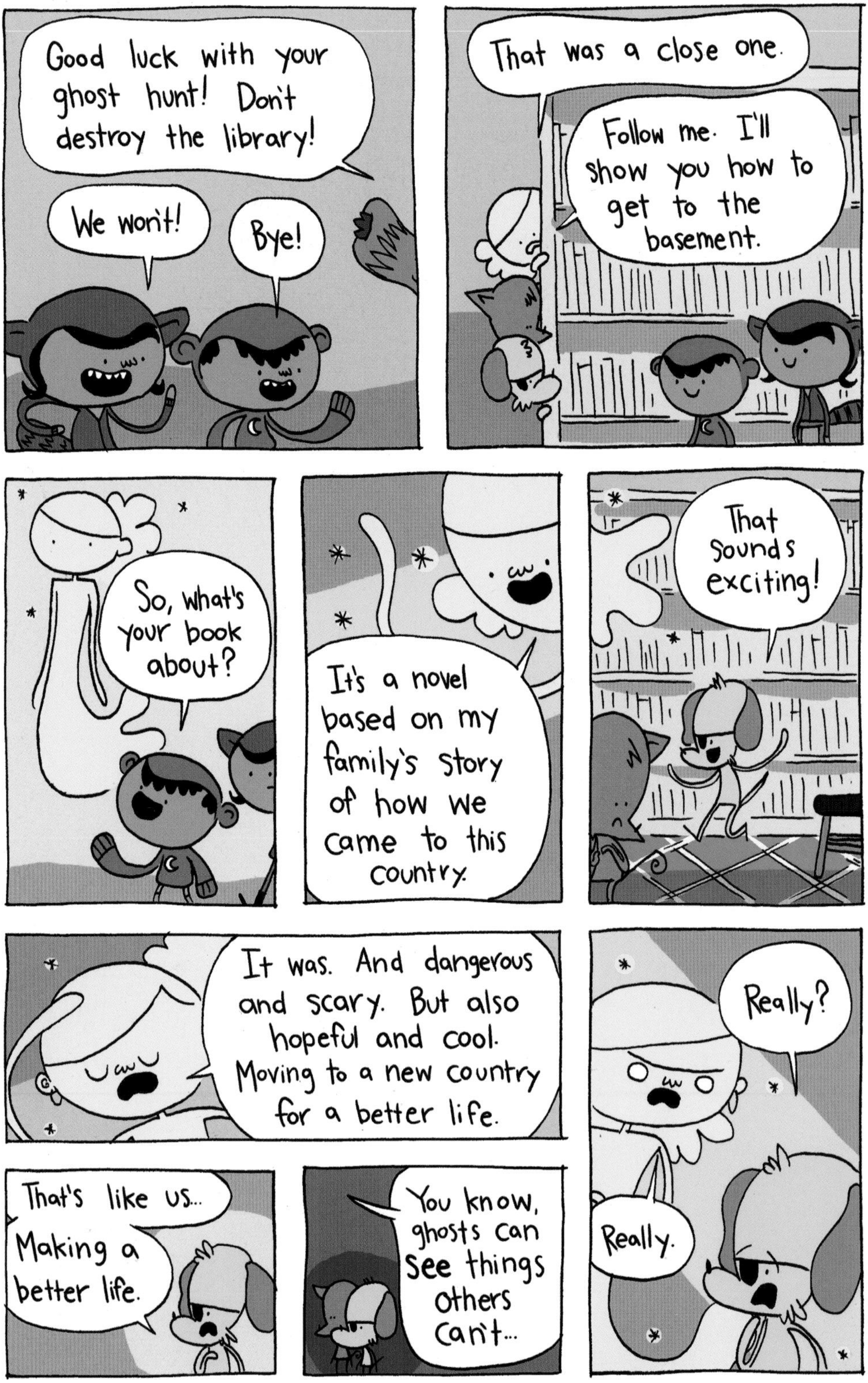
Good luck with your ghost hunt! Don't destroy the library!
We won't!
Bye!
That was a close one.
Follow me. I'll show you how to get to the basement.
So, what's your book about?
It's a novel based on my family's story of how we came to this country.
That sounds exciting!
It was. And dangerous and scary. But also hopeful and cool. Moving to a new country for a better life.
Really?
That's like us...
Making a better life.
You know, ghosts can see things others can't...
Really.

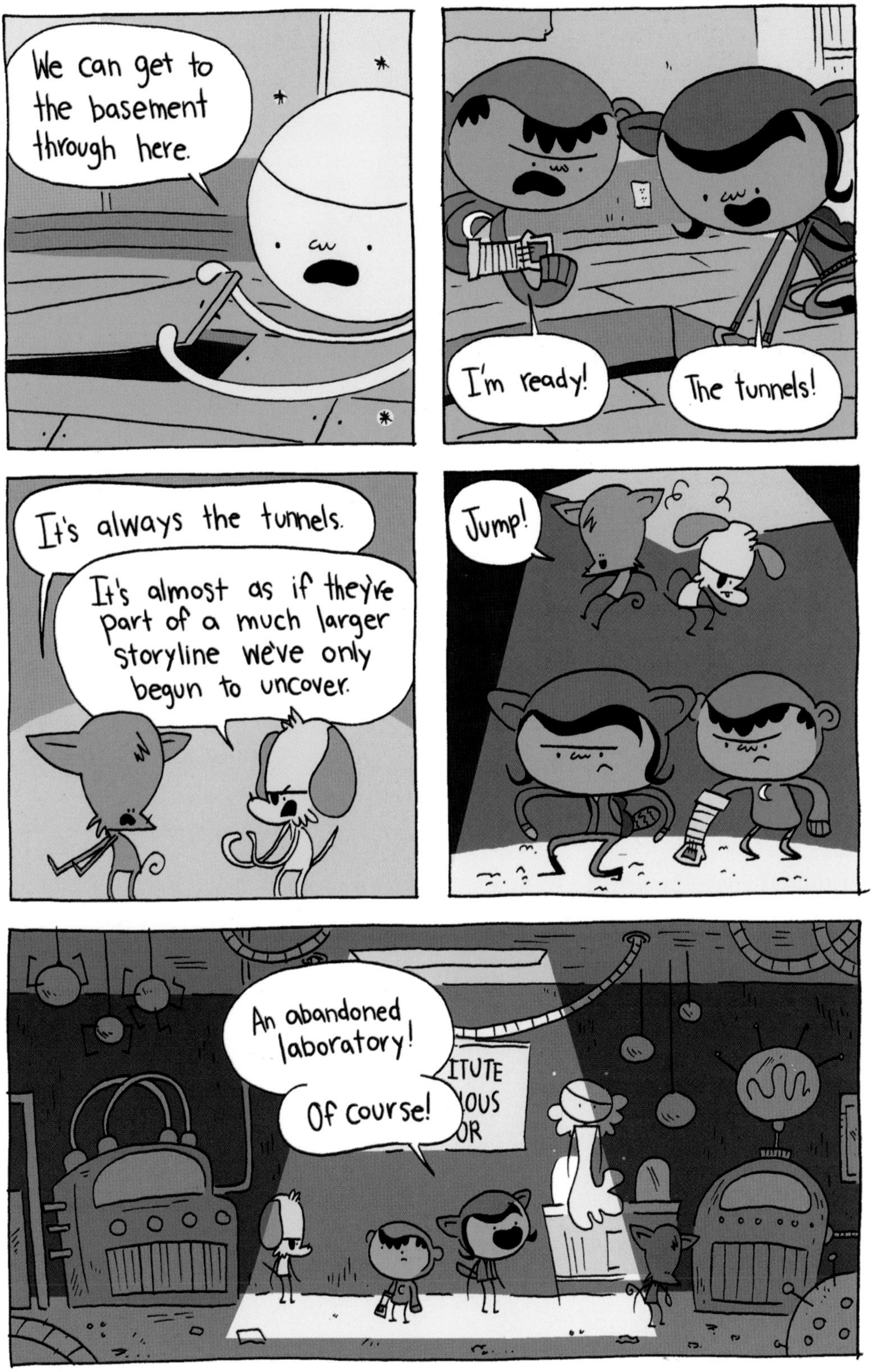
We can get to the basement through here.
I'm ready!
The tunnels!
It's always the tunnels.
It's almost as if they're part of a much larger storyline we've only begun to uncover.
Jump!
An abandoned laboratory!
Of course!
ITUTE
IOUS
OR

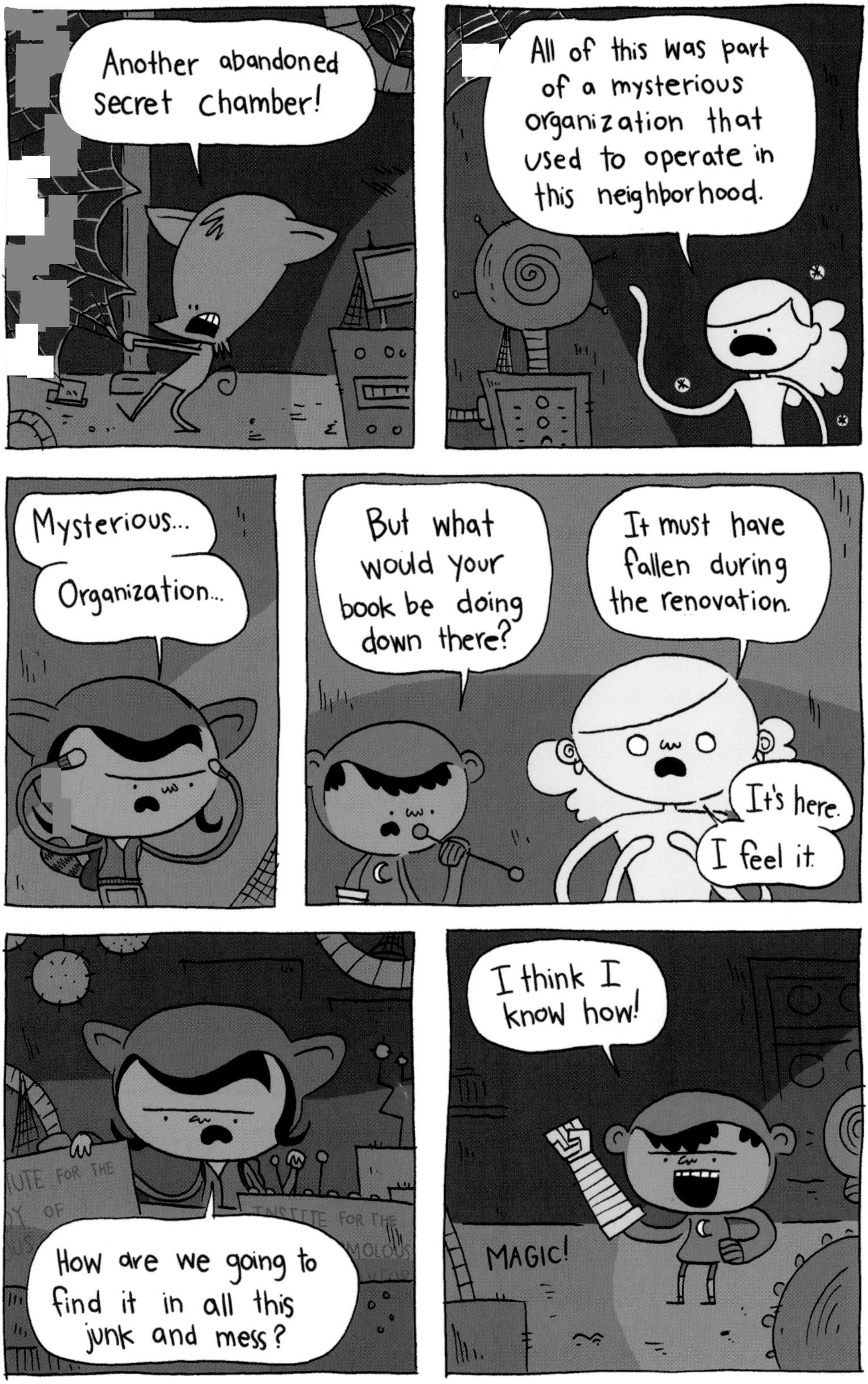

Another abandoned secret chamber!
All of this was part of a mysterious organization that used to operate in this neighborhood.
Mysterious...
Organization...
But what would your book be doing down there?
It must have fallen during the renovation.
It's here.
I feel it.
How are we going to find it in all this junk and mess?
I think I know how!
MAGIC!

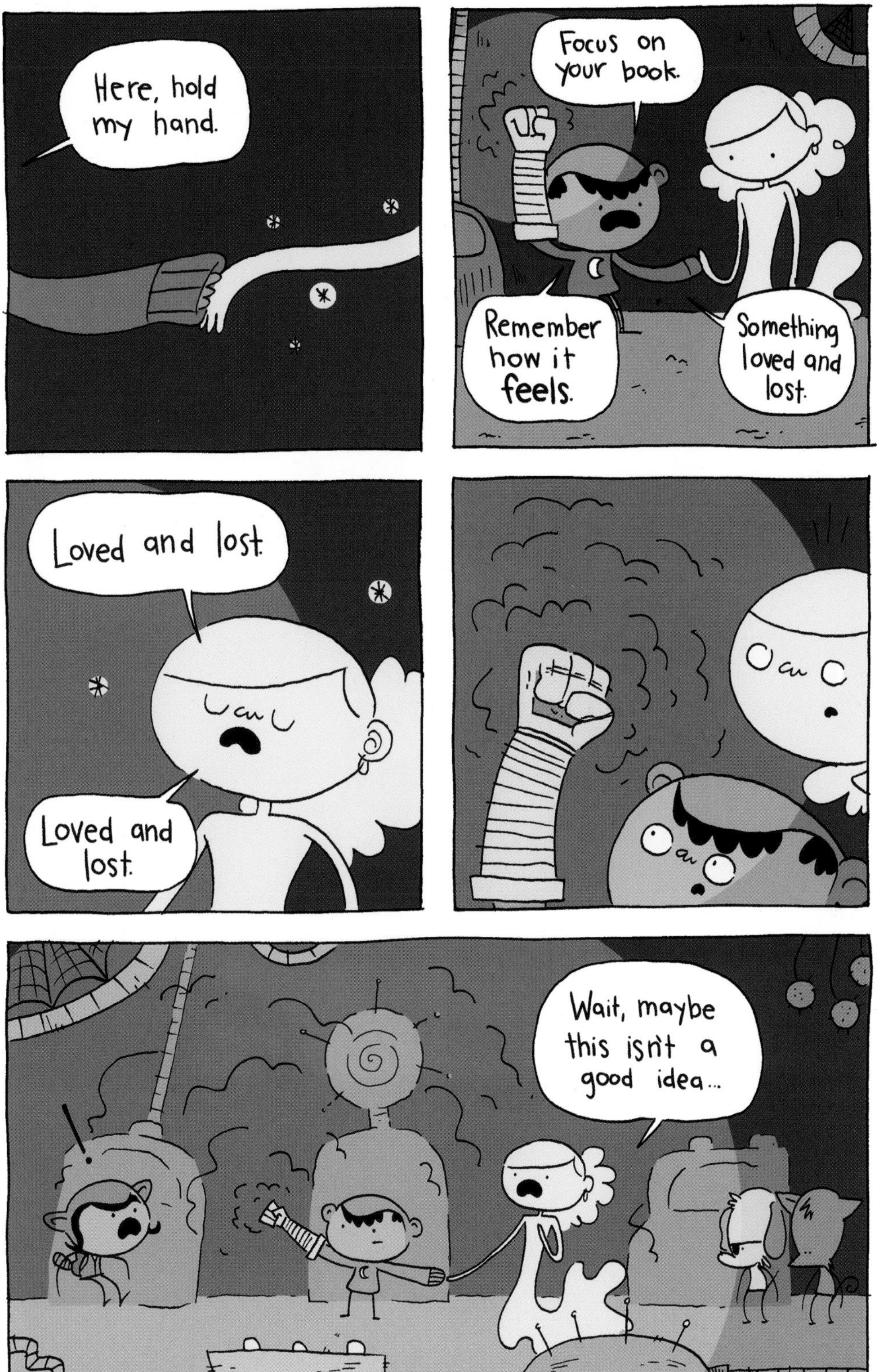
Here, hold my hand.
Focus on your book.
Remember how it feels.
Something loved and lost.
Loved and lost.
Loved and lost.
Wait, maybe this isn't a good idea...

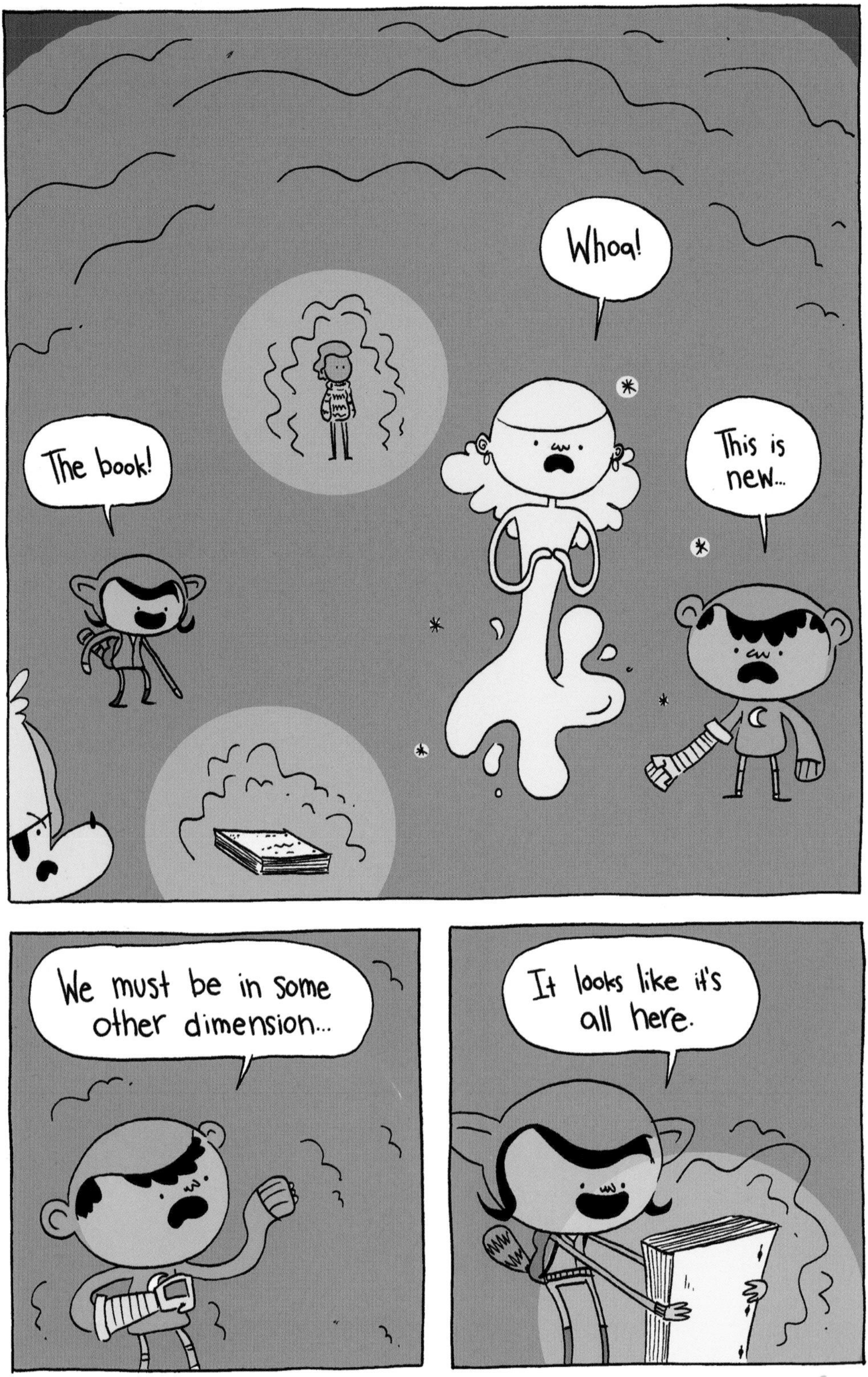
Whoa!
The book!
This is new...
We must be in some other dimension...
It looks like it's all here.

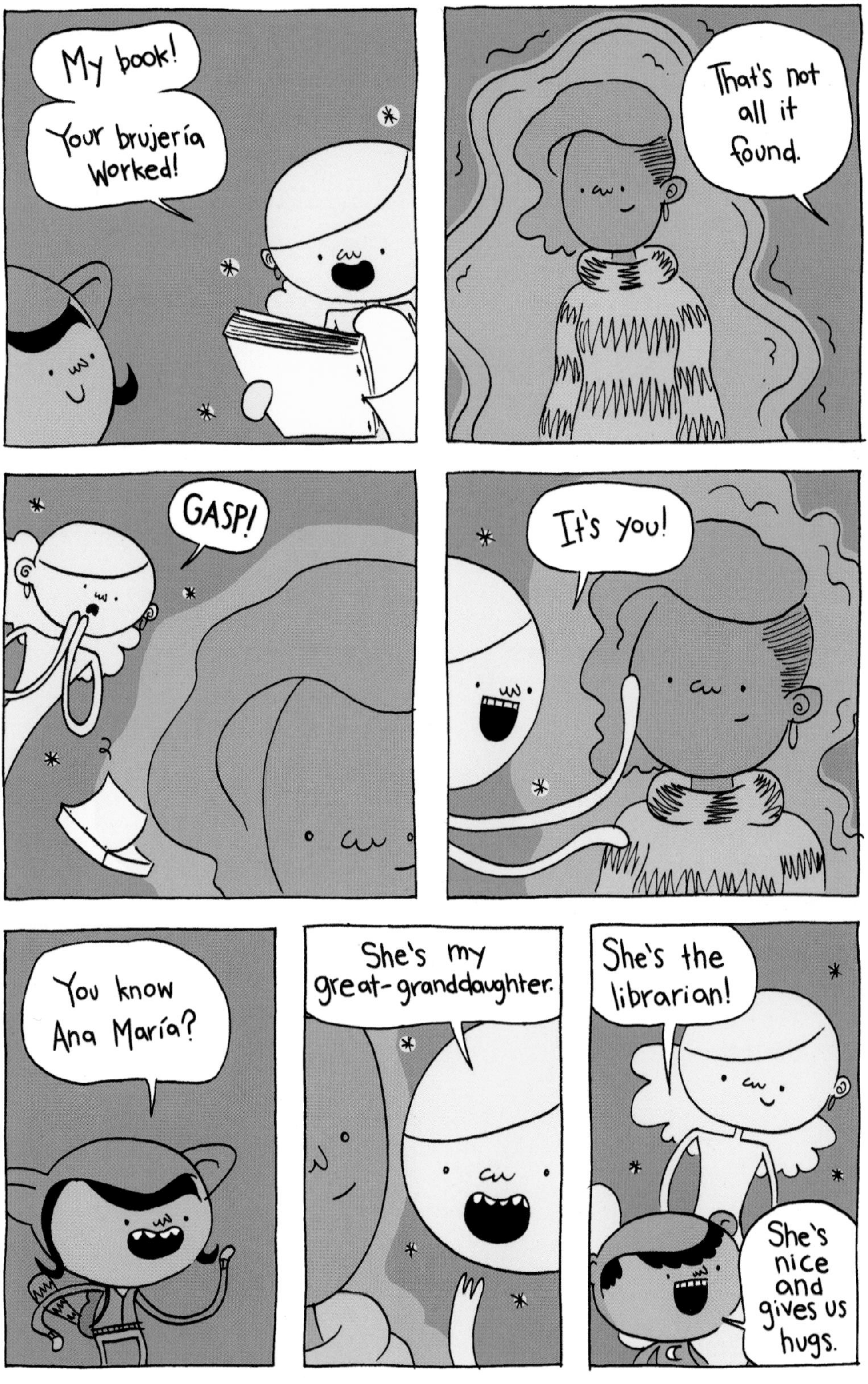
My book!
Your brujería worked!
That's not all it found.
GASP!
It's you!
You know Ana María?
She's my great-granddaughter.
She's the librarian!
She's nice and gives us hugs.

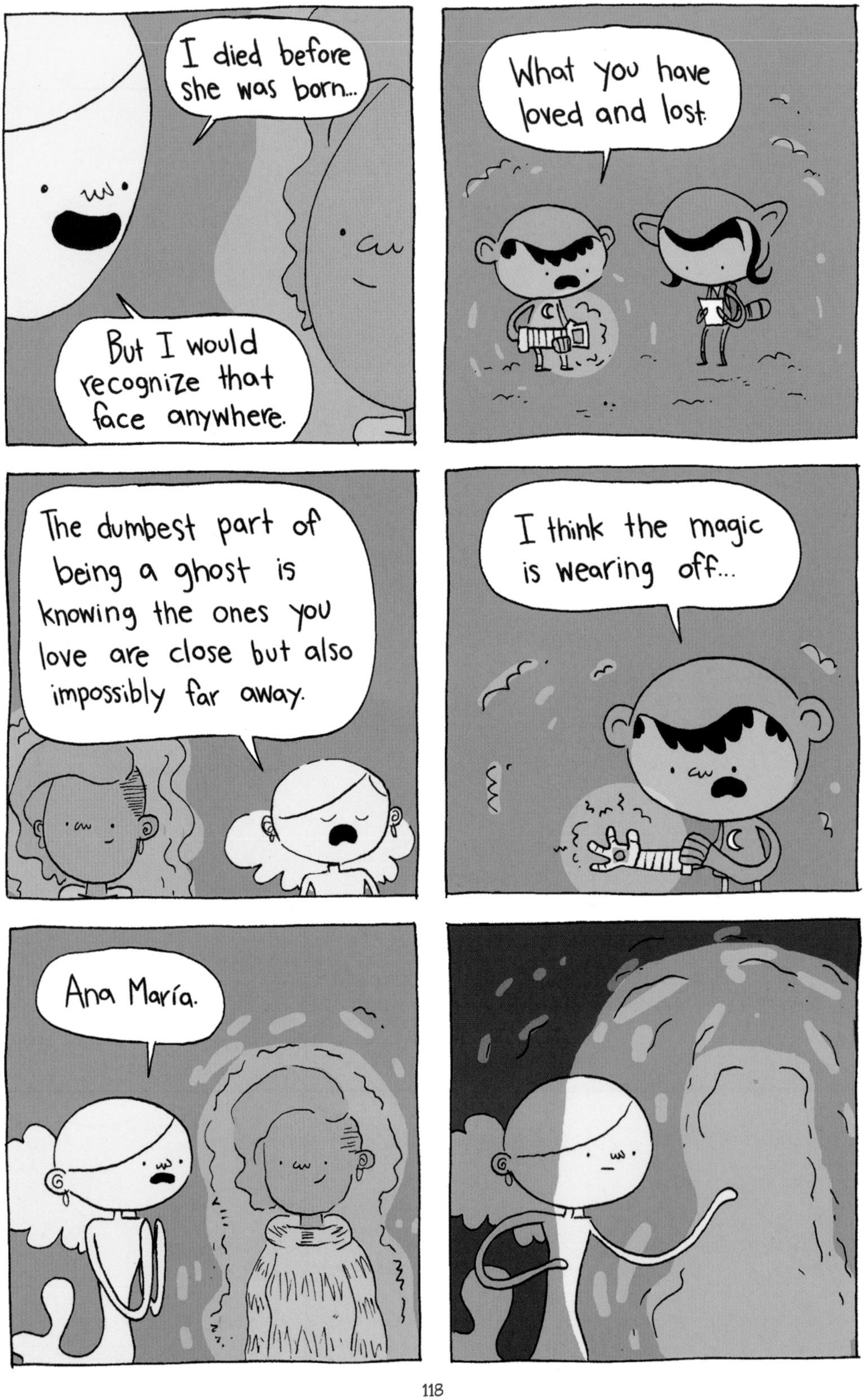
I died before she was born...
But I would recognize that face anywhere.
What you have loved and lost.
The dumbest part of being a ghost is knowing the ones you love are close but also impossibly far away.
I think the magic is wearing off...
Ana María.

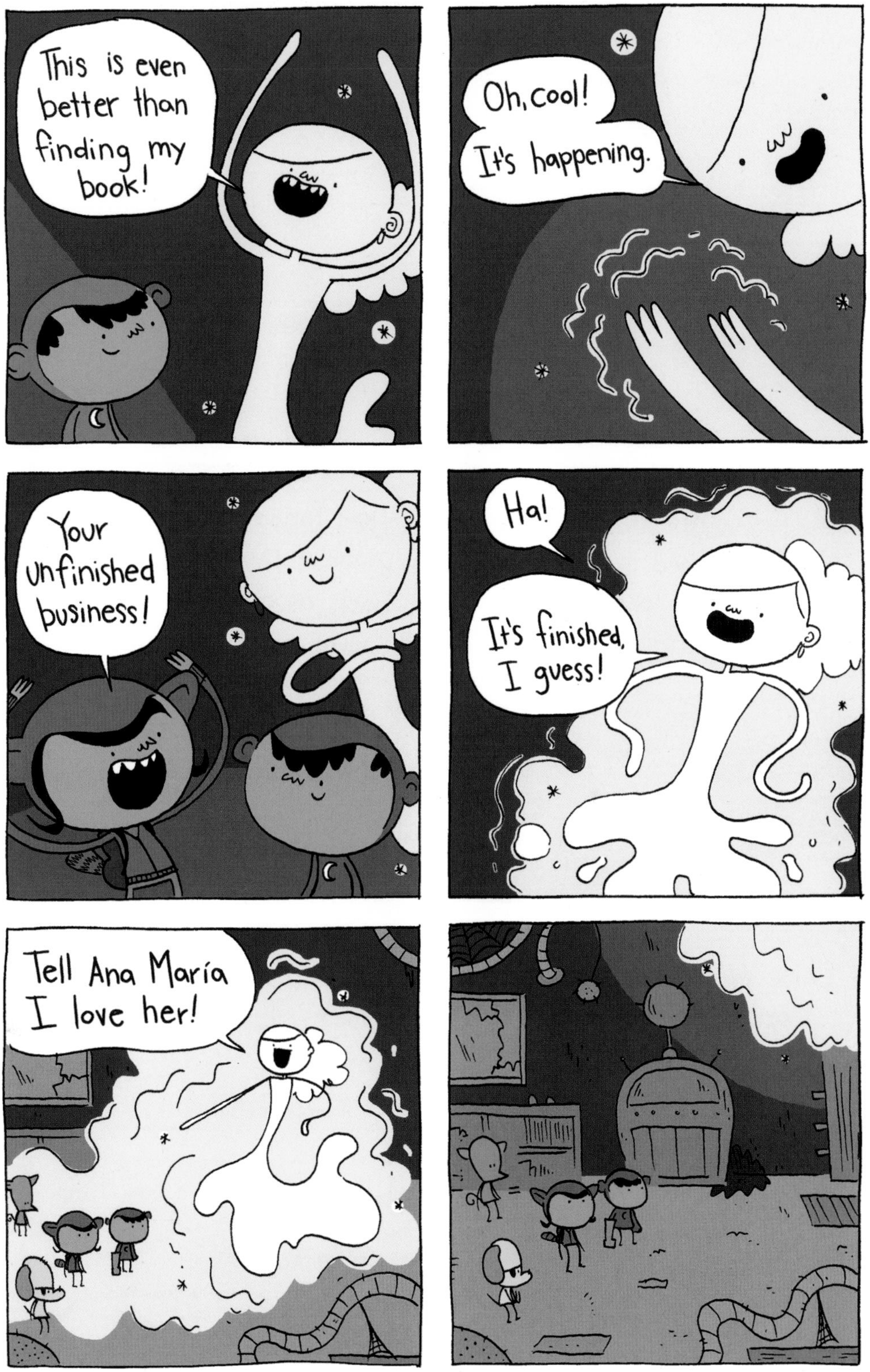
This is even better than finding my book!
Oh, cool!
It's happening.
Your unfinished business!
Ha!
It's finished, I guess!
Tell Ana María I love her!

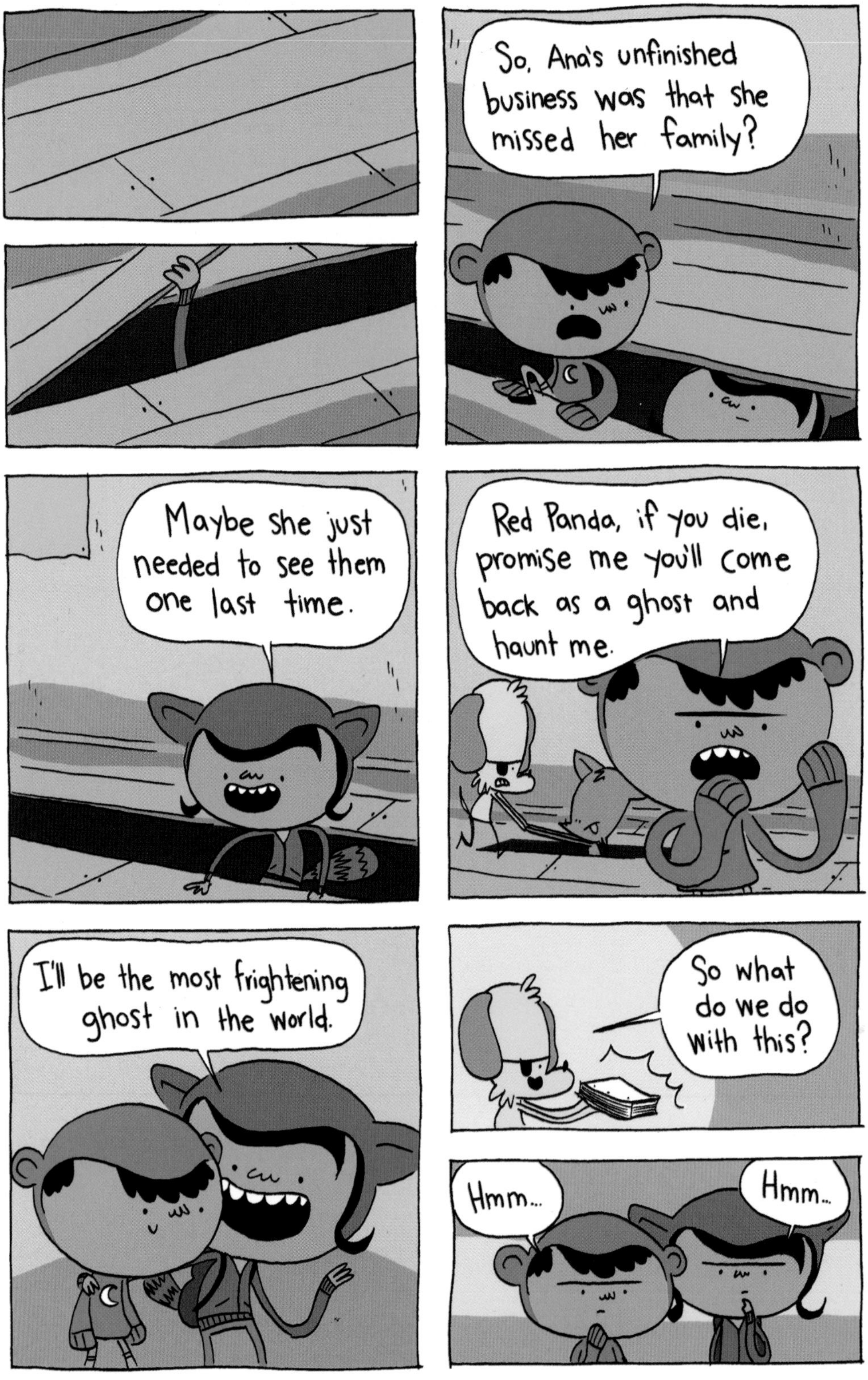
So, Ana's unfinished business was that she missed her family?
Maybe she just needed to see them one last time.
Red Panda, if you die, promise me you'll come back as a ghost and haunt me.
I'll be the most frightening ghost in the world.
So what do we do with this?
Hmm...
Hmm...

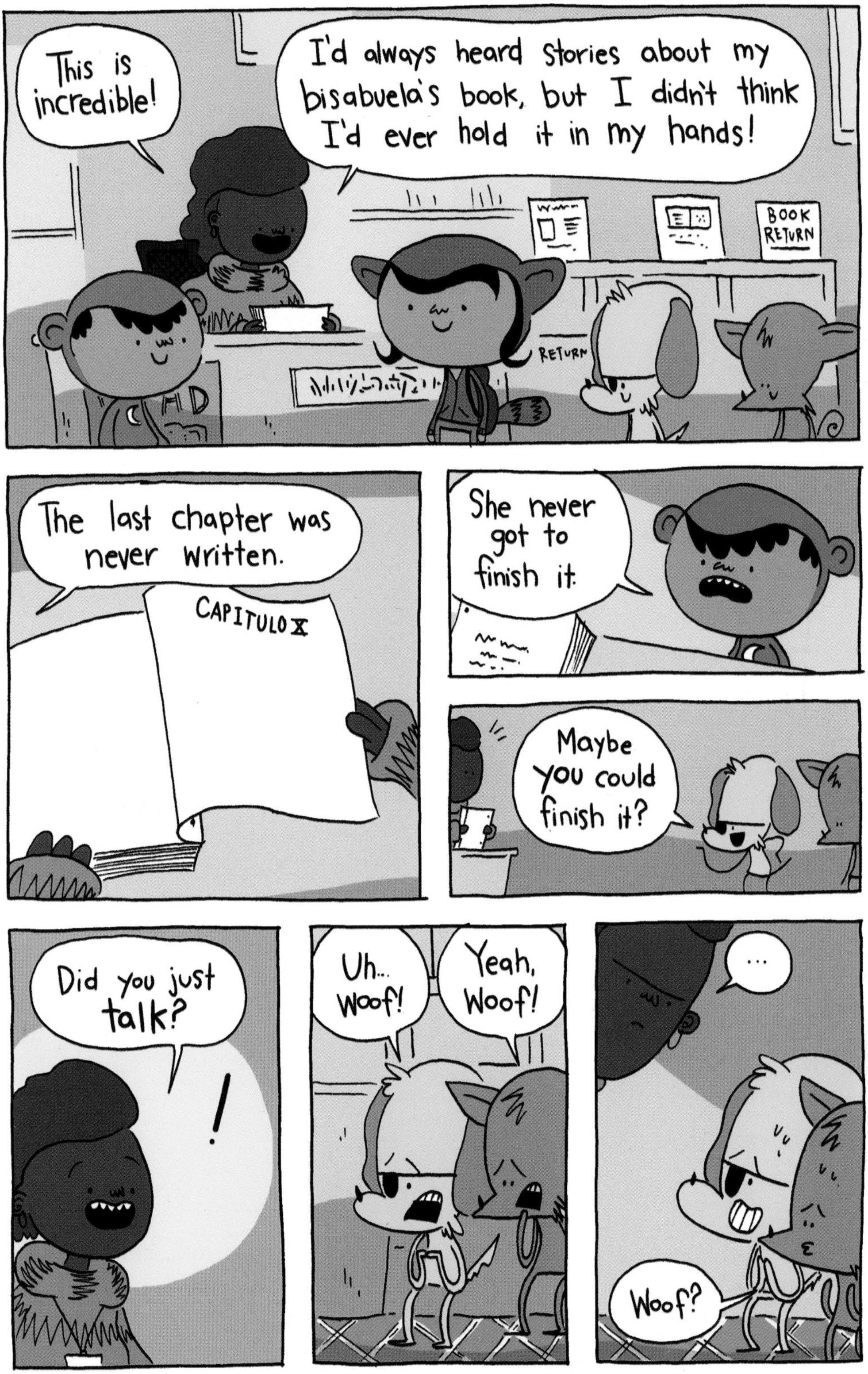
This is incredible!
I'd always heard stories about my bisabuela's book, but I didn't think I'd ever hold it in my hands!
BOOK RETURN
RETURN
The last chapter was never written.
CAPITULO X
She never got to finish it.
Maybe you could finish it?
Did you just talk?
!
Uh... woof!
Yeah, Woof!
...
Woof?

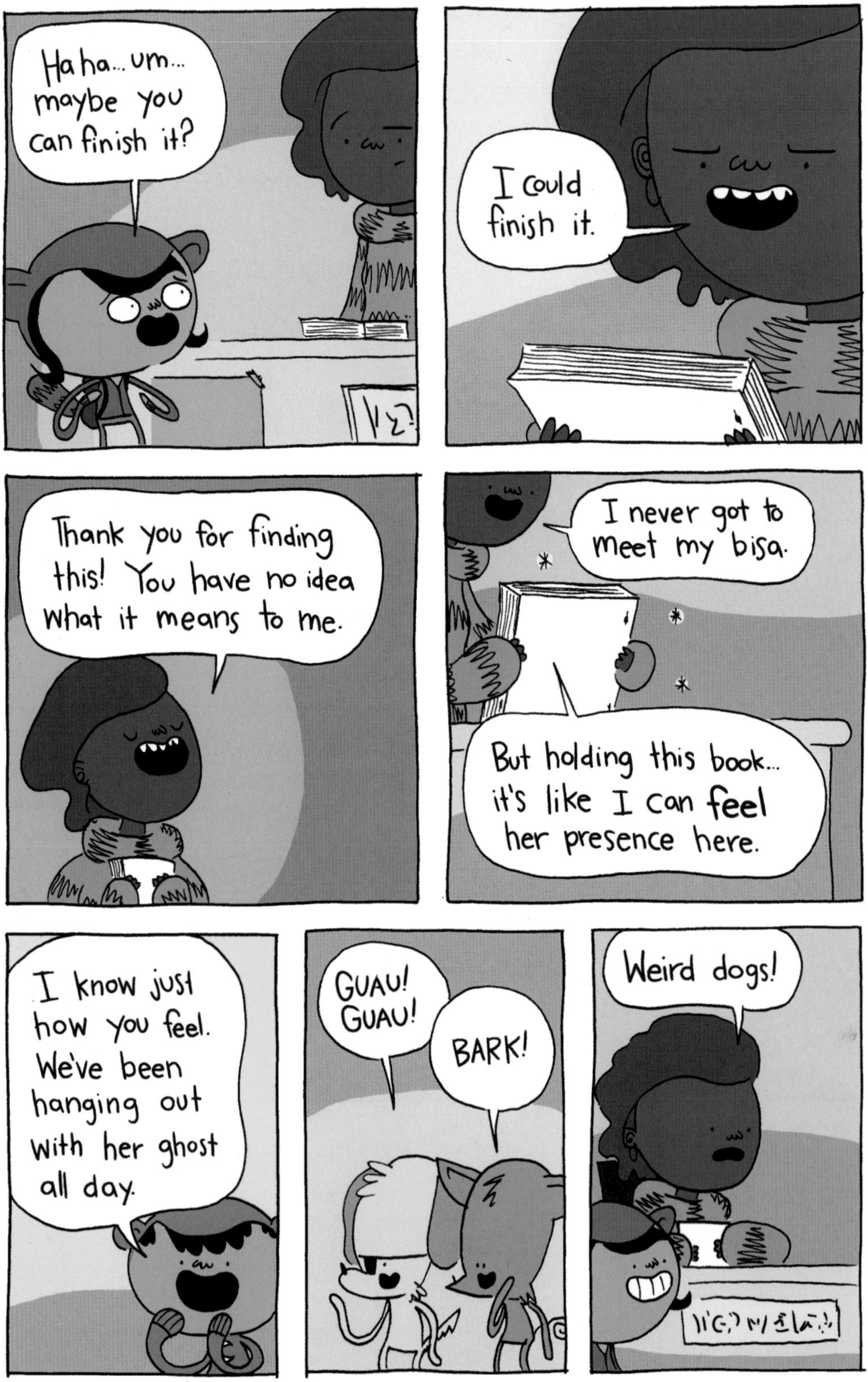
Ha ha... um... maybe you can finish it?
I could finish it.
Thank you for finding this! You have no idea what it means to me.
I never got to meet my bisa.
But holding this book... it's like I can feel her presence here.
I know just how you feel. We've been hanging out with her ghost all day.
GUAU! GUAU!
BARK!
Weird dogs!

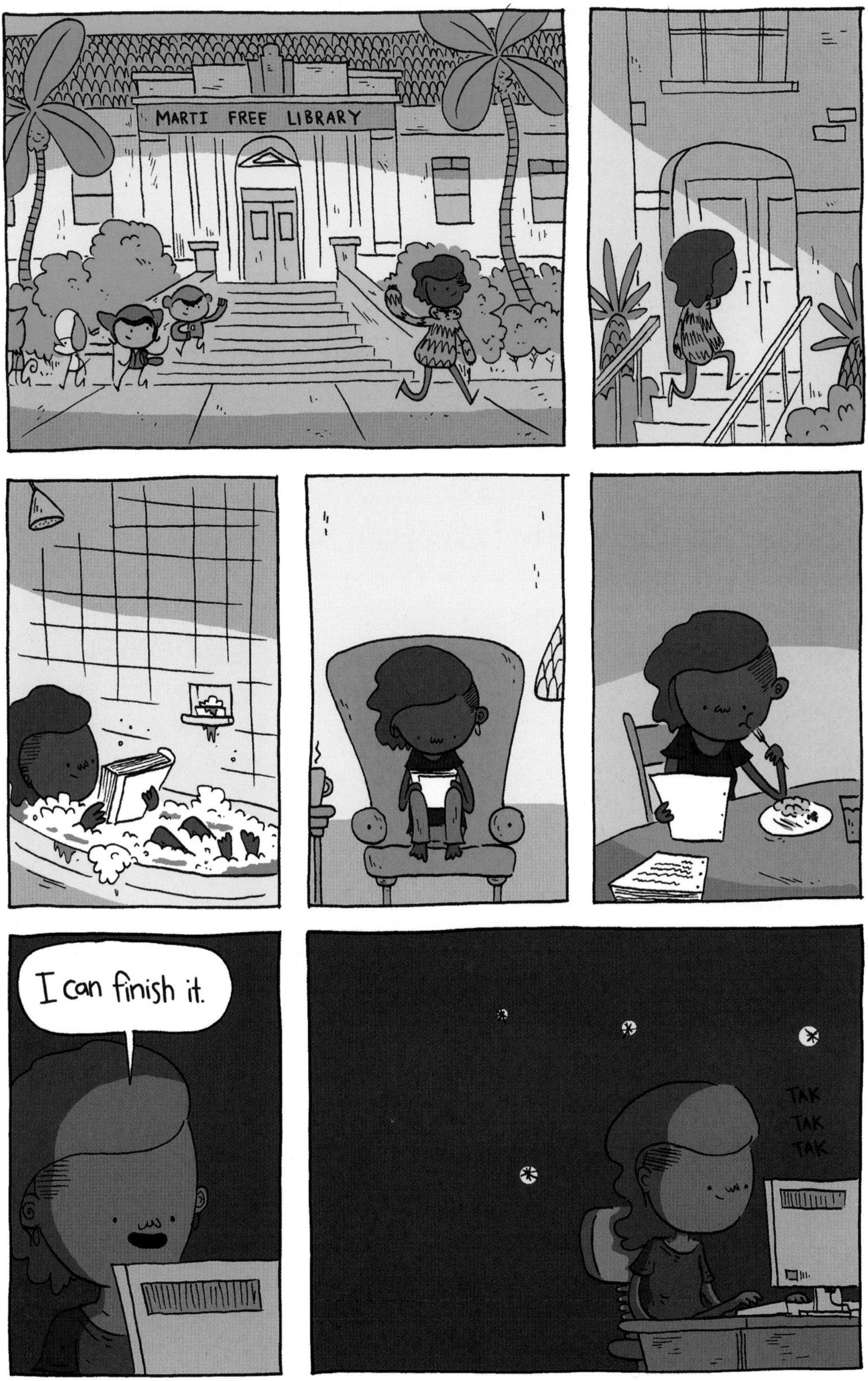
MARTI FREE LIBRARY
I can finish it.
TAK
TAK
TAK

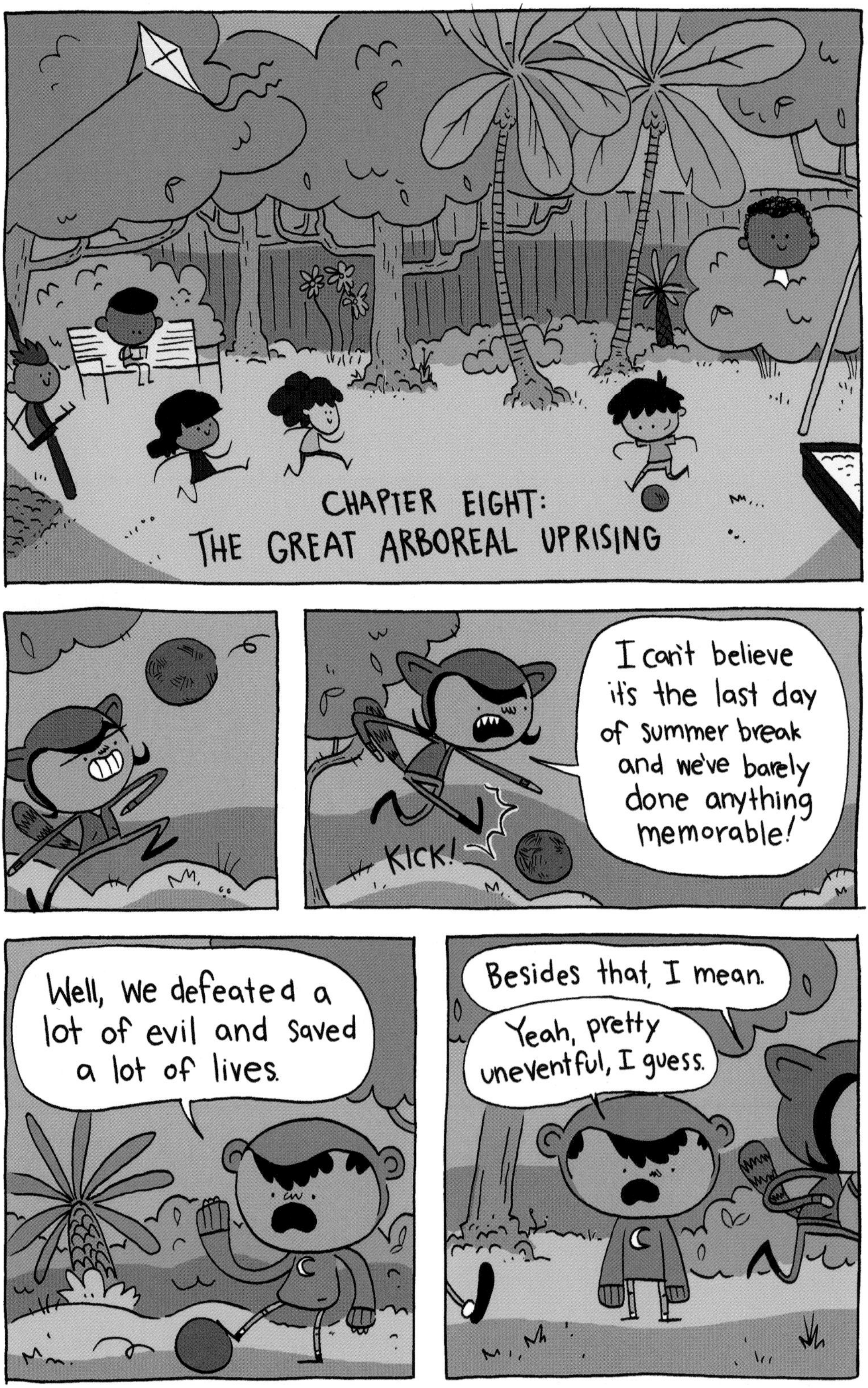

CHAPTER EIGHT:
THE GREAT ARBOREAL UPRISING
I can't believe it's the last day of summer break and we've barely done anything memorable!
KICK!
Well, we defeated a lot of evil and saved a lot of lives.
Besides that, I mean.
Yeah, pretty uneventful, I guess.

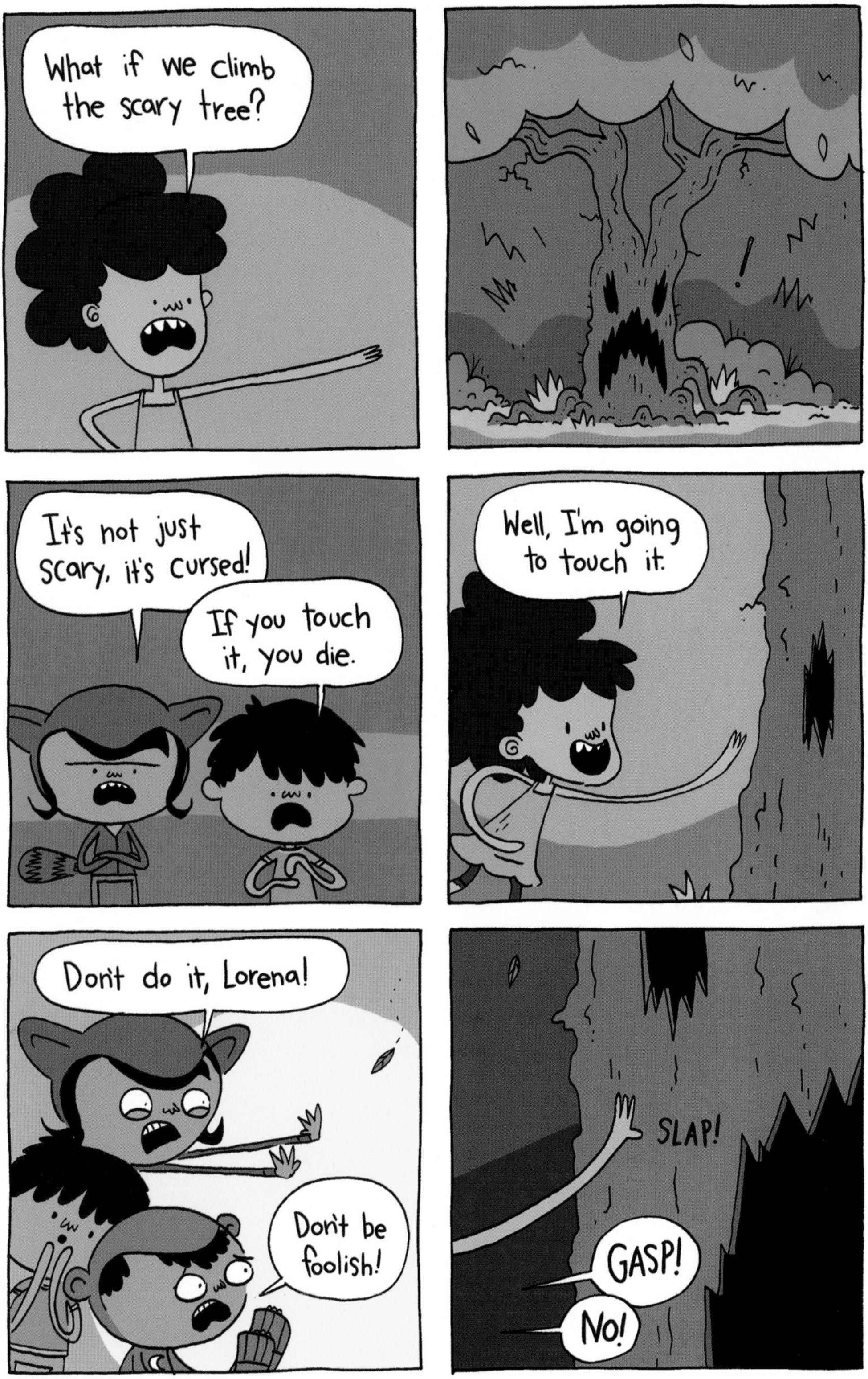
What if we climb the scary tree?
!
It's not just scary, it's cursed!
If you touch it, you die.
Well, I'm going to touch it.
Don't do it, Lorena!
Don't be foolish!
SLAP!
GASP!
No!

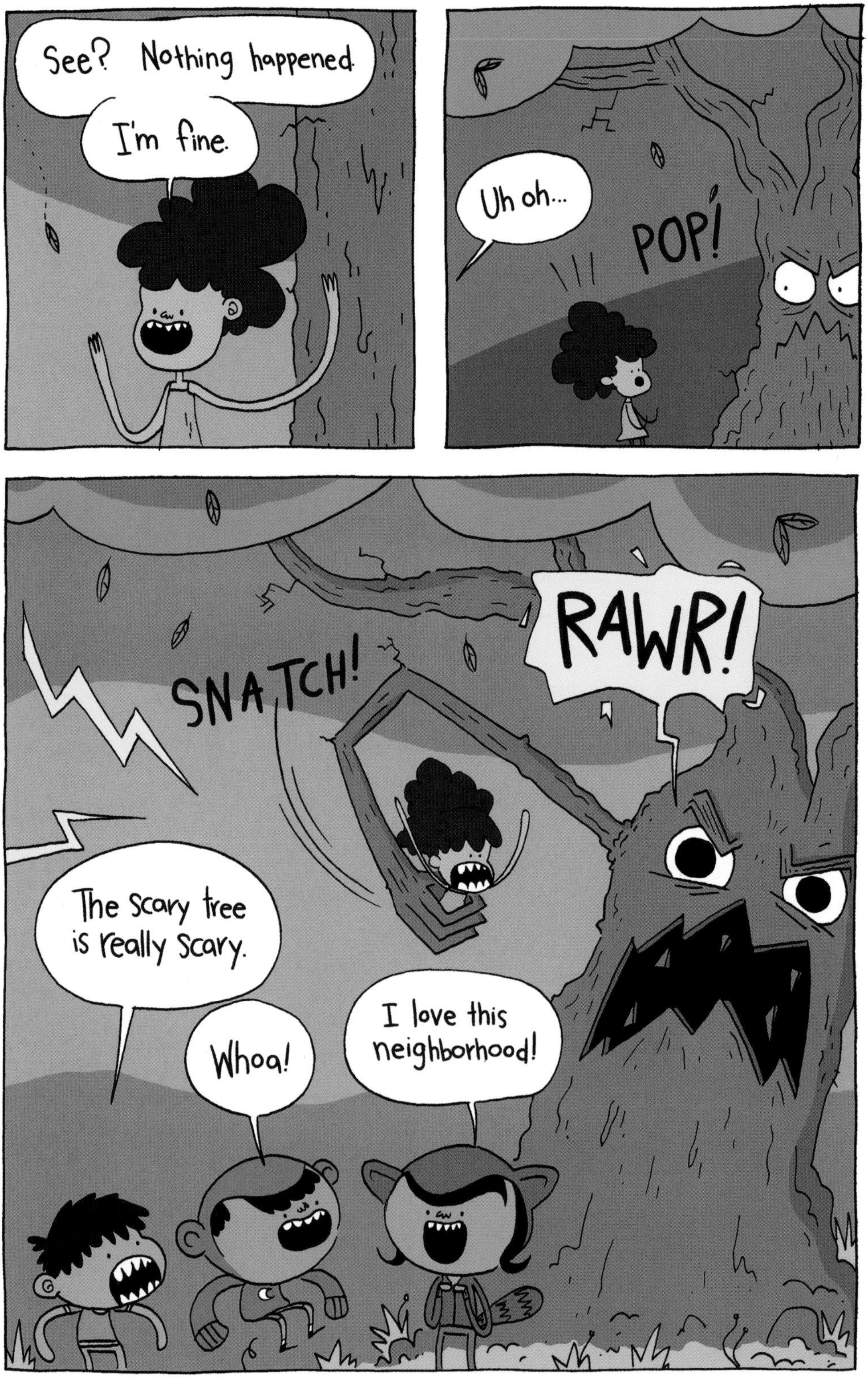
See? Nothing happened.
I'm fine.
Uh oh...
POP!
SNATCH!
RAWR!
The scary tree is really scary.
Whoa!
I love this neighborhood!

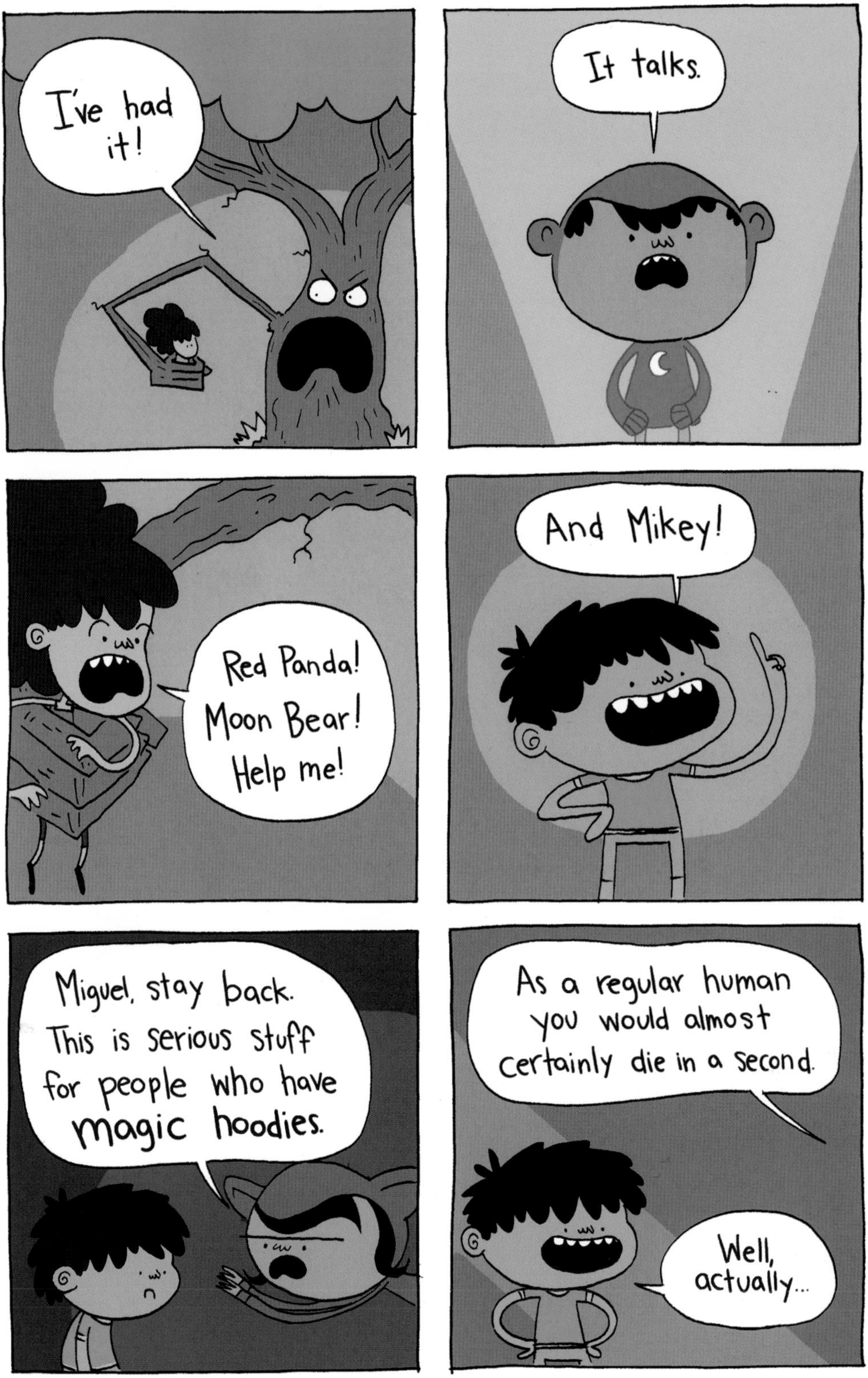
I've had it!
It talks.
Red Panda! Moon Bear! Help me!
And Mikey!
Miguel, stay back. This is serious stuff for people who have magic hoodies.
As a regular human you would almost certainly die in a second.
Well, actually...

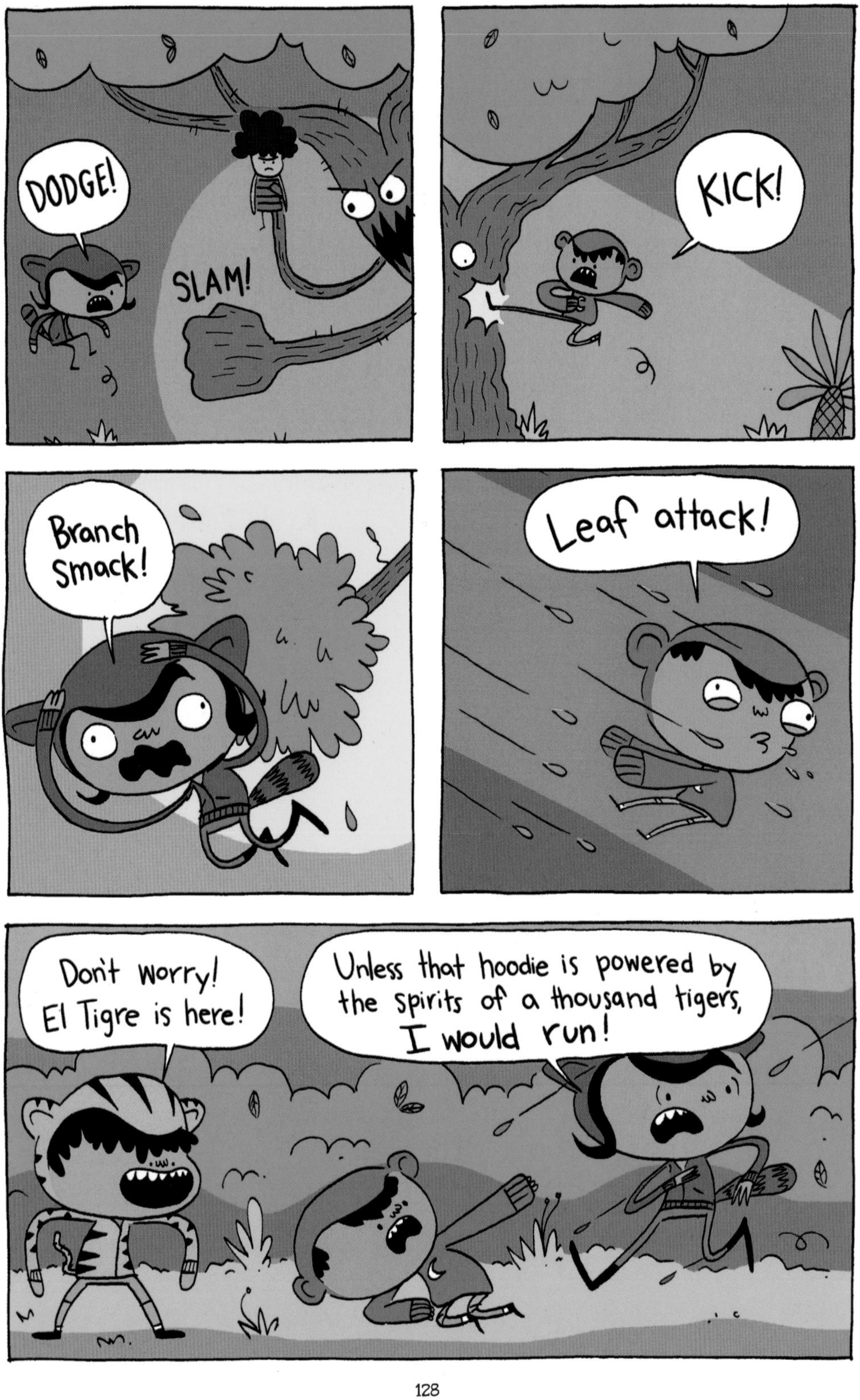
DODGE!
SLAM!
KICK!
Branch smack!
Leaf attack!
Don't worry! El Tigre is here!
Unless that hoodie is powered by the spirits of a thousand tigers, I would run!

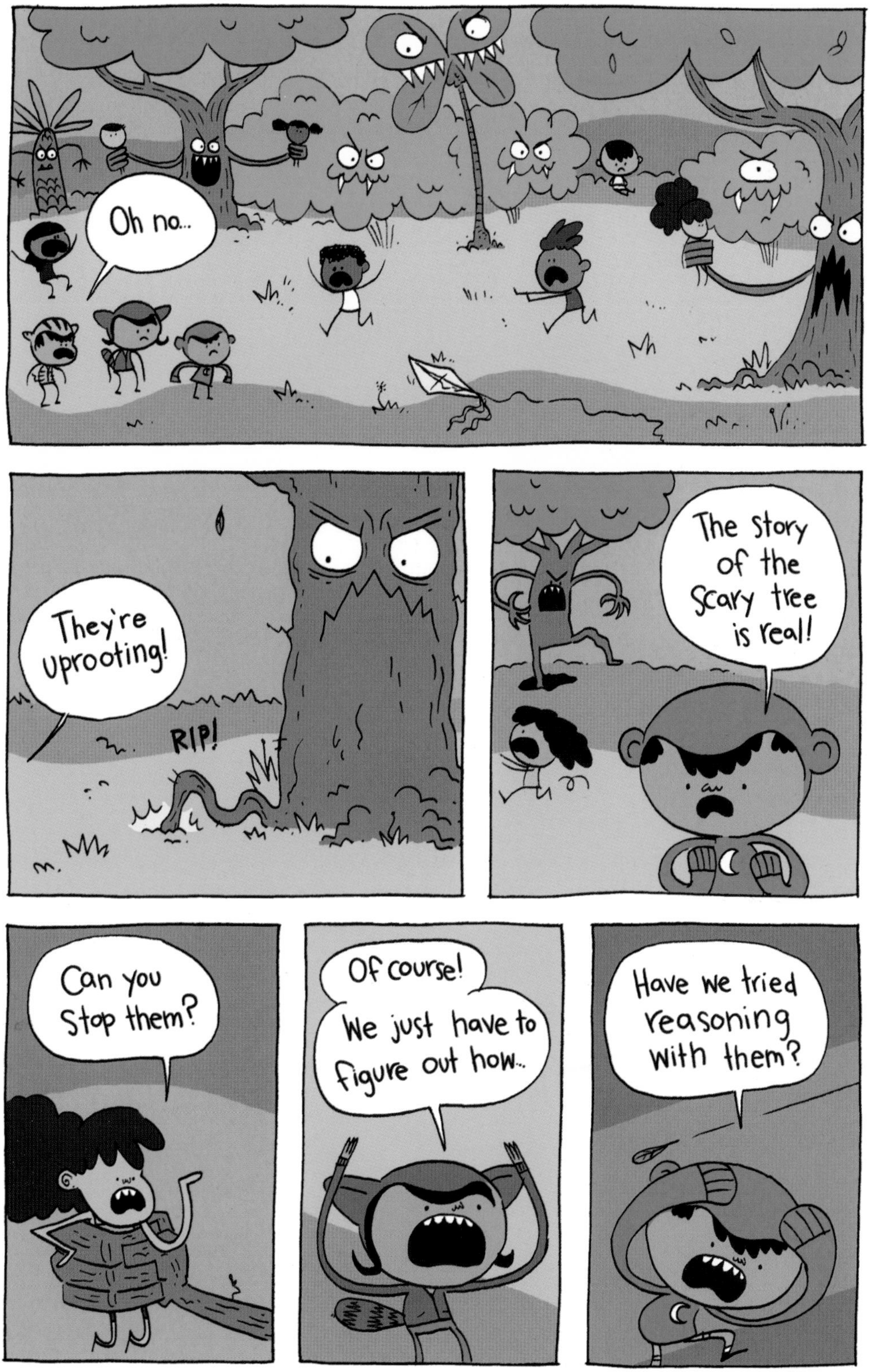
Oh no...
They're uprooting!
RIP!
The story of the scary tree is real!
Can you stop them?
Of course!
We just have to figure out how...
Have we tried reasoning with them?

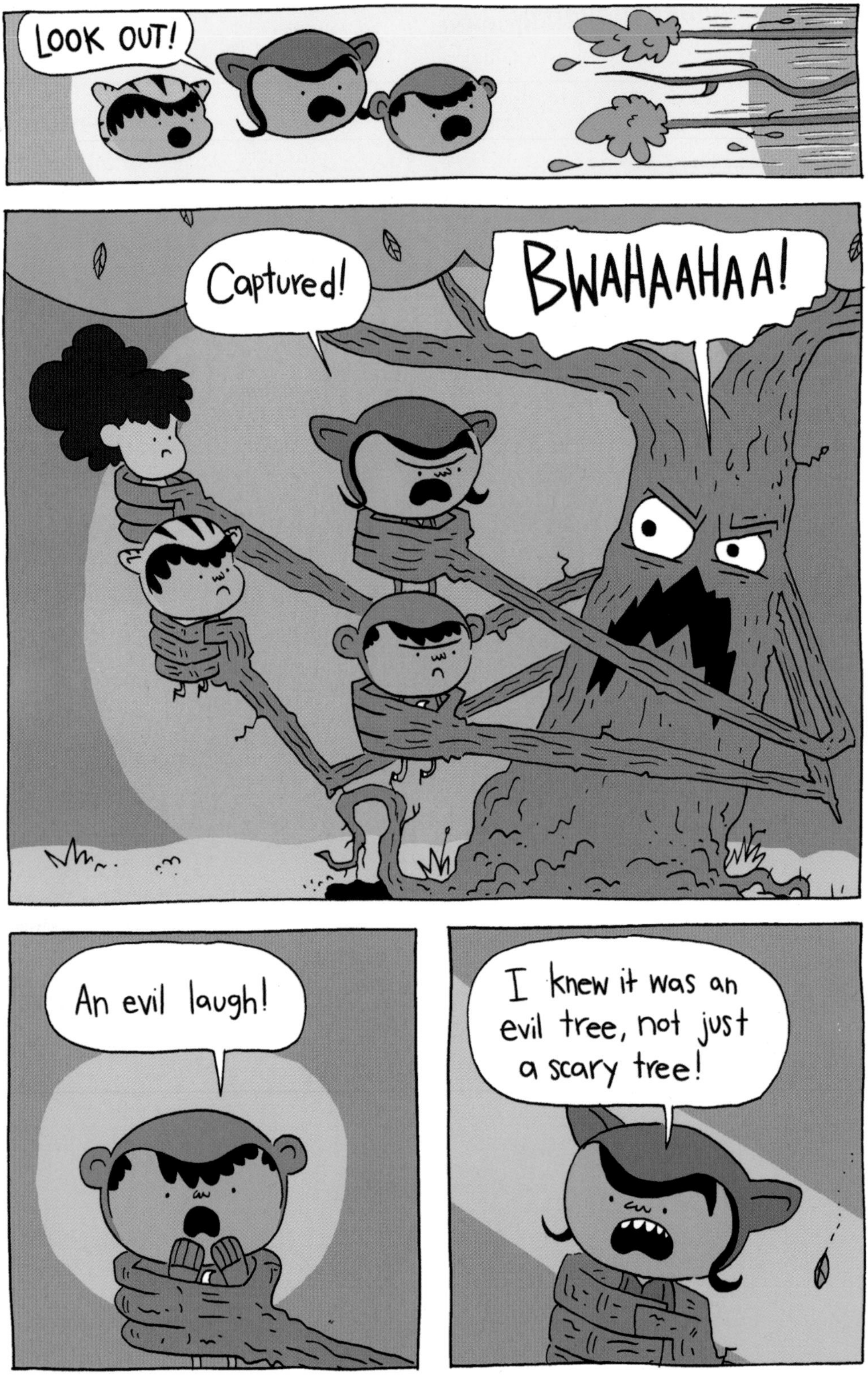
LOOK OUT!
Captured!
BWAHAAHAA!
An evil laugh!
I knew it was an evil tree, not just a scary tree!

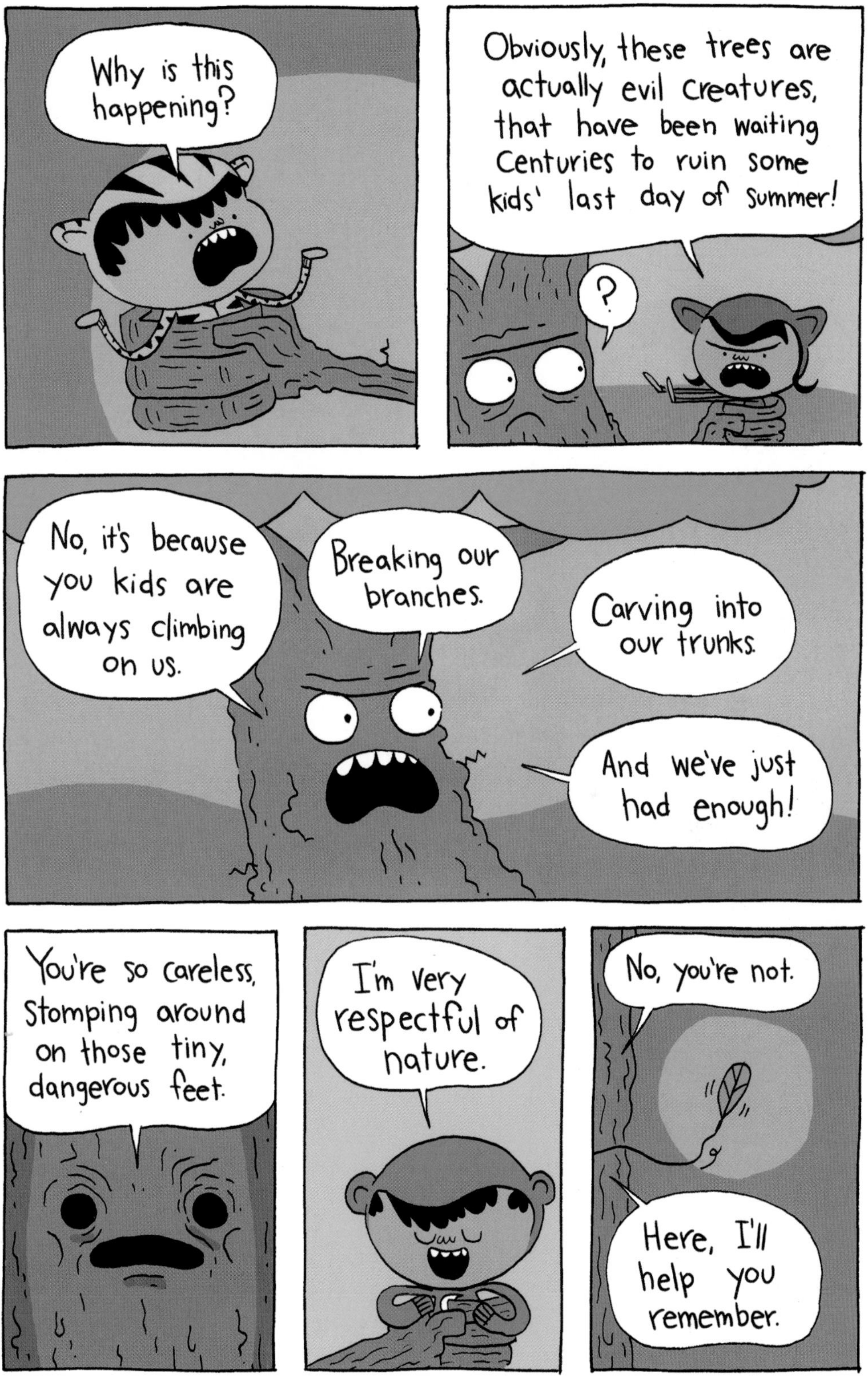

Why is this happening?
Obviously, these trees are actually evil creatures, that have been waiting centuries to ruin some kids' last day of summer!
?
No, it's because you kids are always climbing on us.
Breaking our branches.
Carving into our trunks.
And we've just had enough!
You're so careless, stomping around on those tiny, dangerous feet.
I'm very respectful of nature.
No, you're not.
Here, I'll help you remember.

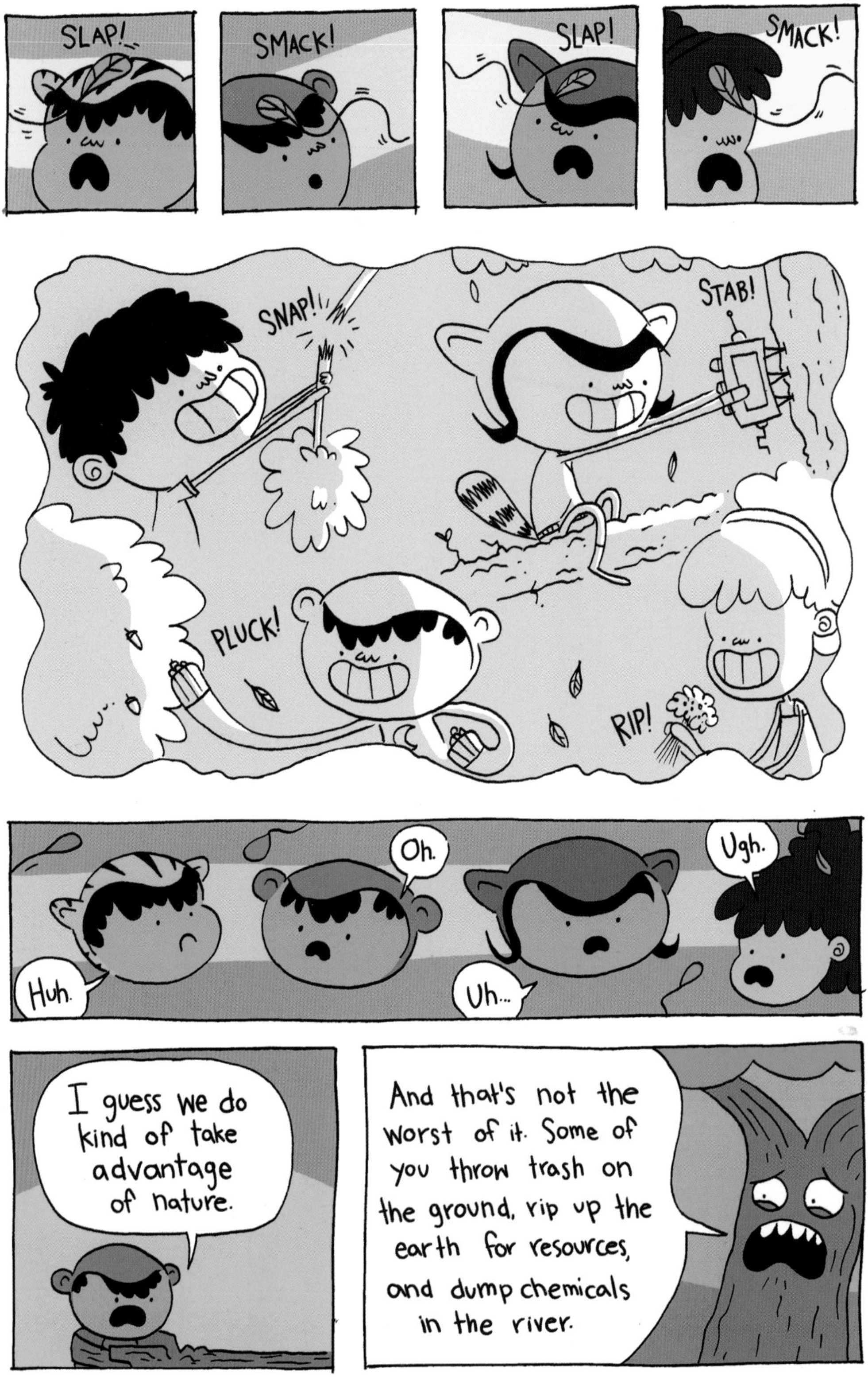
SLAP!
SMACK!
SLAP!
SMACK!
SNAP!
STAB!
PLUCK!
RIP!
Oh.
Ugh.
Huh.
Uh...
I guess we do kind of take advantage of nature.
And that's not the worst of it. Some of you throw trash on the ground, rip up the earth for resources, and dump chemicals in the river.

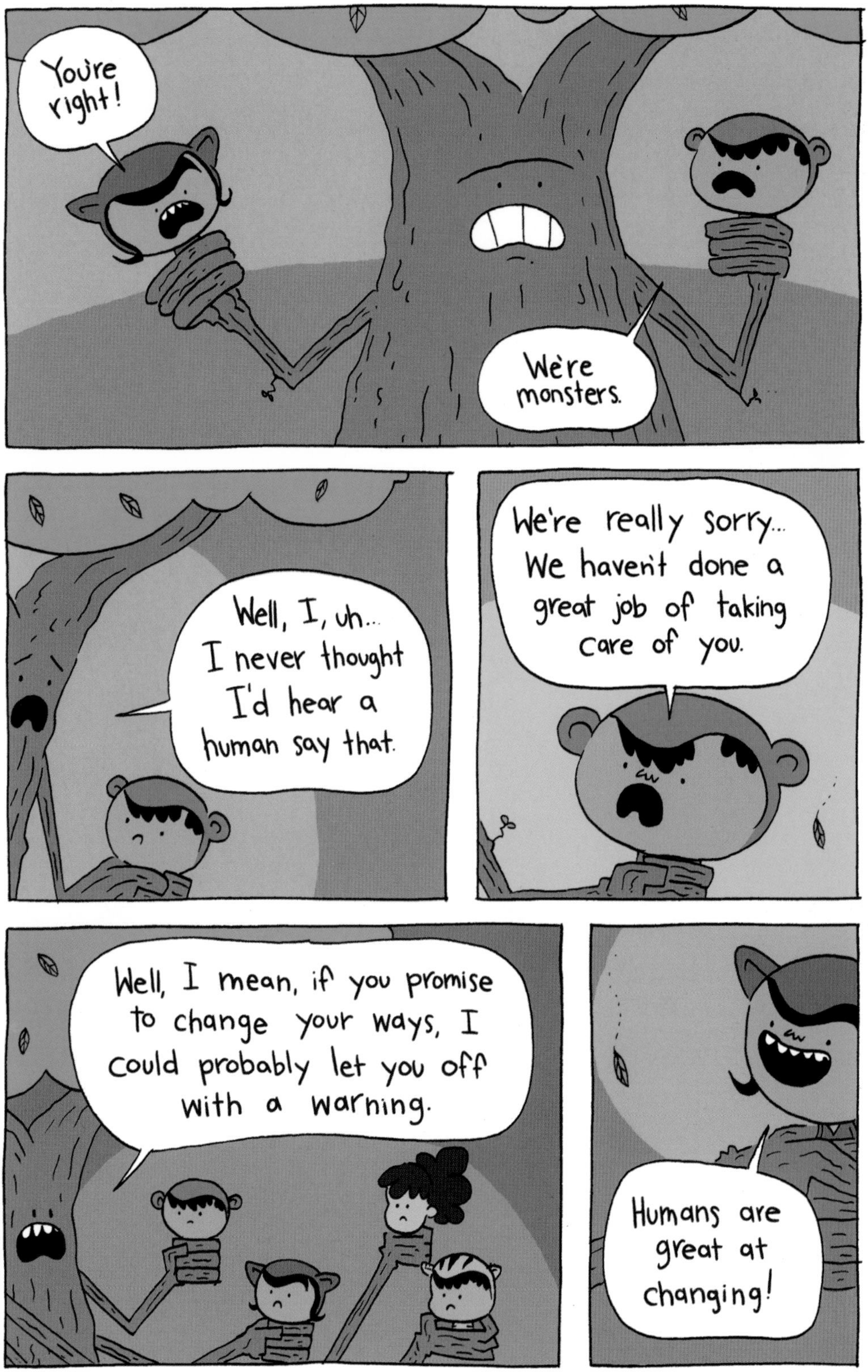
You're right!
We're monsters.
Well, I, uh... I never thought I'd hear a human say that.
We're really sorry... We haven't done a great job of taking care of you.
Well, I mean, if you promise to change your ways, I could probably let you off with a warning.
Humans are great at changing!

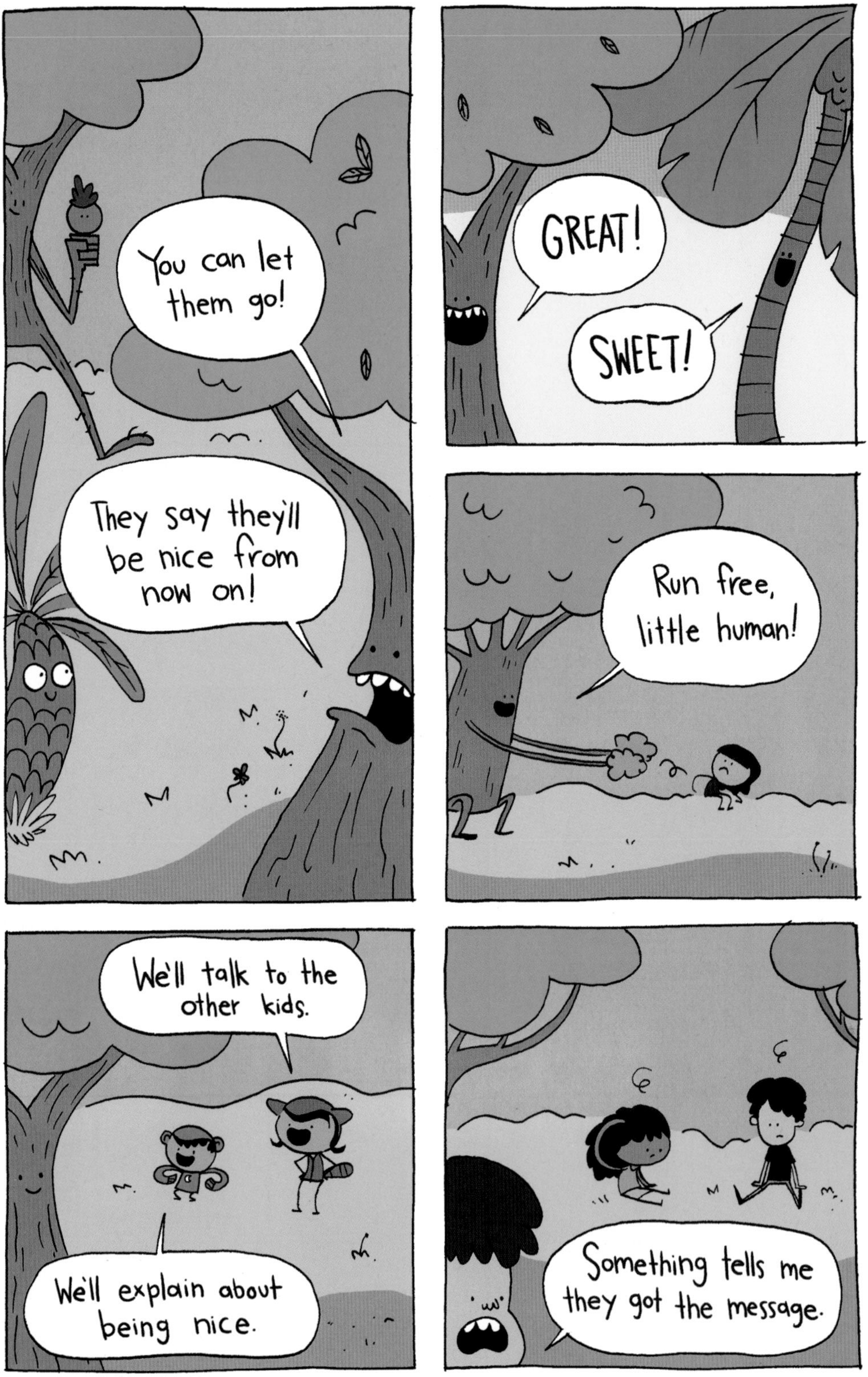
You can let them go!
They say they'll be nice from now on!
GREAT!
SWEET!
Run free, little human!
We'll talk to the other kids.
We'll explain about being nice.
Something tells me they got the message.

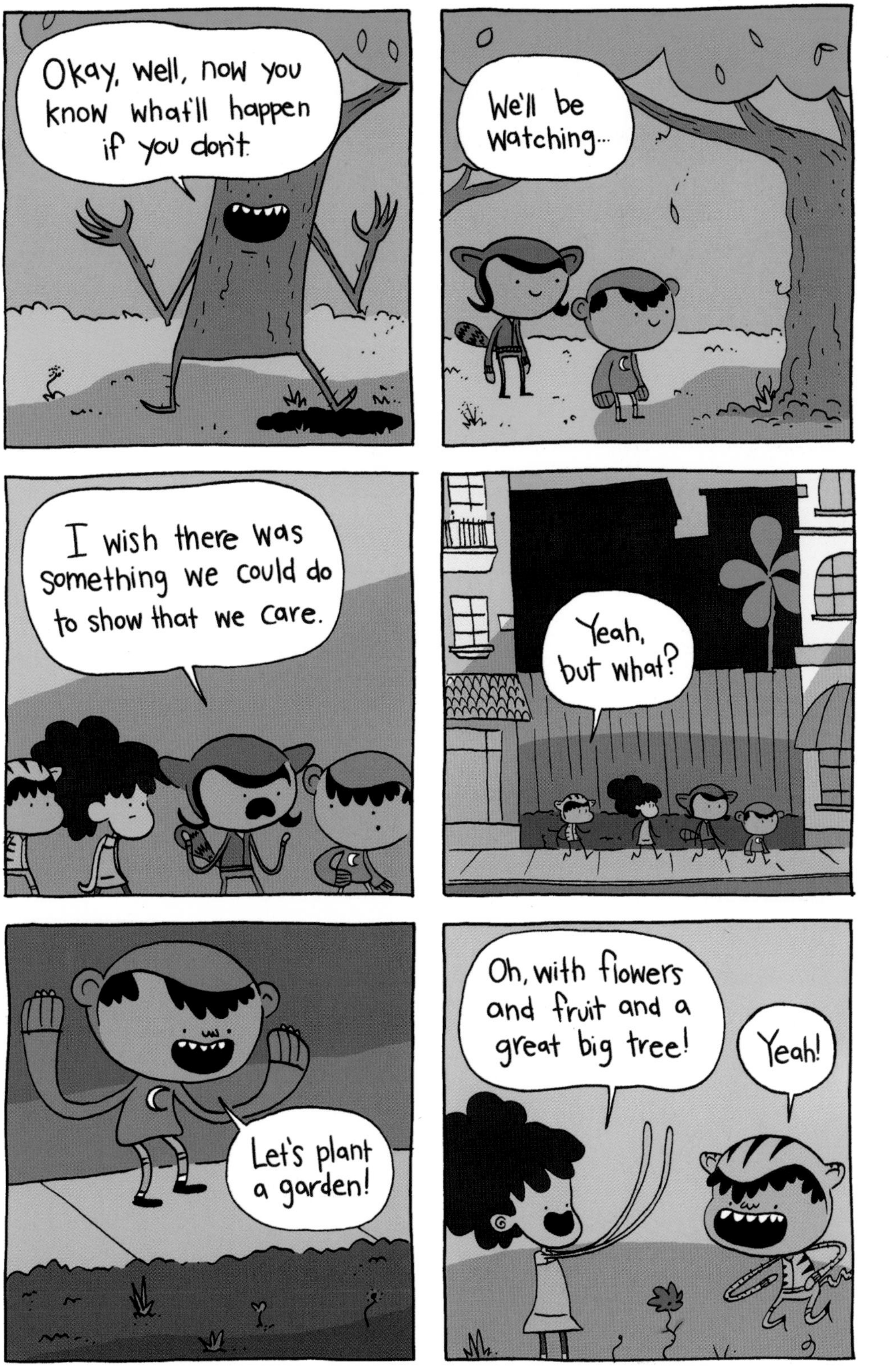
Okay, well, now you know what'll happen if you don't.
We'll be watching...
I wish there was something we could do to show that we care.
Yeah, but what?
Let's plant a garden!
Oh, with flowers and fruit and a great big tree!
Yeah!

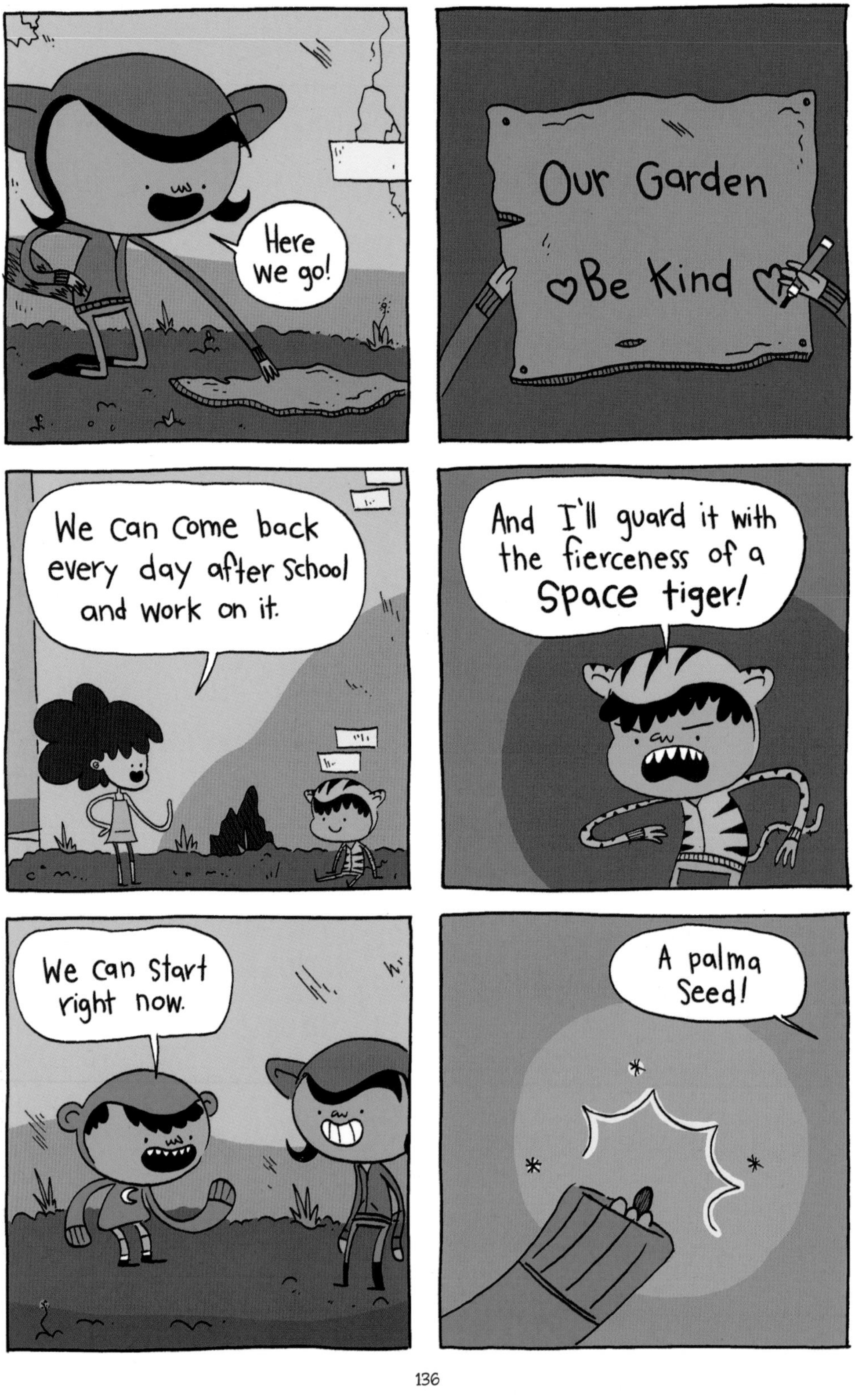
Here we go!
Our Garden
Be Kind
We can come back every day after school and work on it.
And I'll guard it with the fierceness of a Space tiger!
We can start right now.
A palma Seed!

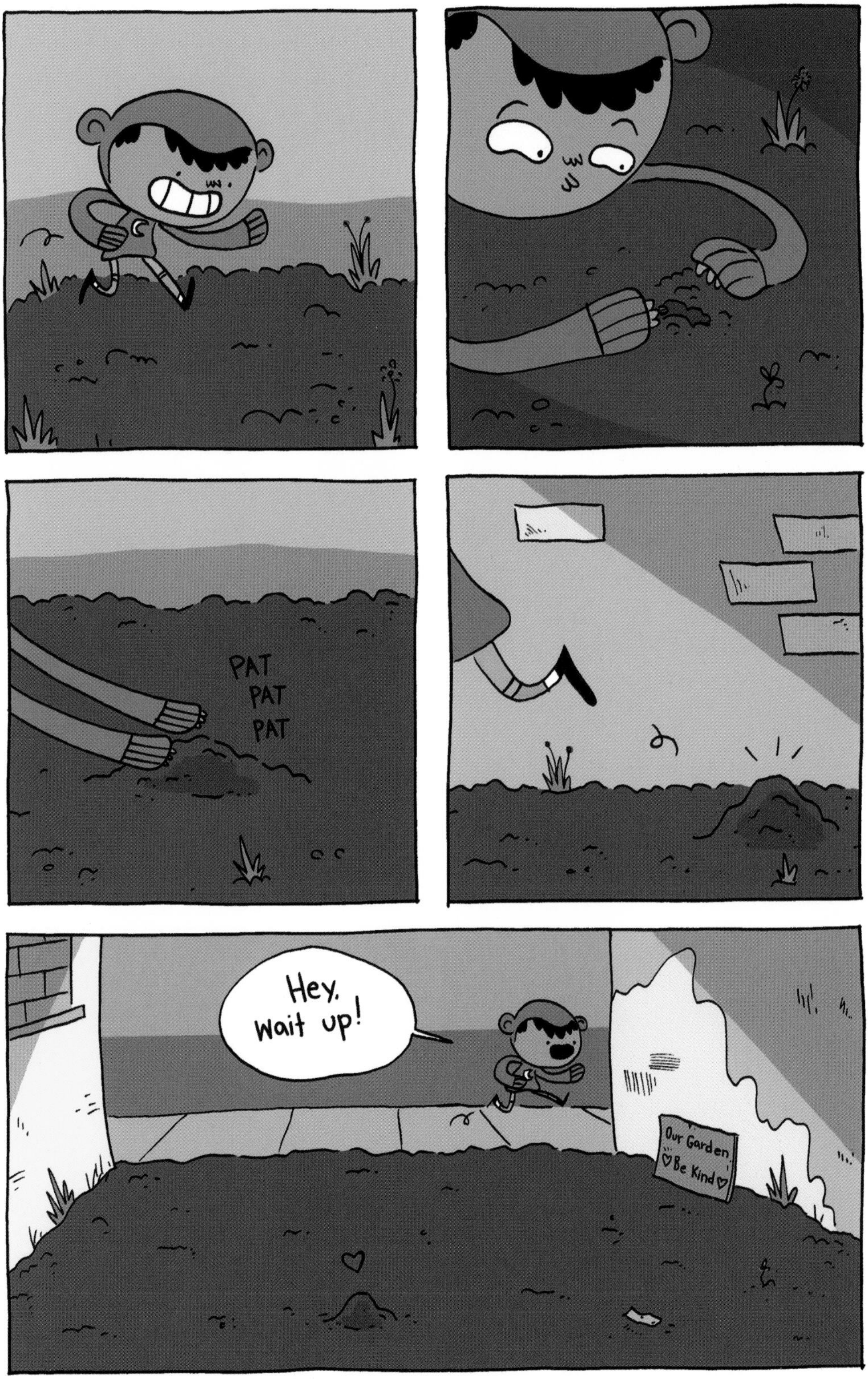
PAT
PAT
PAT
Hey, wait up!
Our Garden
Be Kind

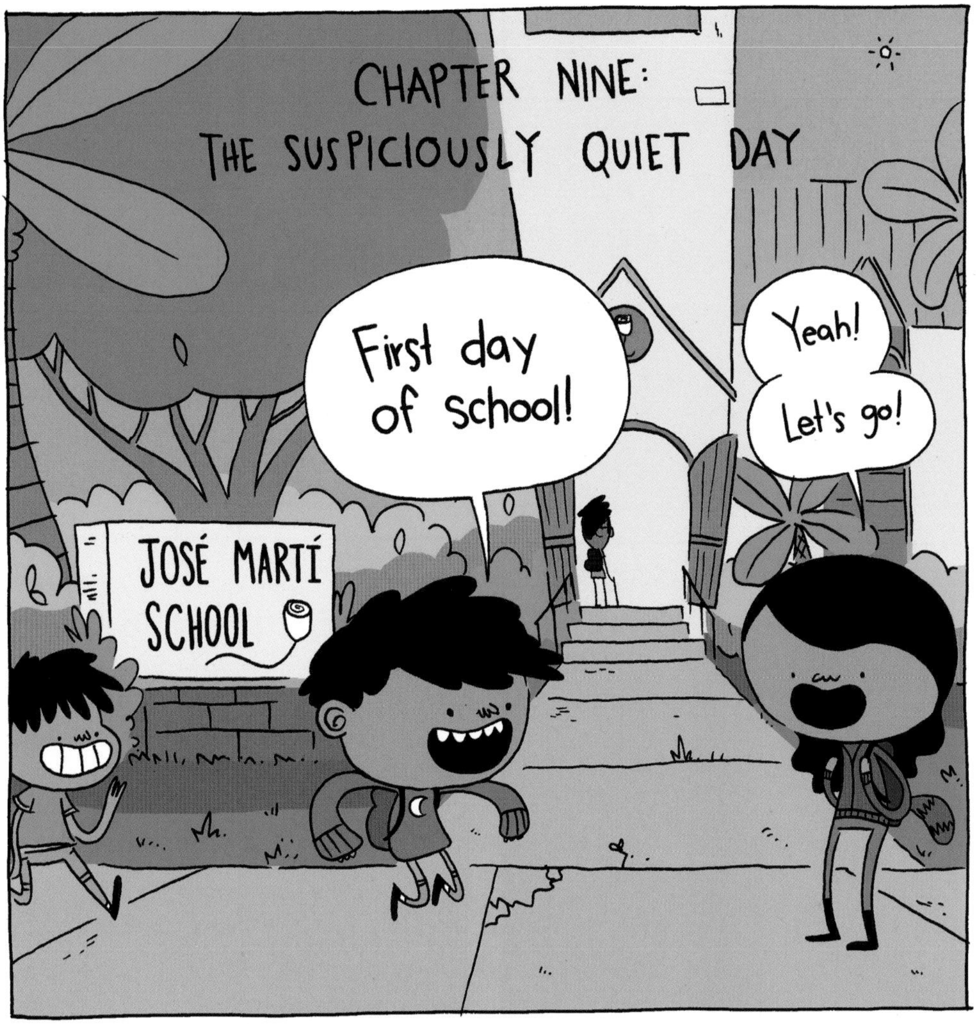
CHAPTER NINE:
THE SUSPICIOUSLY QUIET DAY
JOSÉ MARTÍ SCHOOL
First day of school!
Yeah!
Let's go!

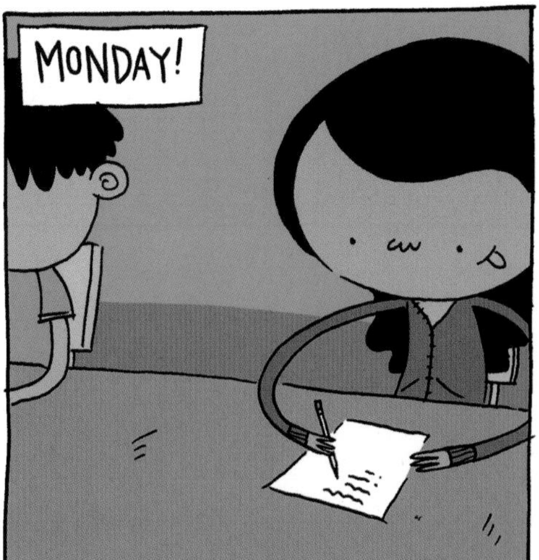
MONDAY!

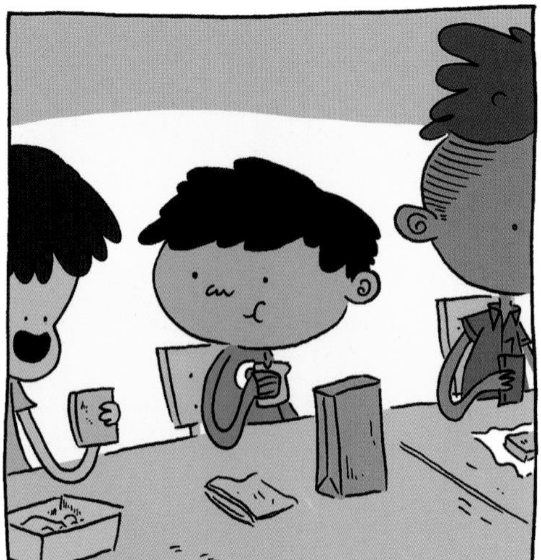

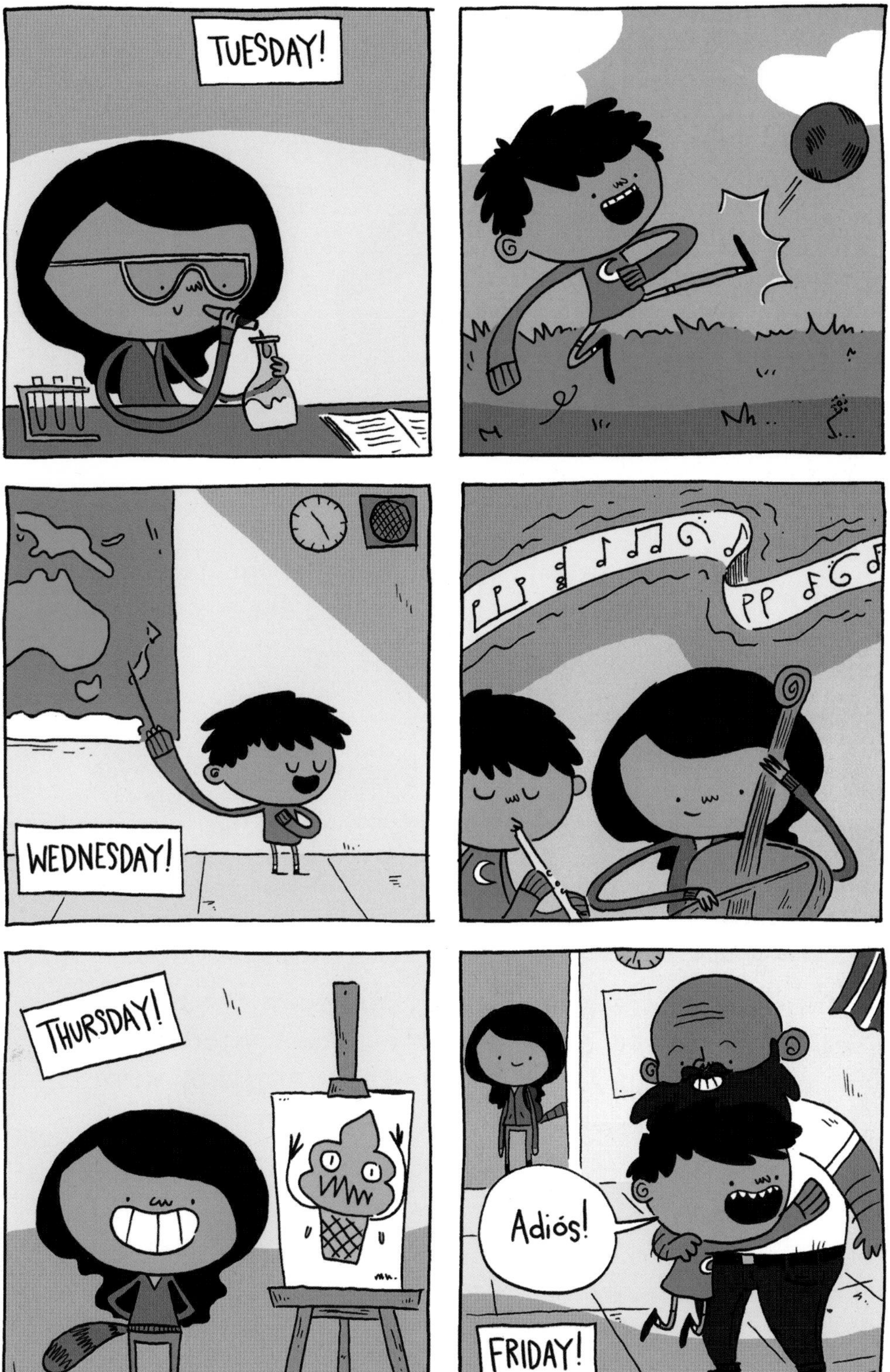
TUESDAY!
WEDNESDAY!
THURSDAY!
Adiós!
FRIDAY!

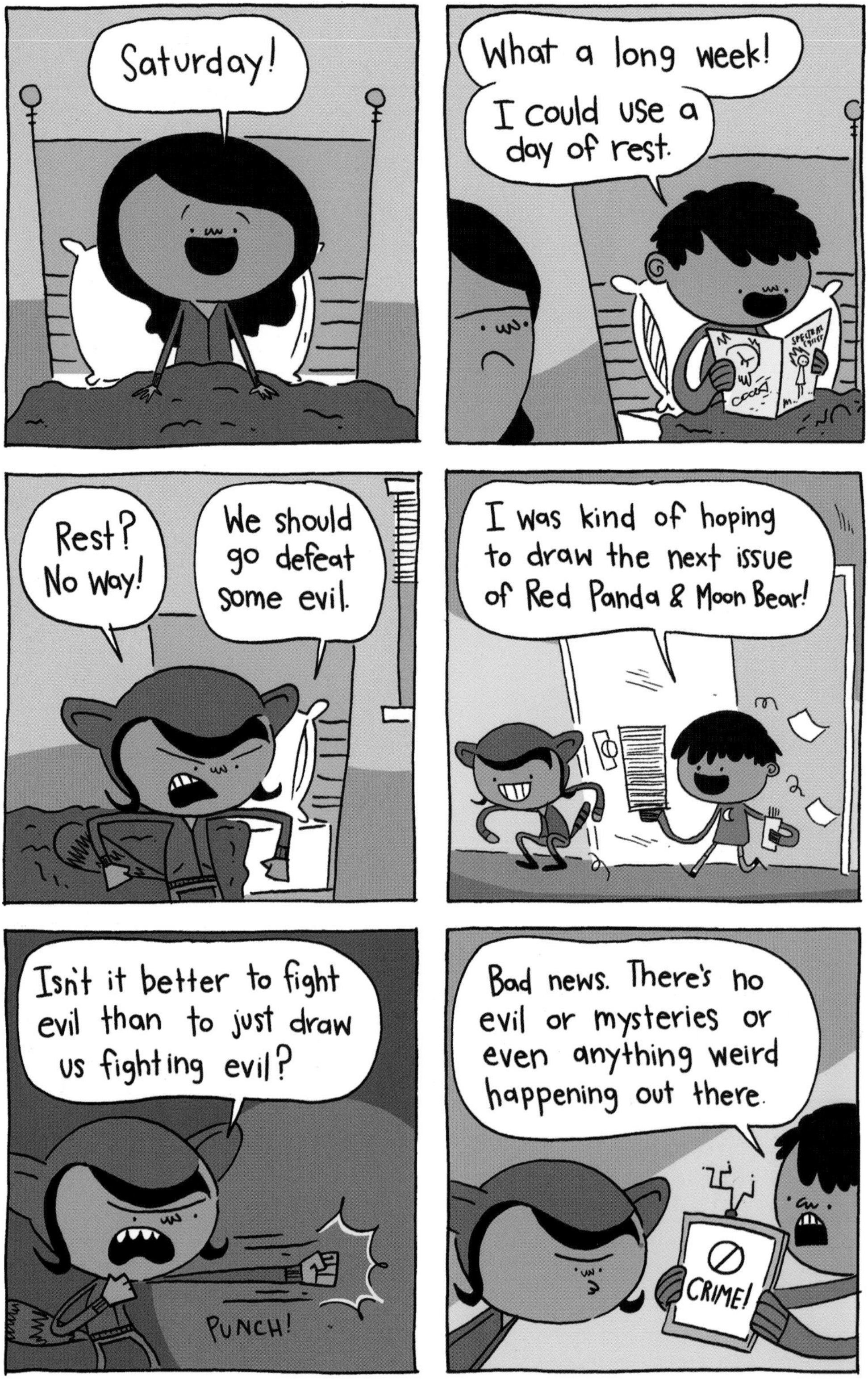

Saturday!
What a long week!
I could use a day of rest.
Rest? No way!
We should go defeat some evil.
I was kind of hoping to draw the next issue of Red Panda & Moon Bear!
Isn't it better to fight evil than to just draw us fighting evil?
PUNCH!
Bad news. There's no evil or mysteries or even anything weird happening out there.
CRIME!

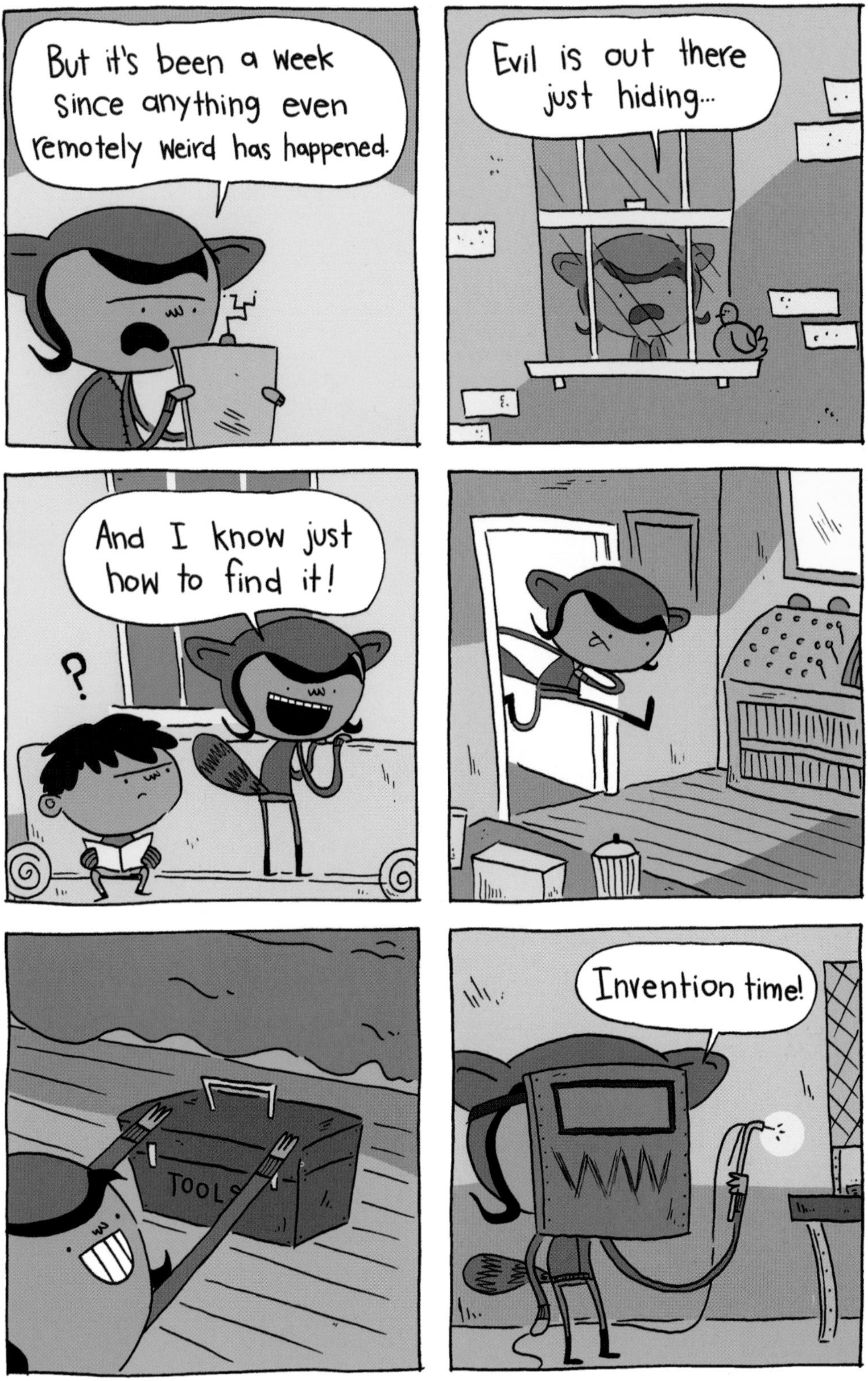
But it's been a week since anything even remotely weird has happened.
Evil is out there just hiding...
And I know just how to find it!
?
TOOLS
Invention time!

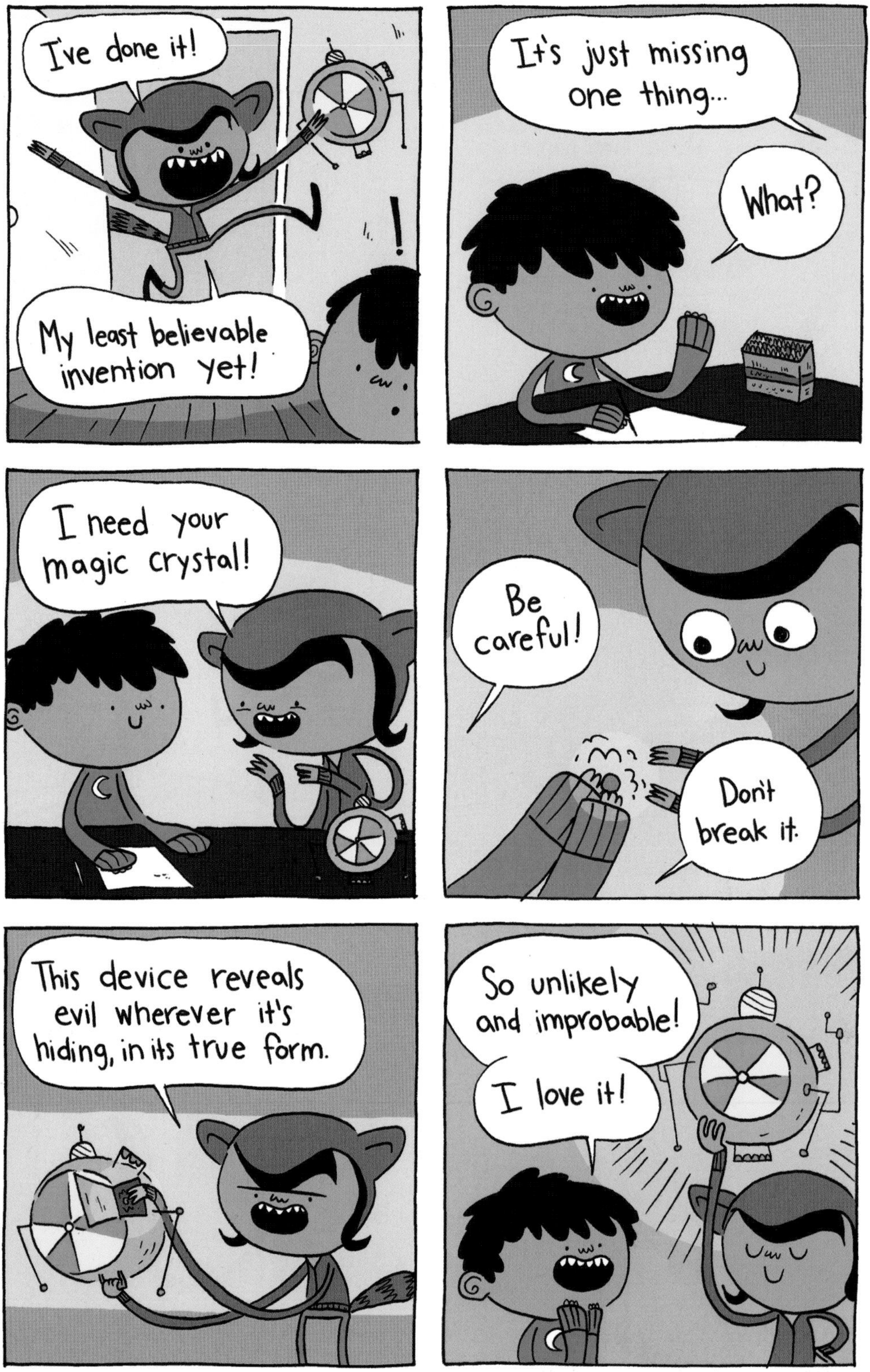
I've done it!
My least believable invention yet!
It's just missing one thing...
What?
I need your magic crystal!
Be careful!
Don't break it.
This device reveals evil wherever it's hiding, in its true form.
So unlikely and improbable!
I love it!

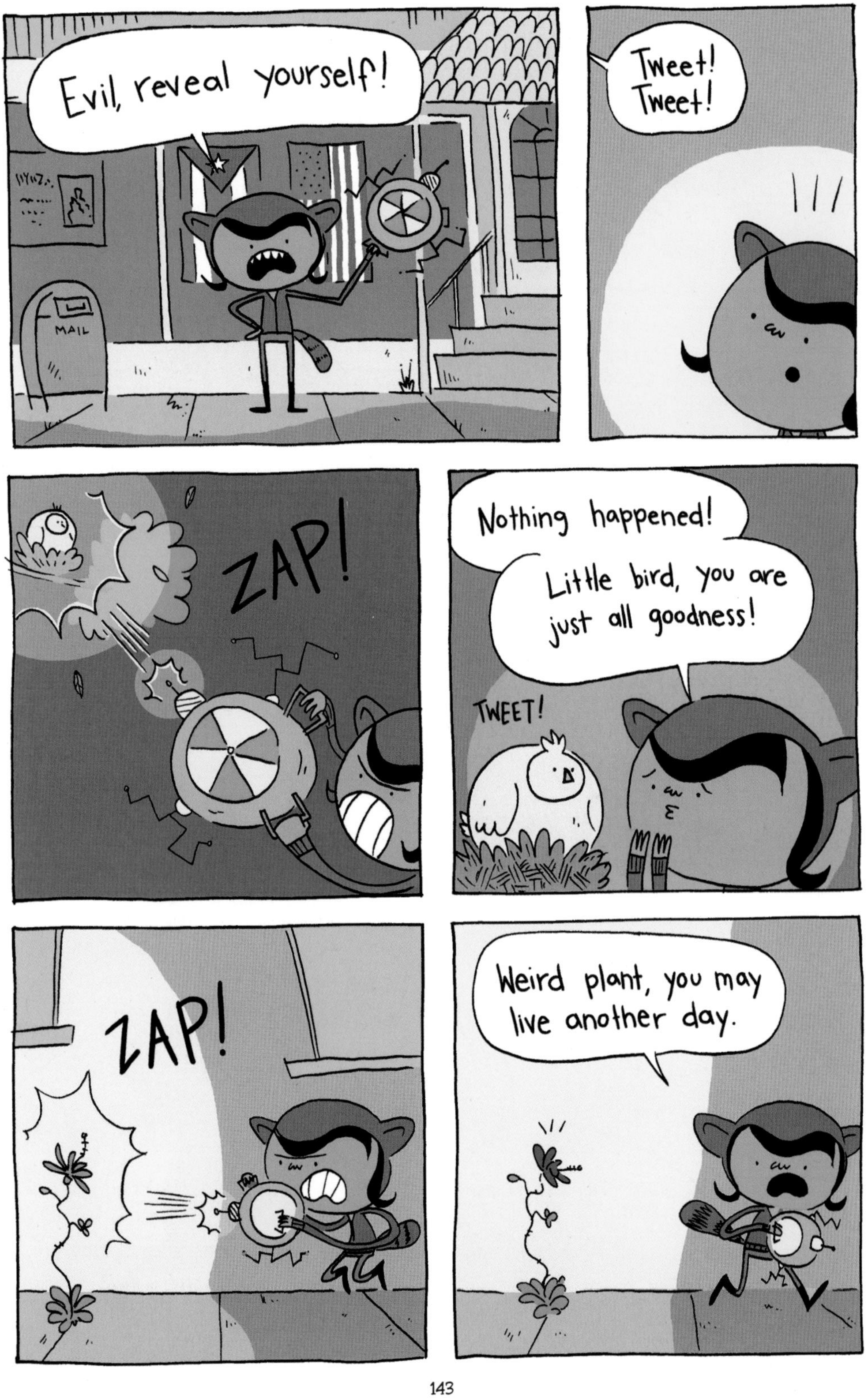
Evil, reveal yourself!
Tweet! Tweet!
ZAP!
Nothing happened!
Little bird, you are just all goodness!
TWEET!
ZAP!
Weird plant, you may live another day.

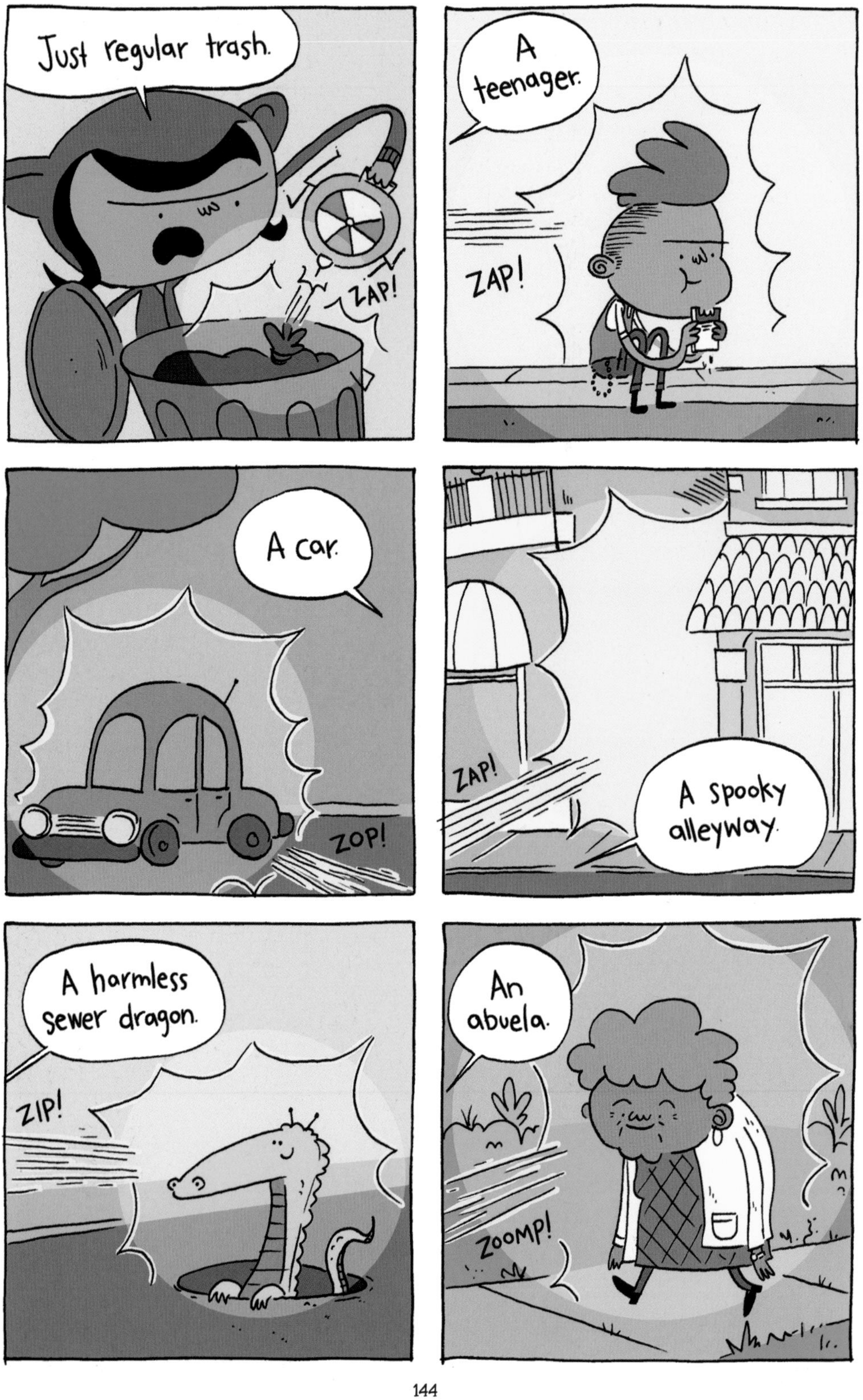
Just regular trash.
ZAP!
A teenager.
ZAP!
A car.
ZOP!
ZAP!
A spooky alleyway.
A harmless sewer dragon.
ZIP!
An abuela.
ZOOMP!

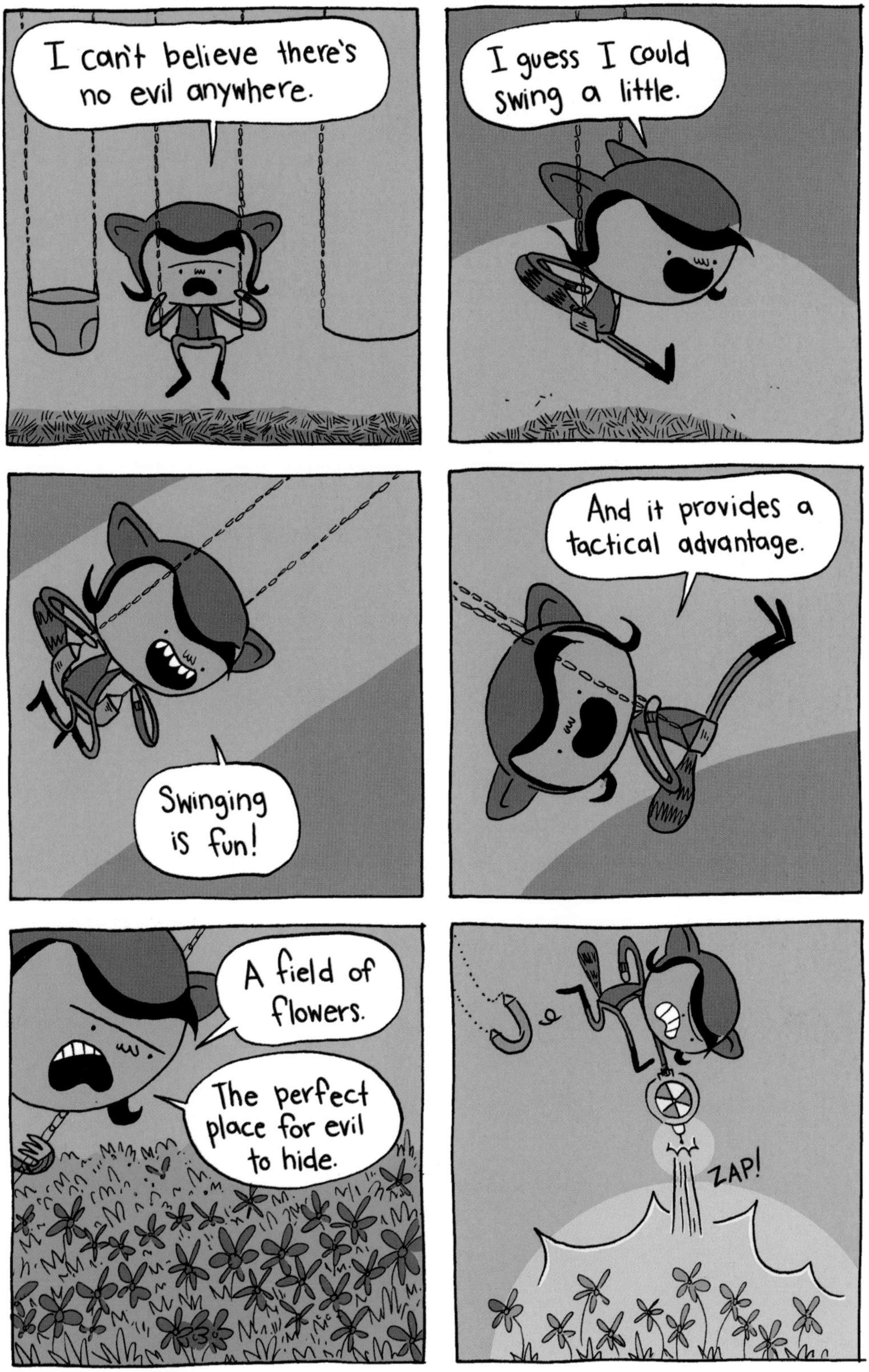
I can't believe there's no evil anywhere.
I guess I could swing a little.
Swinging is fun!
And it provides a tactical advantage.
A field of flowers.
The perfect place for evil to hide.
ZAP!

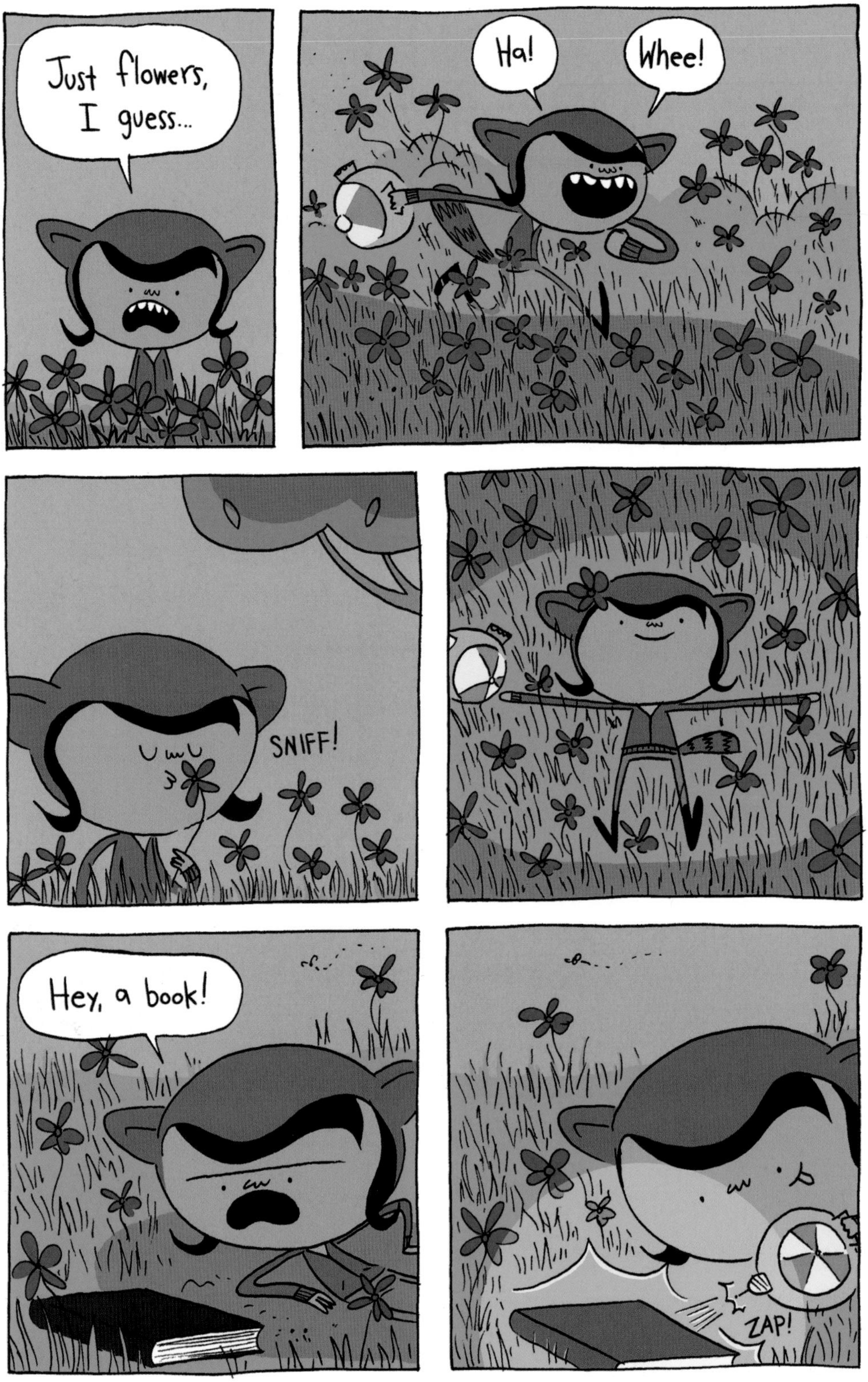
Just flowers, I guess...
Ha!
Whee!
SNIFF!
Hey, a book!
ZAP!

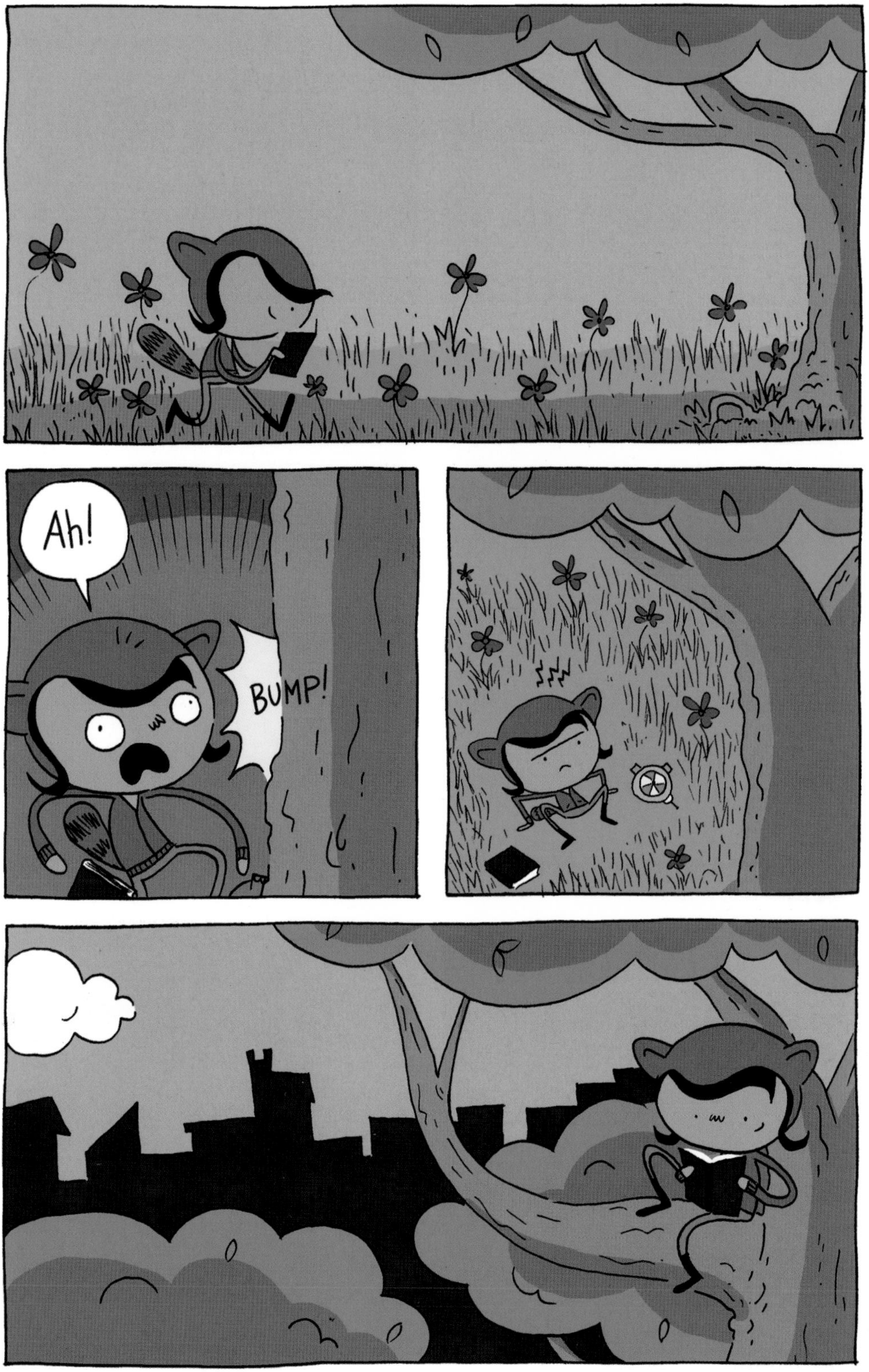
Ah!
BUMP!

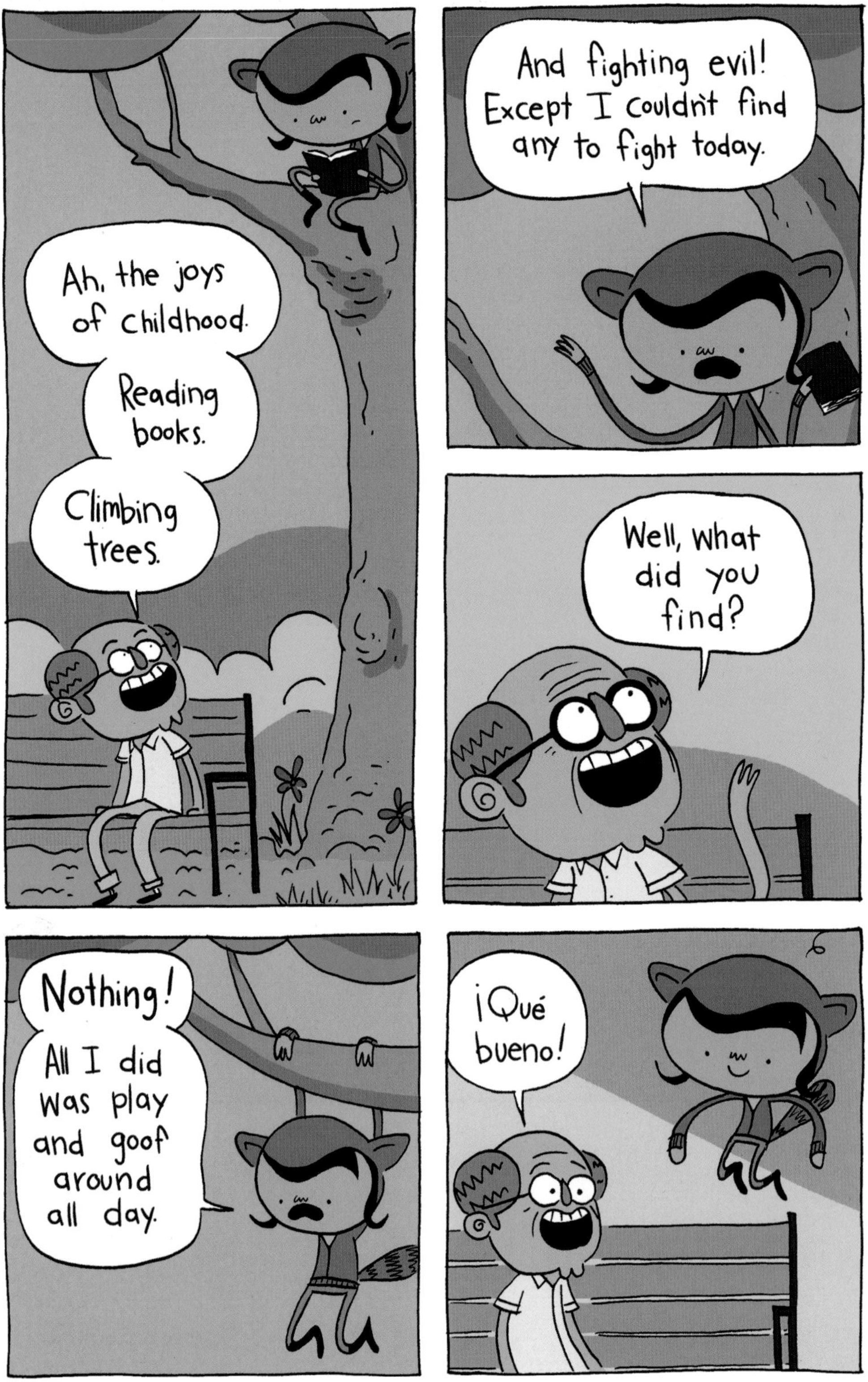

Ah, the joys of childhood.
Reading books.
Climbing trees.
And fighting evil! Except I couldn't find any to fight today.
Well, what did you find?
Nothing!
All I did was play and goof around all day.
¡Qué bueno!

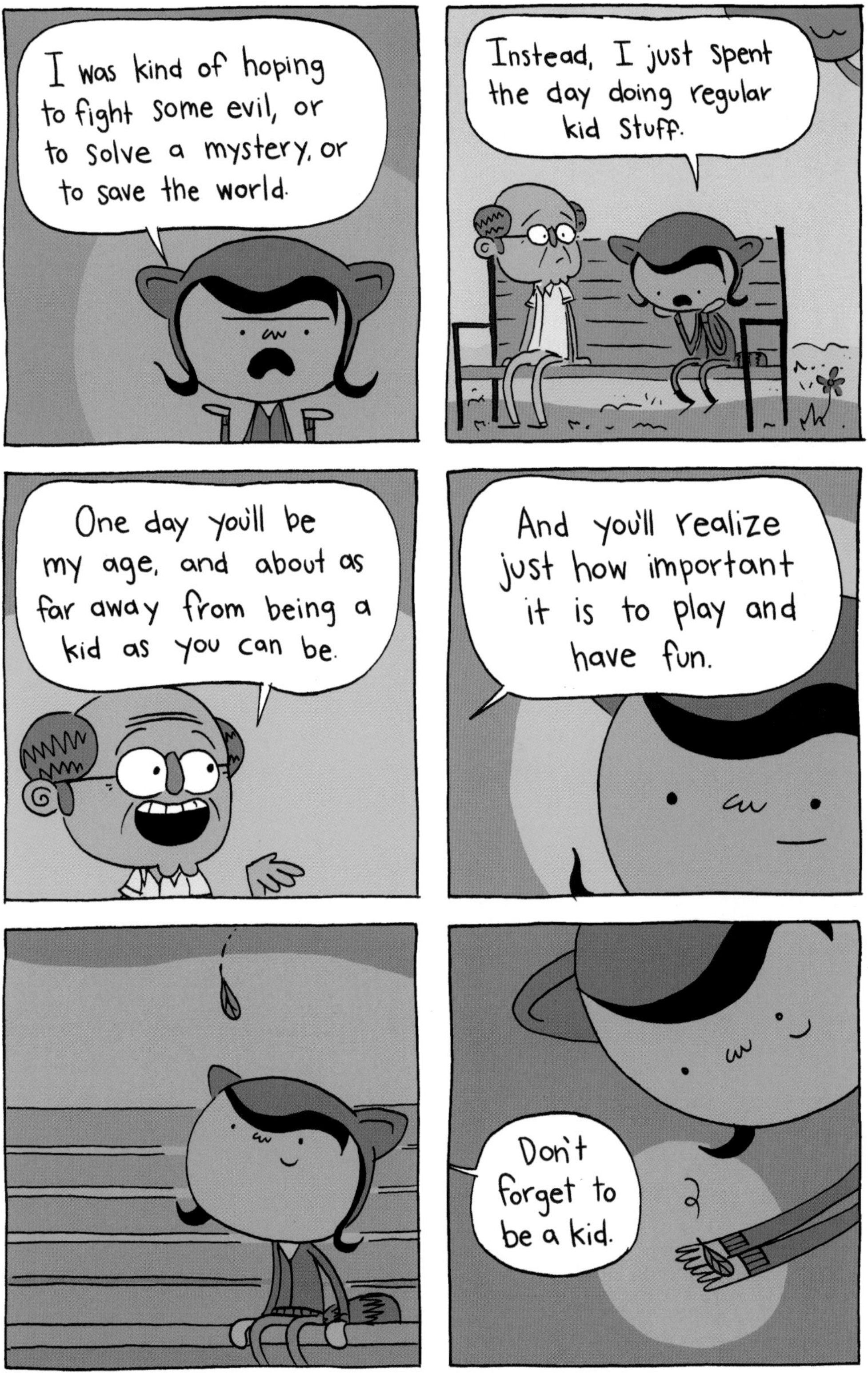
I was kind of hoping to fight some evil, or to solve a mystery, or to save the world.
Instead, I just spent the day doing regular kid stuff.
One day you'll be my age, and about as far away from being a kid as you can be.
And you'll realize just how important it is to play and have fun.
Don't forget to be a kid.

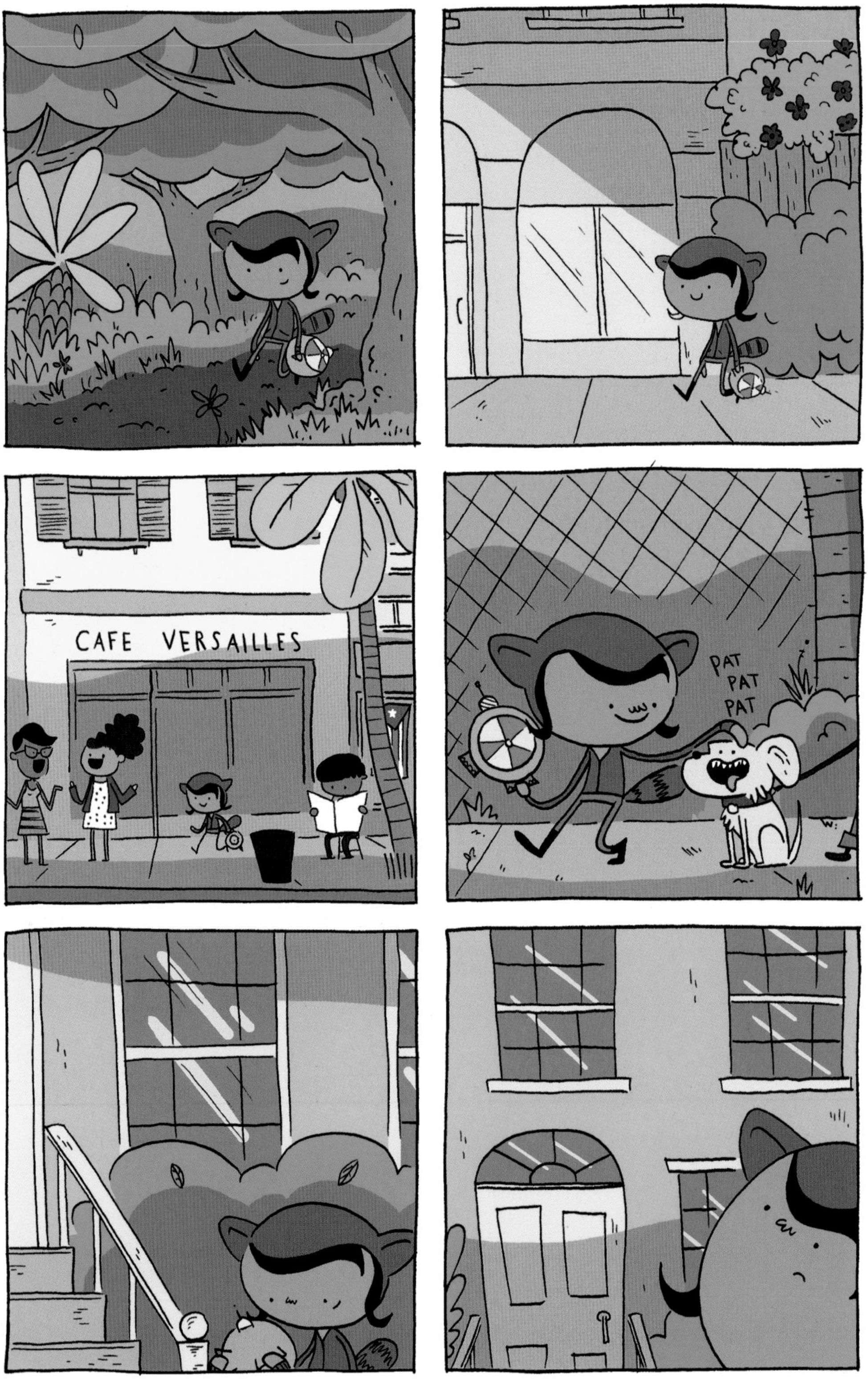
CAFE VERSAILLES
PAT
PAT
PAT

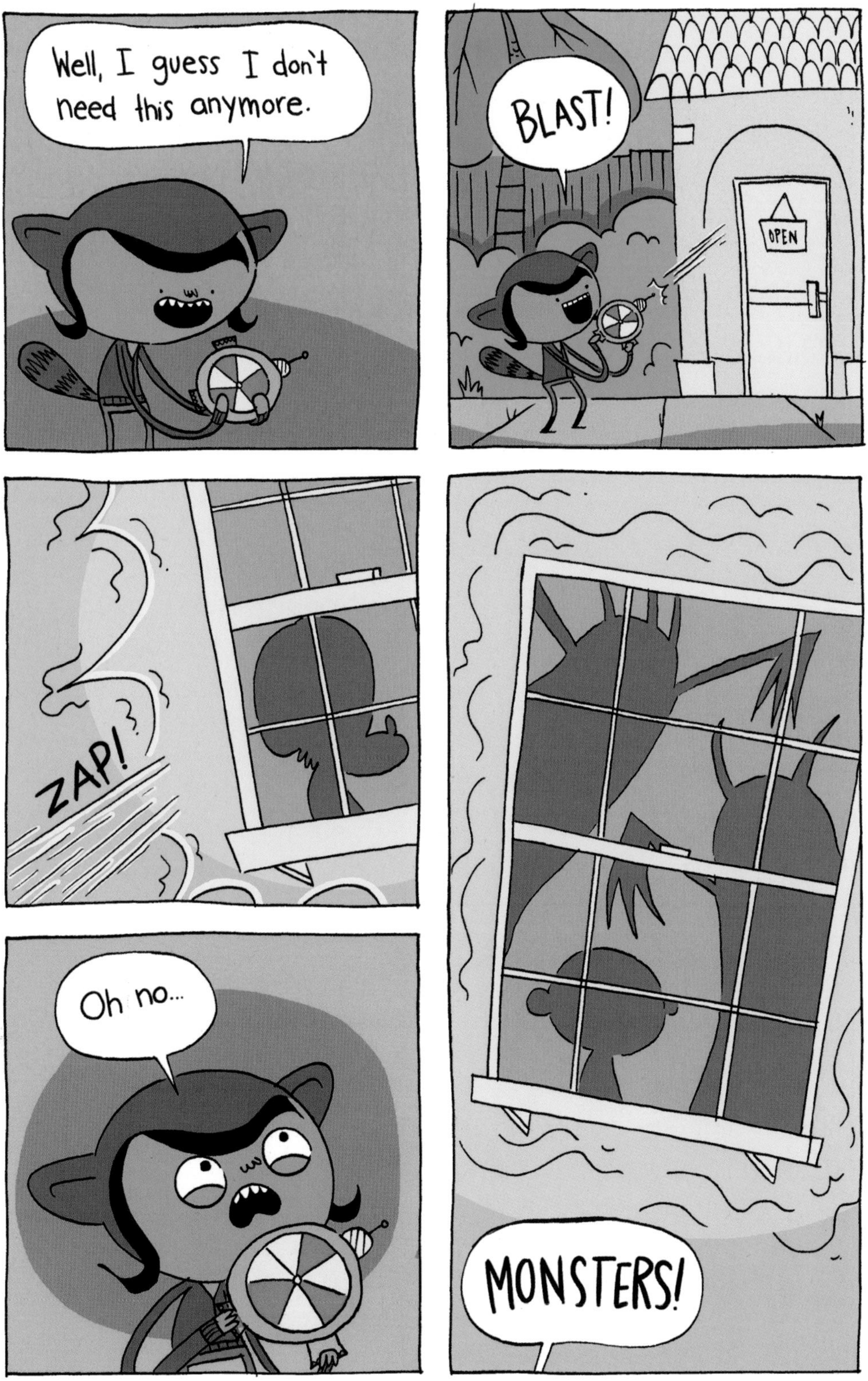
Well, I guess I don't need this anymore.
BLAST!
OPEN
ZAP!
Oh no...
MONSTERS!

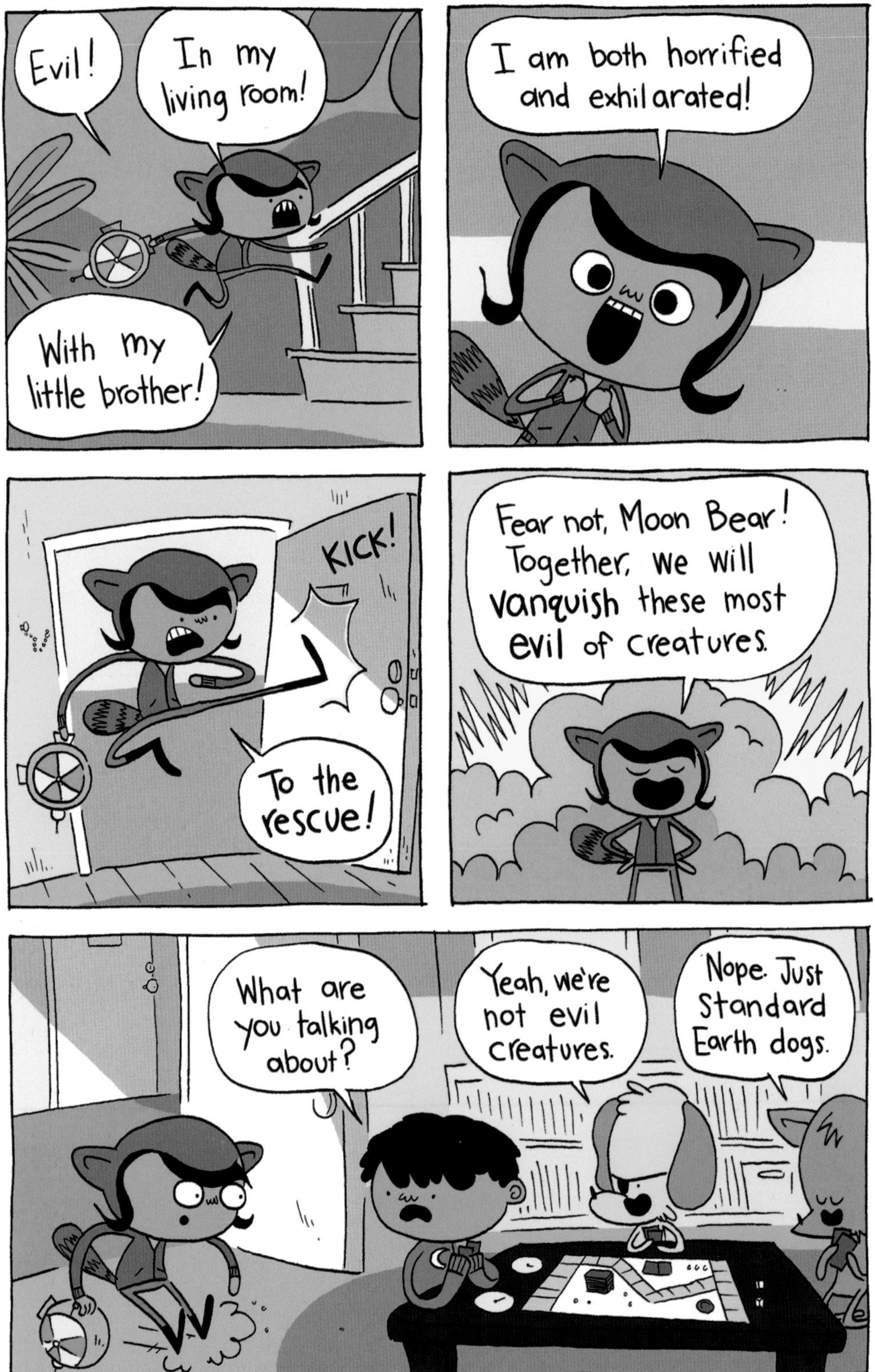
Evil!
In my living room!
With my little brother!
I am both horrified and exhilarated!
KICK!
To the rescue!
Fear not, Moon Bear! Together, we will vanquish these most evil of creatures.
What are you talking about?
Yeah, we're not evil creatures.
Nope. Just Standard Earth dogs.

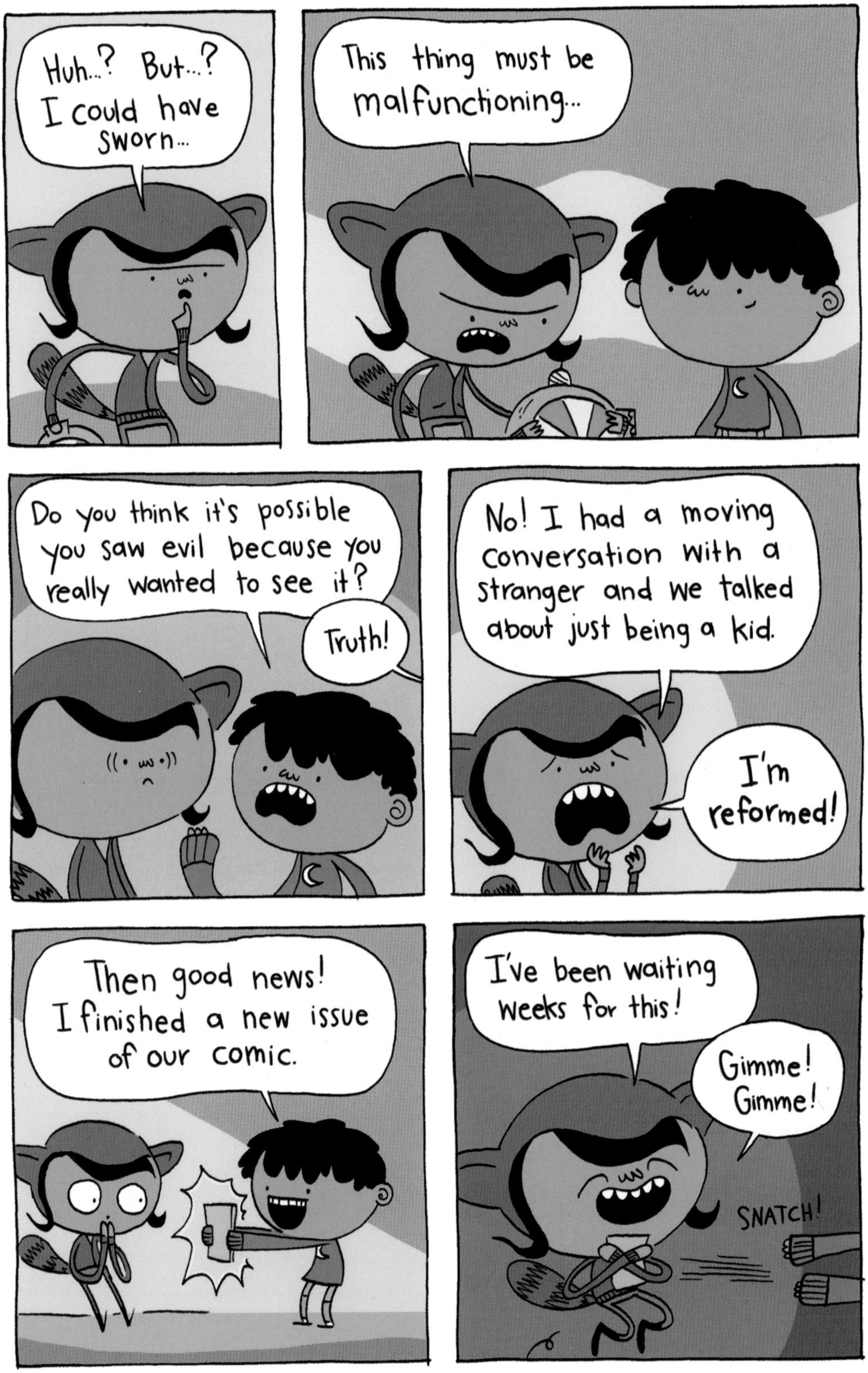
Huh...? But...? I could have sworn...
This thing must be malfunctioning...
Do you think it's possible you saw evil because you really wanted to see it?
Truth!
No! I had a moving conversation with a stranger and we talked about just being a kid.
I'm reformed!
Then good news! I finished a new issue of our comic.
I've been waiting weeks for this!
Gimme! Gimme!
SNATCH!

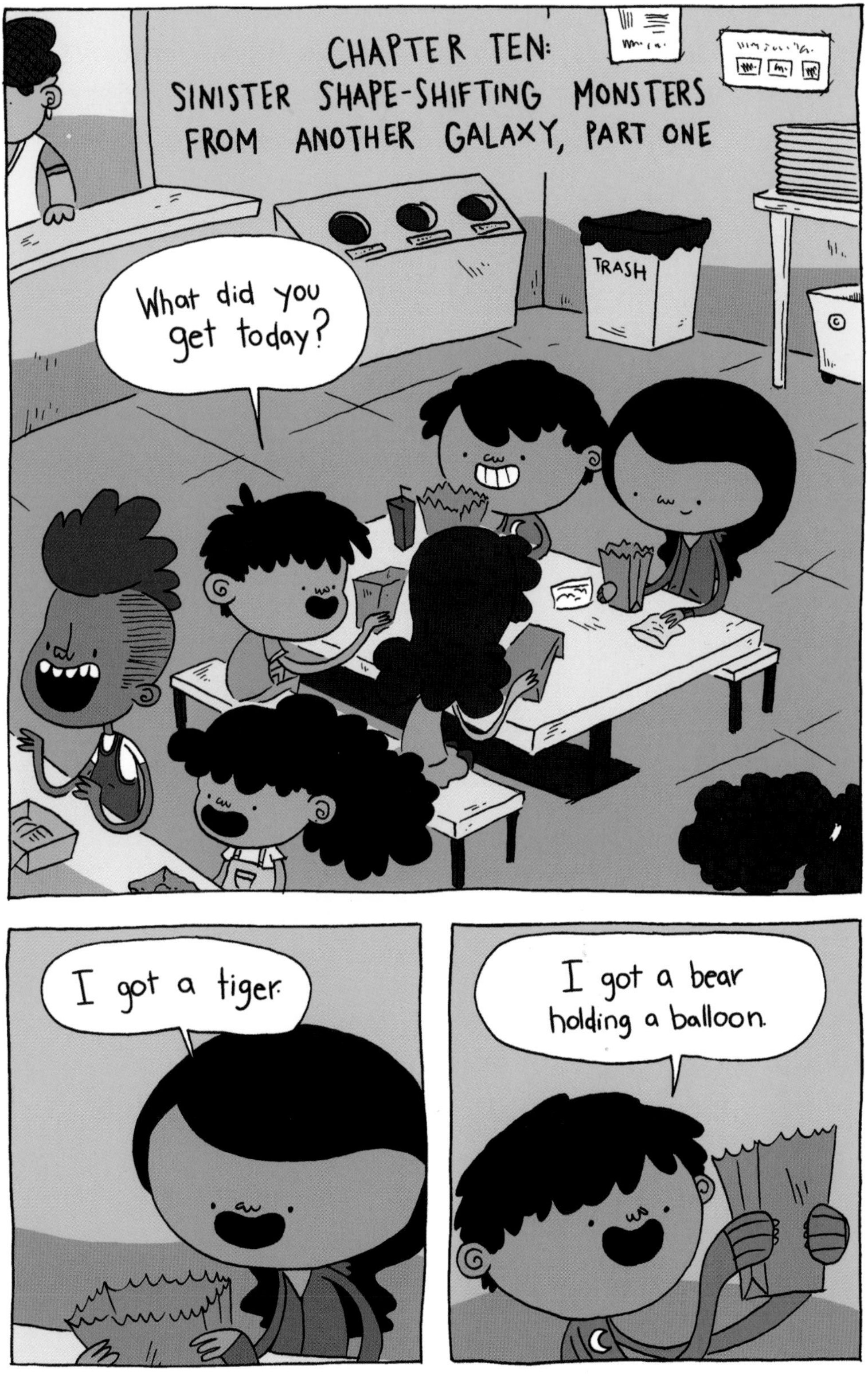
CHAPTER TEN:
SINISTER SHAPE-SHIFTING MONSTERS FROM ANOTHER GALAXY, PART ONE
TRASH
What did you get today?
I got a tiger.
I got a bear holding a balloon.

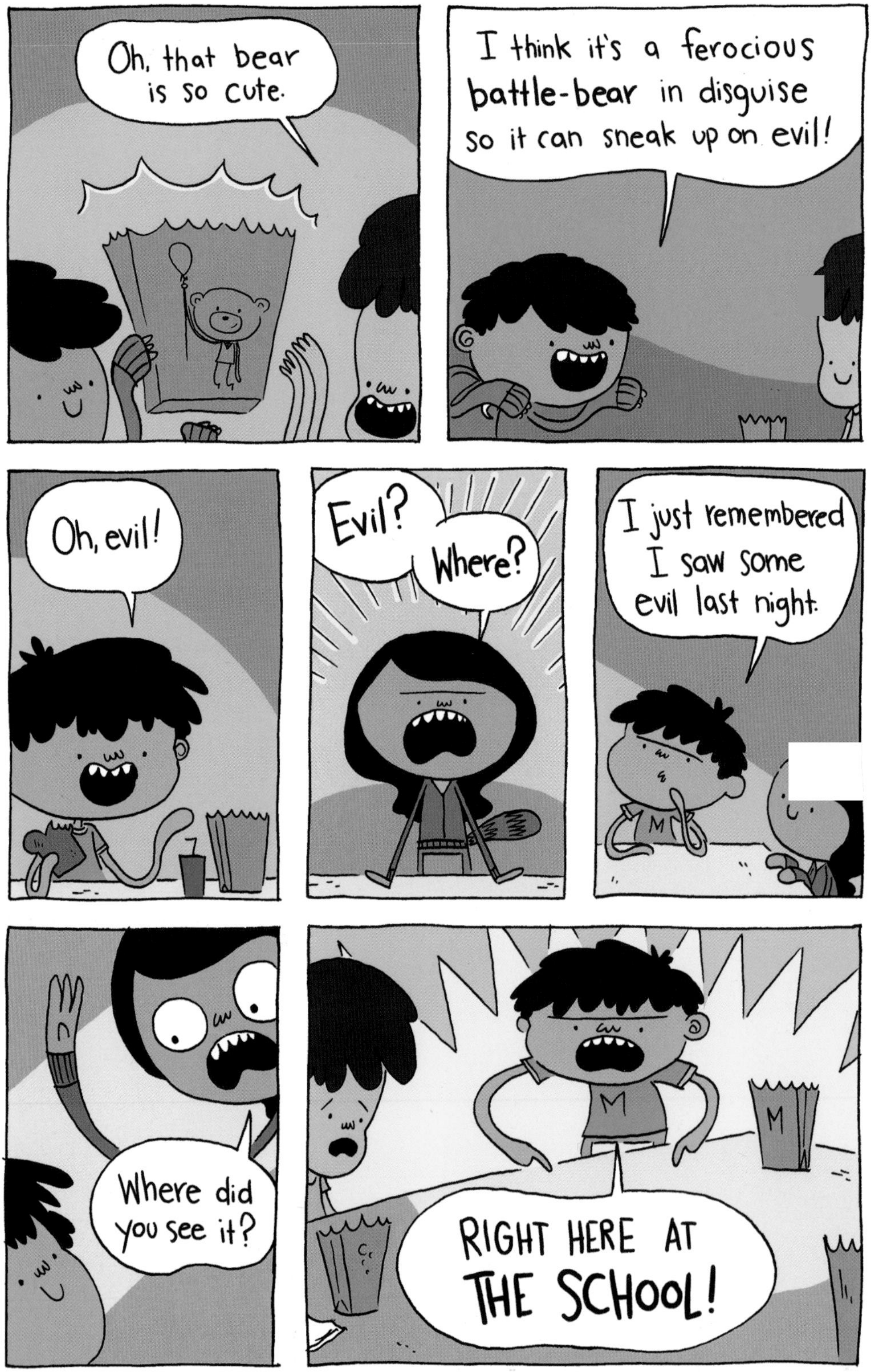
Oh, that bear is so cute.
I think it's a ferocious battle-bear in disguise so it can sneak up on evil!
Oh, evil!
Evil?
Where?
I just remembered I saw some evil last night.
Where did you see it?
RIGHT HERE AT THE SCHOOL!

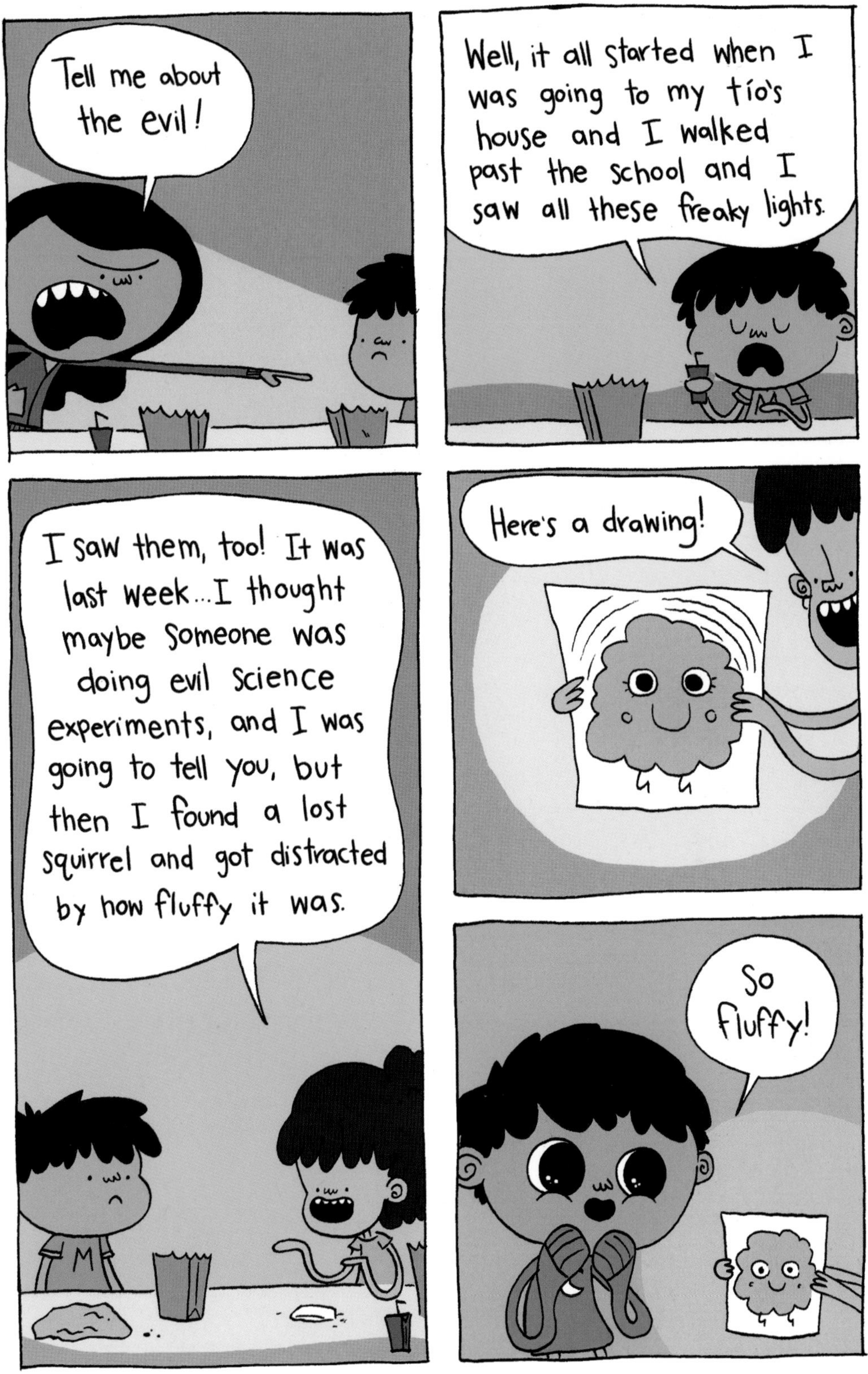
Tell me about the evil!
Well, it all started when I was going to my tío's house and I walked past the school and I saw all these freaky lights.
I saw them, too! It was last week...I thought maybe someone was doing evil science experiments, and I was going to tell you, but then I found a lost squirrel and got distracted by how fluffy it was.
Here's a drawing!
So fluffy!

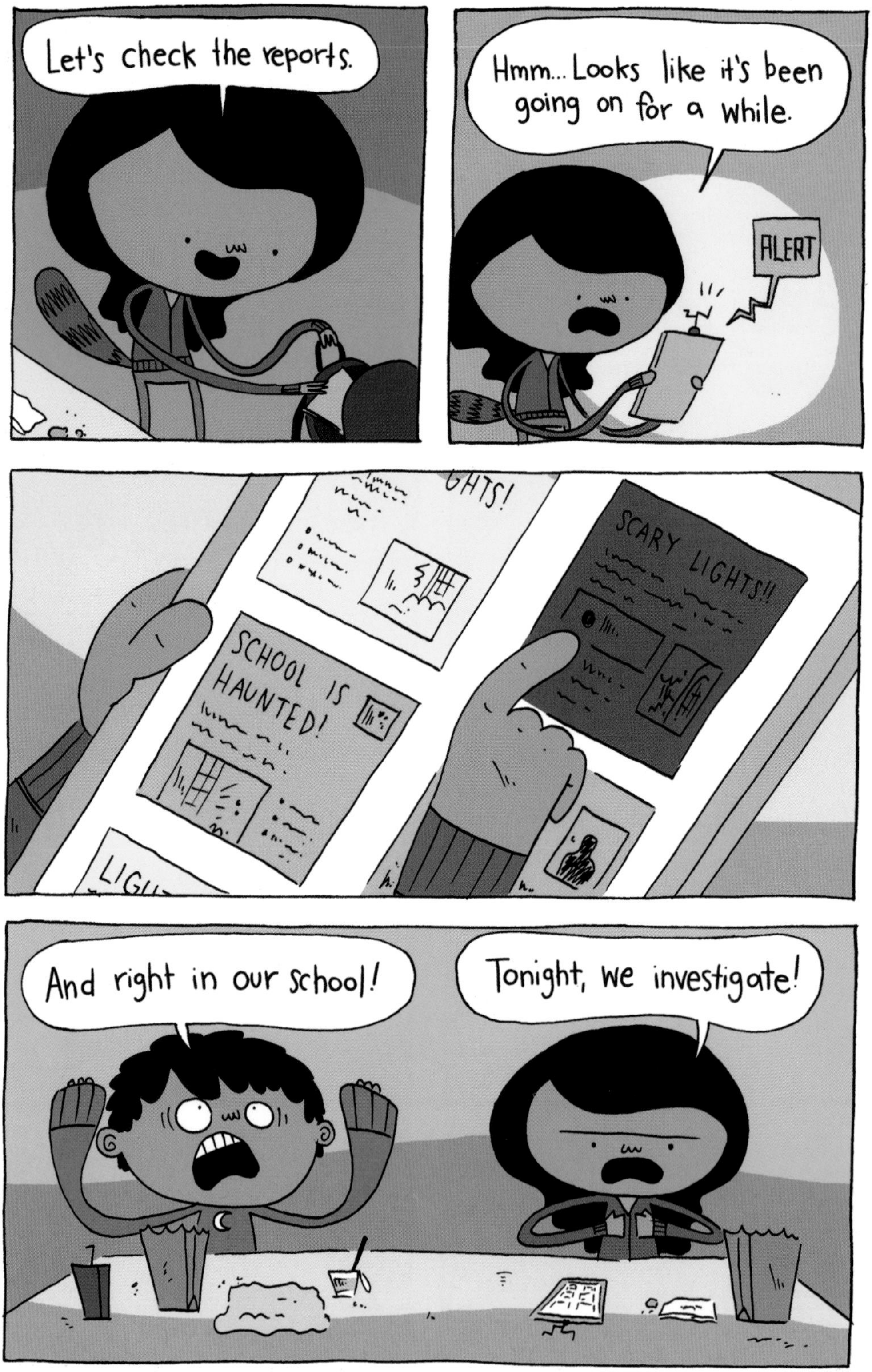

Let's check the reports.
Hmm... Looks like it's been going on for a while.
ALERT
GHTS!
SCARY LIGHTS!!
SCHOOL IS HAUNTED!
And right in our school!
Tonight, we investigate!

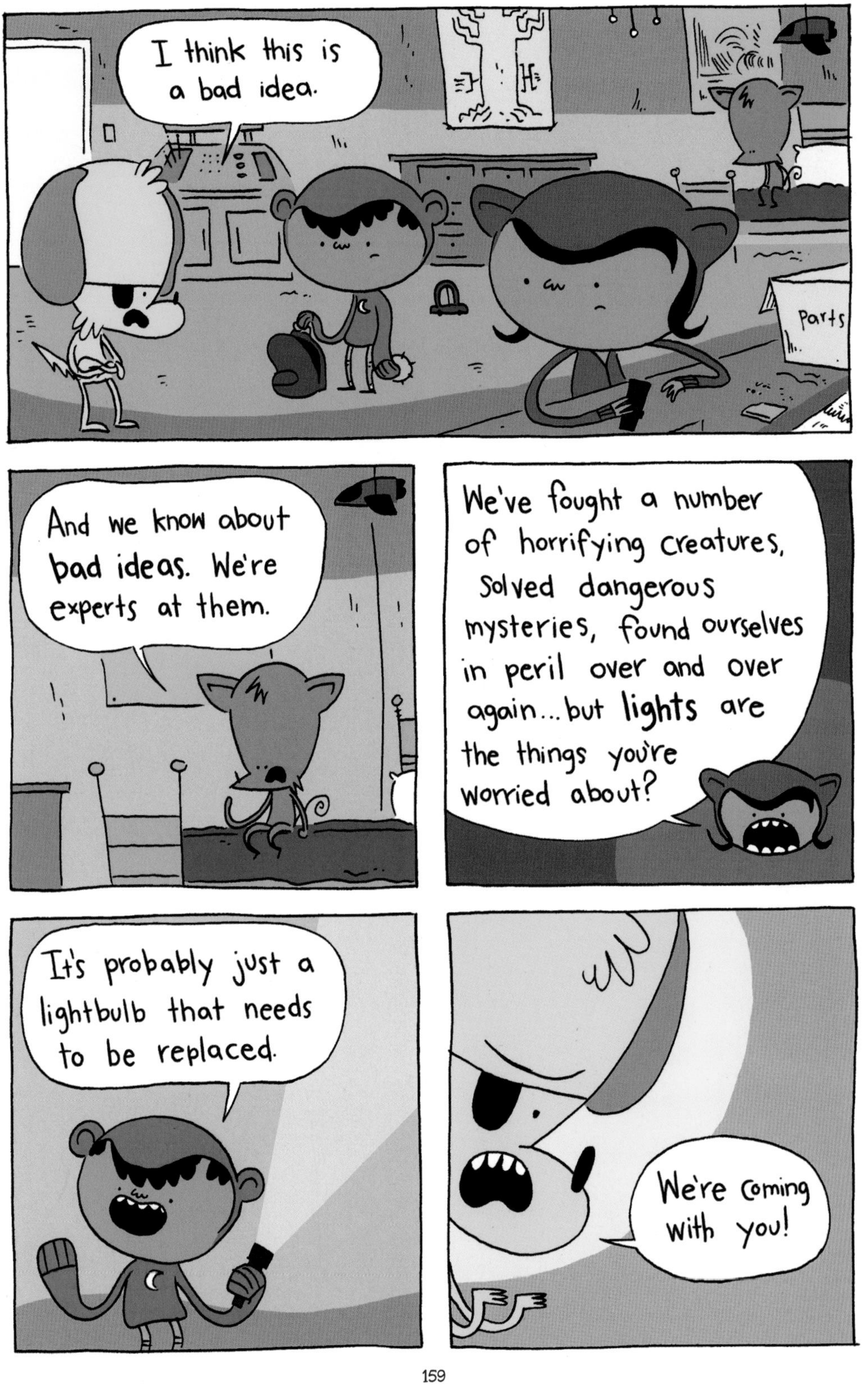
I think this is a bad idea.
Parts
And we know about bad ideas. We're experts at them.
We've fought a number of horrifying creatures, solved dangerous mysteries, found ourselves in peril over and over again... but lights are the things you're worried about?
It's probably just a lightbulb that needs to be replaced.
We're coming with you!

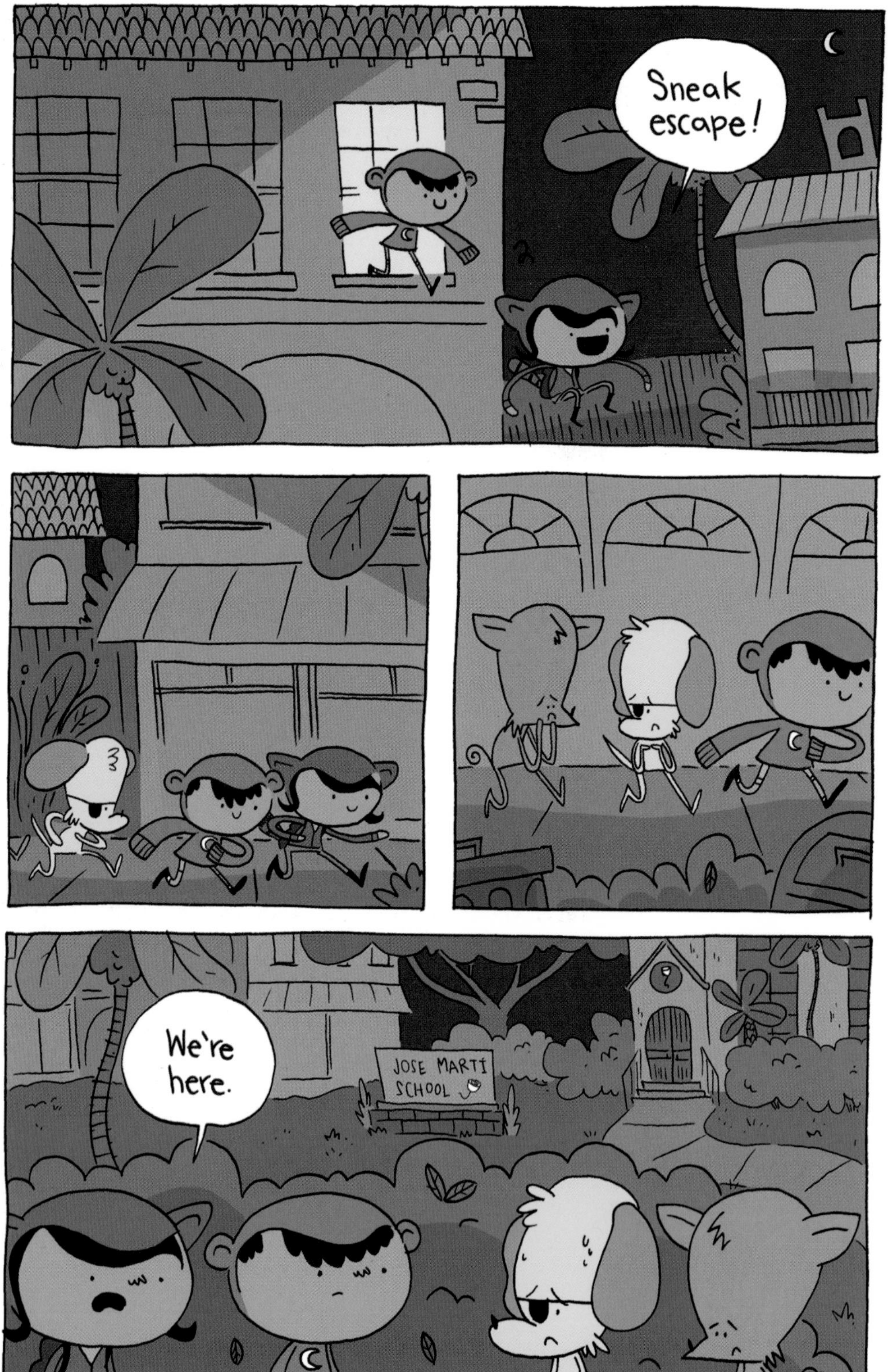
Sneak escape!
We're here.
JOSE MARTÍ SCHOOL

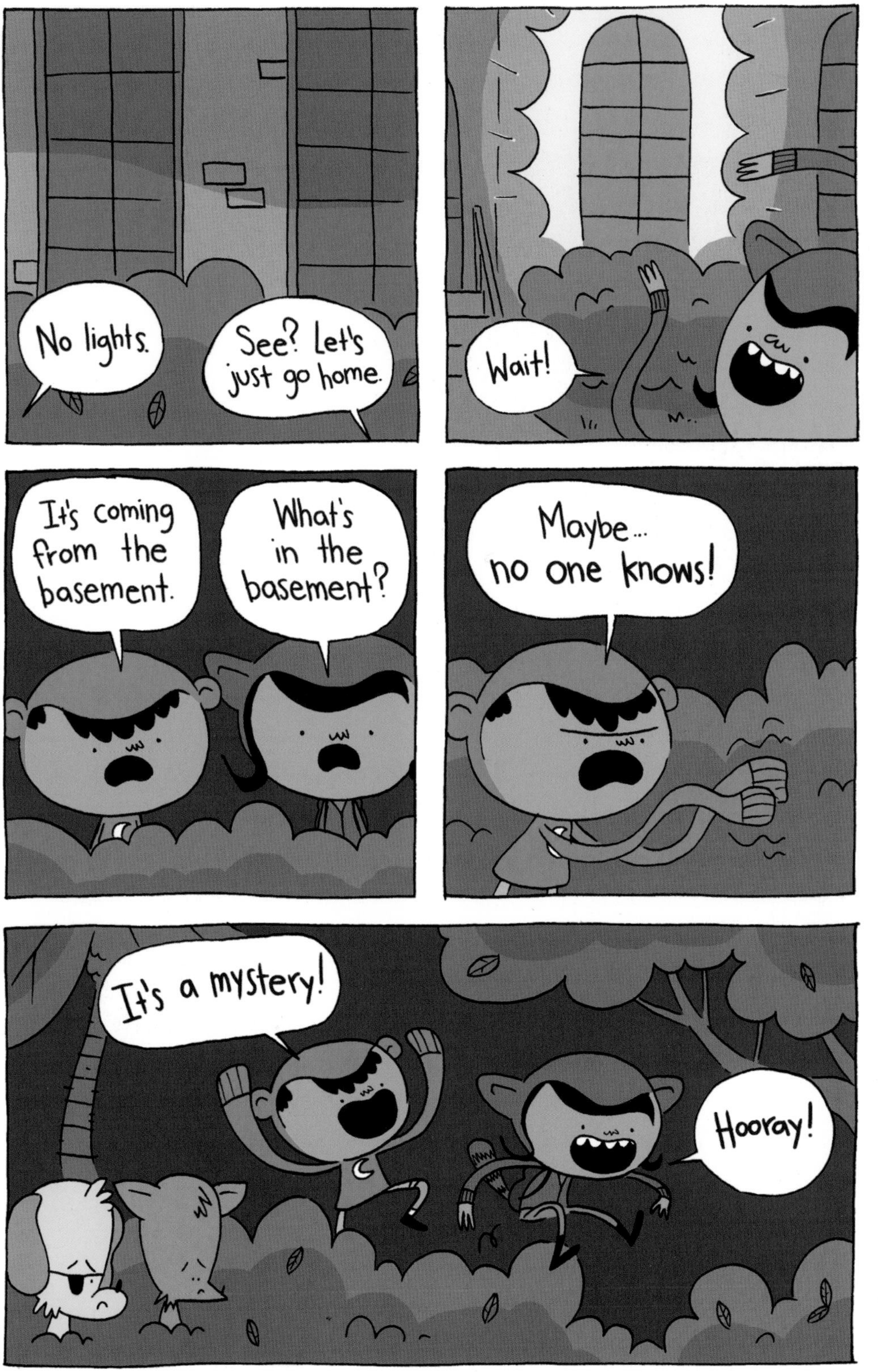
No lights.
See? Let's just go home.
Wait!
It's coming from the basement.
What's in the basement?
Maybe... no one knows!
It's a mystery!
Hooray!

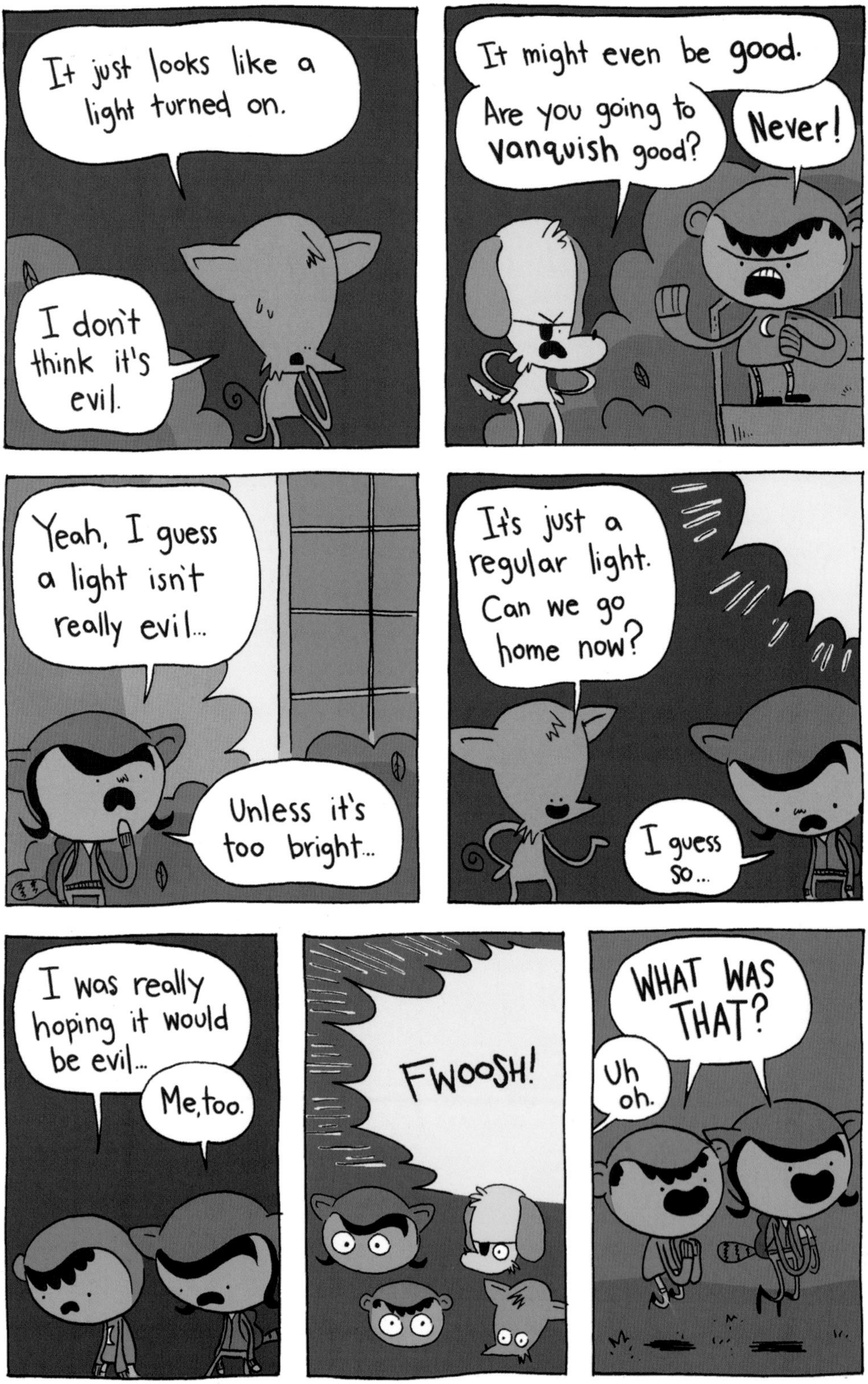
It just looks like a light turned on.
I don't think it's evil.
It might even be good.
Are you going to vanquish good?
Never!
Yeah, I guess a light isn't really evil...
Unless it's too bright...
It's just a regular light. Can we go home now?
I guess so...
I was really hoping it would be evil...
Me, too.
FWOOSH!
WHAT WAS THAT?
Uh oh.

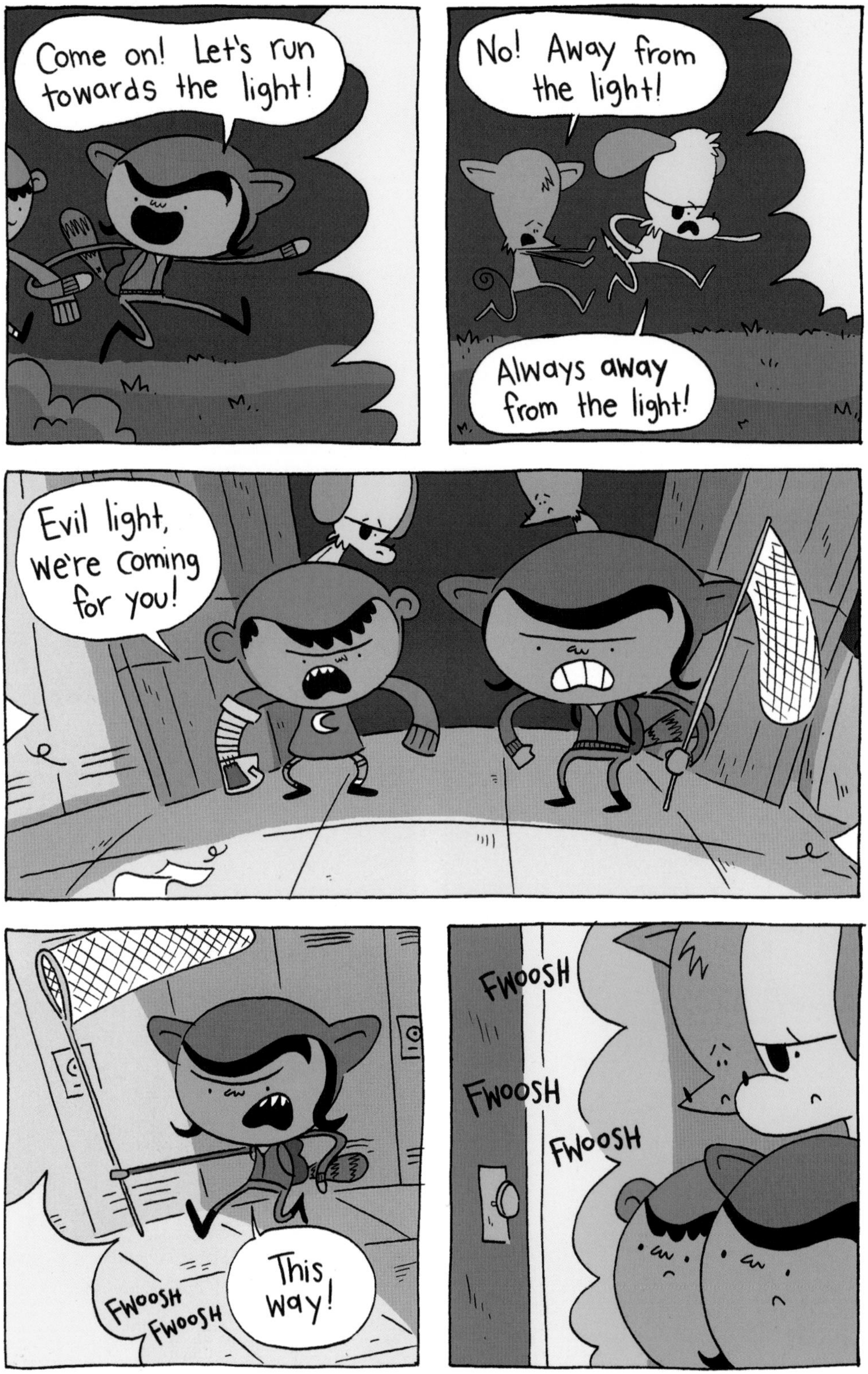
Come on! Let's run towards the light!
No! Away from the light!
Always away from the light!
Evil light, we're coming for you!
This way!
FWOOSH
FWOOSH
FWOOSH
FWOOSH
FWOOSH

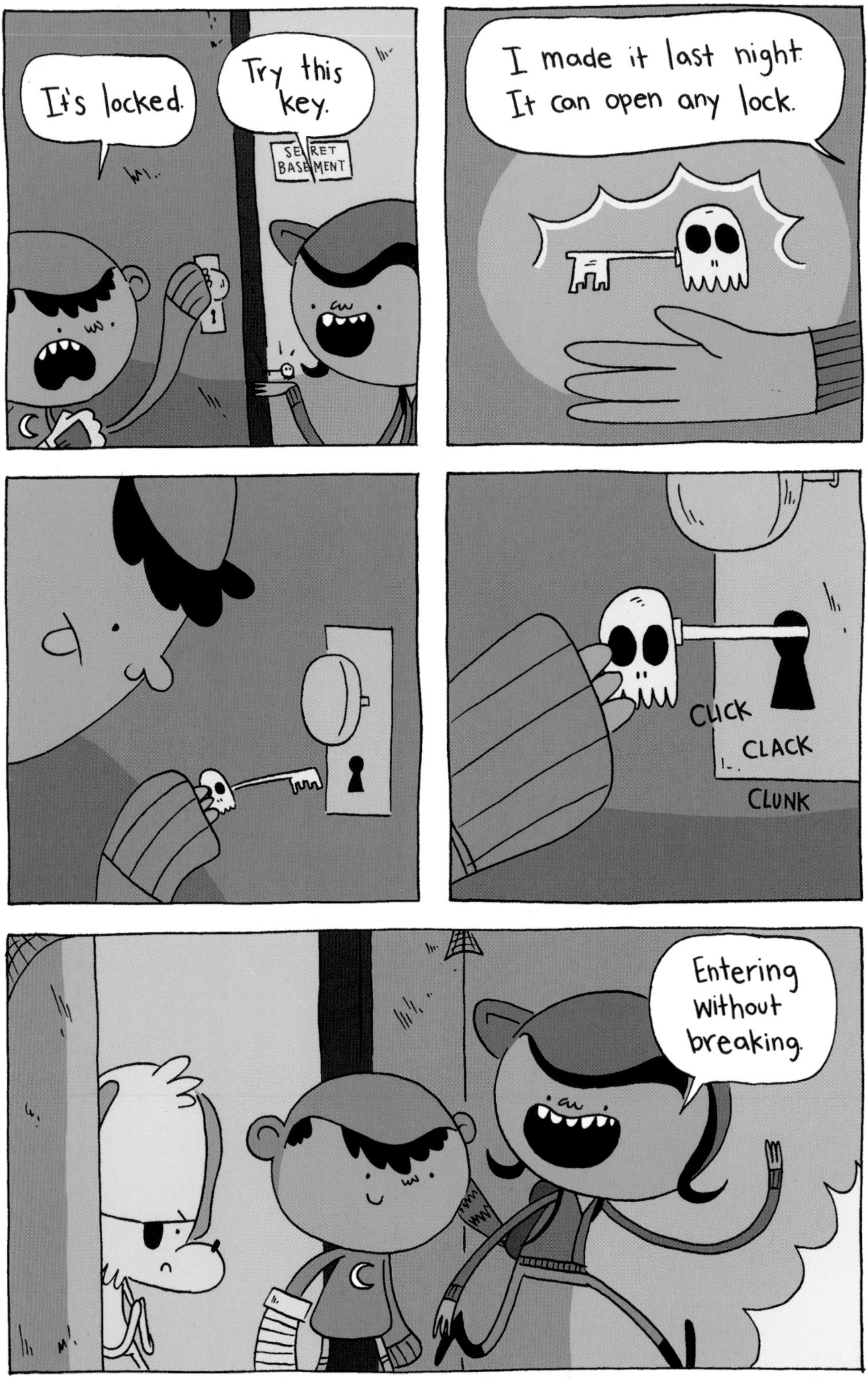
It's locked.
Try this key.
SECRET BASEMENT
I made it last night. It can open any lock.
CLICK
CLACK
CLUNK
Entering without breaking.

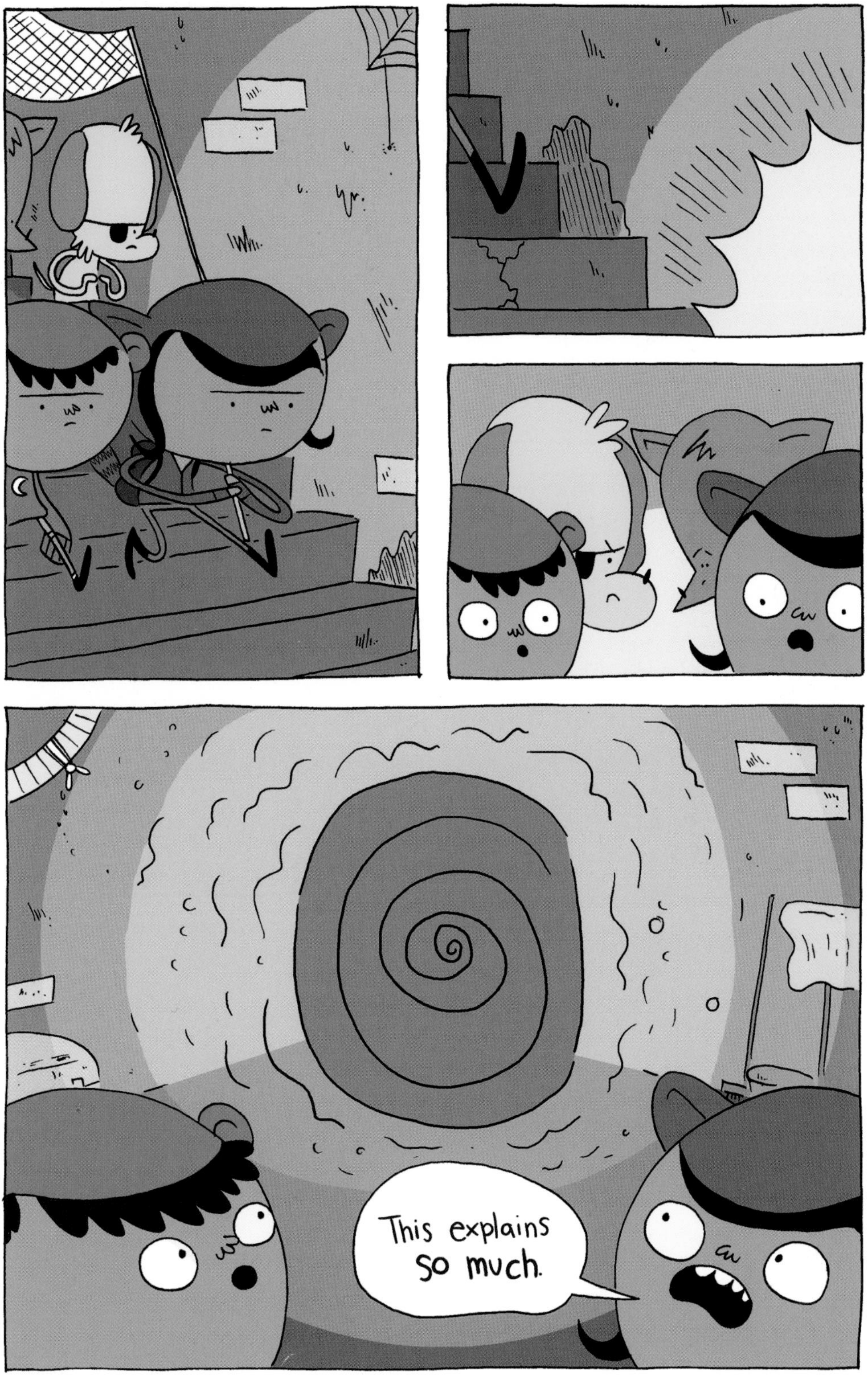
This explains so much.

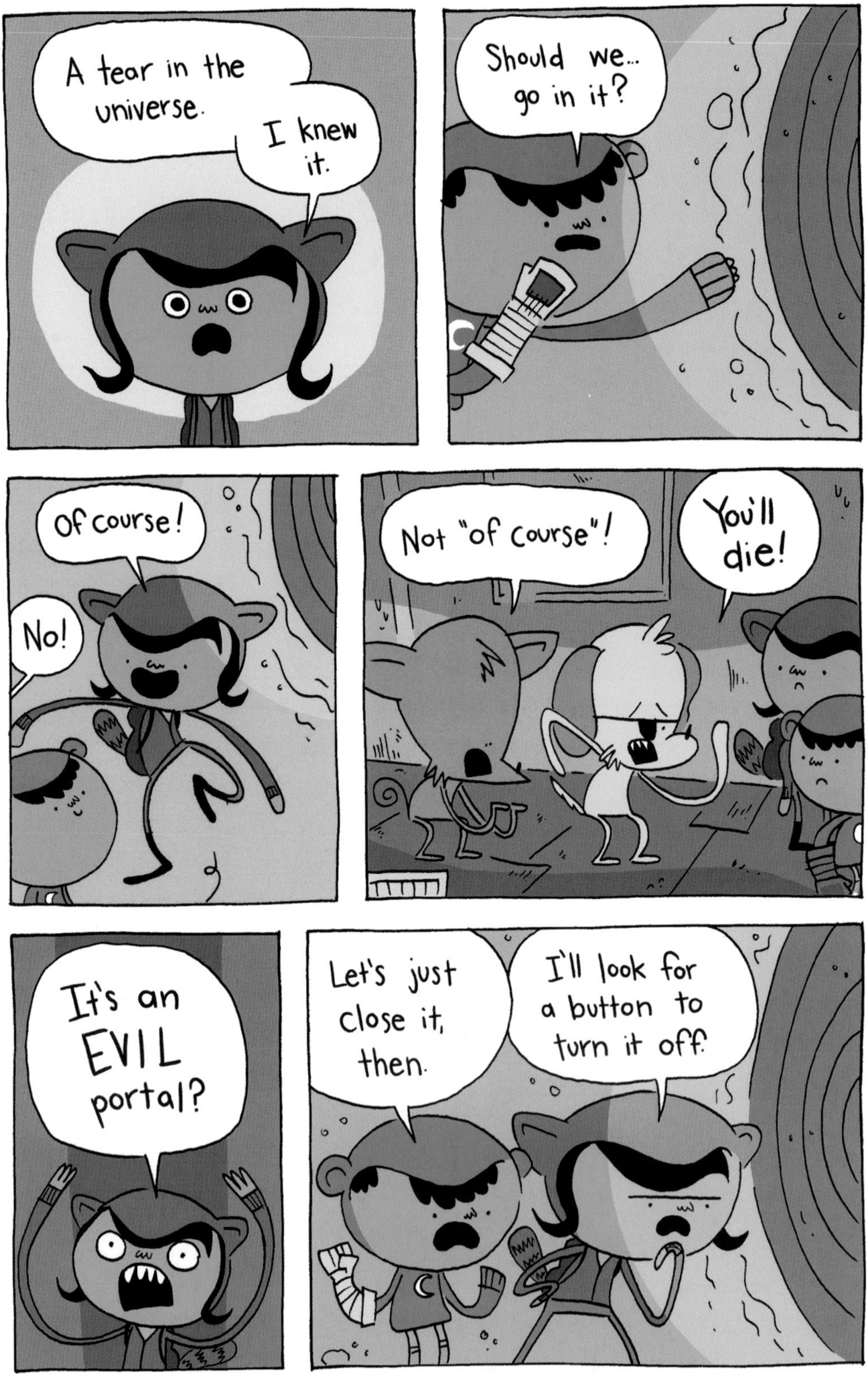
A tear in the universe.
I knew it.
Should we... go in it?
Of course!
No!
Not "of course"!
You'll die!
It's an EVIL portal?
Let's just close it, then.
I'll look for a button to turn it off.

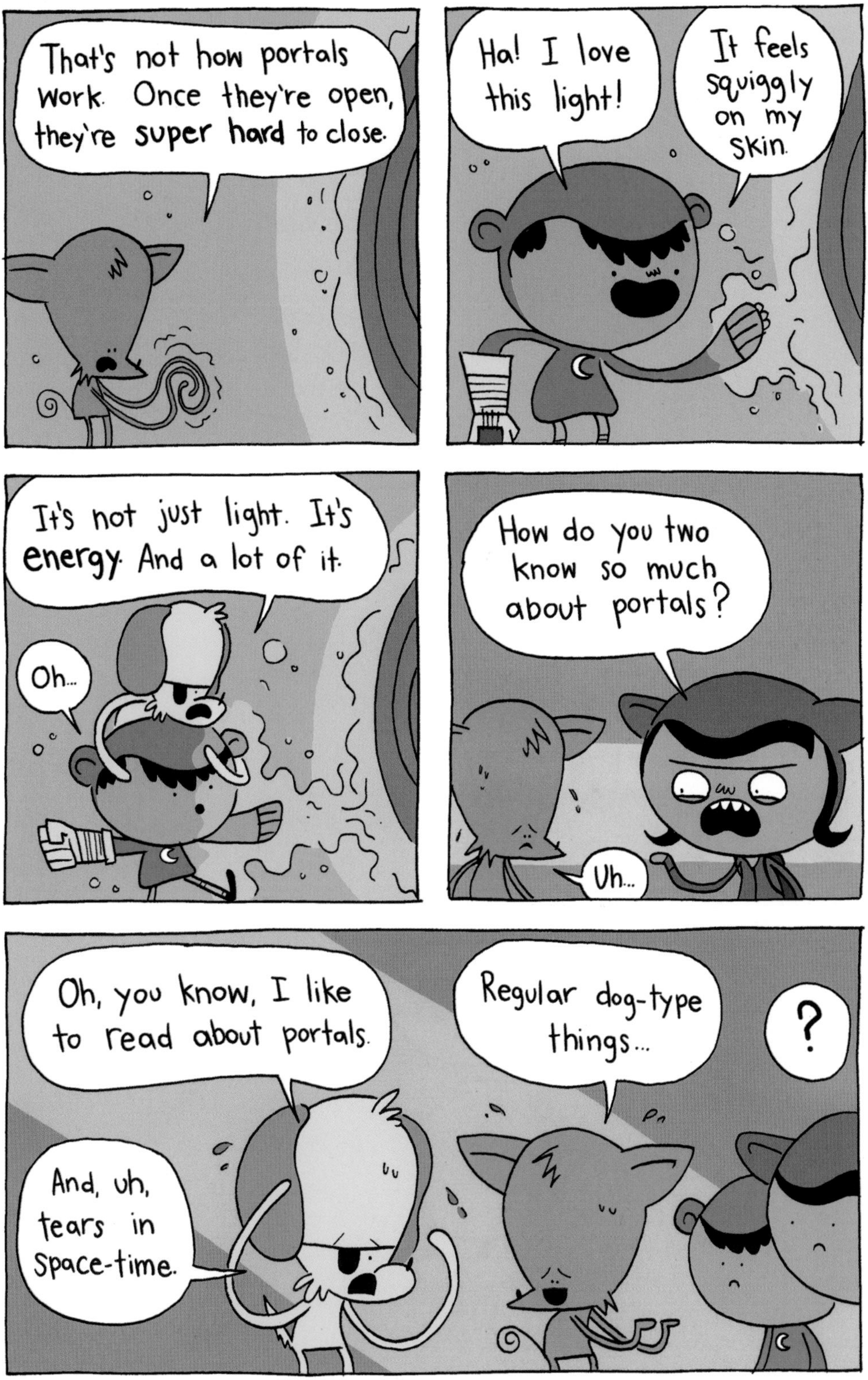
That's not how portals work. Once they're open, they're **super hard** to close.
Ha! I love this light!
It feels squiggly on my skin.
It's not just light. It's **energy**. And a lot of it.
Oh...
How do you two know so much about portals?
Uh...
Oh, you know, I like to read about portals.
Regular dog-type things...
?
And, uh, tears in space-time.

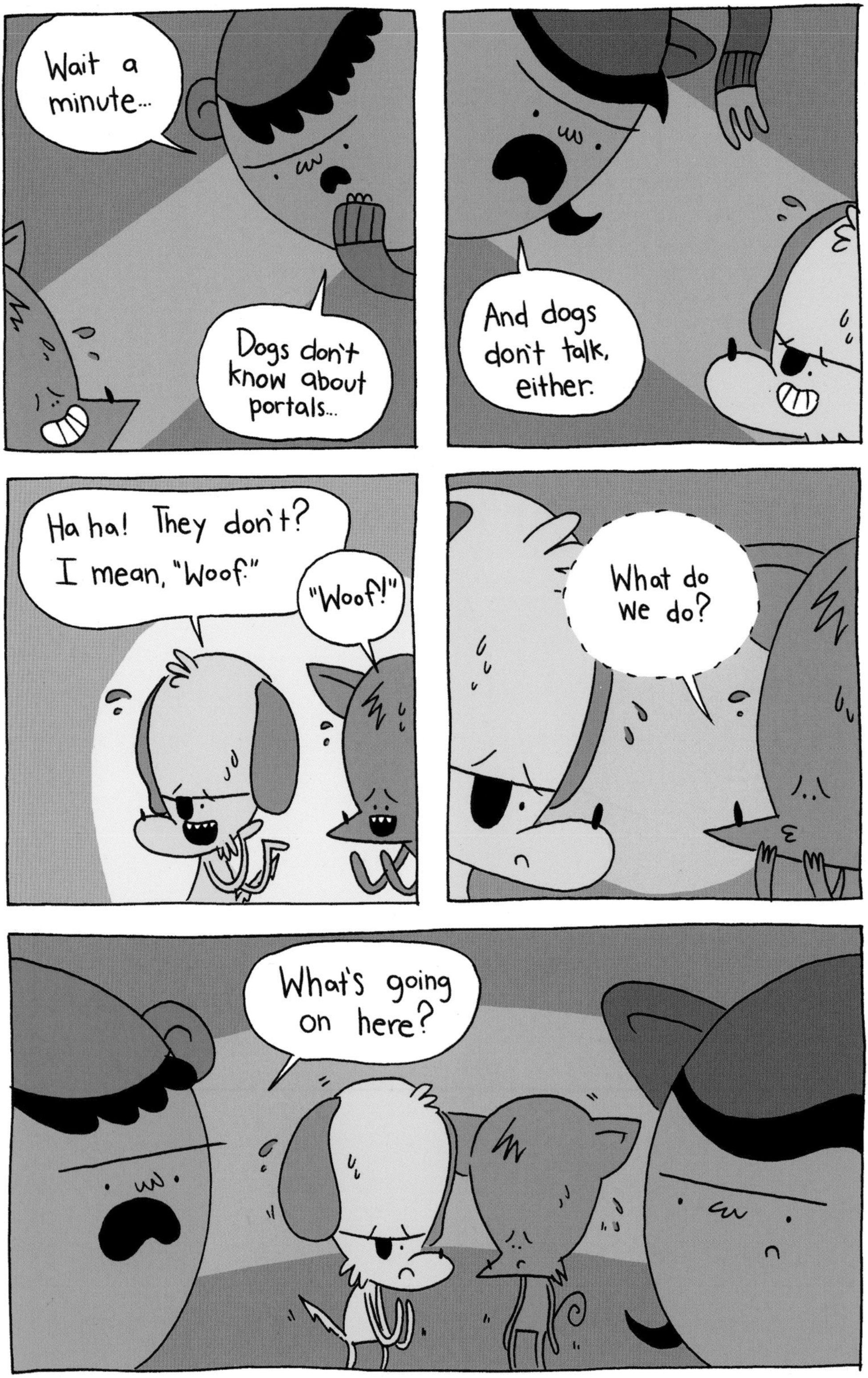

Wait a minute...
Dogs don't know about portals...
And dogs don't talk, either.
Ha ha! They don't? I mean, "Woof."
"Woof!"
What do we do?
What's going on here?

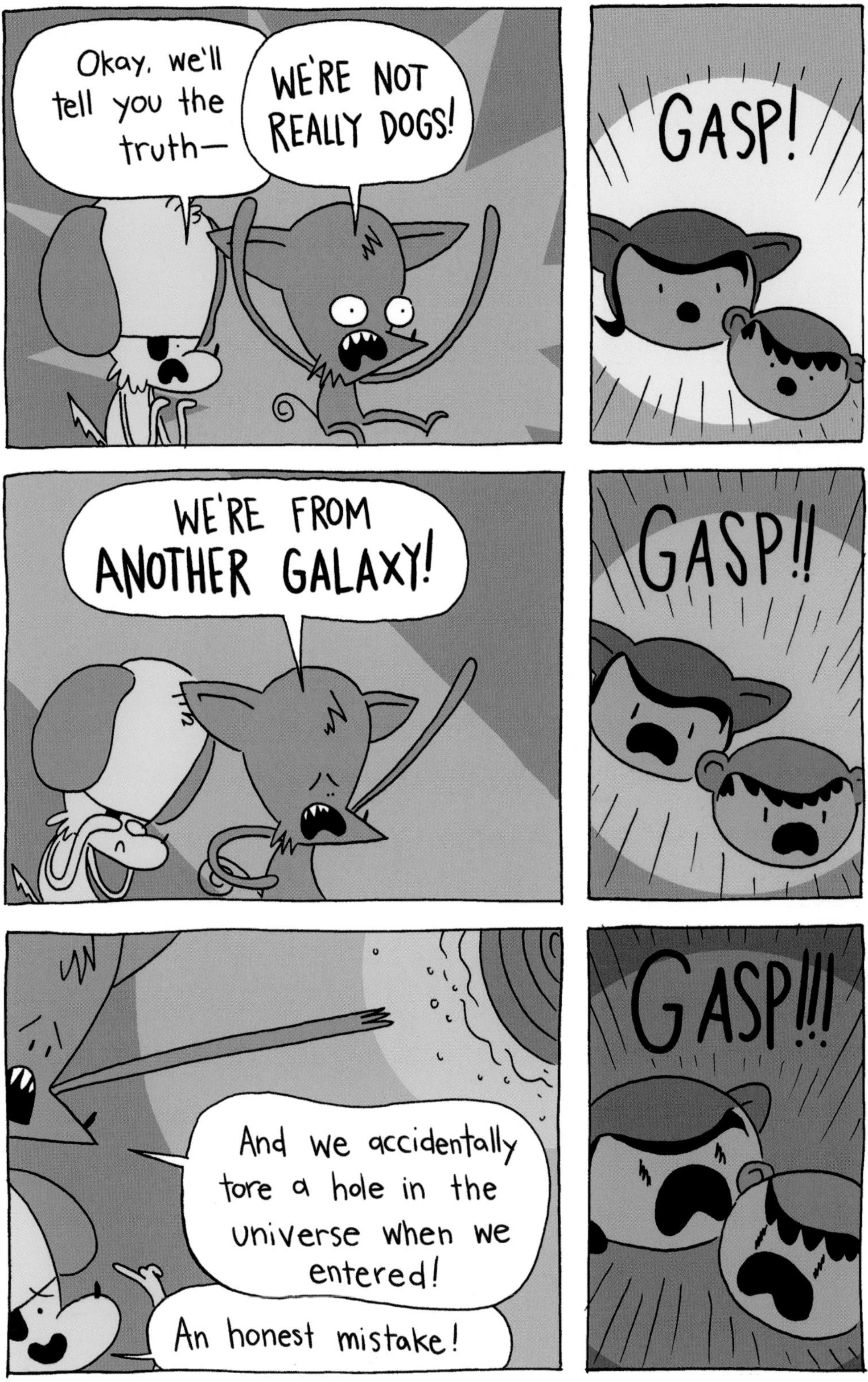
Okay, we'll tell you the truth—
WE'RE NOT REALLY DOGS!
GASP!
WE'RE FROM ANOTHER GALAXY!
GASP!!
And we accidentally tore a hole in the universe when we entered!
An honest mistake!
GASP!!!

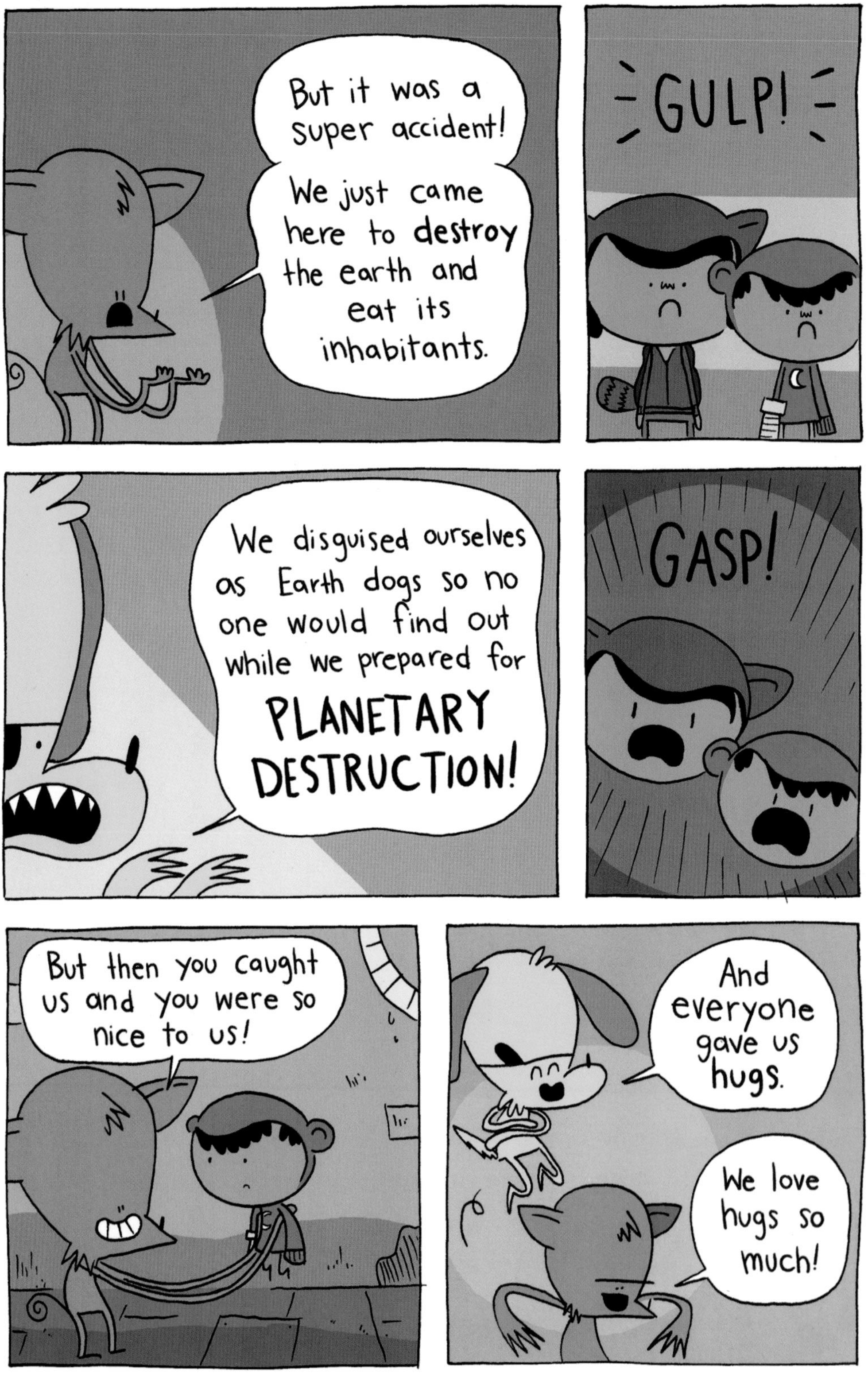
But it was a super accident!
We just came here to destroy the earth and eat its inhabitants.
GULP!
We disguised ourselves as Earth dogs so no one would find out while we prepared for PLANETARY DESTRUCTION!
GASP!
But then you caught us and you were so nice to us!
And everyone gave us hugs.
We love hugs so much!

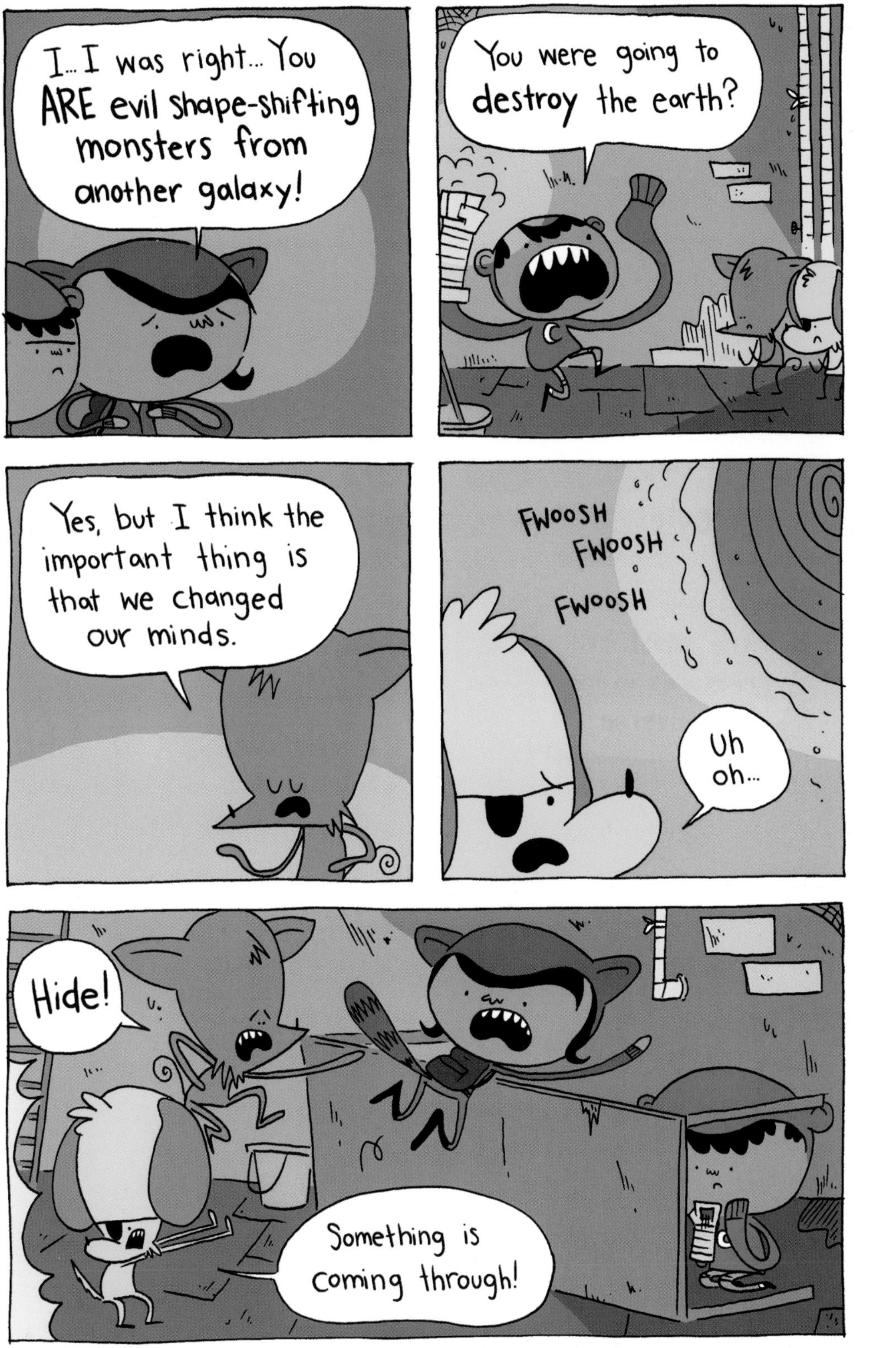
I... I was right... You ARE evil shape-shifting monsters from another galaxy!
You were going to destroy the earth?
Yes, but I think the important thing is that we changed our minds.
FWOOSH
FWOOSH
FWOOSH
Uh oh...
Hide!
Something is coming through!

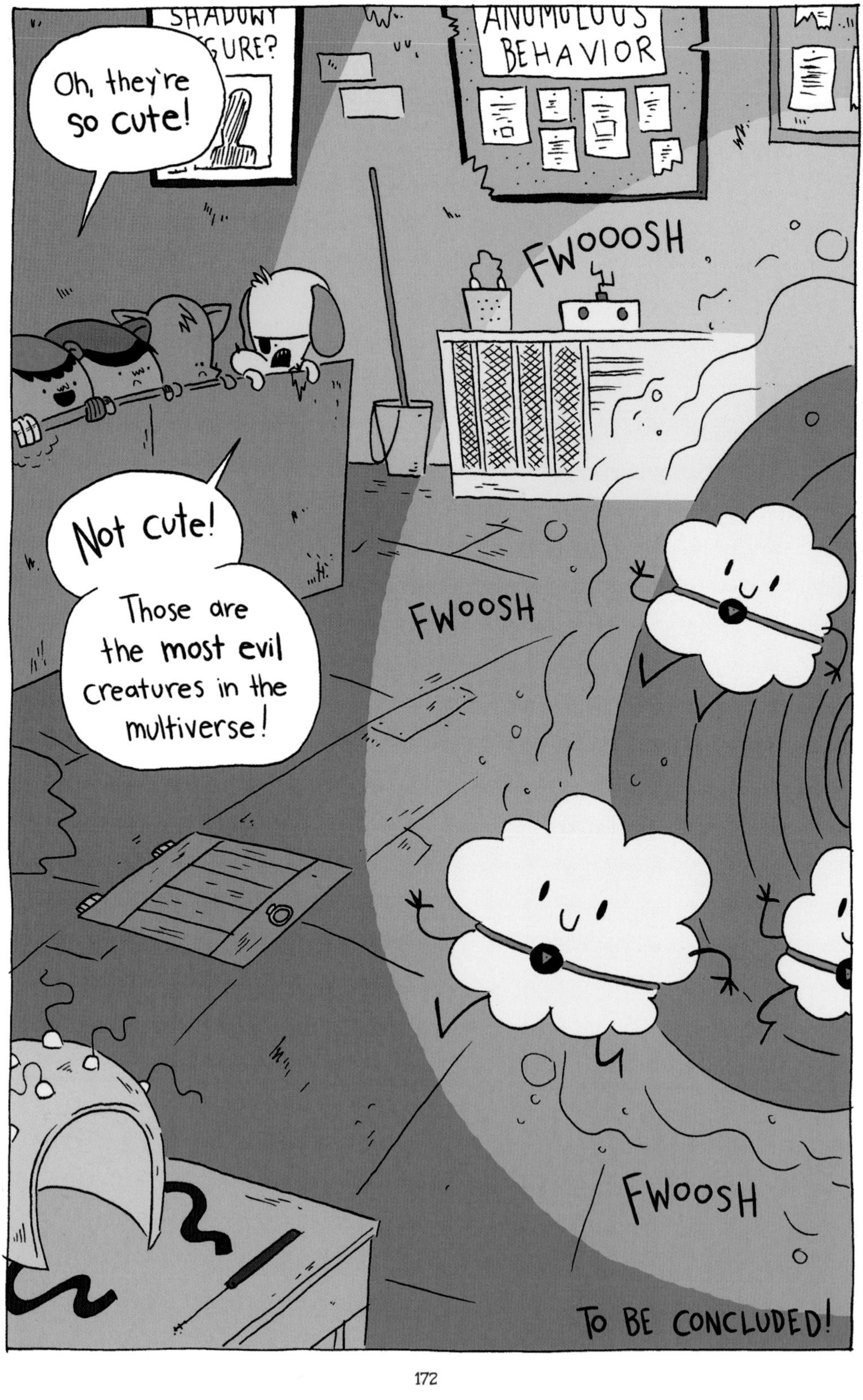
SHADOWY
GURE?
ANOMOLOUS
BEHAVIOR
Oh, they're so cute!
FWOOOSH
Not cute!
Those are the most evil creatures in the multiverse!
FWOOSH
FWOOSH
TO BE CONCLUDED!

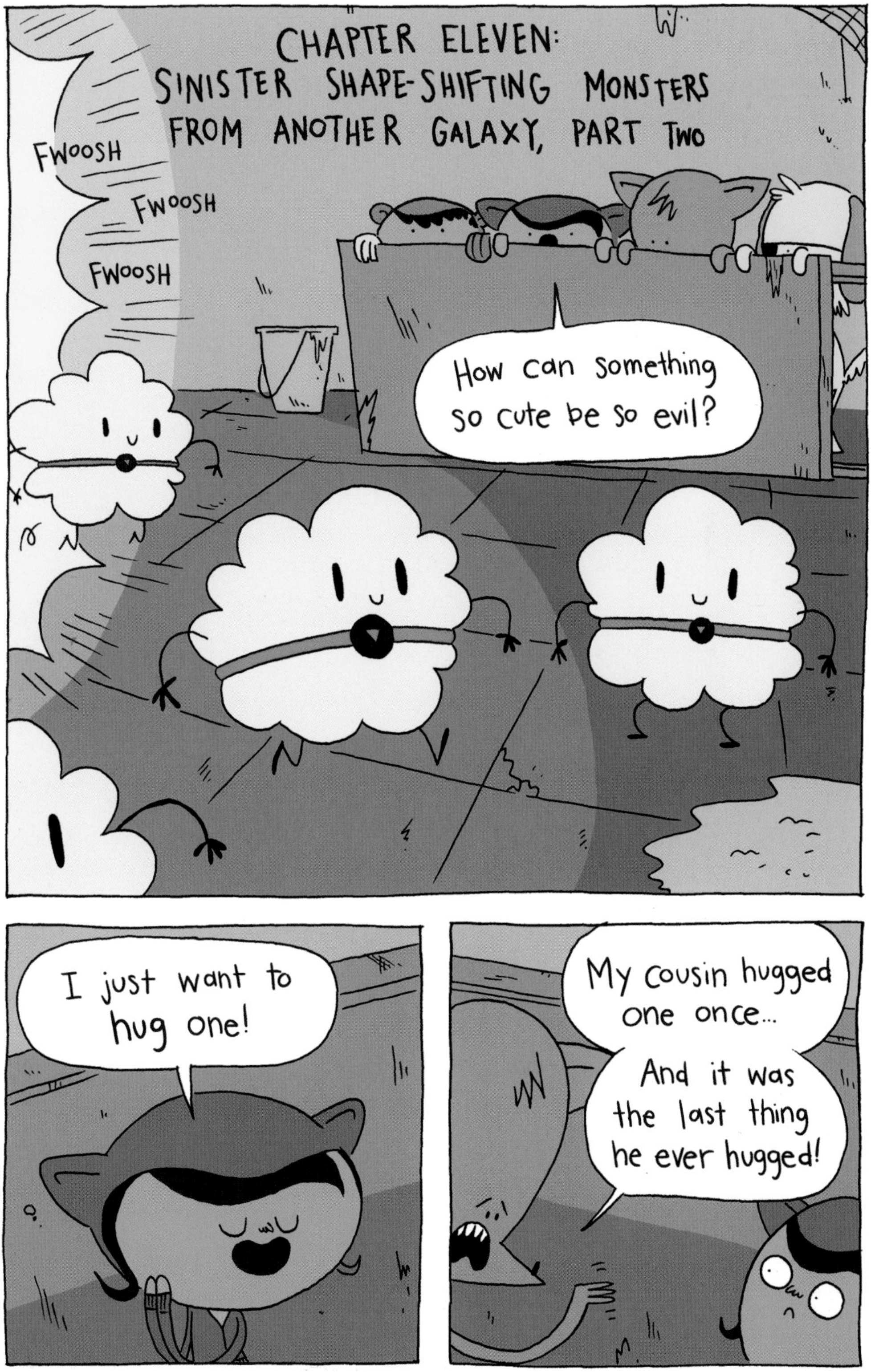

CHAPTER ELEVEN:
SINISTER SHAPE-SHIFTING MONSTERS FROM ANOTHER GALAXY, PART TWO
FWOOSH
FWOOSH
FWOOSH
How can something so cute be so evil?
I just want to hug one!
My cousin hugged one once...
And it was the last thing he ever hugged!

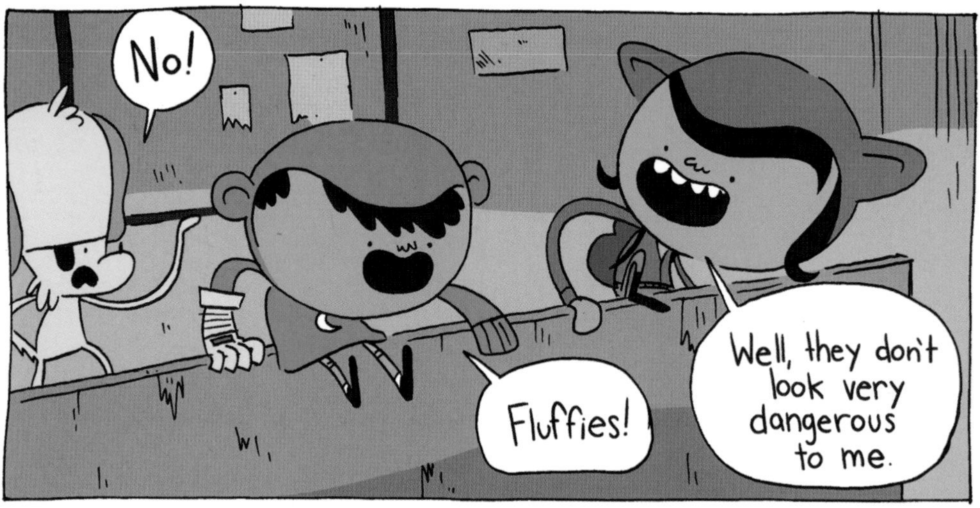
No!
Fluffies!
Well, they don't look very dangerous to me.

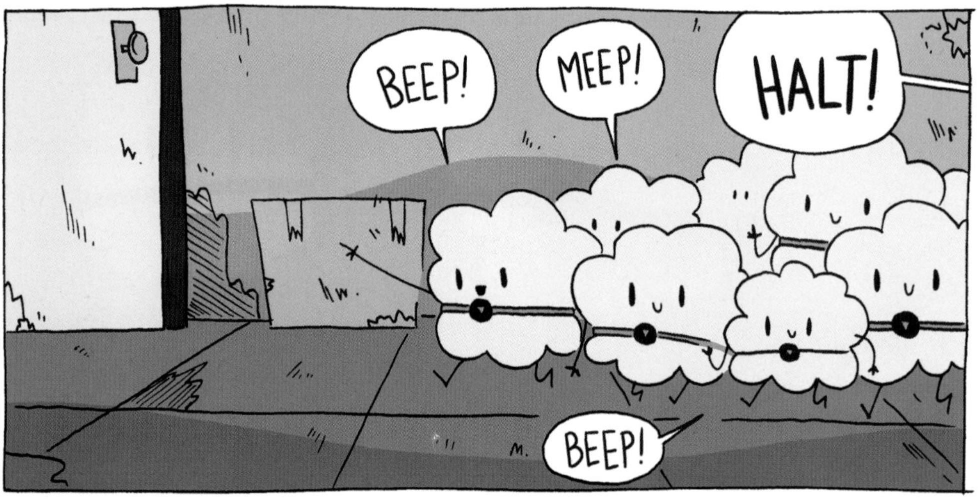
BEEP!
MEEP!
HALT!
BEEP!

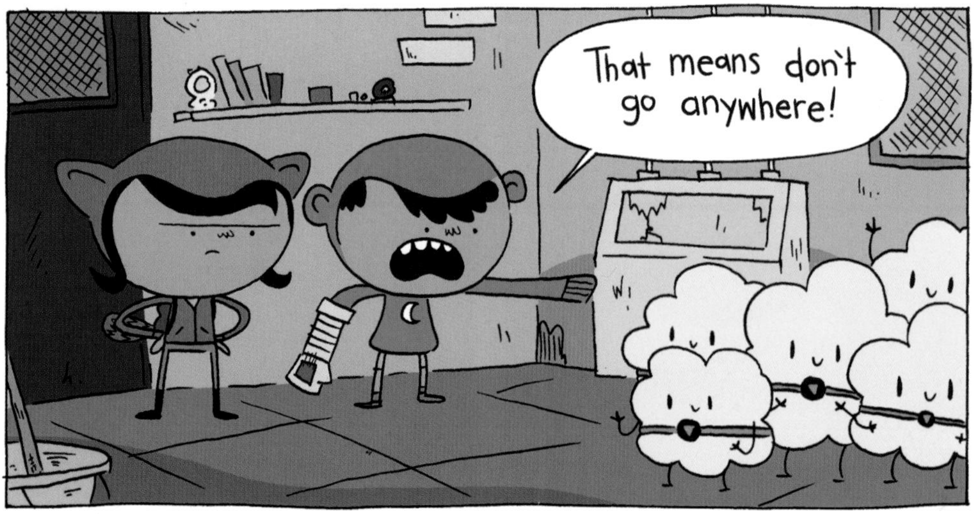
That means don't go anywhere!

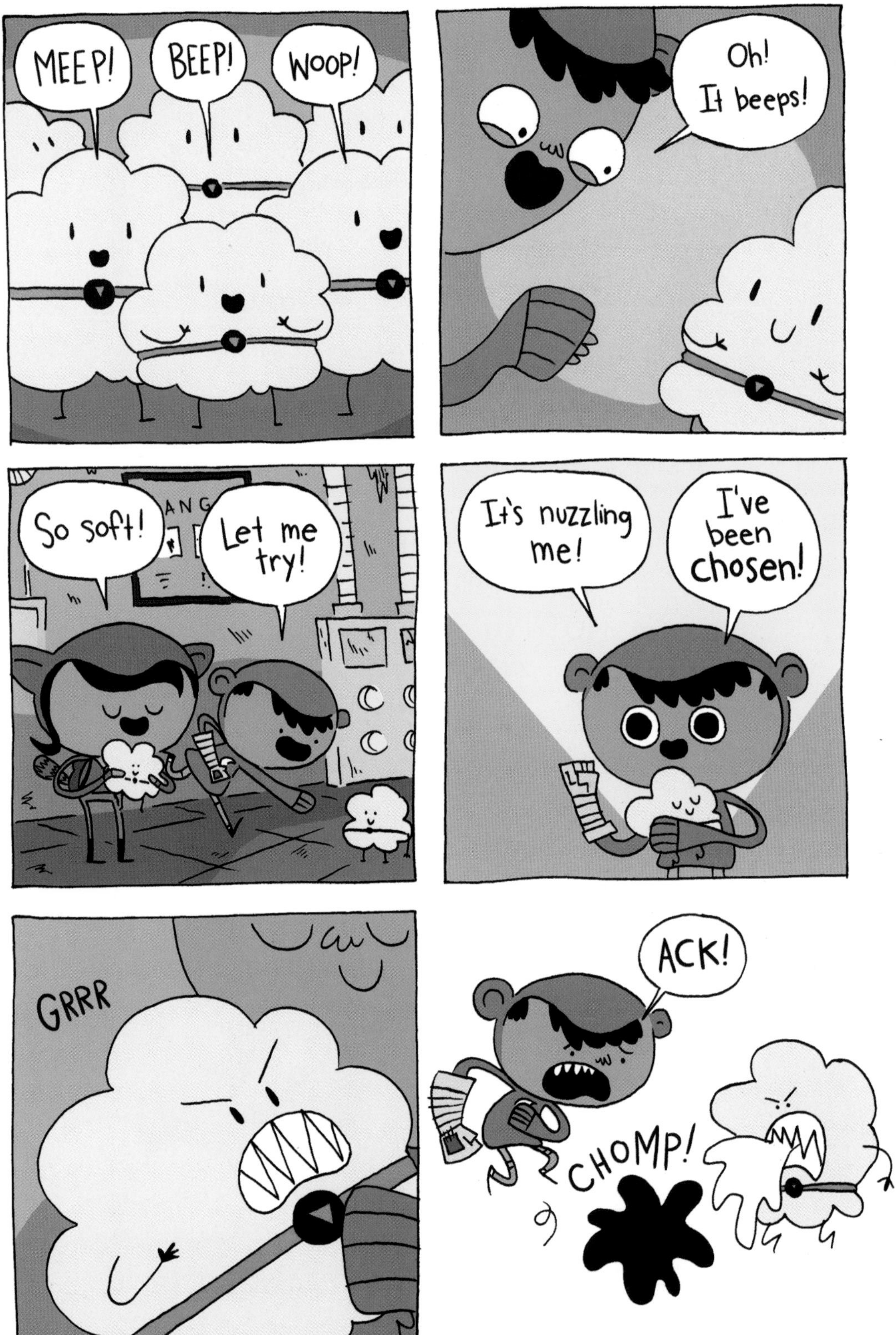
MEEP!
BEEP!
WOOP!
Oh! It beeps!
So soft!
Let me try!
It's nuzzling me!
I've been chosen!
GRRR
ACK!
CHOMP!

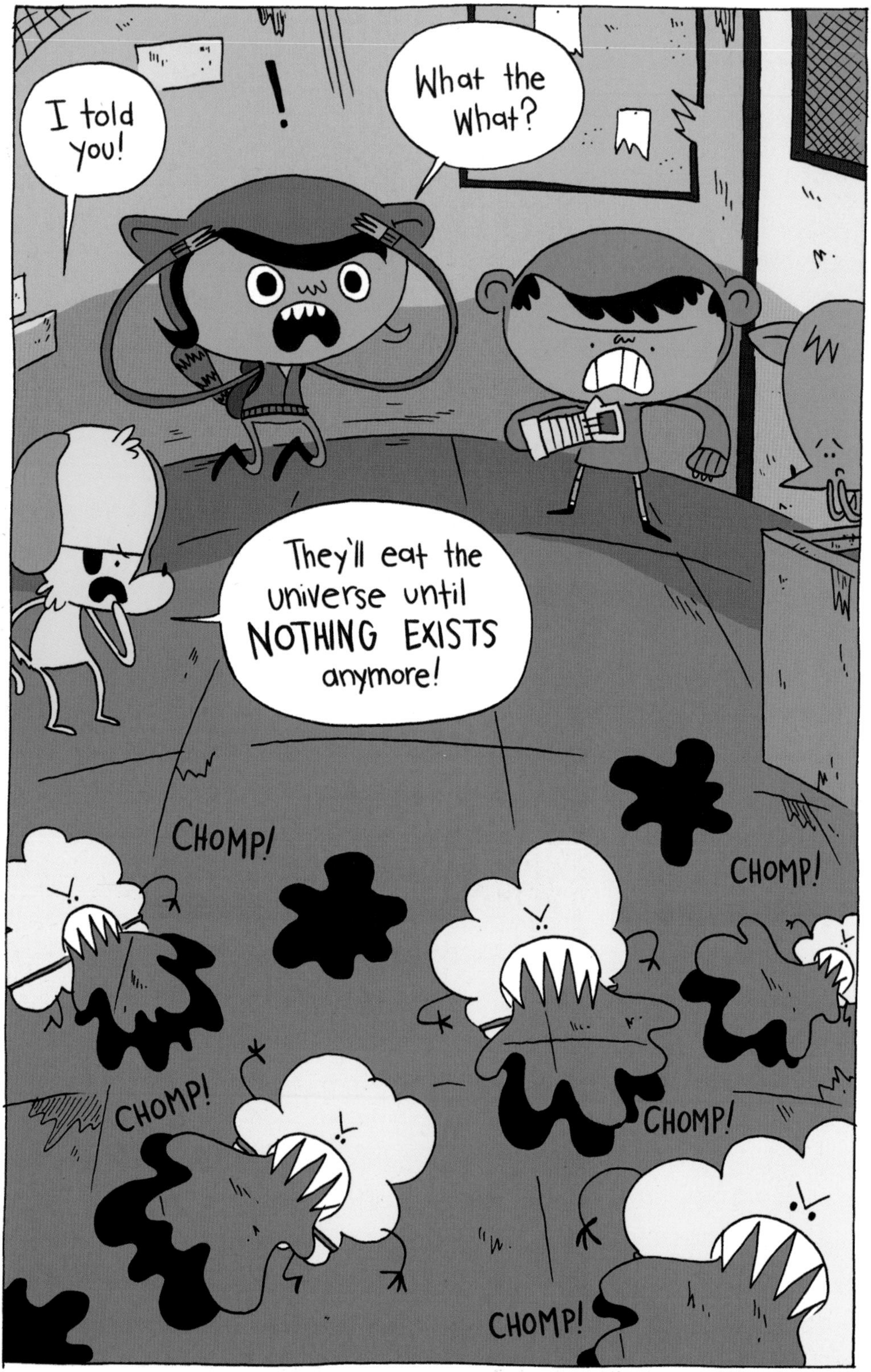
I told you!
!
What the What?
They'll eat the universe until NOTHING EXISTS anymore!
CHOMP!
CHOMP!
CHOMP!
CHOMP!
CHOMP!

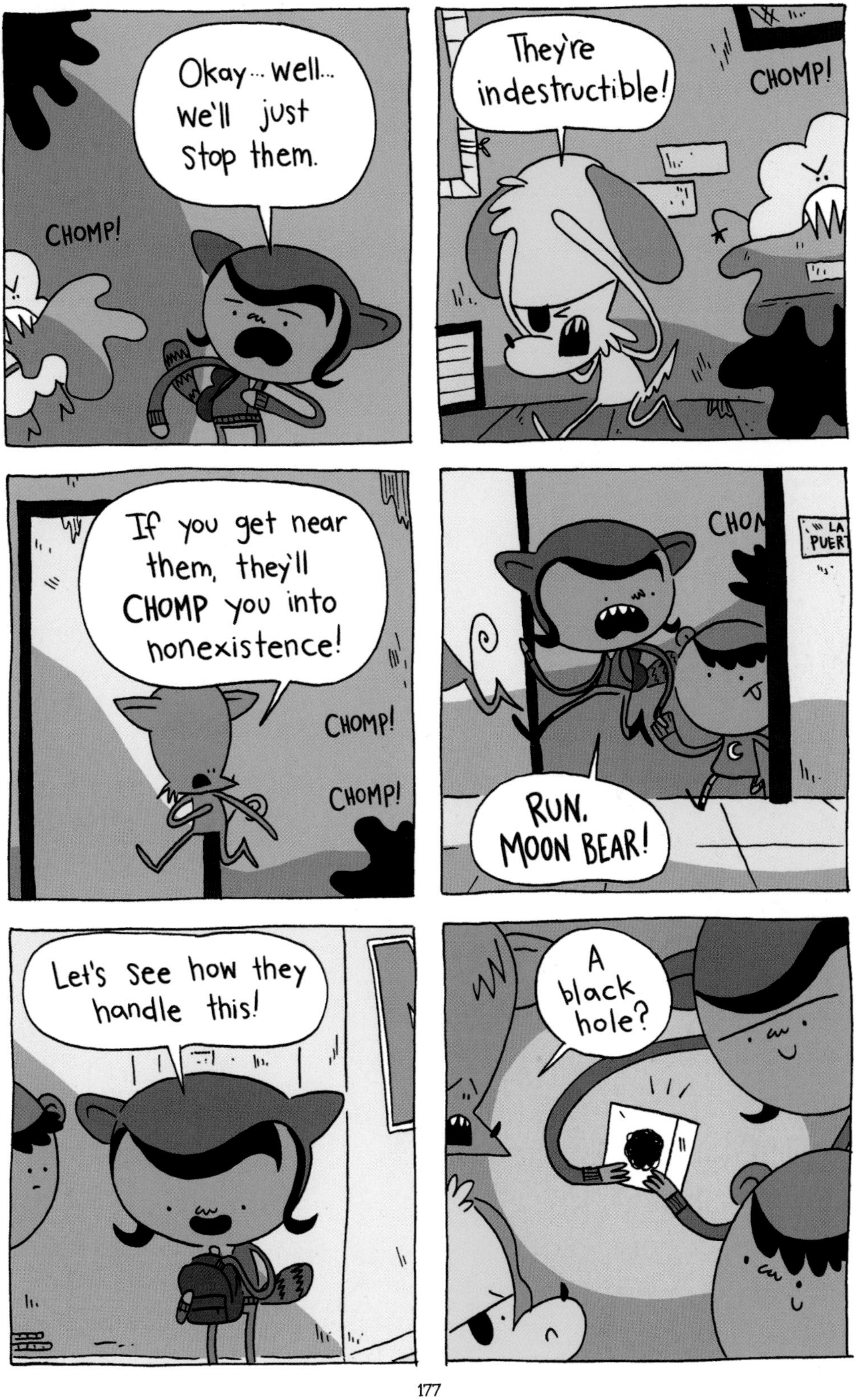
Okay... well... we'll just stop them.
CHOMP!
They're indestructible!
CHOMP!
If you get near them, they'll CHOMP you into nonexistence!
CHOMP!
CHOMP!
CHOM
LA PUERT
RUN, MOON BEAR!
Let's see how they handle this!
A black hole?

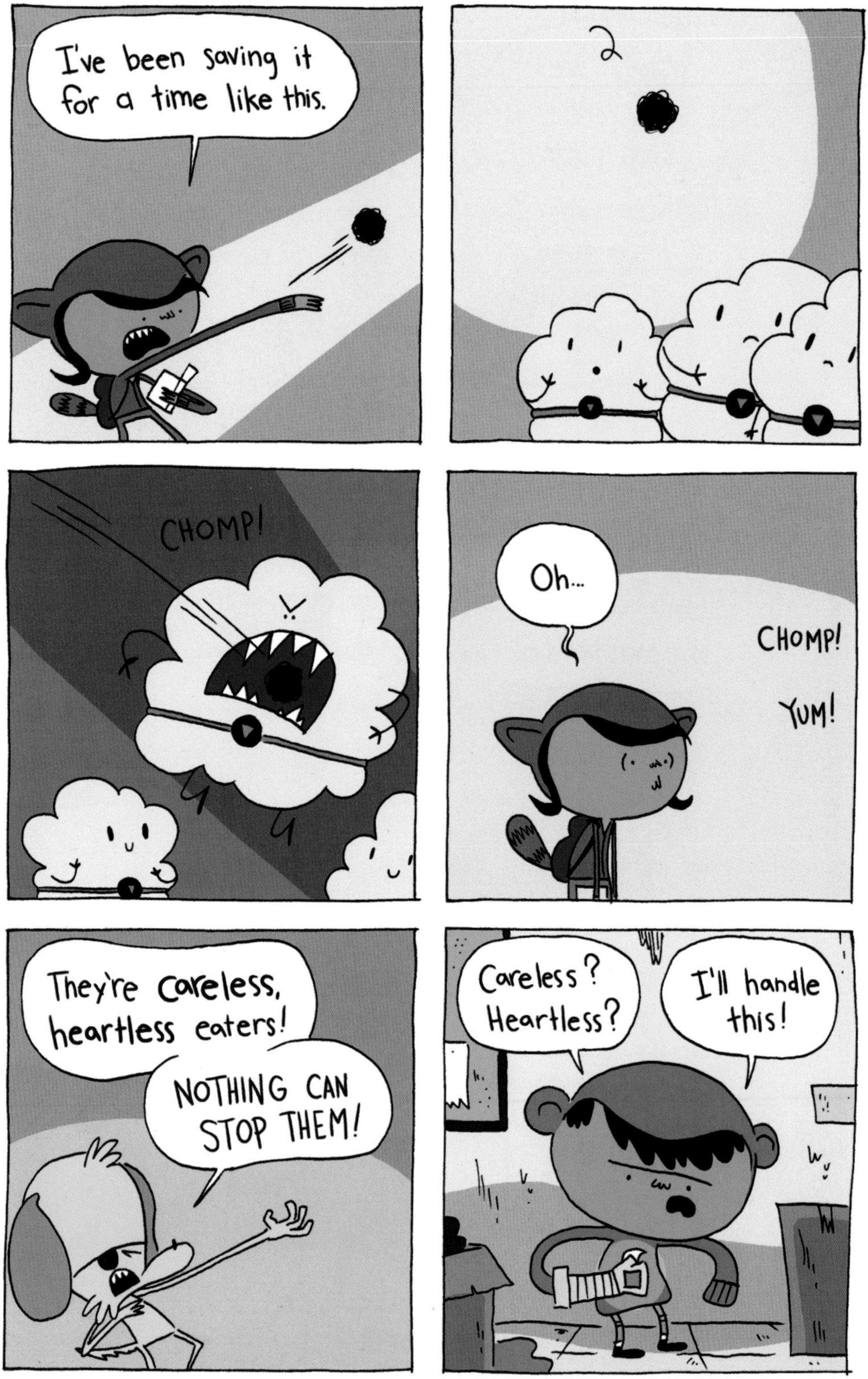
I've been saving it for a time like this.
CHOMP!
Oh...
CHOMP!
YUM!
They're careless, heartless eaters!
NOTHING CAN STOP THEM!
Careless? Heartless?
I'll handle this!

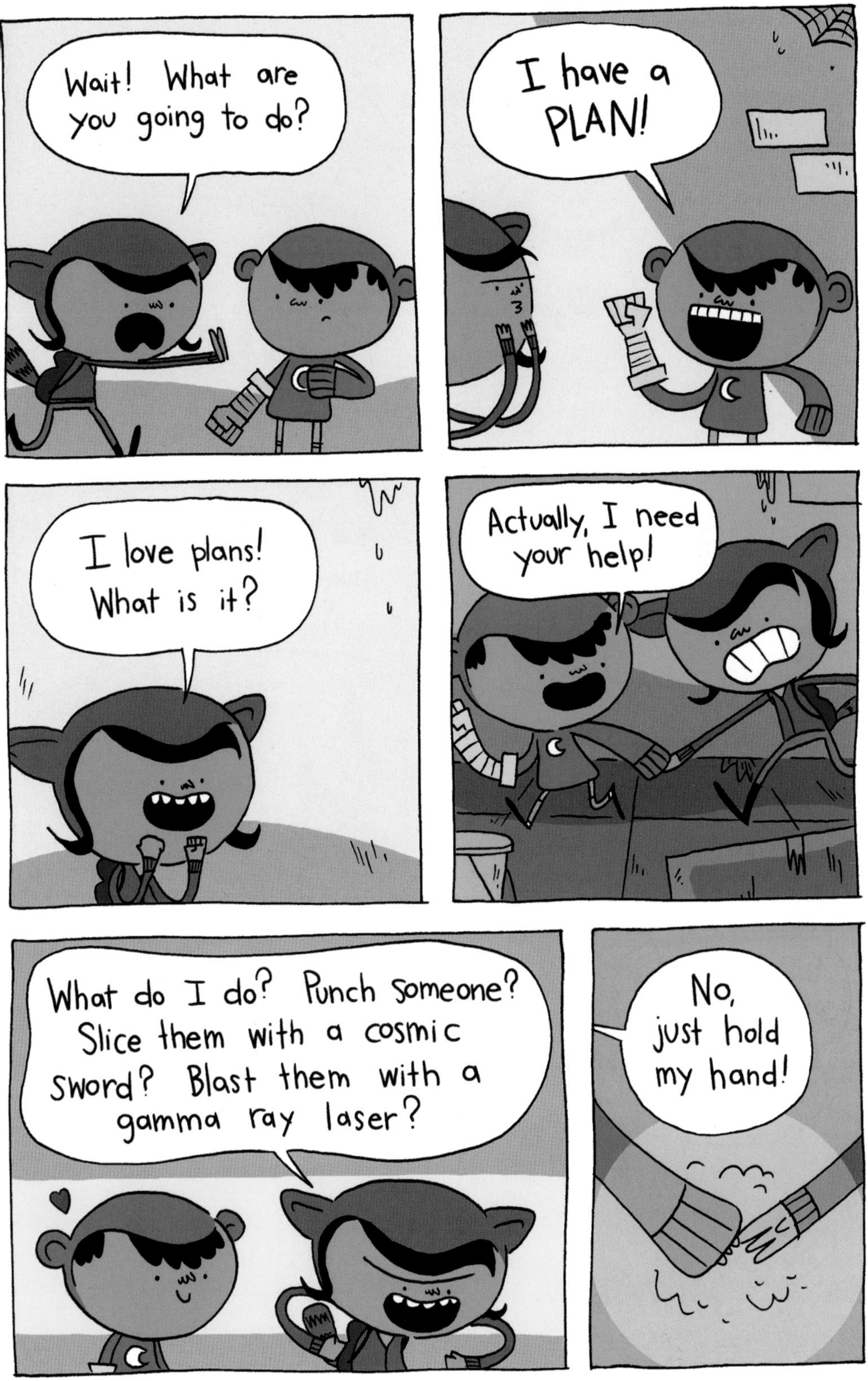
Wait! What are you going to do?
I have a PLAN!
I love plans! What is it?
Actually, I need your help!
What do I do? Punch someone? Slice them with a cosmic sword? Blast them with a gamma ray laser?
No, just hold my hand!

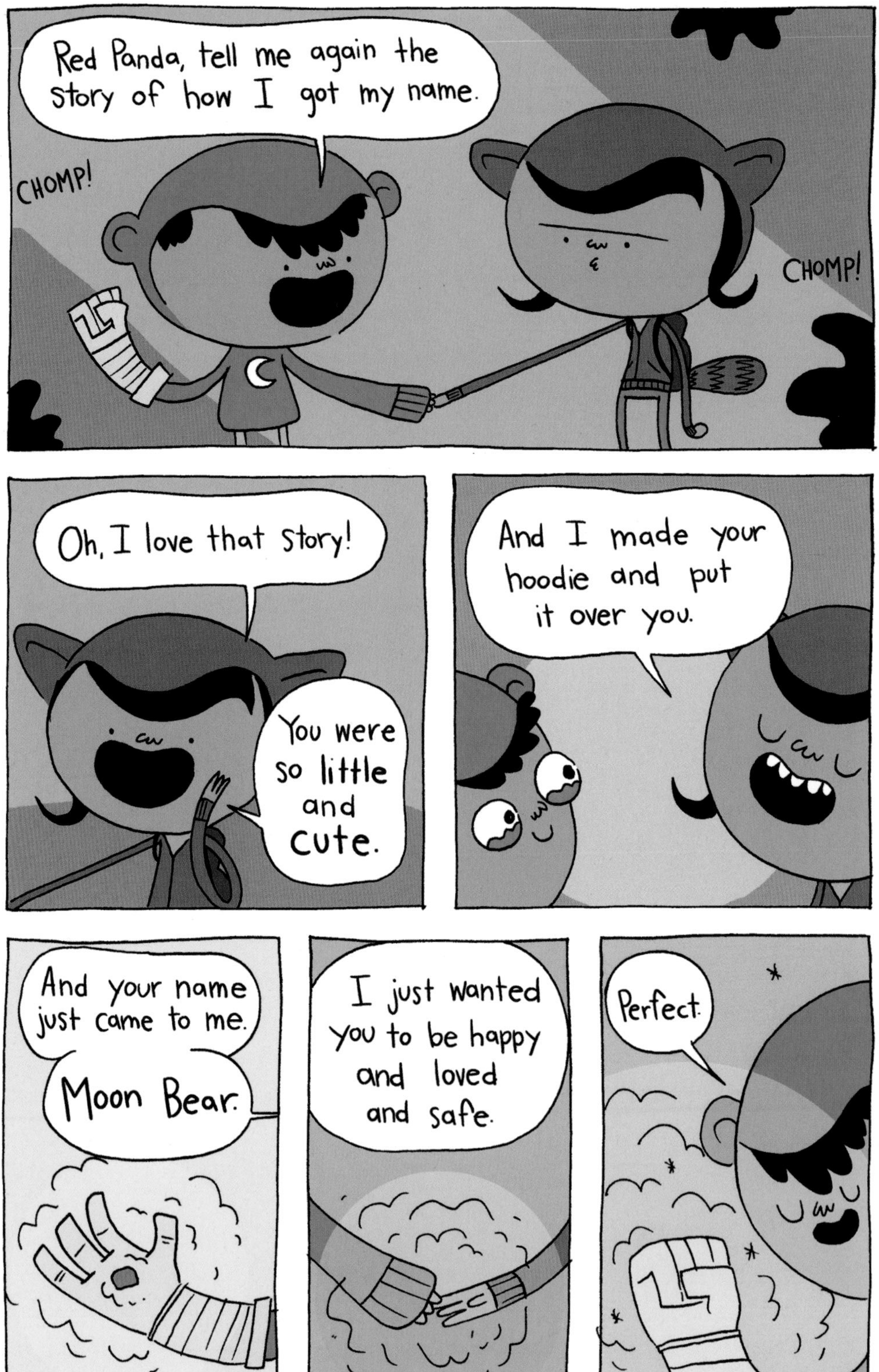
Red Panda, tell me again the story of how I got my name.
CHOMP!
CHOMP!
Oh, I love that story!
You were so little and cute.
And I made your hoodie and put it over you.
And your name just came to me.
Moon Bear.
I just wanted you to be happy and loved and safe.
Perfect.

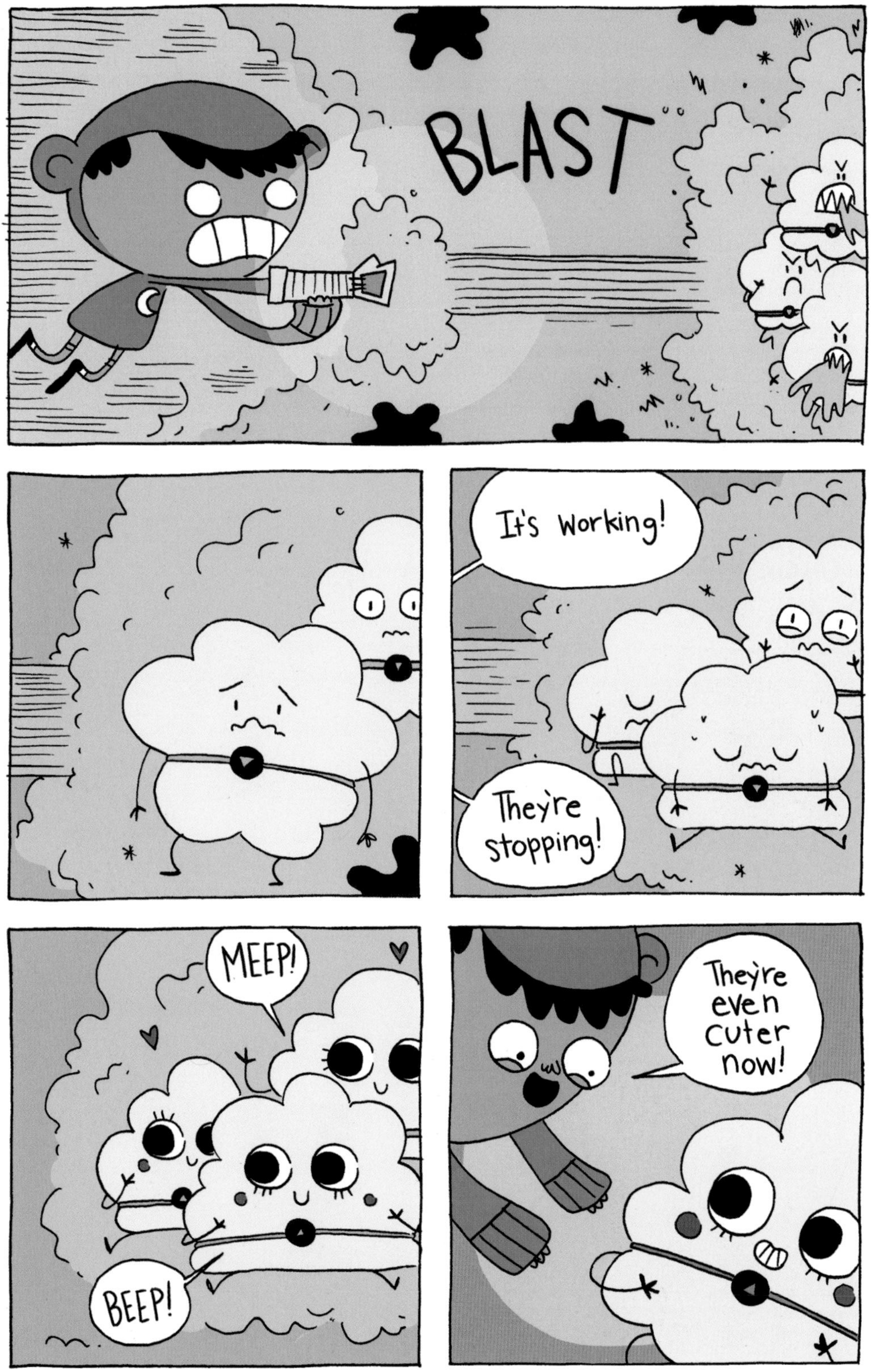

BLAST
It's working!
They're stopping!
MEEP!
BEEP!
They're even cuter now!

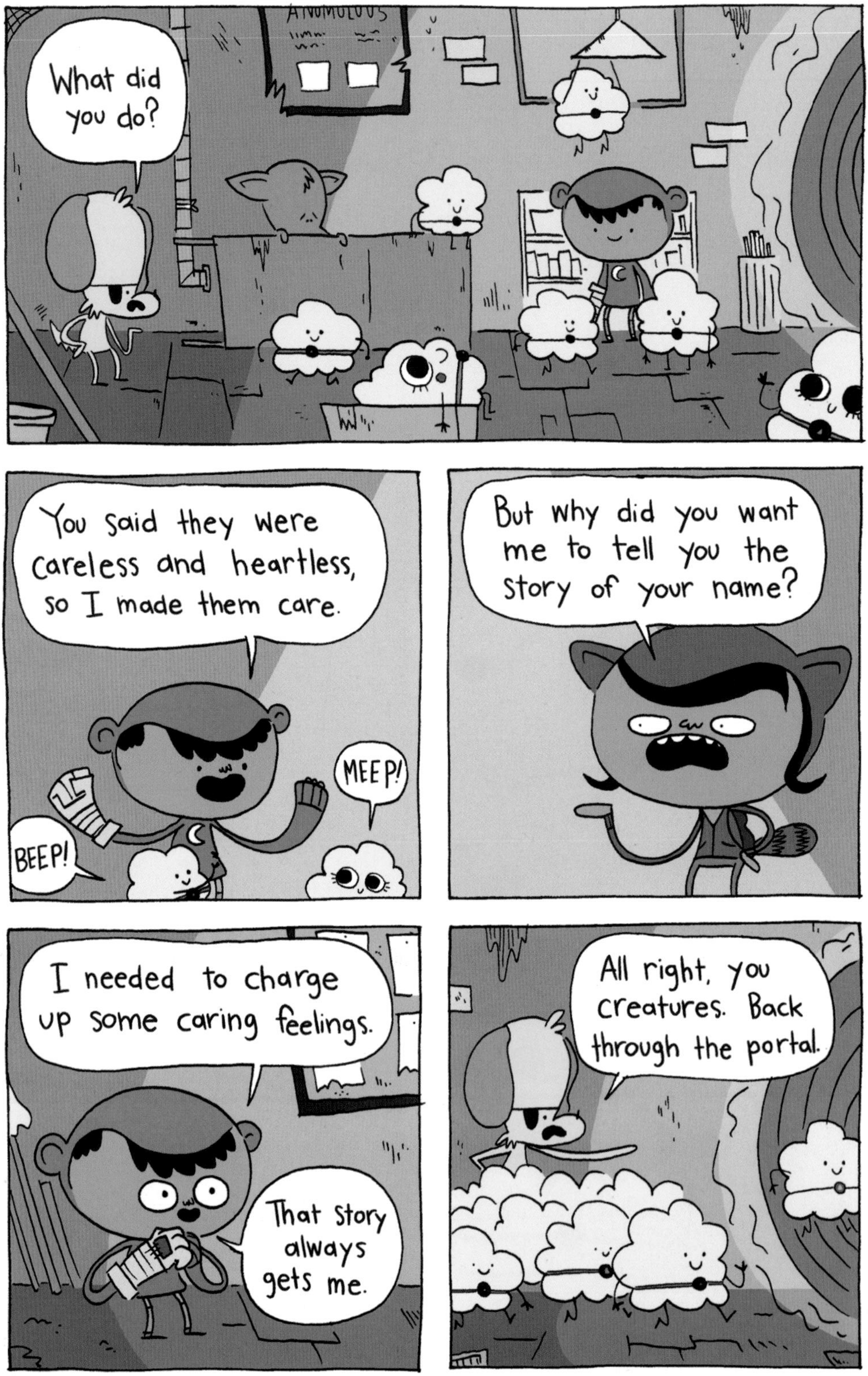
What did you do?
You said they were careless and heartless, so I made them care.
MEEP!
BEEP!
But why did you want me to tell you the story of your name?
I needed to charge up some caring feelings.
That story always gets me.
All right, you creatures. Back through the portal.

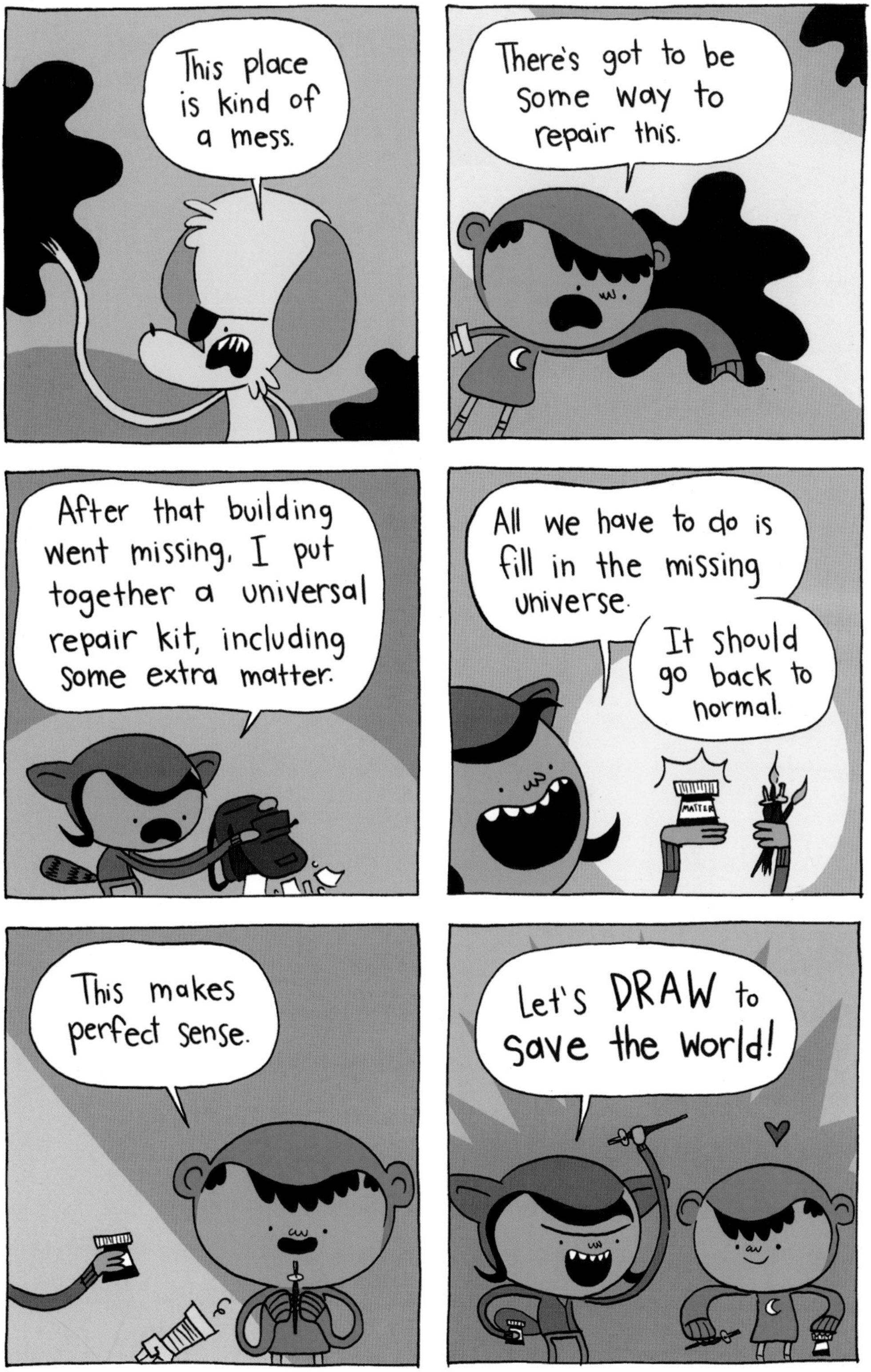
This place is kind of a mess.
There's got to be some way to repair this.
After that building went missing, I put together a universal repair kit, including some extra matter.
All we have to do is fill in the missing universe.
It should go back to normal.
MATTER
This makes perfect sense.
Let's DRAW to save the world!

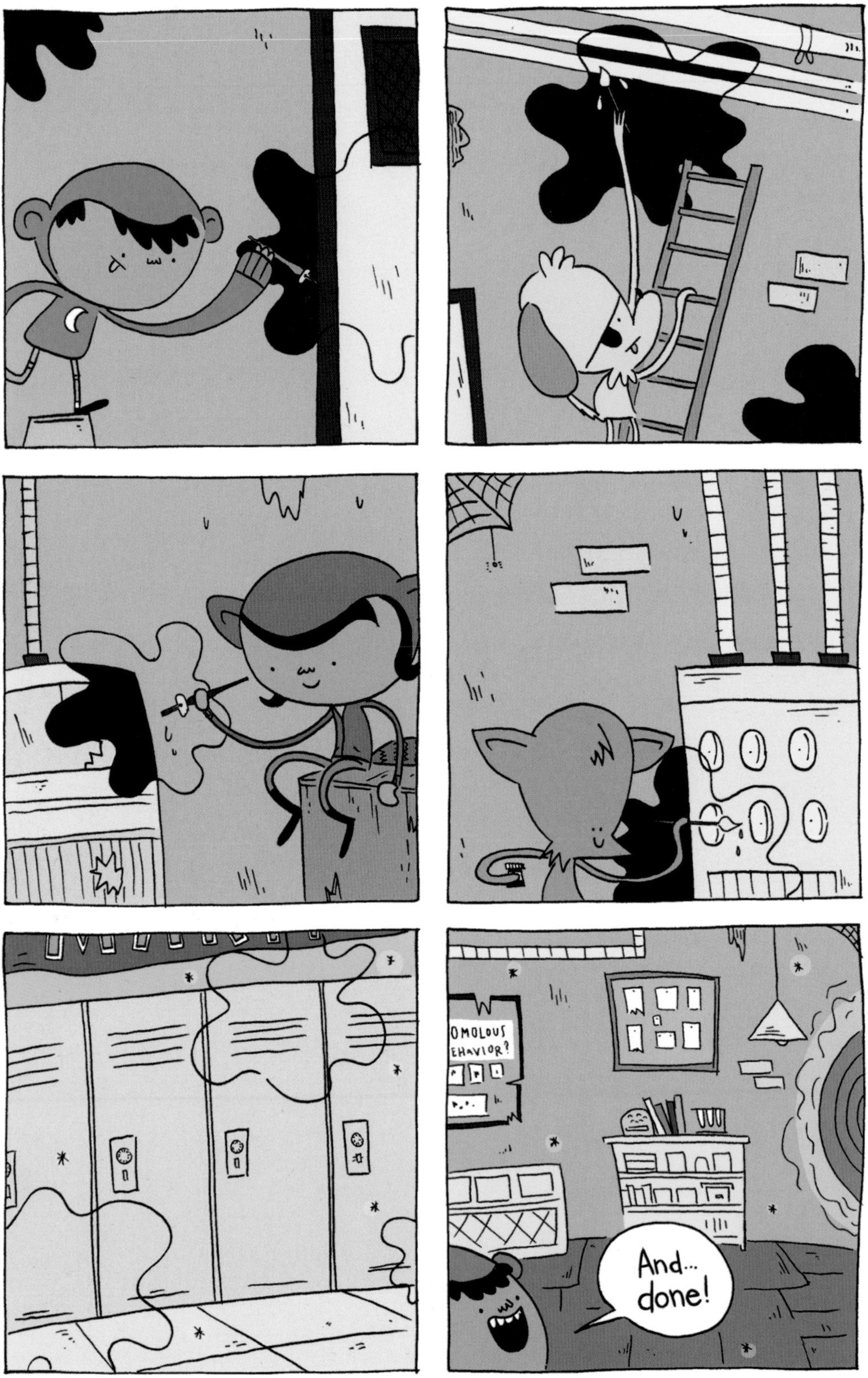
OMOLOUS
EHAVIOR?
And... done!

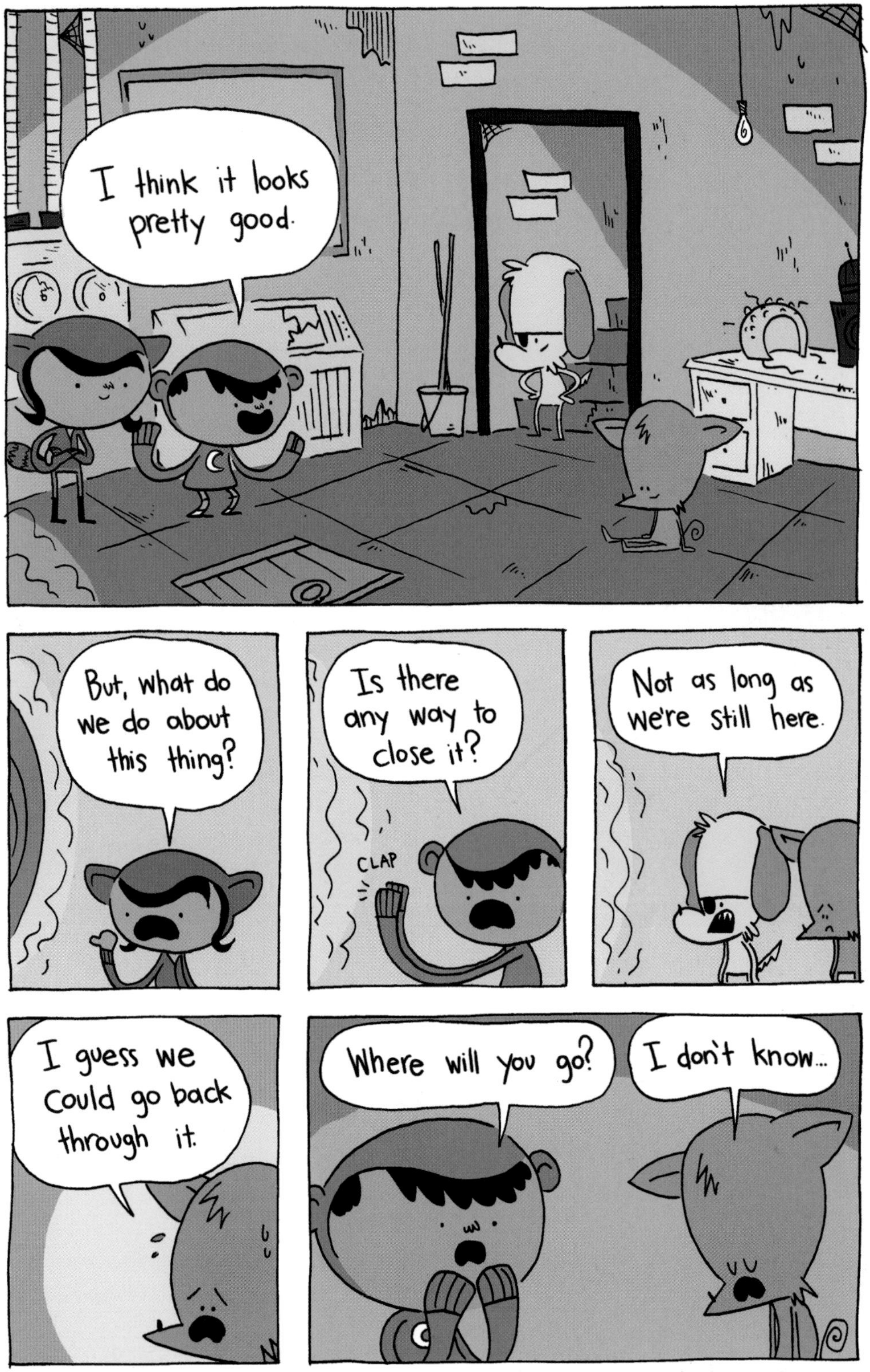
I think it looks pretty good.
But, what do we do about this thing?
Is there any way to close it?
CLAP
Not as long as we're still here.
I guess we could go back through it.
Where will you go?
I don't know...

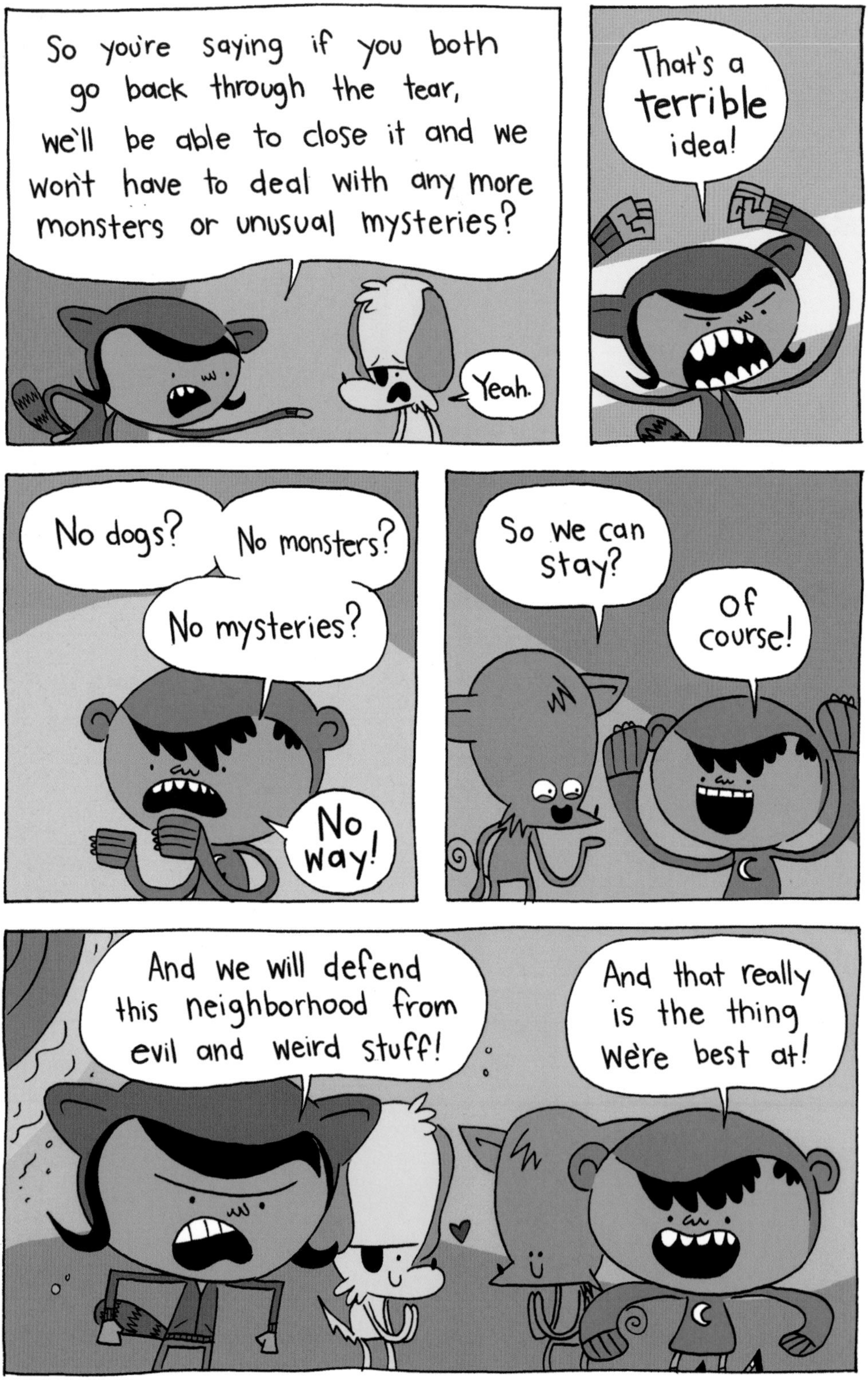
So you're saying if you both go back through the tear, we'll be able to close it and we won't have to deal with any more monsters or unusual mysteries?
Yeah.
That's a terrible idea!
No dogs?
No monsters?
No mysteries?
No way!
So we can stay?
Of course!
And we will defend this neighborhood from evil and weird stuff!
And that really is the thing we're best at!

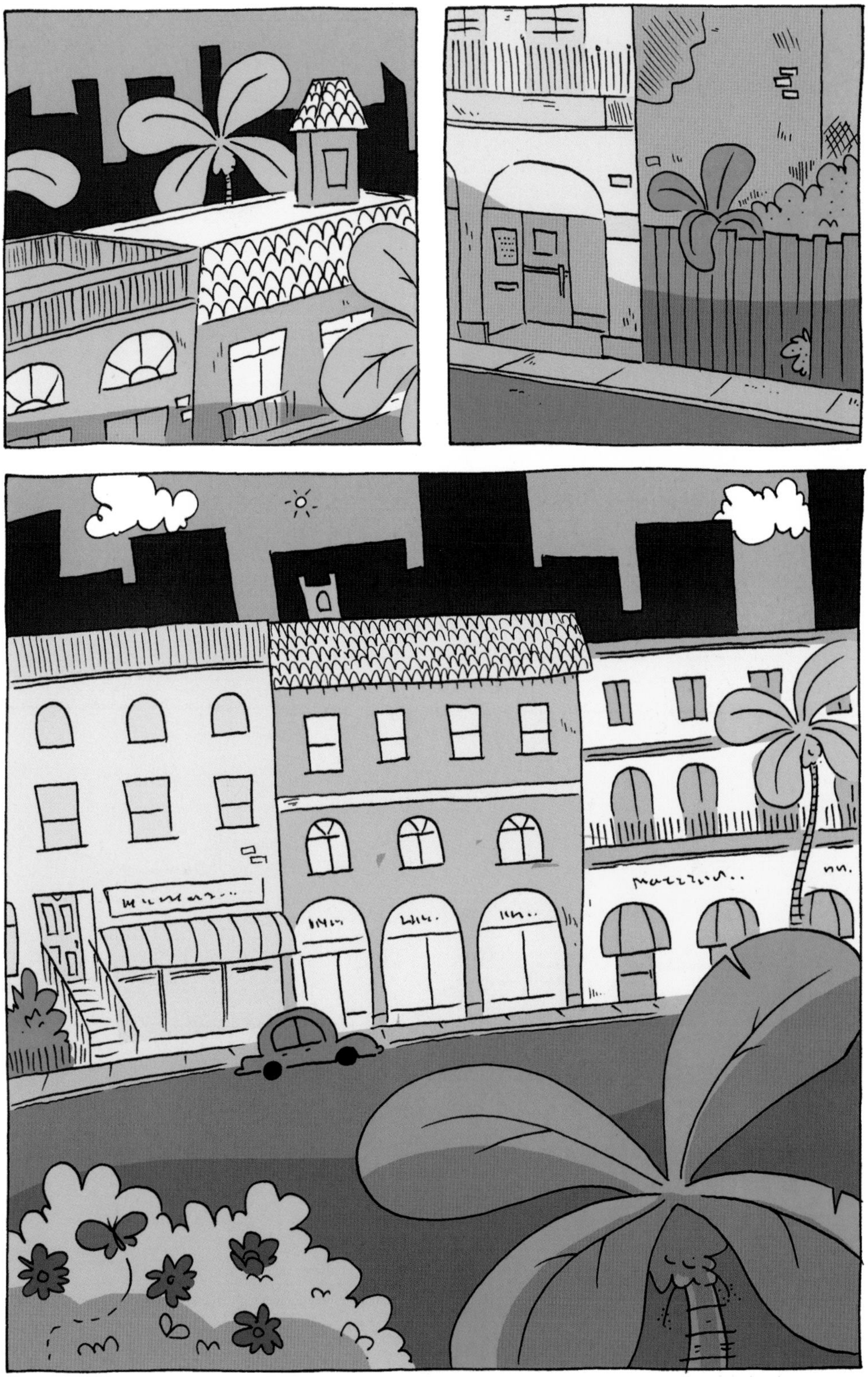

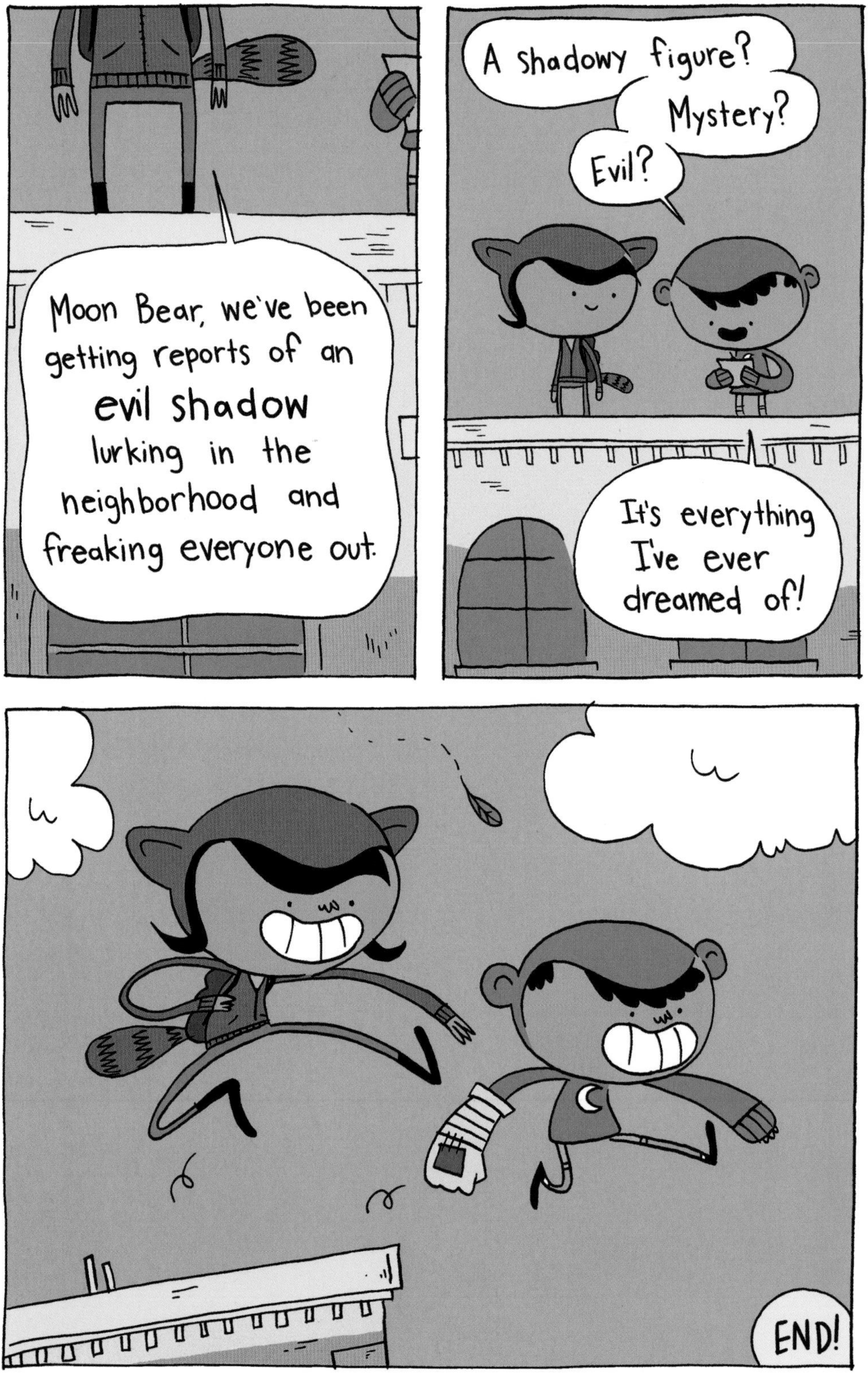
Moon Bear, we've been getting reports of an evil shadow lurking in the neighborhood and freaking everyone out.
A shadowy figure?
Mystery?
Evil?
It's everything I've ever dreamed of!
END!

Thank you to the Florida
Education Fund and the
University of South Florida
Humanities Institute for their
support of this book.